Romance OF THE Ruin

Book 2 of the Branwell Chronicles

Judith Hale Everett

Evershire Publishing

Romance of the Ruin © 2021 Judith Hale Everett
Cover design © Rachel Allen Everett

Published by Evershire Publishing, Springville, Utah
ISBN 978-1-7360675-3-6
Library of Congress Control Number: 2021914876

Romance of the Ruin is a work of fiction and sprang entirely from the author's imagination; all names, characters, places and incidents are used fictitiously. Any resemblance to actual people (living or dead), places or events, is nothing more than chance.

All rights reserved. No part of this publication may be reproduced, stored, or transmitted in any form or by any means without the prior written consent of the author. In other words, thank you for enjoying this work, but please respect the author's exclusive right to benefit therefrom.

*To Elizabeth
who put me on the right track*

*To my readers:
Make sure to read the Author's Note in the back for the historical
background of concepts and events described in the story.*

Romance of the Ruin

Prologue

THE BRICKLAYER'S ARMS, a snug little hostelry within sight of the Kent Road tollgate, London, enjoyed the majority of its custom from the Kent and Surrey stages, and was especially popular with travelers for its flying lunches, got as speedily as the horses were changed, and tasty into the bargain. But the young, bearded man who sat in a brown study over his pint had not come on the stage, nor did he seem interested in any proper food. He had been brooding in the same attitude, and over the same single pint, for an hour and a quarter since he had entered this bustling establishment, and the potman, wiping beer from the tin mugs, began to wonder if trouble might not be brewing.

He was not far afield. Mr. James Ingles, lately of the 51st Foot, had for the past two years been alternately blessing his luck at having lived to see the glorious defeat of Bonaparte, and cursing the day he had been so desperate as to have taken the King's shilling. Feeling in the pocket of his frieze coat, James drew out a folded kerchief, placing it before him on the table and carefully pulling apart the folds. Nestled within was a shiny silver medal imprinted with the profile of the Prince Regent, and hung on a red and blue ribbon. Also within were two new gold sovereigns and a small pile of silver coins, his Private's reward for service at Waterloo.

He regretted nothing of his service. It was with no little pride that he recalled the various battles the 51st had fought and won, both in the Peninsula and in Belgium, and the gratitude of the peoples they had defended and freed from tyranny. It was not the hardships and suffering they had endured on long marches and even longer encampments, in wet and filth and cold and heat, or the horror of bloody and senseless battle, with the cries of the wounded and dying ringing in his ears, that gave him cause to regret enlisting all those years ago. No, if it were only that, he should do it again, and without hesitation.

It was the fickle hand of fate that discouraged him. She seemed always to be waiting in the wings to reverse any good that might come to him. When he had been to go to Oxford, his father had died, leaving him far from home with no means of support. When he had gone to his only cousin in the army, that cousin had soon after been killed in battle. James had lived through Waterloo, but had been discharged with no pension and no home. And the work he had found at the docks was scarcely enough to pay his room and board, let alone his debts, necessitating the sale of his few valuables, including the watch his father had given him as his last birthday present. Was it any wonder he had oftener and oftener found comfort with the bottle?

It was in these dreary times that he most wished that he had tried to work his way home at first news of his father's death rather than throwing in his lot with the army, for if he had done so, he may have had a chance at securing his father's property and something of a future for himself. But wishing paid no toll. He had obeyed his father's insistence that he would be better off away from home, which had been proven wrong—until now.

The medal winked up at him from amid its scanty bed of silver and gold, and he closed the kerchief and its contents in his fist, pushing them back into his pocket. The news he had received this morning seemed too good to be true, even with the grave caveats the solicitor had given. Long experience had taught him not to trust good fortune, for it like as not would turn sour, but he was a gudgeon to think he'd a chance in a million to do better. The docks offered no prospect of security, while the opportunity at Helden Hall was—well, it had possibility, if the solicitor was to be believed. At the very least, he would no longer have to pay room and board, and though the manor was in a sorry state, he would be getting out from under the oppression of his past in London.

Tossing down the last of the beer, he slapped a coin on the table and nodded to the potman—who seemed startled at his activity—and quit the inn. He would give notice at work and pay his shot at the boarding house, and give fate one more chance to lead him aright. Loosening his kerchief against the close September heat, he trudged in the direction of the docks, but checked at the sight of a small boy standing against the wall of the inn, who raised his tousled head and regarded him with large dark eyes.

"Buy a paper, sir?" piped the hopeful voice, and an armful of wrinkled and dirty newspapers were raised for his inspection. They had more than likely been gathered up from the street, and were odds and ends—worth nothing—but the pleading in the dark eyes stirred something deep in James's soul, and he was forced to concede that there were worse things than a handful of coins to his name, and a situation that was at least half likely to make his fortune. With a softened air, he bent and made a show of selecting the best of the mussed papers, placing a whole tuppence in the grubby little hand before moving on.

He had gone only a few steps, however, when he was arrested by the headline on the dingy page. A glance at the date told him the news was weeks old, but he read the short article nonetheless, which apprised him of the knighting of Sir Thomas Stamford Raffles, and that gentleman's intention to return, in the autumn, to the East Indies. The glimmer of hope that had sparked in his chest expanded into an idea as he mechanically folded the paper, stuffing it into his coat. Sir Thomas had known his father, and must still be in London before returning to the East Indies. Perhaps fate was smiling upon him at last.

With renewed vigor, he turned to raise a hand in salute to the small boy still crouched by the wall of the inn before signaling one of the hackney coaches waiting along the Kent Road, and giving the driver an address in Piccadilly.

Chapter 1

LENORA BRECKINRIDGE SAT at the table in the breakfast room of Wrenthorpe Grange, the first volume of the *Romance of the Forest* held open but forgotten before her, as she gazed dejectedly out the window toward the Home Wood. Three weeks had passed since she had joined her mother and new step-father, Sir Joshua Stiles, at his home, and though she loved them dearly, she had never felt so discontented in her life.

The summer months she had passed with her bosom friend, Elvira Chuddsley, in preparations for that damsel's wedding, and the constant flow of engagements, shopping, and shared fantasizing over the romance in store for Elvira had staved off for a time the depressing truth that Lenora was to lose her life-long companion. For though they should always be friends, Lenora knew all too well that Elvira's duty was to her husband now, and that she, Lenora, would be obliged to step lower in her friend's esteem.

After the wedding, a sojourn at her brother Tom's estate had served to maintain her spirits for a time, for she was both necessary and welcome at Branwell. Tom had nearly redeemed the estate from ruin—a state the late Mr. Breckinridge had striven ceaselessly to attain before his very timely demise—and Lenora was caught up in the joy and bustle of final arrangements to reclaim the ancestral home from the tenants who had resided there for over a decade. But after six weeks of doing the honors of the cottage where Tom made his abode, the euphoria had begun to pall, and Lenora had fallen prey to a nameless restlessness that would not leave her, at last resolving her to quit her childhood home at Michaelmas, rather than at Christmas as planned, and begin her life at the Grange.

But her mother's happiness with Sir Joshua had recalled Elvira's contentment forcibly to Lenora's mind, and she was again assailed by strong emotions, which she at last recognized as a longing for romance of her own. Her experience of romance had hitherto come vicariously through the heroines in novels, and as her preferred novels were of the Gothic variety, her expectations were not unaccountably tainted with evil Dukes and ghostly castles. But lately, the sensibility encouraged by the genre had too often vied with her own good sense, and she found herself at a loss as to how to reconcile her need for romance with the tepid offerings of the real world.

Her new home served merely to aggravate this frustration, for Wrenthorpe was as typical as it was respectable; the village was charming, the townspeople pleasant, the gentry civil, and the entertainments the height of propriety. And though the neighboring families were all that was kind and welcoming, Lenora began to imagine that she had stepped into a world that revolved within a box, and the feeling of sameness converged with the loneliness she had staved off for the past months, whispering to her that she was everlastingly trapped.

Striving against this notion, Lenora very naturally turned with greater energy to the escape of her Gothic romances, rationalizing that though they had failed her in realism, they never could in virtue, for she, like so many other gently bred young women, had honed her sensibilities on the never-ending supply of maxims, heroic deeds, and stalwart sacrifices obtaining in the books from the lending library. She was cautious in letting her pastime become known, however, for some members of her family could not hold this style of romance to be harmless. They, influenced by Lenora's unwitting part in precipitating certain disastrous events during her first London season in the spring, even considered the genre dangerous.

Thus Lenora, brought back to the present by the sound of a step in the passage, whisked the *Romance of the Forest* into her pocket and reached for the butter dish, innocently spreading butter on her toast as her mother, Lady Genevieve Stiles, joined her. In the exchange of morning greetings, Lenora was quick to catch a distressed note in Lady Stiles's voice, and inquired whether anything was the matter.

Lady Stiles did not answer directly, but went to the sideboard, asking instead, "Did you chance to see the cook this morning, Lenora?"

"No, Mama. Ought I to have?"

Her mother placed a slice of ham on a plate. "Not necessarily, but I confess myself very curious to lay eyes on her this morning. Sanford told me, as she did up my hair, that she is convinced that Mrs. Blaine has been carousing."

"Blaine?" cried Lenora, incredulously.

"Yes, Blaine, whose industry under the circumstances is a source of admiration," her ladyship replied, indicating the range of excellent dishes available for breakfast. "Her nose this morning is red, however—which I have on Sanford's good authority is not the red of one with a cold, as only a simpleton would mistake, but of one lost to inebriety."

Lenora abandoned her knife and fork with a clatter. "Mama, that is the outside of enough! Blaine, foxed? I have known her only a short while, but I cannot think myself wrong in believing that one would as soon accuse Sanford of sliding down the banisters."

"I await that eventuality daily, my dear," said her mother, scooping a poached egg onto her plate. "Blaine is sure to come up with the notion sometime."

"Mama! Am I to understand this is a common occurrence?" Lenora inquired incredulously. "Why do not you put a stop to such a nonsensical contest?"

Lady Stiles brought her plate to the table and poured out a cup of tea. "I fear it will end only when one of them wins, for I own I mishandled the business from the beginning. You see," she said, a dimple peeping in her cheek, "I found it vastly diverting that two grown women could be most civilly at daggers drawn from sunup to sundown."

Lenora pursed her lips and retrieved her fork and knife, shaking her head as she applied herself once more to her breakfast. "I believe, Mama, that the delight of a full staff after so many years of scraping and sacrificing had quite driven you mad. I wonder that my step-father did not take measures for your safety."

Her mother's smile turned rueful. "Perhaps it would have been better if he had, for I have been on pins and needles at wondering if they will come to blows, or keep their attacks strictly verbal. But I do know that I must tread warily, for Sanford has been unceasingly loyal and I should not like to offend her. And as for Blaine, with my being so newly established as mistress of Wrenthorpe, it is only one wrong step to being viewed eternally as a mere usurper."

Lenora was obliged to own the truth in this, and her mother said, putting her chin in her hand, "It makes me rather long for Sally, but if I had brought her from Branwell, then I would be a usurper."

"That and Tom would never have forgiven you for absconding with his cook," replied Lenora.

Lady Stiles agreed, turning her rather pensive attention to her breakfast, but she perked up when one of the footmen entered with the morning post on a tray. Among the bills and invitations was a letter addressed in a schoolgirl hand to Lenora, who pounced eagerly upon it. Her mother watched placidly as the wafer was broken and the pages spread open—multiple pages she perceived, for Mrs. Elvira Ginsham was well able to get a frank for her letter. And even if she could not, it would not signify, mused Lady Stiles smugly, as the recipient was now well able to afford the receipt of an extra sheet or two.

But as Lenora perused the interesting letter, her spirits underwent a rapid reversal, which her mother observed with growing concern. "Elvira is well, I hope?" she asked.

"Oh, yes, she is well," was the quick answer, accompanied by an even quicker smile.

Lady Stiles stole another glance at Lenora's face, which remained bent over the letter, as if to hide its emotion. "Do she and Gregory continue at Chantham Park through Christmas?"

"Yes, and perhaps for the season as well." Lenora neatly refolded the letter, her eyes averted and lips trembling. "I must tell you that they are expecting a happy event in the summer, and so Elvira shall not be disposed for the bustle and noise of London."

"Oh! She will certainly be missed, but how lovely!" cried her mother, watching in dismay as Lenora composed her countenance into one of polite joy.

"Yes, so lovely! I could not be more happy, and so I shall tell Elvira." She stood, smiling brightly. "Pardon me, Mama, I must answer her letter directly."

Walking with a measured step from the breakfast parlor, Lenora held her head high and her smile fixed, leaving her mother to sigh over her tea and toast.

Lady Stiles had not been blind to her daughter's struggling spirits. Lenora had endured a good deal in the past months, what with surviving a plot to ruin her, and seeing her best friend married, and establishing herself in a new home. These experiences were bound to have aroused many and varied emotions in her breast, which must be difficult for a romantic girl of nineteen to assimilate. Her ladyship had done what she could to ease Lenora's transition into Wrenthorpe society, but the true remedy, she was persuaded, would be time and patience, which could not be manipulated.

Thus resigned, Lady Stiles turned her mind to the most pressing of her household responsibilities, and prepared to descend into that apparent den of iniquity, the kitchens. Three quarters of an hour later, she had ascertained that Blaine was indeed suffering from a cold in the head, and had sent her immediately to bed, and subsequently had made her way to Mrs. Pluitt's room to discuss the situation. The housekeeper, whose sage counsel was almost invariably heeded, opined that what the cook had needed for a good while now was rest, and accordingly, the first kitchen maid's mother was brought up from the village for the day or two in which Blaine should recover.

Her ladyship's mind having been entirely diverted by these mundane considerations, and even further by the delightful sensations of observing two footmen, four maids, the butler, and outside a groom and the gardener, all busily at their work, it was with a feeling of complacence that she betook herself to the drawing room with the intention of finishing the hem of a new gown. Though she was no longer poor Genevieve Breckinridge, widow of the profligate Bertram Breckinridge, and could now afford to employ a seamstress if she chose, she did not so choose, taking advantage of her new station to use her time exactly as she wished.

As she entered the gracious room, however, she was drawn, as always, to the window, through which she could see the ancient trees of the Home Wood dipping and rolling into the distance. She fancied she would never tire of the magnificent view from this, or any other window of Wrenthorpe Grange, for they were all hers, every one fresh and unadulterated by dark or dingy memories.

The scrape of the coal scuttle in the fireplace drew her eyes to yet another maid, who was mending the fire, and Genevieve wondered how she could bear such prosperity. This lovely home, her excellent husband, Lenora safe, and her son Tom's estate at Branwell flourishing; the thought of all this made her smile widen into a most unladylike grin.

"You look as if you had eaten a canary," said a solemn voice behind her.

She turned to see that her husband, Sir Joshua Stiles, had entered the room, dressed comfortably in buckskins and shining top-boots, his riding coat open over a somber waistcoat, with a negligently-tied cravat about his throat. He was magnificent to her eyes.

He came to stand beside her at the window, and she put up a hand to tidy the cravat. "I have eaten several canaries of late, Joshua, as you well know," she said, casting him a smug glance from under her lashes, "for you have fed me all of them."

A smile softened his sober expression, and he stilled the work of her hand by clasping it in one of his own. "Had I known you were so fond of canaries, my love, I should have brought home a nesting pair, rather than shooting two fat pheasants for your supper."

"Oh, I shall contrive," she said, watching with delight as he kissed the tips of her fingers in his clasp. "I fancy our cook could dress them any way I wished—except that she is indisposed today, and we shall have Betsy's mama from the village."

"Unfortunate," he said, holding her hand against his chest and looking down at her with a glint in his eye. "Perhaps I may discover another way to fulfill your wishes."

"Sir Joshua," chided Genevieve, demurely withdrawing her hand from his grasp, "We are not alone."

"We were speaking merely of wishes. And I wish," said he in a low tone, pushing back the curtain and bending forward as if to inspect more closely the prospect outside, his lips near to her ear, "that Mary would finish mending the fire so I could show you just what I mean."

Genevieve's appreciative smile was reflected in the window glass as she pressed closer to her husband's side, but was wiped instantly away at the sight of a figure flitting through the formal gardens toward the wood.

"Where is Lenora off to, I wonder?" mused Sir Joshua, having glimpsed the absconding maiden at just the same moment, and leaning closer to the window for a better view.

"To the depths of the Home Wood, I imagine, my dear," replied his wife, the words coming not so glibly as she had hoped. "She has spent many happy hours there, you know, lost in its Gothic fastness. It is the fulfillment of a dream."

"And does she always run into them, like a deer?" asked her husband, looking sidelong at her. "Or has something occurred to upset her?"

"You are so excessively observant, Joshua, that there is no deceiving you, I declare."

"Is it so necessary that I be deceived?"

"Only to save you worry," sighed his wife. "For I fear there really is nothing that can be done. A letter came from Elvira this morning, you see, after you had gone out shooting. Lenora seemed subdued as she read it, but denied that it caused her anything but joy." She stepped away from the window and wandered to an ornate little table, where she turned over the pages of a periodical lying atop it. "It seems we are to felicitate the happy couple once more, my dear. Elvira is increasing."

"Ah." Sir Joshua advanced back into the room, peering over his wife's shoulder at the very interesting periodical. The maid swept up the last of the soot from the hearth and, bobbing a curtsey, left the room. As soon as the door was shut, Sir Joshua's arms went around his wife, and he bent to rest his chin on her shoulder. "At last," he sighed against her neck.

She smiled and leaned her head against his, but did not otherwise change her posture, and nor did he, only tightening his hold around her waist. "Loneliness is a hard companion," he said quietly. "Perhaps Lenora wants excitement, for even I must own that Wrenthorpe is sadly staid and quiet after London, and even Branwell. We might take Lenora off to Bath or to Brighton, and try what a more varied society can do."

"What a splendid notion!" said Genevieve, brightening. "How better to ease her many disappointments than with a holiday?"

He turned her in his arms so that she was obliged to face him. "I believe all those canaries you've eaten have given you indigestion, Genevieve, and you know not what you speak. What are these many disappointments? I own, she did not catch Mr. Whats-his-name last season—that stammering young man—but if the circumstance threw her into dejection, I never knew it. And I rather fancied her dreams were fulfilled by her being abducted and then rescued—moreover, she delivered the quelling blow herself."

"True enough, my love. Yet I do know whereof I speak, for Lenora has been flagging since she came to us." She looked away. "I believe she feels left behind. She and Elvira have never been so long parted since they were children."

"And now Elvira has achieved a romantic ideal in her marriage," observed Sir Joshua. "While Lenora is left to the uncertainty of her own fate."

"Exactly so. Time will lessen her anxiety, to be sure, but growing older and wiser can only do so much for one so entirely given to the craze of sensibility. For all Lenora claims she is cured of romantic notions, I am persuaded it is not so. It's in the blood, you know."

"For which I am eternally grateful, my Genevieve." He kissed her forehead. "For along with an incurable penchant for romance, Lenora will have inherited a deplorable sense of humor and an elastic temperament, which will serve her well through this troublesome time."

"But you must not forget intrepidity, my love, for I fear she has inherited that in abundance!"

He was much struck by this. "Good heaven! I hope that I am equal to rescuing two maidens from ridiculous scrapes!"

"You forget that we are well able to rescue ourselves, Sir Joshua," was the imperious reply.

"For which we must all be grateful," he retorted, eyebrows raised, "as I cannot be in two places at once."

With a wry smile, his lady stood on tiptoe to stop his mouth with a kiss, and Lenora's troubles were suspended, for the time being, from their minds.

Chapter 2

Lenora fled deep into the wood, away from the shadow cast by her dearest friend's joy. Even as she ran, the hood of her cape falling back from her head, she chided herself for being so mean as to resent Elvira's happiness, but every remembrance of her friend's delight set her yearning for something to happen—anything!—that would elevate her from her present humdrum existence to the realization of even the smallest of her dreams.

Pausing for breath against the knotty bole of a chestnut tree, she pressed her forehead to the rough wood, her eyes closed tightly. "You are selfish and ridiculous and... and totty-headed to act in this way," she sternly admonished the tree bark. "Life is not a romance, even if Elvira has achieved her heart's desire and you have not. You have no need to be jealous—you could not be more happy for her!" she insisted, hitting her gloved palm against the trunk in emphasis. "Marriage is no light matter—and a baby—" Here she found it necessary to swallow down a lump in her throat before continuing resolutely, "A baby is a serious responsibility, for all its plumpness and sweetness and tiny fingers and toes—"

But at this her slender self-control deserted her and she slid to the base of the tree, looking forlornly up into the branches. "Is there to be romance for everyone but me?"

The swaying branches above her murmured sympathetically, but she could take no comfort from them, instead pounding a fist into the soft, mossy ground at her side. "All my adventure in London, and what has come of it? I gained acquaintance enough, but Mr. Barnabus's interest was only a fancy, and Lord Montrose was nothing but an impostor." She shrugged a shoulder. "Though I did hit him over the head, which was properly heroic. But that is neither here nor there, for nothing as exciting could ever occur here, I am persuaded."

Since Sir Joshua had first told her of Wrenthorpe Grange, describing the manor in thrillingly Gothic terms, Lenora had yearned to visit. Therefore, her first sight of the venerable house—tantalizingly obscured by the thick stand of the Home Wood, and then bursting upon her vision as the carriage emerged into the full light of afternoon—had been slightly disappointing. Sir Joshua had prepared her for lichen-covered stone walls and brooding casements, with undiscovered secrets lurking behind them, but her own eyes had told her that his was a biased description. Though it was blackened in many places, and one wall was entirely hidden by creeping ivy, the stone was of a much brighter hue—almost golden—than she had been led to imagine. And the windows, besides being fully intact, were sparkling clean in the afternoon sunlight, leading her to doubt the possibility of anything, most especially a secret, lurking within. In good faith, however, she had disdained her own judgment, and embarked upon her new life in the full expectation of mounting horrors—for what else could await her in such an ancient place?

But it was not many days before she was made to realize that she had never been so taken in. There was not a locked door nor an unexplained cupboard in the whole of the house, and search as she might, she could find no evidence of hollows behind the paneling, or of any flooring that could reasonably have been placed to hide an oubliette. She had even tried quite faithfully not to watch for ghostly figures vanishing from the corners of her vision, and had been justly rewarded—there were none. She was forced to the depressing conclusion that Wrenthorpe Grange, despite her persistent hopes and Sir Joshua's assurances, was everything that was proper and comfortable.

Her fingers had been pulling at a clump of moss, and it came away in her hand. "I am doomed to languish in the smooth seas of gentility!" she cried, throwing the clump away from her. But as the words left her mouth, a change came over her mood, as if a beguiling vision had opened before her. The cloud upon her brow eased, and she pushed herself to her feet, vaguely brushing off her dress with a far-away look in her eyes.

"I am cast adrift in unknown waters, friendless, penniless, and without a shore to call my own." She began to walk dreamily, moving deeper into the wood as she mused. "After untold hardships, my boat runs upon a desolate beach, where breakers crash so violently that the craft is broken asunder, and I am dashed onto the rocks." She moved onward, winding around trees and stepping over rocks and creepers as she continued, speaking aloud as if the wood were her bosom friend.

"I awaken in the hovel of a kindly hermit, who nurses me to health, before bestowing upon me a humble gift—" Here she paused to look about herself for a token suitable to the hermit's gift. Spying a burled stick poking up from the underbrush, she pulled it out, wiping the dirt and grass from it with a corner of her cloak and eying it critically. Its proportions, much like a wand, satisfied her, and she held it reverently before her as she continued, "He bestows upon me a humble gift, with the admonition to save it against a time of great need, which circumstance will reveal its magic powers."

Fortified by this knowledge, Lenora strode more purposefully along the path. "Though I wish to repay his kindness, he accepts only a lock of my hair, and directs me into the forest, where he prophesies my destiny awaits. The forest is dark and ancient, full of mysteries and secrets, but my courage shines forth like a beacon, and the Spirit of the Wood guides me on my path."

She ran a hand along the low-slung branch of a tree, which she imagined was the arm of a faerie creature, and walked on, gazing regally about. "The faerie folk peek out from their hiding places to watch me with mingled hope and awe. I am, surely, the One for whom they have waited! Suddenly, a clearing opens up, and in the center, on a greensward like scattered emeralds, stands a prince, whose proud bearing nevertheless pronounces great suffering, and whose gaze pierces me to the very heart."

She advanced into the clearing, which was real enough, and stood in the center, her hand outstretched to the invisible prince. "'Your Highness,' I say, and extend my hand in peaceful greeting, but he falls to one knee before me, bowing over my hand in humble petition. 'My Queen,' he cries, 'I have long awaited thee, and bless the good fortune that has brought you at last to my side.'"

Raising her hand, and with it the gallant—if imaginary—prince, Lenora said, "My lord, I have traveled through untold hardships to find you, and will grant you the boon you seek."

But the prince uttered a groan. "You have already sacrificed much, my Queen! How dare I ask that you risk more?"

"My prince, not all the sacrifice in the world could—"

The prince moaned again, more loudly, and uttered a most unprincely string of curses.

In utmost astonishment, Lenora jerked from her daydream, her eyes darting right and left. The clearing was, indeed, empty, and the gloom of the trees had thickened the shadows beneath them, so that nothing could be discerned within the shapeless darkness. She had often supposed the woods to be haunted, and another moan, accompanied by the thrash and scrape of movement, caused her to take an involuntary step backward, her skin prickling. But as her gaze searched the shadows, a light breeze shivered through the gold-tinged leaves overhead, allowing a sprinkling of sunlight to penetrate the gloom. There, in the underbrush beyond the clearing, was the distinct outline of a man—a real and ordinary man—lying face downward in the dirt.

She blinked at the figure. He was surely in distress, as the groans attested, and she weighed the prudence of investigating against that of running away. Curiosity and concern, and perhaps, as her mother had lamented, her intrepid nature, convinced her feet to carry her forward, and she made her way to the man's side. He lay at the base of a low hill, his frieze coat and breeches stained and covered with dead leaves and other debris, as if he had rolled down the hill and into the brush.

"Sir?" she asked, and was mortified at the quaver in her voice. There was no answer, and Lenora, asserting herself, cleared her throat and said in the strong, brave voice worthy of a queen, "Sir, are you hurt?"

Another moan issued from the fallen man, and he tried to lift himself, but after an abortive effort, he again lay still.

"May I be of assistance, sir?" she pursued, taking tentative hold of one of his arms and pulling. This proved utterly ineffectual, as he was larger than she and dead weight into the bargain but, undaunted, she tugged insistently at the arm and urged in an encouraging tone, "Sir, if we both try at once, you may be able to rise—"

His arm suddenly swiped out in an arc, ripping itself from her grasp, and the man flung himself into a sitting position, facing her. "Don't need any assistance, you," he bellowed through a full, matted beard, with fumes of strong drink billowing on his breath and into Lenora's horrified face.

"Good heavens!" she cried, stumbling backward. "You're drunk!"

Her exclamation gave him pause, and he squinted hard at her through tangled black hair, evidently making a discovery. "Ladies present!" he said, his hand going to the kerchief knotted about his neck, and patting down his coat in a cursory self-inspection. "Pleasure, ma'am. No wish to contradict, but only slightly disguised," he slurred, his accent coarse. He touched his cap. "Word of a gen'leman."

"Gentleman!" exclaimed his outraged companion, wide-eyed at this absurd speech. "No self-respecting gentleman looks—or smells— as you do, sir!"

He blinked down at his attire, then surged to his feet, achieving a bow that threatened to topple him onto his head. By dint of windmilling his arms in rather a haphazard fashion, however, he miraculously righted himself, and said, nodding in a conciliatory way to this angry, yet percipient young lady, "True. Not a gen'leman. Soldier."

"Well," huffed Lenora, her arms crossed sternly as she surveyed the disgraceful personage before her, from his unkempt hair and stained clothing to his mud bespattered boots. "Any man claiming to be in

His Majesty's service ought to be ashamed to be seen in such a state!"

"Fallen on hard times," he mumbled sullenly, swiping at his nose with his sleeve. "Old Boney drew in his horns. Wellington gave us marching orders. Had to come here." He wheeled around and stumbled toward the path. "Nowhere else to go."

Lenora had heard of the sad lot of noncommissioned soldiers, who were turned out of the army with no pension, and often with no home to return to, after the long years of the Peninsular War. He was young, as well, not much older than Tom, which somehow made his plight the more pitiable. Discomfited, she watched him go, wavering between disgust and compassion for him. After all, how just was it to condemn this poor soul, who had sought refuge in drink from his not insignificant troubles?

His toe suddenly hit a root, pitching him forward onto his knees, and she cast aside her scruples, hurrying forward to help him to his feet. "Sir, take care," she said, holding tight to his arm as he swayed alarmingly.

He swatted at her hand, as if it were a fly. "Not fitting for a lady to take care of me."

"Certainly, under normal circumstances," she persisted, keeping step with him as he started once more down the path. "But you are not yourself, and I feel I should see you safely home."

He stopped again to gaze blearily into her face. "Much obliged, but can't be done. Raffles can't help me, and nobody answers my letters." He plunged onward.

Lenora, standing bemused for a moment at this cryptic utterance, hastened forward to right him as he nearly toppled into the brush, and stumbled alongside him as he wove from side to side along the path. The gloom of the wood deepened, and she glanced up through the burnished leaves at a cloudy sky, wondering how long she had been gone from home, and how much longer this ill-advised adventure would continue.

The third time she found it necessary to haul him to the side, to prevent him from breaking his head open on a low-hanging branch, she inquired in a tense voice, "How far is your home, sir?"

But her inebriated companion merely waved a hand in a vague forward direction and trudged on, obliging her to continue with him. Lenora, fast repenting the compassion that had decided her to accompany a stranger—and a drunkard at that—into the forest, was forming the determination to leave him to his fate and seek her own home, when the trees opened onto the most fantastic vision she had ever beheld.

An undulating field of unmown grass, interspersed with patches of thistle, autumn gentian, and Queen Anne's lace, fell away from the wood, down a slight decline, and across a wide expanse, where it ended at the sloping and bedraggled walls of a hedge-maze. This was surrounded by a riotous garden of sweet pea and rambling rose, with spikes of hollyhock and delphinium, all tangled in russet-leaved bramble and ivy, with ragged clumps of lavender and geranium clinging about the edges.

But the sight that held Lenora dumbstruck was a fine old Palladian mansion that rose up beyond the gardens in three storeys, its rain-blackened Cotswold-stone walls splotched with lichen and overgrown with vines, and its pocked roof line stretching the cracked teeth of chimney pots into the clouded sky. The building extended in a great, brooding block with the blank eyes of several boarded or bricked-in windows staring outward, as if in sightless resignation.

Her drunken companion trundled forward into the high grass, and Lenora, rooted to the spot, breathed, "You live here?"

But he shook his head ponderously. "Not the Big House," he mumbled. "Only ghosts there. Gatekeeper's lodge," he finished succinctly, and swerved abruptly away from the mansion, onto an unseen path.

Lenora's heart leapt at the mention of ghosts, and she scarcely heard the rest. This could not be real—this could not be happening to her! An actual haunted house, within a walk of her home—she pinched herself to be sure, and the answering pain became a shiver of terrified excitement. Her eyes scanned the Gothic perfection of the mansion—all blackened stone and ivy and despair—and she resolved that she must know everything about this place. What was its history? How had it come to be abandoned? How was it possible that such a place existed at all, within miles of Sir Joshua's home—and why had he not told her of it?

She broke from her reverie to hasten after her drunken companion, who had weaved his way around the corner of the fantastic house. He must be the caretaker, or some such, and would have the answers to her questions. Indeed, he had owned himself obligated to her, for she had rendered him a signal service in ensuring his safe journey through the wood, without which he would surely be lying unconscious after walking smash into a tree, and would very likely have died of it. Yes, he felt he owed her a debt, which could easily be paid upon his satisfying her curiosity.

She followed after him through the grass, around the mansion, and finally caught him up on a weed-strewn gravel sweep at the front of the house. But again she was distracted by the splendor of four ivy-wrapped pillars flanking the huge double doors at the top of a short flight of wide, cracked steps, and she gazed with unrestrained wonder upon its ruined beauty. Oh, to know the secrets of this house, perhaps to go inside—these thoughts forced her to command herself enough to drag her eyes from the mansion and address the caretaker.

"Sir, I must ask you—"

He spun to face her, bristling in outrage. "Where'd you come from? Why're you following me?"

"Following—" cried Lenora, taken aback. "I did not follow you— that is, I did, but you would have caught your death in the forest had I not attended you!"

The soldier's head reared back, his eyebrows, or what she assumed were his eyebrows under all that hair, drawing together over beetle-black eyes. "Why?"

"Why, because you are in no state to go—"

"Why did you follow me?" he elucidated, swaying slightly with the effort. "Do you know me? Do I know you?"

"No, you do not, for you are too castaway to walk straight, let alone allow an introduction," she answered with asperity.

He wagged his head as he regarded her. "Highly improper."

"I should say so, sir, and imprudent, too—"

"Lady shouldn't introduce herself to a man. Highly improper."

Lenora was temporarily stricken dumb by the irony of this truth. "I—I would never press for an introduction. That is not why—Circumstances forced me to—" she stammered, but he reeled away and down the gravel drive.

Lenora scrambled after him, hardly knowing why she did so, except that the notion that she must know the history of the manor had taken firm root in her mind, and she felt as strongly that she was perfectly justified in asking the caretaker of it now, though he was foxed, for she had no way of knowing whether he was not perpetually so, and she did not know when she should have the chance again.

"Sir, I beg you to stop, for only one moment, please, and hear me out."

To her surprise, he did stop, but he did not look at her, only standing, staring gravely ahead at the door of the lodge.

"Sir, though you do not seem to clearly recall it, the fact remains that you owned yourself obliged to me today, and you would be able to repay me in a very small way."

"No."

Only slightly daunted, Lenora persisted. "It would be only a trifling favor, and should not incommode you in the least—"

He turned on her again, towering menacingly over her. "I said no. I've troubles enough without vandals and trespassers wasting my time."

"I mean no harm," Lenora insisted, standing her ground. "I wish only to know about the house, sir."

"No!" he almost shouted, whirling to yank open the door and enter the lodge. "Go away!"

"Sir, I beg you to—" began Lenora, but he closed the door in her face, and before she could protest further, the bolt slammed home.

Chapter 3

SHE STOOD IN shocked indignation for several moments, the fantasy of having at last been granted a promise of romance crumbling in the face of the caretaker's irrefutable rejection. The more she considered, the more she was convinced that he would very soon be flung unconscious upon his bed, and any memory of her—and her very reasonable request—would be lost in the bleary aftermath of his potations.

The injustice of her situation struck her forcibly, and she squared her shoulders, knocking at the door and calling imperatively, "Sir! Come back!" There was no response from inside the cottage, and she knocked again, raising her voice. "Sir! Please, it will take but a moment to tell me the history of the Big House! Sir! Please open the door!" But it was to no avail. The door remained shut, and the rooms behind it were as silent as the grave.

As she gazed in dejection at the locked door, her sense reasserted itself, and she became aware of the gross impropriety of her actions. She had forced her company upon a total stranger, and resented his rejection of her wishes. Though she had undoubtedly been useful to him while in the forest, with tree limbs and trunks standing ready to brain him, once he had cleared the wood he had been safe enough, and she could, with perfect propriety, have counted her Christian duty fulfilled and left him.

But the house! That wondrous house had eclipsed her reason, and she had seen nothing but its perfection. It had taken her under its spell, and drawn her on to commit these improprieties in the name of romance. Romance! Why did she crave it so? Why could she not be satisfied with reading it in books, and living a quiet, ordinary, genteel life? Perhaps her mother and step-father were not so unreasonable as to mistrust the power of Gothic novels. It was a lowering thought.

With a heartfelt sigh, she turned her unwilling feet back toward Wrenthorpe Grange, determined to act rationally. But as she meandered past the enticing decrepitude of the mansion, every lichen-bound stone and blocked up window frame beckoned her with promises of ghostly figures and clanking chains, and the skeletal remains of prisoners in an oubliette. As she passed through the romantically overgrown gardens, a host of visions assailed her, of faeries and witches and hulking ogres invading the gardens by moonlight, or of nefarious villains swathed in black, plotting in the tangled darkness of the maze. Her heart longed to elaborate on these visions, but her mind warned her against it, and it was with great self-control that she quickened her pace, fairly flying through the overgrown lawn and into the safety of the Home Wood.

Wending her way to the Grange, she thought mournfully that if Sir Joshua had kept the existence of the mansion from her knowledge, he had only had just cause. What a hoyden she had been! If the matter should ever come to her parents' notice, they would be horrified and so terribly disappointed. Even the caretaker, in his inebriated state, had recognized her actions as "most improper," and, when sober, would have some very wrong notions of her upbringing. She shuddered at the very real possibility that he could ruin her reputation by noising their encounter abroad, and could only hope that he would not remember it, or count it as a drunken dream.

With such thoughts to humble her, she was not long in concluding that the whole of the experience was the hand of Providence, for nothing else could have opened her eyes to the severity of her weakness for sensibility, and convinced her of the necessity to distance herself from romance.

Thus, after changing her dress, Lenora went dutifully to the drawing room with her mother and plied her needle with scarcely a thought for the tangled, forgotten pleasure garden at the ruin, where there were sure to be fae creatures, or poisonous plants awaiting concoction into sundry potions for the entrapment of man or woman. In the afternoon, she quietly set herself to writing a letter to Elvira, and let the ink dry upon her pen only four or five times in succession as she stared unseeing at the wall above the writing desk, envisioning the bulk of the mansion rising up into the pale sky, its stark and haggard stone walls interrupted by bricked-in window frames, like the pitiless eyes of a phantom. And at dinner, her thoughts were not so caught away by the tantalizing mystery behind the Big House's dereliction that she was more than twice remonstrated for her inattention to the conversation, before her mother put down her fork and regarded her with concern.

"My dear child," Lady Stiles said, "what has come over you?"

Lenora jerked into motion, scooping peas onto her fork. "Nothing, I assure you, Mama."

"My dear, you have not listened to two words I have said together. What can you be thinking of?"

"I cannot tell," she said, not looking up as she hastily temporized. "I suppose I am merely distracted by Elvira's news."

Her parents exchanged speaking looks, and Sir Joshua cleared his throat. "Lenora, my dear, what would you say to our removing to Bath for the winter?"

Lenora's abstracted gaze flew to his face. "Why do you wish to leave Wrenthorpe?"

"Your mother has suggested that a change of scene would do you good."

"Oh, no, I cannot leave now. That is—"

Her parents both looked their astonishment and she blushed in confusion, sensible that her reticence must appear to them utterly unreasonable, as well it was. She ought not, and would not, return to the ruin, but somehow the idea of leaving it entirely was impossible for her to contemplate. Perhaps she had been unwise to attempt an abrupt renunciation of her romantic notions, for it had not answered—the train of her thoughts all afternoon was a testimony to that. Would it not be more effectual to wean herself gradually from them?

"I do not wish to seem ungrateful, Sir Joshua," she said after a moment, "for such a scheme would be delightful, to be sure, but just now, I feel that I ought to remain here. I have only just arrived at Wrenthorpe, and—and have been looking forward to bettering the acquaintance of our amiable neighbors. Would it not seem odd if you were to carry me away so soon after I have come?"

"I suppose it would, my love," said her mother, with a searching look that inclined Lenora not to meet her eye. "You must know that we wish for you to be happy here, of all things. But in light of recent events—"

"There is nothing in the world to make you anxious on my account, Mama," declared Lenora, with what she hoped was a bright smile. "If anything, I have been moving about too much of late; another move may rob me of my peace altogether."

Her mother looked uneasy, but Sir Joshua gave her an infinitesimal shake of the head before rather deliberately pouring himself another glass of Madiera and water. "It needn't signify, my dear. If you do not wish to leave Wrenthorpe, you shall not. I own I had liefer stay at home, for the autumn at Wrenthorpe is quite spectacular." And he applied himself to his plate without further comment.

This victory fortified Lenora to carry off a tolerably cheerful evening in her parents' company, and she retired to bed exhausted. Her dreams were plagued by visions of the ruin worthy of Mrs. Radcliffe's pen, and she awoke before dawn with such tumultuous emotions that she was at some pains to make head or tail of them. An effort to brush them aside and assert her native cheerfulness failed utterly, and after a quarter of an hour spent gazing into the shadows, all she could discover was that she wanted more than ever to be acquainted with the mansion's history, and had reason to believe she would go mad if she could not find it out.

But she could not ask Sir Joshua, for he had kept the knowledge of it from her for a reason, and she suspected that if she evinced her curiosity over the subject, her parents would do all in their power to distract her from it. How to find the answers to her questions, then, she must puzzle out.

Her dejection over the problem was observed by her maid with growing interest, for Tess was wont to believe any sudden fit of the dismals to be a sure sign of dire illness—having herself weathered no fewer than five epidemic complaints that had carried off various members of her village over her distressingly robust eighteen years.

As she arranged Lenora's hair, Tess remarked, "If I may be so bold, miss, I trust you ain't been taking the evening air, for you oughtn't to do it! My very own Uncle Robert was struck by the influenza after he'd spent the evening outside—" she added in an under voice, "in the open air."

Miss was unresponsive, except for the deepening of the cleft between her brows, and Tess felt the certainty of doom envelope her. "Are you faint, miss? Do you have palpitations, or sweats?" Dropping the hairbrush and grasping her mistress's hands, she hissed, "Please, miss! Don't fall into a swoon!" She then breathlessly awaited events.

After a long moment of incomprehension, Lenora blinked, shaking herself free of Tess's grip. "For heaven's sake, Tess, why should I swoon?"

"I thought you was ill, miss, for all you've been moping," replied the maid, in some disappointment.

"Well, I am not ill," said Lenora, looking away. "I am merely thwarted." But then an idea suddenly struck her, and she asked, "Tess, you were born hereabouts, were not you? Do you know the ruined mansion on the other side of the Home Wood?"

"Oh, yes, miss!" replied the maid, startled. "But how came you to know of it?"

"I stumbled upon it yesterday," Lenora said. "I had no idea such a place existed, and so near."

"Aye, you wouldn't, miss, for none go nigh the place if it can be helped, and we daren't speak of it," Tess confided, lowering her voice, "for it is haunted, and no denying!"

Lenora was all rapt attention, and Tess, to whom a haunted mansion was hardly less fascinating than illness or death, needed no further prompting to unfold the dramatic history of Helden Hall and its doomed occupants. Dropping to her knees at Lenora's side, she explained that Old Lord Helden was the most diabolical man on God's earth, whose wife had died half a century earlier either from terror and torment—the facts were rather fuzzy here—or from childbirth. Lord Helden, being heartless, had neglected the child in its cradle and despised him in his youth. Were it not for the brave intervention of the housekeeper, the boy should almost certainly have lived out his days in a forgotten garret, with only stale bread and fetid water for nourishment. As it was, the boy's spirit showed itself in the rebellion of growing to hale and hearty manhood, but overstepped itself when he went so far as to attempt to claim his freedom.

Though speculation was vague as to his motivations, his lordship had flown into a towering rage, locking the young man up in irons and spiriting him away on a ship bound for Foreign Parts, in the hopes that he should not survive the passage. But the young man not only lived to step foot on Heathen Soil, but further enraged his sire by taking one of the natives to his bosom in marriage, and producing a son. This impudence was too much for the Old Lord and his reason deserted him. From that moment, he began tearing up his manor, turning off his faithful retainers, and threatening his tenants off his land. In true Gothic style, this course had broken his health, and within fifteen years, he was brought to his death bed. Not to be outdone by fate, he cursed what was left of the estate with his dying breath, and his housekeeper had sworn that he had died with a ghastly smile on his lips.

"Though why he did, she couldn't say, for none mourned him—not even she," explained Tess, "and with everything wasted, he got no more than a pauper's burial by the vicar of the parish."

"How horrid!" whispered Lenora, mesmerized.

"Yes, miss, but there's more," Tess went on in thrilling tones. "No sooner was the Old Lord dead and gone, than his housekeeper found a letter that told how the son and his family had died of the plague in that Heathen Country, so it was all for naught. That was four or five years ago, and from that day to this, their ghosts walk the Big House, moaning and groaning for what was lost."

Lenora, who had sat spellbound throughout this recitation, thought that no history could have more fully answered her expectations. Indeed, it had exceeded them, for only yesterday she had become resigned that such things did not occur in real life. That it had, and in such proximity to her new home, was so near an omen that Lenora, putting aside the warnings of her good sense, determined not to discount it.

"What of the heir, Tess? Does he do nothing?"

Tess regarded her, blinking. "The heir? He's not stepped foot in the place, and ain't done nothing for it, save sending that horrid Mr. Ingles to watch over it, and more shame on him, to be carrying on like the Old Lord and letting the place go even worse."

This information, corroborating everything Lenora knew of the owners of crumbling mansions—for they invariably employed gruff and coarse retainers, just like Mr. Ingles—sealed her decision. Dismissing Tess, she betook herself to the breakfast parlor to gaze absently out the window at the Home Wood while her mind revolved with plans. She must discover the fate of the estate, and more about the heir—for she was persuaded that he was the victim of tragedy, just as the two heirs before him had been, and that was why he had grown so distant from his duty. If she could but meet him, it was only a step to saving him, and then, in accordance with the narrative that had so amazingly proved true thus far, he would fall madly in love with her, and they would redeem Helden Hall together.

Chapter 4

Feeling it would be unwise to trust either Sir Joshua or her mother with her plans, Lenora judged it best to look to the young people of the neighborhood to enlighten her as to Helden Hall's fate. Her first attempts with the young ladies on an outing to nearby Jack's Hill produced an account nearly identical to Tess's, which gave Lenora to believe that it may be more difficult to get the unadulterated facts than she had imagined. However, just as she had determined this, Mr. Dowbridge requested the honor of escorting her home, remarking dryly, "All you'll get there is tittle-tattle, Miss Breckinridge. Best not listen to them."

Mr. Frank Dowbridge, scion of the house of Mintlowe, had accompanied his mother on her call of ceremony when Lenora had arrived in the neighborhood, and had apparently been prepared to admire her. He was very handsome, and obliging—if a trifle overbearing—with a determined, confident air. His first meeting had established him as a man of information, and Lenora wondered that it had not occurred to her to approach him before, wasting no time in asking him what he knew of Helden Hall as they settled into his well-sprung curricle.

His brows raised. "I wonder what could interest you about that old ruin? I suppose it is a curiosity, though there is little mystery about it. Everybody knows all there is to know of Helden Hall."

"Not everybody, Mr. Dowbridge. The Misses Littleford know only gossip, as you observed, and I, who had not the advantage of having lived next the ruin all my life, am at the mercy of what I can find out—and I am agog to know if it is half so romantic as it is made out to be."

"I seriously doubt it, though I cannot conceive of what she has told you. The lower orders are so prone to superstition and other such nonsense, one never can tell. But Sir Joshua can acquaint you with the particulars. I am only surprised that you did not apply to him."

Lenora waved Sir Joshua's authority away. "My step-father does not concern himself with such things. But I, personally, am excessively curious as to Helden Hall's history, and even more about its present circumstances. I imagine any stranger would be."

"Certainly. It is the only scandalous subject we have to discuss hereabouts," he said with a wry smile. "I am glad to satisfy you, but if your mind is already filled with absurd fancies regarding the Hall, the truth may only disappoint you. I know how young ladies dote upon romance."

This bland attitude was quite damping, but Lenora was determined, and merely retreated a bit from her sensibility in order that she may prevail. "Pray, do not be anxious on that head, Mr. Dowbridge. I am aware that the rumors of ghosts and curses and such—as romantic as they seem—are pure nonsense."

"As you say," he said, clearly unconvinced. "But do not blame me if my information disillusions you."

He launched into the tale; however, his exposition was cut short by their arrival at the Grange and, as he was unable to stop for refreshment, Lenora was at pains to mask her disappointment at being obliged to wait.

"My humblest apologies, Miss Breckinridge, but you cannot expect that I should give up all my interest at once," he said, helping her to descend from the curricle. He pressed her hand with a knowing smile. "I must give you a cause to admit my company again."

Then he bowed over her hand and set his horses to, and Lenora was to wait two entire days before he returned to call. Lady Stiles was in, which filled Lenora with consternation, for the three of them sat primly discussing the unexceptional topic of hunting for a quarter of an hour, and Lenora inwardly despaired of ever discovering more about Helden Hall.

Therefore, as Mr. Dowbridge rose to leave, she made a desperate bid, inquiring, "Mr. Dowbridge, I wonder if you would be so good as to accompany me on a ride tomorrow. I have been on short rides through the village, but do not know the country so well as to trust myself farther afield, and should be grateful for your escort."

Lady Stiles eyed her askance, but added her approbation to the scheme, and Mr. Dowbridge, a pleased lilt to his lips, pronounced himself honored.

The scheme worked charmingly, for Lenora got the remainder of the story from him during the hour-long ride, but she also garnered some interested stares from villagers and gentry alike as she and Mr. Dowbridge rode along the village high street chatting in what many chose to term an intimate manner. The quizzes eagerly took up speculation as to the probability of the heir to the Mintlowe title taking up with a mere Miss Breckinridge, and when the two continued to meet one another with particular friendliness, rumors began to circulate.

Lord and Lady Mintlowe, who might have been said to have had cause to dislike such a match, surprisingly, and contrary to their usual condescending manner, smiled upon their son's fascination.

"Such a pretty-behaved young lady, and so unassuming!" Lady Mintlowe was heard to exclaim at more than one gathering. "One cannot but hope that one's offspring should have the good fortune to attach just such a genteel partner—I speak generally, mind! I do not pretend that dear Frank is quite ready to marry—if he has been in love once he has been in love a thousand times, poor boy! But if he were to form a lasting attachment to a pretty, lively girl such as Miss Breckinridge, well, a mother's heart could not but be softened toward the match."

But Lady Stiles watched her daughter's apparent courtship with a more jaundiced eye. While Mr. Dowbridge seemed unexceptionable in his attentions, she had observed a marked indifference in Lenora's demeanor toward him, which seemed at variance with the interest with which she welcomed him. Her ladyship was uncertain what to think of this, for twice she had joined the young people after the visit had commenced, and both times been impressed by a sudden, hurried tempo to the conversation—exactly as if the subject had just been changed. Her curiosity, of course, being piqued, she did as any well-bred woman would do when next she came upon one of these tete-a-tetes, and listened at the door before making her presence known. Her relief was not greater than her confusion when no lovelorn expressions of undying devotion smote her ears, but eager undertones regarding a certain Helden Hall and its villainous master.

A repetition of these events served to persuade her that Helden

Hall and its master not only held some sort of interest for Lenora, but was the sole purpose for her entertainment of Mr. Dowbridge. This conviction did little to reassure her, for she did not like the idea of Lenora toying with a young man's affections, but worse, she was persuaded that with Lenora's penchant for romance, she was winding herself into a fantasy regarding the Hall, which could very well be dangerous, as the adventure of last spring attested.

With these thoughts striving in her motherly bosom, Lady Stiles tapped on her husband's study door one afternoon, while Lenora was safely away on an outing. Sir Joshua welcomed her into his sanctum with a smile, which quickly devolved into a quizzical look as he took in her somber expression.

"I fervently trust Sanford and Blaine have not declared open war, my love," he said gravely.

"Oh, no, Joshua," said his wife, taking a chair opposite him. "I have not come to you for such a trifling matter as that. Indeed, Sanford has called a truce, for she has had the headache these three days and has required Blaine's assistance in brewing a tisane to relieve it, and you would not conceive of her forbearance in listening to Blaine's veiled insinuations while they must continue in the same room together. But, my dear, I desire your advice, for I have heard snippets of the most astonishing tale, and I wish that you will give me the right of it."

"And what story would that be?"

"The horrid history of Helden Hall."

He blinked at her. "I should have expected Lenora to inquire after that story before you, my dear."

"That is exactly the issue, Joshua. Lenora has been inquiring after it, but not from you or from me."

"I see," he mused, rubbing his chin. "I had hoped she would not find out about that particular history so quickly, but I should not be surprised that it has come out, for Lord Helden was just what Lenora would style an Evil Duke."

"Which is the heart of my anxiety, my dear. I fear she is fascinated, and will tumble headlong into just the sort of scrape she got into with Lord Montrose."

"Oh, do not be anxious, my Genevieve," said her husband with a comforting smile. "Beside being no duke, Samuel Engleheart, Viscount Helden, is far from capable of doing our Lenora harm, for he is dead, and his son also."

Genevieve was silent for a time, considering this. "Why, then, I wonder, is she so interested in his story?"

"Is she so terribly interested?"

"Oh, yes, my dear. It is my opinion that she has encouraged Mr. Dowbridge purely to learn about Helden Hall. The poor thing believes she is only intent on hearing him talk, and seems to be oblivious to the fact that Helden Hall is all she cares to hear about. I have only overheard parts of the conversations that have taken place in the drawing room, but I fear that every ride with the hapless young man is filled with sordid details that cannot be good for her to know."

He smiled again. "I will endeavor to set your mind at ease, then, my dear, for the truth is not so terribly sordid that it has not been canvassed at least a hundred times a year in every drawing room in the county for a decade. The Helden estate, which is not far from here, is not overly large, but was lovely and prosperous, with several tenants and a good farm. But from the day his son sent word of his marriage to a lady of whom he disapproved greatly, Lord Helden did everything within his power to see that the estate would be of no worth to its next master. It is said he never lifted a finger again for the benefit of the estate, but locked himself away, ignoring the claims and petitions of all those under his stewardship, selling off everything of value in the house, and using up every guinea that came in without investing a single penny back." He took a ruminative breath. "And by my observations, the rumors were nothing but true. The servants all left one by one, and the poor devils on the estate were forced to give up their farms and find another livelihood, as their homes fell into such deplorable disrepair they weren't fit for wild animals to live in."

"And his lordship simply ignored them?" cried his wife in disbelief. "How despicable!"

Sir Joshua nodded. "Indeed, it was, and proved one of the most enduring lessons I learned as a young man, for the very thought of so much good property, wasted for mere revenge, filled me with such repugnance that I resolved never to be guilty of anything resembling profligacy as long as I lived."

"But revenge, Joshua? What filled him with such hatred? Was his son's marriage so untenable?"

Sir Joshua absently ordered the papers on his desk. "It was not simply the marriage, Genevieve. Lord Helden was a cold, selfish man, whose only thought was for his own consequence. My mother often commented that his wife was never happy, poor woman, and most thought it a mercy when she died in childbirth. She gave him a son, but even this could not satisfy her lord, for the boy never seemed to measure up." He looked up at her with sadness in his eyes. "Poor Matthew Engleheart was the most browbeaten boy I've ever known. We were nearly contemporaries, you know, but he was extremely solitary—the only boy in the neighborhood who went happily back to school after every holiday, even when he faced torment there."

"Oh dear, Joshua," murmured Genevieve, her mother's heart wrung. "Had he no relations to help him?"

Sir Joshua considered. "I believe he had some cousins, on his mother's side, who took him from time to time, but they lived far away, and their situation in life didn't suit Lord Helden's consequence."

"And then—I believe I heard—he was sent abroad?"

"Just before Matthew came of age, he quarreled violently with his father, and vowed not to collude with him to break the entail—for his lordship desired that some of the land be sold off, and planned to stage a common recovery. Lord Helden flew into a rage, said Matthew had been nothing but a disgrace, and that he would have to learn what it was to fend for himself. Then he shipped him off to India."

"India!" Genevieve's eyes widened as the truth began to dawn. "Oh, my—was it there he met his wife?"

Sir Joshua nodded. "Yes, my love."

"Oh, Joshua!" cried Genevieve. "That a father could be so intolerant as to cast him off for that! I have known of many such marriages that have been perfectly well accepted."

"And I—but in this case there was some doubt as to the lady's birth, something which a man of Lord Helden's kidney could not countenance even in an English lady, and it was the last straw with him. He cut Matthew off, and the young man never set foot on English soil again, and died before he could discover in what a state the manor was left."

Genevieve's forehead creased in disgust and consternation. "What a horrid waste! I wonder that his lordship went to such measures. Could he not simply have disinherited the boy?"

"He could not for the entailment. It was also rumored the union produced a son."

"So the tyrant destroyed his property just for spite," spat Genevieve, standing and pacing about the room. "Oh, I have no patience for that sort of pride! I sincerely hope he got his deserts, and that his grandson—I suppose he must be of an age with Tom—was able to turn something of his inheritance to account!"

"You have one part of your wish, my love, but not the other. Lord Helden's health failed as soon as he began to neglect his estate, but four years ago he received the news that Matthew had died in an outbreak of plague. None in the house survived, and no word was received as to whether the child was involved. Lord Helden died two years later, leaving the estate in probate, for his grandson was the last of the Engleheart line."

"What a terrible tale, Joshua!" cried Genevieve. "But what is to become of the estate, and the title? Is there no one to claim it?"

"That I do not know. But I understand that the grandson's death must be incontrovertibly determined before another heir may make a claim, and with travel to India taking many months, it could conceivably take years before the estate, and the title, are settled." He leaned back, interlacing his fingers before him. "What with the gross neglect of its last occupant, and the rather energetic efforts of vandals, the solicitor was obliged to send up young Ingles some months ago to watch over things until the rightful heir can lay claim."

Genevieve shook her head. "I suppose I need not worry overmuch about Lenora's fascination, then, if there are no longer any Evil Dukes to lure her. The romance of a ruin is exciting enough, I daresay, and I cannot complain of the result. She has not been so lively since she came to us."

Sir Joshua came around the desk and took her hand, bending to kiss it. "Yes, my dear, and I only hope that her suitor will not misconstrue her liveliness."

"As I do, Joshua," Genevieve said, standing. "Though I fear it may already be too late."

But by the end of October, she detected a shift in the nature of Lenora's relationship to Mr. Dowbridge that eased her worries. Indeed, Lenora's initial persuasion that her swain looked with indulgence upon her curiosity regarding Helden Hall had been forced to give way to the conviction that the Hall held no fascination for him whatsoever, for she had begun to perceive what seemed to be resentment to her continual references to that place. It was not until she received from him a rather snappish response regarding her insatiable appetite for haunted manors, however, that she began to suspect that his motives for satisfying her had been, from the outset, entirely contrary to the disinterested friendliness to which she had attributed them. She imagined that he had even, perhaps, hoped to deaden her interest in the Hall by supplying her with nothing but the facts, and could only conclude from this that he was not in the least romantic. This discovery rather sunk him in her esteem; however, as he had shown himself a constant friend, she felt that he need not be of a mind with her on that head. She did judge it best to be decidedly more cool with him, however, and when the Princess Charlotte died suddenly in childbirth, she retreated into the national mourning with little regret.

Chapter 5

At the end of the two-week mourning period, Lady Stiles found herself overwhelmed with an accumulation of postponed duties, and requested Lenora to dispatch some errands for her in the village. Lenora, whose prowess in the saddle had yet to be proven at the reins, elected to bring Tess along with her in the gig, for that damsel—unlike the footman—could be relied upon to scarcely remark the times they swerved up the berm, and to give only a squeak whenever they nearly collided with a farm cart. The young ladies made their purchases, stowing them in the gig, and had just resolved upon entering the sweet shop for necessary restoratives when a commotion down the street drew their attention. A cart horse had reared up, and was being scolded by its driver, while several onlookers, mostly men from the nearby pub, were drawing close to regard with apparent derision something huddled in the road.

Lenora, perceiving that the dark bundle was a person, hurried toward the group, pushing her way through the jeering men, and stopped short at the sight of Mr. Ingles crumpled beside the stamping horse's hooves. She hesitated, recalling the exact tenor of their relationship, but she could not turn her back on a fellow creature in need, and marched forward to kneel in the road by his side. He was unconscious and smelled atrocious, of sweat and spirits and blood and dirt, and she was obliged to press her handkerchief to her nose. A cursory inspection revealed a severe blow to his hairy head, and a nasty-looking wound on his thigh, both of which would require proper care to heal. Removing the kerchief from his neck, she tied it around the leg, and pressed her folded handkerchief to his brow, looking about for someone to help her.

The crowd, by this time, had dispersed, but the cart driver was just backing his horse away. "Sir," she called to him, "will you go for the surgeon?"

He cast her a look of disapprobation. "He's off Cranham way, miss. Saw him go this morning."

"Is there no one else who could attend Mr. Ingles?" she asked, undaunted.

"Gor, miss, why?" was the disdainful response.

Her indignation aroused, she stood, assuming her loftiest air. "We cannot leave him in the street. His injuries are serious, sir, and no matter his past offenses, he is not dung to be trampled at will."

"He got hisself knocked down, miss," replied the man defensively, though he removed his hat respectfully. "He walked right a front of me horse. A menace to society, that one."

"Be that as it may, sir, if you and I do not do something, he may die. Someone must take him back to the lodge, and someone must tend his wound." When the carter still looked as if he would demur, she fished in her purse for a shilling and proffered it, adding, "Once he is laid up in his bed, he will give the village a respite from his irksome presence."

The good sense of this notion, strengthened by the shilling, struck the carter forcibly enough that he called a man over and they hefted Mr. Ingles between them into his cart. Lenora hurried over to the gig, where Tess had been watching the proceedings in awe, and climbed up, instructing the carter to take Mr. Ingles to the lodge of Helden Hall and place him upon his bed, while she went to find someone to tend to him. The carter tipped his cap, but saw them off with a dubious shake of the head.

"He looks mortal bad, miss!" exclaimed Tess, twisting around in her seat to gaze at the carter's load as they passed. "Do you expect he'll die?"

"No, though he may run a high fever from practically pickling himself in gin," replied Lenora.

Tess was undaunted. "All that blood—my cousin Joe got just such a wound, and it turned green and swelled up big as a melon!"

This earned her a horrified stare from her mistress. "Did he die?'

"Oh, no, only they cut off his leg." Tess shrugged. "He walked with a crutch, leastwise 'til the typhus carried him off last year."

Lenora swallowed but did not reply, having returned her gaze to the road just in time to avoid a signpost. Tess continued to chatter.

"If anyone's like to die, it'll be him, miss, for he's evil, he is."

"Mr. Ingles, evil?" replied Lenora, startled. "He may be odious and filthy, but he is not evil, I am persuaded, Tess."

The maid turned a knowing gaze upon her. "Begging your pardon, miss, but he must be. All he done since coming here is sell off the game from the manor and be disagreeable. He started friendly enough, but my cousin Theo says he's in the pub more often than not, and it's turned him sour. He didn't even see fit to mourn the Princess, miss! Imagine that! Not so much as a black riband about his arm! A man in his position, putting on airs." She huffed virtuously. "Strong drink is the Devil's snare, and Mr. Ingles is fairly caught, I say. No doubt he'll be struck dead, and that'll show him."

As Lenora listened to these interesting insights, several images revolved in her mind: of Helden Hall rising magnificently into the sky, of Mr. Ingles warning her off the grounds, and of the same odious man flat in bed, unaware of who may be trespassing on the manor. She would have been less than human had she not entertained this idea even a little, but to her credit, she made a valiant effort to stifle it, instead seizing on the far more exciting notion that the present Lord Helden, wherever he may be, would no doubt be grateful for her intervention on his retainer's behalf. Indeed, in committing to her present course, she had left behind the role of spectator in the stirring drama of Helden Hall, and had taken up the heroine's part.

They arrived at the Grange and handed the gig off to the groom, and Lenora, hastening into the house, called to her mother.

"Good gracious, Lenora," cried Lady Stiles, starting forward from the library into the hall, "I had just determined upon sending the servants after you! What can have happened to detain you for so long?"

Lenora immediately set her parent's mind at rest by pulling her back into the library and regaling her with a highly-colored account of the accident in the high street, and her subsequent heroic rescue.

"And now, Mama, I confess that I am in a quandary, for Mr. Ingles will need immediate attention to ensure his recovery, but there is none to provide it."

"But my dear, of course we shall supply all his needs!" responded her mother, in just the tone Lenora had hoped for. "The poor man. He is a discharged soldier, you say? It is too bad, that so many have fallen on hard times, after having given their hearts and souls to the defense of liberty."

"Recollect that he is a drunkard, Mama," Lenora said, wishing to make the matter entirely clear.

Her mother paused, but only for a moment. "There is that, my dear, but it only makes the poor man more deserving of our compassion. And who knows but what we shall cure him? Come," she said, standing resolutely and sweeping out of the library, with Lenora right behind. "I shall discuss with Blaine what we may take to him, while you gather such things as will make him more comfortable. And send a groom to fetch the doctor, as well, my dear."

With righteous fervor in her bosom, Lenora flew to find blankets and lint and basillicum powder and bandages, dispatching a maid to inform the groom of his errand, and met her mother in the hall within a half-hour, ready to return to the gatekeeper's lodge and its injured occupant. They packed their offerings into the gig and were off, Lenora relinquishing the ribbons to her mother while she gave the direction.

The lodge was very quiet when they approached the door, and Lenora was uncertain whether she hoped to find their patient still asleep, or awake and aware. A tap on the door elicited no response, so Lady Stiles opened it and stepped inside, and Lenora followed.

The house was simple, with one open room on the ground floor and stairs climbing to an attic above. A large fireplace meant for cooking as well as heating reposed in the far wall, the remains of a fire smoldering within and a kettle caked with something on the hob. Under the window on the right-hand wall was a rough-hewn table with dirty dishes and empty bottles strewn across it, and a bed with greasy linens lay against the other. The carter and his assistant had laid the still unconscious Mr. Ingles atop the bedclothes and the ladies could not tell if it was only he or the room as well that reeked of spirits and sweat.

Lady Stiles, stopping for several moments to take all this in, squared her shoulders and moved briskly forward to inspect her patient's wounds. "Hmm," she said, retrieving her handkerchief and holding it to her nose. "You were not exaggerating the seriousness of this business, Lenora. I shall tend to his wounds while you tidy up."

Lenora, whose vivid imaginings of angelic ministrations had been entirely overthrown upon entering the room, moved mechanically to obey her mother's directions. Lady Stiles busied herself in removing the patient's soiled nether garments and boots before setting to cleaning both wounds and binding them with lint and bandages. Lenora put her back to the now indecent patient, muttering indistinctly about men's horrid notions of cleanliness, and puttered about the room, arranging empty bottles in a row against the wall and tossing trash into the fireplace, until her mother pulled the bedclothes up over his chest.

These duties finished, the ladies went together out to the gig to retrieve the food and extra blankets they had brought with them, and to take a breath of fresh air. As they lingered on the gravel drive, Lady Stiles glanced toward the Hall, which rose up behind the trees.

"So that is Helden Hall?" she mused. "Such a somber prospect, though I cannot help but pity the house."

Lenora glanced at her mother in surprise. "You pity it?"

"After all," said Lady Stiles, "it is not at fault for the horrors that it has seen. How wrong that it should bear the brunt of the consequences. It looks a noble place. What a shame."

Lenora was made to feel that she had wronged her mother, for she had never considered that Lady Stiles could be romantic enough to pity a ruin, and with a heart warmed toward her, led the way back inside to their patient. Mr. Ingles was sitting up in his bed when they reentered, and he regarded them hazily from under his tangle of hair.

"I see you are up," said Lady Stiles in a capable tone, bustling forward and planting the basket the cook had provided on the table. "Now, if you will eat some of this good food, you will feel more the thing."

"I'm thirsty," said Mr. Ingles thickly, and he attempted to rise.

Lady Stiles and Lenora both hurried to push him back down. "Please, sir," said Lenora, "your head and leg are injured. You should not try to walk. I can get you some water."

"Gin," he grumbled, swiping at their hands.

Lady Stiles motioned Lenora to get water, and filled the bowl on the table with warm soup from the basket. "You'll not be getting any gin while we are here, Mr. Ingles, but here is some good, healthy food to give you strength."

"I don't want food," said Mr. Ingles, crossly, pushing away the bowl. "I'm thirsty."

Lenora returned with a mug of water and put it on the table next to the bed. "If you are thirsty, sir, then water will do you good."

"How can you tell what will do me good?" he growled, throwing off the blanket and lurching to his feet, but his leg collapsed beneath him and he fell back on the bed, clutching his head and groaning.

Lenora had spun around, blushing furiously at sight of his bare legs under his shirt tails, and Lady Stiles hastened to help him, but she was cursed for her pains, her hands pushed away in the roughest manner as she attempted to settle her recalcitrant patient back under the bedclothes. She was at last successful and stepped quickly away, out of his reach, while he glowered at them both.

Lady Stiles drew her daughter away into the corner. "My dear, this is the way with drunkards, as you may perhaps remember from your papa. It will be a day or two before he is reasonable. If his manner disturbs you, perhaps you could return to the Grange and desire Tess to come to me with a groom."

Though the reality of Mr. Ingles' situation had tarnished her romantic visions, she could never relinquish the cause in the name of mere squeamishness. "It does not disturb me, Mama!" she said, lifting her chin. "I can help, perhaps to better purpose than Tess, for I do recall Papa's episodes. In any event, it was I who brought this upon you, and I will not leave you to it alone."

"Very well, my dear," said her mother, not unpleased.

Mr. Plympton, the village surgeon-apothecary, arrived near three o'clock, and pronounced the patient in good hands. "We will watch for signs of brain injury, for that is a very nasty blow to his head, but the leg wound is only superficial, and the young man ought to be good as new with a bit of rest and good care." He drew Lady Stiles with him toward the door and added in an under voice, "And it wouldn't hurt if he was kept from the bottle while he's in bed. The drier he is, the faster he'll recover."

Lady Stiles, well-versed in the consequences of spirits on health, nodded her understanding and, tapping the side of his nose conspiratorially, the doctor was gone.

Chapter 6

For the remainder of the afternoon, the two ladies took it in turns to patiently remonstrate with their patient, and were at last able to coax and cajole him into taking the water and a few spoonfuls of soup. When their own dinner time drew on, they built up the fire and tucked the new blanket around him, Lady Stiles quietly gathering up all remaining liquor in the house while Lenora cheerily advised him that they would return the next day, to which he responded with a resentful grunt.

And return they did, for four days, until their patient no longer shook nor raged, nor complained at taking water instead of spirits, but only somberly gazed on them as they bustled about his house, and even occasionally muttered a word of thanks. He had caught a chill, which Lady Stiles informed him briskly was common enough in those who took no care for their health, but he had shown no symptom of brain injury, and the leg wound bade fair to heal completely, inducing Lady Stiles to relinquish the burden of the remaining few visits to the lodge to Lenora's capable shoulders, if she could prevail upon Tess to accompany her.

This Lenora greeted with mixed emotions, having endured the preceding five days in a heroic spirit of long suffering, and having felt a material diminution in her eagerness to be of use to the odiously hairy caretaker, whose surly attitude had not much softened toward her through her ministrations. Having had experience with her own papa in his drunken periods, however, she could not much blame him, and palliated her reflections by dwelling on the fact that she would be fully justified in approaching the gatekeeper's lodge through the Home Wood, which would take her once more past the Hall. Thus resolved, she approached Tess in full expectation of a debate, but Lenora's heroic manner over the preceding week had so impressed the maid that she had long desired to try her hand at ministering to a Lost Soul, and she greeted Lenora's request with elation.

Thus, with Tess in tow, Lenora emerged from the forest the next day onto that fascinating prospect of the wild lawn, with the overgrown gardens beyond, and the decaying mansion rising up into the afternoon sky. After standing at the edge of the forest with Tess, breathlessly surveying the picturesque scene and refreshing its imprint in her memory, she boldly set off with a righteous sense of impunity through the very landscape to which she had so long been denied access.

They traversed the path through the high grass, Lenora reaching her hands out to feel the feathery seed-heads against her palms, and thrilling to hear the swish of her skirts against the stems. They reached the maze of bramble and ivy which had grown up to support the bristling hedge like some magical barrier against intruders, and rather than go around, Lenora pronounced that they would go through, for they were there by tacit permission and it would do no harm for them to wend their way over the property, in the event they should not have the chance again.

They were obliged to seek for an inlet that would not leave their skirts in shreds and their hands bleeding, and at last, after much poking and prying, they discovered a narrow opening that must have been the original entrance to the maze. They slipped through it, their feet crunching lightly on the weedy gravel, and pushed their way through the now nearly impassable maze, but after only a few false turns, and at the expense of Lenora's shawl, which caught and was frayed on an unhandsome briar, the path at last opened to the broad veranda.

Lenora gazed at the somber facade of the house, her mind alight with visions of the various horrors it had seen, and she greatly desired to catch a glimpse of the shadowed rooms, to determine if there could be hidden treasure or secret passageways. Knowing this to be impossible—much as she would like it, she could not justify tacit permission to go poking about the house—she and Tess continued on their way around the outside of the mansion, voicing their various speculations regarding the state of the interior, the probability of its entertaining ghostly inhabitants, and the likelihood of their swooning should they ever have cause to meet one.

They arrived at the lodge in a mood of gaiety, and in the bustle of their entrance did not at first notice the strange silence that reigned in the room. But when Lenora turned to greet their patient, she discovered the bed was empty, the blankets swept off, and Mr. Ingles huddled on the ground.

With a cry the girls flew to his side, calling his name, but he did not respond. Lenora touched his cheek, which was flushed and hot, and tried to brush the hair away from his neck.

"He is burning with fever, Tess! His wounds may have become infected. Help me roll him onto his back."

They managed it with a great heave, and Lenora peeked under the bandage on his head, but the wound was calm and healing nicely. She bent to inspect his leg, rolling up his breeches to where that wound, neatly bandaged, seemed entirely undistressed. Lenora sat back, regarding her patient in bewilderment. From where had the fever come?

Then Mr. Ingles' body shook with a paroxysm of coughing, and she instantly recalled his slight chill of the previous few days. "Oh, good gracious, Tess! He must have taken an inflammation of the lung! We must get him back into bed, and summon the doctor!"

With many a heave and a strain, the two young ladies managed to pull him up between them and topple his inert body back onto the bed.

Flopping into a chair, Tess fanned herself with the edge of her apron. "Oh, miss! He must weigh a tonne! We'd like to have killed ourselves, and for what?"

"We could not leave him on the floor, Tess," replied Lenora, catching her breath. "There can be no question that our exertions were necessary."

"He'll surely die now, miss, what with the inflammation of the lung. My neighbor Bessie was took off just three years ago by—"

"Enough, Tess!" cried Lenora. "I've worked too hard for him to die now. How can you be so careless for his welfare? I shall not give him up!"

With renewed vigor, Lenora set about making the patient more comfortable, and one touch of his burning skin reminded her that time was of the essence. "Tess, you must fly to Wrenthorpe and send one of the grooms for the doctor, at once."

The maid, stung into action by her mistress's unequivocal tones, hurried to the door, but she abruptly turned back. "But miss! I can't leave you alone with him! Tisn't proper!" she cried, wringing her hands in the doorway.

Lenora, all efficiency, glared at her henchwoman. "He's no more fit to compromise me than a lamb, Tess! His life is worth more than your scruples—now go!"

Tess bit back any other qualms she felt and turned, flinging out of the cottage and up the drive, toward the Home Wood. Lenora worked quickly and methodically, her mind only once becoming distracted by the thought of how romantic was the circumstance of her saving a young man's life, if only he had not been the most odious, smelly, hairy young man she had ever met.

Pulling the blanket over him and tucking it up around his chest, she was again struck at how young he was beneath all that hair. He could not be much older than herself, she thought, perhaps of an age with Tom, a realization which gave her a strange sensation beneath her breastbone. Shrugging this off, she hurried to find a cloth and bowl of cold water with which to bathe his fevered brow. He moaned and tossed his head from side to side, which made it difficult for her to do her work, and after twice bathing the pillow rather than his face, she found it necessary to remonstrate with him.

In no real expectation of a response, she was rather surprised when he snatched her hand and held it to his chest, moaning, "Forgive me, Mata, but it is too hard, too hard." Lenora blinked at this, wondering who Mata could be, but he did not speak again, relapsing once more into restless sleep.

As the minutes dragged by, and her patient continued to toss and turn, she wished for the hundredth time that the doctor would come, and that Mr. Ingles was a shaving sort of man, and had not so much hair for her to contend with as she bathed his face. She absently brushed at her skirts, which were speckled in clinging sanicle seeds, and in her impatience bent to pull them off, murmuring against the unkempt lawn, which had suddenly lost all its fascination. But as she turned to toss the handful of seeds into the fire, she was checked by the recollection of a novel in which a stricken maiden had been nursed to health by a potion of boiled sanicle.

"Sanicle heals all," she murmured, recollecting having seen sanicle on the shelf at the village apothecary, and she resolved to try if it would help.

Mr. Ingles stirred fretfully as she poured the tisane into his mug, and she hastened to his side to calm him, brushing back that reprehensible hair from his face with a cool hand. His eyelids flickered open and he gazed hazily at her with eyes that she had thought were beetle black, but were quite a warm brown in the light of the fire.

"You are an angel," he murmured, his accent strangely softened. "Have I died?"

"You are safe, Mr. Ingles," Lenora replied gently. "The doctor will come at any moment, but you must drink this medicine I have made for you."

He clasped her wrist urgently, his eyes burning. "It will kill me!" Lenora hastened to reassure him, but he shook his head in despair. "The Hall! It is cursed! I am cursed!"

Lenora's hand came up to cover his on her wrist, her eyes nearly as intent as his own. "Calm yourself, Mr. Ingles. You speak of Lord Helden's curse?"

"Yes, and now it is mine," he said, releasing her and easing into his pillow once more. "Perhaps it is better that I die."

Lenora gripped his clammy hand tightly. "You shall not die, Mr. Ingles!" she declared, with sincerity in every syllable. While there was breath in her body, she vowed that the evil Old Lord's curse should not triumph, even over someone as odious as Mr. Ingles.

Her patient spoke no more, but with some coaxing, he was induced to take the spoon that she held to his lips, and he drank down much of the sanicle tisane with his burning hand over hers, before finally turning his head away and closing his eyes. Lenora sighed and put the cup on the hob, sternly subduing her rampant desire to make him tell her the particulars of the curse, and secretly fearing that there was nothing that was not already known by the entire neighborhood.

Presently, the crunch of hooves sounded on the gravel outside, and Lenora hastened to open the door. Mr. Plympton hurried into the room, followed closely by the faithful Tess, who eyed her mistress surreptitiously as if to discern whether Mr. Ingles had kept the line while alone with her. She was apparently satisfied, for she quickly busied herself making a wholesome broth for the invalid, at the doctor's orders.

An inspection with a wooden tube, which the doctor proudly proclaimed to be a stethoscope "direct from France, miss," confirmed the diagnosis of an inflammation of the lung. Such a malady was serious, and would require even more attention, but Lenora's determination was fortified by the likelihood that, if she were to perform that care, she would be on hand to receive any more of Mr. Ingles' revelations.

The doctor, having finished his examination, noticed the cup on the hob and sniffed it, turning to Lenora with brows raised. "Well, Miss Breckinridge," he said, eying her with something like respect, "I must congratulate you on your nursing skills. Not many young ladies would think to use sanicle in this case."

She blushed and disclaimed, and he rose to collect his tools, adding, "Tess has told me how matters stand, and considering the service you have already rendered, I expect you will be glad to give over management of Mr. Ingles to another nurse."

"On the contrary, Mr. Plympton," Lenora cried, believing that wild horses could not have dragged her from her patient's side after his fevered disclosure, "I feel a particular responsibility for Mr. Ingles, and should consider it a dereliction of duty to leave him to another's care, merely for my own comfort!"

The doctor endeavored to relieve her mind on this head, expressing his full confidence in her unexceptionable behavior, as he added, "This is a hard case, miss. Mr. Ingles will need constant care for several days, including linen changes, which will hardly be appropriate for a young lady to perform."

Lenora scorned this notion, informing him that if propriety was what concerned him, she should have her mother, or some other respectable female with her, to perform such tasks.

He seemed unconvinced. "Her ladyship ought not to waste time on such a case as this, miss, and nor should you. I can promise to visit him once per day, but I will only have a few minutes to spare. It would be best to hire one of the village matrons to sit with him."

"None would care to come, I fear," rejoined Lenora. "The village thinks just enough of Mr. Ingles as to leave him lying in the street like so much refuse. If I had not insisted on his being removed into a cart and transported here, he would very well have died."

This seemed to give the doctor pause, and Lenora, recognizing victory within her grasp, swept on, "To be sure, doctor, we are happy to be of service to a fellow being, especially one who has none else to care whether he lives or dies. It is the least we could do for a man who has given his all in the defense of liberty!" she added impressively.

In the face of this declaration, the doctor could not do otherwise than to agree, and left instructions until the following day, when he promised to visit again and see how the young man fared. Lenora, in turn, requested him to take word to the Grange of what had passed, then saw him out, barely concealing her exultation at having won the day—and all rights to Mr. Ingles' inevitable confidences.

For the ensuing three days, the ladies of Wrenthorpe Grange took it in turns to stand vigil over Mr. Ingles' bedside, ably assisted by the laundress, who declared that the poor boy was no different than her own eldest boy, who'd seen such horrors in the Peninsula as would give the best of men a fractious disposition, and if he couldn't be forgiven his tendency toward a good grip on the bottle, he ought at least to be pitied for it. This conviction rather overthrew Lenora's views on the temperament of the villagers, but it was a circumstance in which she found she could not repine, though the good woman's involvement did lessen Lenora's chances of being on hand for the anticipated revelations.

In an attempt to forestall disappointment, therefore, Lenora gathered the courage to request her mama—who it had been decided would pair with Tess on these visits, while Lenora accompanied the laundress—to apprise her of any communications Mr. Ingles happened to make. Her mother seemed surprised at this entreaty, and inquired as to the reason.

"Mr. Ingles hinted to me that he feels a certain dread," replied Lenora carefully, "and as I feel a degree of responsibility for him, I wish only to ascertain that his mind is healing, in addition to his body."

Lady Stiles agreed to the request, but with a crease between her brows, and was rather tight-lipped the remainder of the day.

As it transpired, Mr. Ingles's communications were limited to unintelligible moanings, until at last, on the third day, his fever broke. Made pliant by weakness and fatigue, the patient obeyed his nurses' every stricture and recovered apace, while never again making reference to anything akin to curses or dread. Indeed, he was a further disappointment to Lenora in his almost rude manner when she was his nurse, hardly looking at her, and saying as few words to her as possible during her stay. When the doctor pronounced the patient recovered, Mr. Ingles offered his thanks to the ladies with gruff sincerity, but seemed as though he would be more than satisfied to see their backs.

The ladies, three of whom were pleased enough with the happy result of their labors, returned to their usual employments and entertainments, but Lenora could not help but feel bereft. With no expectation of a recrudescence of the caretaker's symptoms—indeed, she could not wish there to be—she had lost all possible connection with the beloved Hall, and feared that her all too briefly glorious part in the story was finished. Mr. Dowbridge had imparted all the information he possessed, Tess, while sympathetic, could offer only conjecture, and Lenora still did not trust her romantic fascination to her parents. Therefore, the only course open to her was the relinquishment of Helden Hall—a course that filled her with dejection.

Chapter 7

THOUGH LADY STILES had been decidedly in agreement with her daughter's determination to champion poor Mr. Ingles's recovery, she could not but have noticed the girl's tenacity in the project, and a dark suspicion had taken hold of her imagination as to its cause. Having observed Lenora's tender patience with Mr. Ingles's secondary indisposition, and received her astonishing request to relate his communications, it was not surprising that her ladyship would come to the distressing conclusion that her daughter's subsequent malaise was caused by unrequited love.

"It defies reason, Joshua!" cried Genevieve one night as she burst in upon her husband in his dressing room. "I cannot conceive how a girl of Lenora's sensibility could fall in love with such a—such a hairy man!"

With a knowing smile, Sir Joshua dismissed his valet—whose disdain for all such sordid matters as love showed plainly on his pinched face—and drew his wife into a chair by the fire, settling into another opposite as she ranted on.

"He has not spoken to Lenora but to criticize or grumble—he plainly has no opinion of her, even after having been brought back from the brink of death by her intervention—and yet she would not leave him to the care of others, though given every opportunity. She is besotted, Joshua!"

Her husband's eyes gleamed, and he leaned back in his chair, musing, "Perhaps Mr. Ingles—I assume he is the person to which you refer, my love—reminds Lenora of a Bluebeard. I have it on good authority that pirates are excessively romantic."

Genevieve regarded him with pursed lips. "I wish you will be serious, Joshua. Mr. Ingles is a landbound, penniless drunkard, who has as much romance to recommend him as a mongrel dog."

"Ah, but appearances may be deceiving, my dear. We must not make assumptions about a man who has endured the hardships that poor James Ingles has been called upon to endure."

Chastened by this generous view, she nevertheless cast him a darkling look. "Next, I suppose you will assert his unfortunate circumstances secure poor James Ingles' right to my daughter's hand, notwithstanding they are decidedly beneath her own!"

"My darling, you leap too far ahead! If Lenora does have a tendre for James Ingles—of which I am not yet convinced, mind you—it does not mean that marriage must be the result. As you well know, Lenora's sensibility must be taken into consideration, and though it has carried her into strange waters in the past, it has never carried her completely away. I cannot believe that her present infatuation—if that is, indeed, what it is—will be her only, or her last. Her good sense will see her through."

With this Genevieve was obliged to agree, and she called upon this conviction to quiet the fluttering voices in her mind whenever she came upon Lenora gazing longingly out the window at the Home Wood—toward Helden Hall, and the gatekeeper's lodge, and the incredibly hairy Mr. Ingles. Her chief consolation was in the recollection that Lenora had fancied herself in love before, with a Mr. Barnabus—a worthy young gentleman, to be sure—and had emerged from the experience unscathed, but also wiser.

Lady Stiles was not the only person to detect a marked difference in Lenora's demeanor; her abstraction could not pass unnoticed by Mr. Dowbridge, who was determined to reinstate himself after her protracted absence from society. His advances were met with such detached friendliness that a less assured individual would have succumbed to a similar conclusion as had her mother, and relapsed into grumbling acceptance of his fate, with many ill-wishes upon the head of whatever sneaksby had captured Miss Breckinridge's heart. But Mr. Dowbridge, with an in-bred belief in his own worth, suffered few such illusions, and continued his attentions to her with the happy conviction that any other contender for her affections could not stand against his better claim. Had he been given to understand that his rival was a crumbling, haunted mansion, whose history, destiny, and present mysteries would not leave Lenora's mind in peace, his feelings would have been difficult to determine.

Mr. Ingles's emotions during this time were likewise difficult to determine. He had been exceedingly grateful to the Wrenthorpe ladies for their unmitigated kindness—he had not received such treatment since his days at school under his landlady, Mrs. Swaythe's, motherly care. He had been rendered distinctly uncomfortable, however, by the presence of Miss Breckinridge during his most vulnerable moments, and the awareness that she was a most genteel, pretty girl was not made less unnerving by the vague recollection of his having taken her hand and uttered—he knew not what.

Despite this challenge to his equilibrium, or perhaps because of it, Mr. Ingles found within himself a feeling of determination that had been lost some years past, in the depths of the War, and which had had no chance of revival while he had been utterly alone and without prospects. With this determination, he set to his work on the manor with a new will, spending his energy on improvement rather than brooding over a bottle, and always, always ruminating over what he should do about Miss Breckinridge.

After some two weeks, he resolved to seek her out—and Lady Stiles, too, of course—and attempt to convey once more his gratitude to them, while trying to determine if what he had said to Miss Breckinridge had been inappropriate or imprudent in any way, so that he could explain it away. He set forth, but he had gotten only ten paces into the shelter of the wood between the estates when he came upon Miss Breckinridge herself, with her maid, coming the opposite way. This so disconcerted him that he merely stopped still and stared at her—them—until he recollected himself, and retreated into his habitual impassivity.

Lenora, who had that morning conceived the notion that as Mr. Ingles had, in fact, acknowledged his indebtedness to his nurses for his present state of health, perhaps he would not grudge her and Tess coming—through the Home Wood so that the Hall must be circumnavigated, of course—to see him on a visit of disinterested goodwill. When he met her, however, his grave manner, with his arms crossed uncompromisingly over his chest, and his beard clean but bushy as ever, he looked every inch the landbound pirate her step-father had envisaged, and she faltered to a stop.

"Good day, Mr. Ingles. I was coming to see how you get on."

"You see that I'm very well, Miss Breckinridge," he said.

Refusing to shrink from his abrupt manner, Lenora replied, "And I am glad to know it, sir. I suppose I have come to feel responsible for you, and felt anxious to confirm your welfare."

He gazed at her, apparently unmoved. "You'd do better to come by the road."

"I—I thought to gather some sanicle on my way," she offered, "so that should you feel a relapse imminent, you would have enough for another tisane."

He grunted. "Hot drinks don't suit me."

"I had gathered that," she answered a little tartly. "Perhaps you have been thirsty of late, having nothing stronger than tea in your house."

He shifted on his feet. "I've not been to the village."

"Oh," said Lenora, observing upon earnest inspection that, for the first time in their acquaintance, he did seem remarkably in command of himself. If he had gone all this time without strong drink, of his own volition, perhaps he was cured of that odious habit, and she was pleased for him, to be sure.

She rocked a little on her feet, her gaze darting past him to the mansion. "It was quite a shock to find you unconscious in the road, sir."

He regarded her gravely. "You oughtn't to have bothered with me."

"You could hardly expect me to leave you to die—"

"You didn't know as I would die."

"No, but as a Christian, it behooved me to make certain you did not, sir," she said with some asperity. "How could I reconcile it with my conscience not to help you, when I had already behaved toward you in the most improper manner—That is, when anyone could see your injuries were most serious, and that you hadn't a friend in the world? You must have a poor notion of my principles, sir, if you believe—"

"I don't, Miss Breckinridge," he interrupted, quite gently. "I'm not used to speaking with—people." He scratched the back of his neck. "What I meant to say was that it was kind of you to help me, when I'd only ever been rough with you. Thank you."

Lenora, astonished, murmured something proper, then averted her eyes, her gaze landing on the Hall behind him.

After another silence, Mr. Ingles asked, "Why do you have such an interest in the Big House?"

Her eyes shifted quickly to his face. "I—I had no notion you would have recollected that."

"You did make a point of it, and you can't take your eyes off it now."

The color rushed into her cheeks, and she began to feel incredibly foolish. "It—it is only—" she stammered, frantically searching for a reasonable answer. Recalling her mother's words, she said at last, "It is such a noble house that I find its state shameful. Something ought to be done."

He regarded her inscrutably for some moments and she wished she had not come. He thought her nothing but an encroaching busybody, and would tell her so at any moment.

"Should you like to go around the house?" he asked.

She blinked. "Go—go in, you mean?"

"Only if you'd like."

Her heart thumping with incredulous joy, Lenora was obliged to compose herself before replying, "I should like that excessively, Mr. Ingles."

"Today suits me," he said. "Now, if you wish."

She gaped at this utterly strange version of the caretaker and burst out, "You're certain you aren't foxed?"

He huffed, his eyes twinkling briefly before he replied, "I'm sober as a judge, ma'am. On my honor."

"To be sure, sir, indeed!" cried Lenora, coloring. "Forgive me, I ought not to have questioned—Yes! Yes, that will do very well. We are at leisure, are we not, Tess?"

Tess, who was gazing wide-eyed over Mr. Ingles's shoulder at the mansion, did not seem to be much excited by this prospect, but nodded at Lenora's prodding.

With a wry glance at Tess, Mr. Ingles led the way through the fallen grass and around the hedge maze to the veranda, but Lenora scarcely noticed the journey thither, so thrilled was she to be once more a player in Helden Hall's story. The great house brooded before her, dark and forbidding, marking her approach with its sightless eyes, sending a shiver of fear up her back as she imagined it was daring her to enter its mottled stone portals. Mr. Ingles placed his hand on the knob of the door and turned it, and Lenora and Tess held their breath as the door swung wide. Then he stepped aside, motioning the two round-eyed young ladies into the forbidden house.

Lenora blinked at him. "You do not come with us?"

"I'll go for candles," responded Mr. Ingles. "But you may go on ahead if you like. There's quite enough light in the main rooms."

A twinge of dread had seized Lenora's stomach at his words. She had envisioned Mr. Ingles as their guide through the Hall, and had never doubted the assurance that, as the rightful caretaker, he would stand between them and any irascible specters that should come in their way. But the shadowed recesses beckoned enticingly to her, and she reached out to grip Tess's hand. Tess, who had never once desired to enter the haunted mansion in her life, was nevertheless determined to stand by her mistress come what may, and pressed Lenora's hand with her own. With a dignified bow of their heads to the caretaker, she and Lenora stepped forward, into the darkness of Helden Hall.

The room they entered was large, almost cavernous, and extended right and left into the shadows. Motes of dust danced in the shafts of sunlight that filtered through the boards over the windows, and cobwebs clung to the casements. Their footsteps echoed as they moved cautiously into the vast chamber, their skirts sweeping up dust as they went.

"This must have been the Grand Saloon," observed Lenora in a low tone, but echoes reverberated back to her.

Tess nodded, her eyes darting back and forth as if ghostly visions chased just beyond her vision. They attained the middle of the room and, their eyes adjusting to the dimness, could descry the medallioned ceiling that rose above the first floor, where a gallery overlooked the room.

"See, Tess? There would the musicians have sat to play, and Lord and Lady Helden would have danced here with their guests—"

"But the Old Lord never danced, miss," put in Tess.

Lenora breathed in sharply. "Of course you are right, Tess. To be sure, he'd not have allowed his lady such delight. She would have walked the gallery in solitude, yearning for the lost joys of her youth while he gloated in the shadows."

Something fluttered on the balcony railing, and the room felt suddenly colder. Lenora's gaze flitted about the gallery, certain the desolate Lady Helden would at any moment make an appearance, but there was only shifting dust on the air. Refusing to submit to a growing sense of unease, she renewed her hold on Tess's arm and moved purposely toward one of several open doorways leading from the room. Her progress was slow, however, for Tess seemed to have acquired leaden feet.

"It's my belief that wicked Mr. Ingles is set on doing away with us," hissed the maid, as the floorboards creaked beneath them. "He's sent us in here to be gobbled up by vampires, that all live in the cellar, and any moment they'll leap through the floor to feed their monstrous appetites!"

For a moment, Lenora's gaze was locked on the floor. "That cannot be. Recollect, Tess, that though Mr. Ingles is, in general, disagreeable, I cannot believe that he would deliberately guide us into danger."

Tess agreed to this, but without conviction, and the two continued forward, emerging into a wide, low corridor that ran the width of the saloon. At either end, a grand staircase wound upward, and before them arches opened onto an immense hall, with tall pillars running down either side which supported the galleries on the first floor. Light cascaded from the partially boarded windows above, an illumination that seemed only to enhance the pervading eeriness.

"The Great Hall," whispered Lenora. "I am persuaded that, after his wife's death, his lordship took his meals here in solitary state, while his poor son languished in a tiny cell somewhere in the farthest reaches of the house."

"It's said he hated the boy from the moment he was born," supplied Tess, "and short of murdering him, made his life as miserable as could be."

The girls hovered in one of the archways, clinging to one another as they reflected upon the wretchedness of the lives that had been so lately lived in this place. Daunted by the vast emptiness of the hall, Lenora considered whether her courage would extend to exploring up the staircase, but at her slight movement Tess grabbed hold of her arm.

"I can't, miss, I can't go farther in this great, dark house!" she hissed. "It's evil, it is, miss, and I fear for our souls!"

"Calm yourself, Tess," returned Lenora, her voice barely above a whisper. "It is only an oppression of spirits you feel, depend upon it, from the imposing size of the rooms, and their darkness and decrepitude."

"There are ghosts, miss!" insisted Tess. "It's no use denying. They flit away before I can see them but it's true all the same—I can feel them watching me!"

A breeze sighed through one of the high windows into the hall, stirring the cobwebs that festooned the balcony like bunting, and sending the dust eddying at their feet. It swirled up behind the girls, as if in a ghostly caress, and of one accord they darted away from it, scurrying forward into the hall. The vastness of that chamber instantly overpowered them, however, and they sought refuge in the nearest corner.

Pressed up against the wall, Lenora shivered, her sensations having suffered a complete reversal, from excitement to fear. As her eyes darted about the dim hall, she imagined she could see the pale form of Lady Helden floating behind the pillars, and the Old Lord's sinister figure peering at them from the balcony above. Her skin crawled, and she thought with detached horror that these were the same dreadful sensations she had experienced time and again reading Gothic novels, but without the delightful sense of impunity provided by the barrier of the page.

"Perhaps we ought to turn back, Tess," she whispered, endeavoring not to betray how near she was to terror. "We need not penetrate farther without Mr. Ingles."

Tess's answering whimper was in eloquent agreement, and the two began sliding along the wall toward the nearest archway.

"It is not as though we are forced to remain, as are the heroines in books," continued Lenora, feeling it necessary to fill the silence.

They slipped through the archway to be confronted by the seemingly immense width of the corridor.

"Indeed," she said, swallowing valiantly, "we are more brave than those heroines in books, for we chose to come to this place, knowing it was haunted, and entered of our own volition."

Eyes flicking back and forth, up and down, they inched away from the wall, moving slowly but deliberately across the terrifying expanse.

"And if no other writes a book of our exploits this day," Lenora chattered on as they neared the closest doorway to the saloon, "we must certainly—"

A groan echoed through the corridor, followed by a sharp creak, and both girls screamed as the floor fell away beneath Lenora.

Chapter 8

JAMES HAD JUST rounded the back corner of the Big House when Tess's frantic screams assailed his ears. He bounded across the veranda and through the open door, but was forced to stop, blinking away the darkness until he could assimilate the scene. Tess stood rigid, eyes screwed shut and screaming without cessation, while Miss Breckinridge looked at first to be crouching on the floor, but as his eyes adjusted, he could plainly discern that a floorboard had given way beneath her, and that she was at least partially suspended over the hole with her hands braced on either side.

Her face was pale, and her wide eyes flew to his. "Please, sir, help me before—before something—" He stepped quickly forward, but she cried out, "Don't! The floor may not support you, and then we shall both be eaten by vampires!"

Her situation required that he not waste mental energy in translating that last, incoherent message, but he moved forward cautiously while testing the boards beneath his feet, until he came close enough to grasp her under the arms.

"Ready now?"

"Do take care!" she said breathlessly. "I fear something has me by the foot."

"I'll go slowly, never fear. Only advise me if you feel anything amiss."

Tess, who had stopped screaming when it had become apparent that Lenora was not lying dead and broken in the nether regions, moved her hands to cover her mouth, and watched fixedly as Mr. Ingles eased Lenora out of the ragged hole and lifted her in his arms to carry her to a safe spot in the saloon. Placing her gently on the floor, he asked if she was unhurt, to which she responded by feeling her leg through her skirts and nodding her head.

"They took my half boot," she said, rather mournfully.

Tess, flying to her side, took her hand and pressed it to her cheek. "Oh, miss! I told you there was vampires, just as sure as there was ghosts!"

"Forgive my disbelieving you, Tess," said Lenora with a little sob. "This house is assuredly cursed."

"Aye, miss, so it is! We ought never to have come!"

"I felt them all in those dreadful moments I was trapped," Lenora said on a shiver. "The Old Lord and his lady, and the poor son."

"I could see them, miss! Leastwise, I would've if I'd kept my eyes open—but they was all here, staring at us with their cavernous eyes!"

"Oh, that they knew we could only wish to help them!" cried Lenora. "So much tragedy—so much despair!"

As Tess was entering into these feelings, a strange sound made them pause. They turned instantly toward the spot where the floor had given way, but it soon became clear the sound was not emanating from there. It was a rhythmic huffing, that became a wheeze—Lenora looked to Mr. Ingles and gave way to astonished dismay. His shoulders shook and his eyes crinkled, and the wheeze transformed to a deep chuckle, which he strove to suppress but evidently could not.

"Mr. Ingles!" exclaimed Lenora, shifting away from him. "Whatever can you be laughing at?"

He did not answer, but as the girls looked on in indignation, he laughed until the tears ran from his eyes and soaked into his bushy beard. He covered his eyes and rocked back and forth, gasping for breath and uttering occasional inarticulate words, until at last, after several minutes, he composed himself.

"Pardon me, ladies," he said, swiping an arm across his eyes. "Pray accept my sincerest apologies—I could not help it."

"We are all happiness to oblige you, sir," said Lenora stiffly. "Perhaps you may oblige us in return by telling us what in our situation could have struck you as humorous."

"Only that you frightened yourselves silly. Ghosts and vampires? A curse?" He chuckled again. "I fancied you liked this house, ma'am."

"It is ungentlemanly of you to poke fun when it was yourself who told me it was cursed, sir," replied Lenora, tight-lipped.

After a ruminative pause he asked, "Did I, then?"

"You did," said Lenora, on her dignity. "And unless you did it for a joke, sir, I do not see how you could have imagined I would not take you at your word."

He rubbed his jaw. "Would this have been when I was taken sick, ma'am? In a fever, perhaps?"

Lenora gaped at him, struck by his meaning, then looked away. "Perhaps it was, sir, but you cannot blame me for believing your words, even if you were out of your senses, when all the neighborhood had corroborated them already."

"Aye, so they have," he agreed amicably. "And I suppose what a lot of people say makes it true."

"Odious man," muttered Lenora under her breath. Louder, she said, "There is nothing about this place to suggest otherwise, sir!"

"Only you've not gone past the passage, ma'am, so how can you think that? Perhaps there's something farther on that will change your mind."

Tess started so violently at this that Lenora was moved to protest. "We no longer wish to tour the house, sir," she sniffed. "We will return home instantly."

He shrugged and helped her as she struggled to stand while holding her unshod foot off the floor. Motioning to the foot, he said, "Does it pain you?"

"No, but having lost my boot, I do not wish to ruin my stocking as well," was the curt reply.

He scratched his beard. "It seems a shame to leave the boot in the cellar. I'll fetch it for you, if you'd like."

Lenora, supported by Tess, was taken a bit out of her angry stride. "That is very kind of you, sir, though I do not believe Tess should like to wait another moment in this room."

"Thank you, miss," whispered Tess, tugging her arm.

"You both may wait outside, Miss Breckinridge," he said, folding his arms across his chest. "But I must own to disappointment. I did not take you for such a faint-hearted miss."

Lenora favored him with a withering glance. "If it were only me, I should go in a trice, but Tess is in no state to remain."

"But miss, are you wishful of going on?" asked the incredulous Tess.

"I could wish for nothing else, Tess, as you must know, but I cannot go on without you."

Tess, conflicted, dubiously eyed the doorway to the passage, and the vast hall beyond. "I suppose Mr. Ingles will protect us, miss, if we come across any ghouls."

Reassured by Mr. Ingles on this point, Tess resigned herself to whatever gruesome fate awaited them, and supported her mistress back into the corridor separating the saloon and the hall, carefully skirting the hole that gaped across the last doorway. Mr. Ingles helpfully indicated a patch of damp in the ceiling above the hole, and rot was readily apparent on the splintered remains of the broken floorboard, a circumstance which served to bolster both girls' spirits.

Through a door beyond the formal staircase was a slim servants' hallway where, lighting them each a candle, Mr. Ingles led the way down into the rabbit-warren of the basement. He took them directly to a pantry, where Lenora's half boot lay in a pile of splinters and plaster. Her footwear restored, Lenora boldly indicated her readiness to explore the basement, whispering to Tess that they never knew but that it might yield a dungeon or secret passage.

They exited the pantry into the kitchen, which was spacious and had apparently been well-appointed before its plunder by the Old Lord. One entire wall, where Lenora imagined some cabinets had once stood, was now empty, and a small chopping block graced a space large enough for a sizable table. A pair of pots sat forlornly atop a rusting iron stove, their shadows from the candlelight flickering against a buffet, whose cupboard doors hung open to reveal cobweb-festooned remains of food.

"Lord Helden's last meal, I expect," observed Lenora in a low voice.

Tess eyed the food with undisguised fascination. "It's a shame what's gone to waste here. That honey pot would still be good, I'll guess."

Mr. Ingles plucked the pot of crystallized honey from the shelf and held it out to her. "Take it, and welcome."

Tess stepped back, glancing warily at the pot. "I've no wish to steal from the dead."

"It's no longer the property of the Old Lord," he said, still proffering the pot. "The new orders are to use what can be used. Take it."

After a pause wherein she strove between fear and frugality, Tess took the honey pot from Mr. Ingles, and Lenora led the way through the scullery, the buttery, and the larder, intent upon her secret passage. Her triumph was great upon the discovery of a locked door between two cellars, but Mr. Ingles was able, after a search through his pockets, to produce the key, and the much anticipated opening of the door revealed nothing more than a closet with one forlorn broom leaning like a forgotten child in the corner.

Lenora's disappointment was patent as she thrust her candle into all the empty corners of the closet, and Mr. Ingles inquired of her what she had hoped to find.

"Nothing! Nothing," she insisted, suddenly conscious.

But Tess burst out with, "A skeleton, to be sure, sir! Or at the very least, a black veil."

While Lenora, blushing hotly, disclaimed this, Mr. Ingles, prudently keeping his inevitable reflections on the nonsensical turn of female minds to himself, merely suggested they continue the tour above stairs.

"I can promise at least one horror to interest you there, if you can spare the time," he offered handsomely, "for all it's not a skeleton or a black veil."

"What is the time, pray?" asked Lenora, snatching at the opportunity to change the subject.

Mr. Ingles said, "I have no watch, ma'am, but unless I'm much mistaken, it cannot be past three o'clock."

"Very well, let us go upstairs," Lenora said with decision, and she hurried toward the stairs before he could twit her more about black veils.

They ascended to the ground floor and began to make the circuit of the rooms. In constant expectation of the promised horror, Lenora felt the return of her earlier dread, which was only amplified as they moved from drawing room to parlor to study, for the atmosphere was heavy with tragedy. Each dusty apartment, bare of anything that was not part of the structure of the house, seemed to press its wretchedness upon the visitors, whispering of its innocent violation and entreating them to envision its past glories.

Twice Mr. Ingles misled them into believing themselves on the brink of terror, when he stepped suddenly to a spot at the wall and opened a hidden door. As the wall gaped open, Lenora and Tess both clung to one another, knowing not what could be hidden in the black compartment, but each time, Mr. Ingles calmly rekindled the flame of his candle and led them forward into nothing more sinister than a servants' hallway.

Their tour bringing them once more through the Great Hall, Tess and Lenora remained close beside Mr. Ingles, while craning their necks to remark anew the vast proportions and stark emptiness of the chamber. No specters assailed their vision, until on the far side, still glancing over their shoulders, they stepped through a corridor and into another room, and stopped still upon the threshold.

The room was not empty, as all the other rooms, excepting the kitchens, had been. A large four-poster dominated the space, its hangings coated in dust, and the bed unmade. A candlestick with a stub of wax graced a dusty table at the head of the bed, and a large wardrobe stood alone along a far wall. The young ladies, absorbing these eerie details, never doubted that this must be the late Lord Helden's apartment.

As they considered whether to flee to the Great Hall, Mr. Ingles walked slowly past them into the room and around it, as if considering its possibilities. He stopped to regard the unmade bed. "He died here, you know," he said, in a matter-of-fact tone.

Lenora, her arm around a clinging Tess, murmured, "They say he tried to sell his bed to the vicar at his last confession, but the vicar declined."

"And no blame to him!" whispered Tess, eying with fascination the furniture left in the room. "Who'd sleep in a bed his lordship died in?"

"Nothing wrong with that piece there, though," Mr. Ingles said, as he walked over to the wardrobe and knocked on it. "It's sound, and fine workmanship." He opened the doors rather dramatically, one at a time, to reveal a few drab suits of clothing, and a pair of rusty buckled shoes.

Lenora shuddered. "Lord Helden's own clothing!" she observed in thrilling tones. Mr. Ingles watched her, an amused gleam back in his eye, and she turned wide eyes to him. "You promised horrors, and horrors they are, sir! The very clothes that Lord Helden wore! His evil taint can be felt even from here."

"It's rare fortune they left all this for us to see, miss," remarked Tess, drinking in the mordant scene.

When they had shivered their fill, Mr. Ingles led them out of the room and across the hall to the front door, releasing the young ladies into the fresh air, where they stepped out of the porch to receive the welcome rays of the sun on their faces.

Lenora turned her head to squint up at Mr. Ingles, who had stopped beside her. "Had you planned all along to show us that room?" she demanded.

"Not until I'd taken your measure, ma'am."

"Odious man," she said, primming up her mouth and turning away again.

"Would you rather that I had kept it from you?" he inquired, earning himself a quick glance of disdain. His answering sidelong smile gave her to realize that he was not to be deceived.

"I should never have forgiven you if you had, Mr. Ingles," she declared roundly. "It was the best part of the tour. Indeed, I must thank you."

"For protecting you from vampires?"

She arched an eyebrow. "For saving me from falling through the floor, and for accompanying us through the house. I own I was not equal to the task at first—indeed I was utterly unprepared—that is, I thought I knew—"

"It was my pleasure, Miss Breckinridge," he said, saving her the trouble of getting hopelessly lost in her explanation.

She smiled gratefully and cast one more long look at the facade of the Hall. With a gusty sigh, she said, "Then goodbye, Mr. Ingles," and extended her hand.

He regarded her hand silently for a moment. "There's more to be seen yet," he said. "The first floor and the attics. Bound to be where all the ghosts and ghouls are hiding."

She took this roast in good part and answered blandly, "Very well, sir, if you will promise ghosts and ghouls."

"I shall do my poor best," he said, taking her hand and shaking it. "Tomorrow, then?"

She agreed and took her leave of him, setting off with Tess back around the mansion. As they passed the now familiar walls, Lenora considered how odd had been her experience inside them. She had gone from excitement to terror to curiosity to thrilling pleasure, but none of it had been what she had expected. Indeed, looking at the blackened and lichen-strewn stones and boarded up casements, she discovered they no longer held mystery for her, now that she knew they hid nothing but emptiness and neglect.

Tess shuddered pleasantly by her side. "It is an evil place, to be sure."

"Indeed it is, Tess," Lenora replied, rather mechanically. But as they made their way through the maze and out onto the riotous lawn, she could not help but feel that Helden Hall had been irrevocably changed for her.

Chapter 9

THE NEXT AFTERNOON, Lady Stiles was in conference with Blaine—who insisted that Sanford had been flirting with the head groom—when she spied Lenora and Tess flitting over the lawn to the Home Wood. She let out an exasperated sigh.

"Now, your ladyship, what's wrung your withers?" said Blaine, sidling over to the window and craning her neck to look out. "Ah, there goes Miss, off to pay a visit to that caretaker again." With a sideways glance at her mistress, she added, "I do trust he is gaining his strength."

Lady Stiles, annoyed at having exposed her daughter's imprudence to a servant, fervently hoped Blaine would keep a still tongue in her head and adjusted her air to that of authority. "The apothecary tells me the poor man could not have survived without Lenora's excellent nursing, and also your fine soups."

This last had the effect Lady Stiles had hoped for—turning the cook's attention from whatever might be brewing at Helden Hall, to the rosy self-gratulation of her own charity—and her ladyship gratefully escaped the kitchens.

Mr. Ingles met Lenora and Tess once more at the edge of the wood, walking with them across the wild lawn and around the hedge maze to the veranda of the Hall, and Lenora felt that her eyes had been opened. She could no longer desire to unearth horrid secrets within, for the house now seemed more frightened than it was frightening. The persona of menace and horror she had formerly attributed to the Hall had utterly dissipated, leaving behind the impression of an abused thing that craved life and love, and dreamed of once more being made useful and necessary. As they entered and wandered down dreary passages that seemed to cling hopelessly to life, and through vast chambers that echoed with distant memories of grandeur, Lenora was moved to pity, much as her mother had been.

They ascended the grand staircase to the first floor, and Lenora put out a hand to touch the top of the newel post, where the finial had been removed. "I wonder what it looked like in its heyday," she mused, running a finger over the shorn post. Following Mr. Ingles into the first of the bare rooms, a graciously proportioned bedchamber, she gazed speculatively about her. "Was Lord Helden parsimonious or was he gracious—before he set himself to ruin his heirs? Was his lady given rein for her genius or was she restricted by his impecunious temperament?"

"My Ma says his lordship was ever so close with his money, especially to those as were beneath him," offered Tess, who also seemed to have broken from the spell of terror.

Lenora went to the wall, lifting a curl of wallpaper and inspecting it closely. "And yet, this paper is of the finest quality. Methinks his lordship kept himself in very good style, if only to preserve his own consequence."

Peeking into the adjoining dressing room, Tess observed, "It's ever so sad, all these rooms with nothing in them, when it's plain as my nose they must've been right grand in their day."

Lenora's mind was suddenly assailed by an image of his lordship, in the throes of his success in outwitting the entailment, parading in the first style of elegance through his barren house. The picture struck her so forcibly that she paused in the hallway, ruminating on the pride that had caused a man with so much to throw it all away.

"Mr. Ingles, I wish you will tell us more of the late Lord Helden," she said, moving once more to peer into yet another bare chamber.

He shrugged. "I've nothing to tell, Miss Breckinridge."

"Oh?" she replied, raising an eyebrow. "I suppose the solicitors told you nothing of this place before sending you here to guard it."

"Only what state it was in, and that it was the fault of the dead lord."

"And you've not heard any of the stories, I collect?"

He lifted a hand, indicating their surroundings. "It don't need stories to tell me Lord Helden was a muckworm and a rip."

"How true!" cried Lenora, bestowing an approving look on her host. "This house has seen enough to tell us volumes about his lordship. Take this room, for instance," she said, walking speculatively into a room with the vestiges of a fine, floral wallpaper peeling from its walls. "It speaks of a desperate attempt by my Lord to appeal to the female sex—most assuredly after the death of his wife. You see that even in his pride, he saw the usefulness of cultivating fair company."

Tess blinked at her as she swept from the room and down the hallway.

Warming to her role, Lenora stepped into a small, dim chamber and declared, "This room must have been something special, I am persuaded. Note the dimensions, and the excellence of the light! I have it! It was My Lord's Mirror Chamber, for such a man must needs have had not one, but many mirrors with which to view himself, to ensure that no detail was overlooked." She gazed at Tess with eyes half-lidded in hauteur. "One can never repose one's entire trust in one's valet, he being of the lower orders, you comprehend."

A scandalized grin broke over Tess's face, and she glanced uncertainly at Mr. Ingles, who winked back at her before following her mistress down the hall.

"Here we have the Grand-Duchess's bedchamber," intoned Lenora in the next room, a large one with a dressing room and a sitting room attached, "made up especially—to curry favor during her sole visit in the late '80's—in green and ivory stripes, as you see, to match her favorite gown. An unfortunate notion," Lenora said in a confidential aside to Tess, "as it turned out, for her Grace was quite invisible when situated in front of the wallpaper, and frightened the housemaid out of her wits with a demand for hot water."

Tess, stifling giggles, followed her mistress as she glided away, her hand held gracefully ready to direct her companions' gazes. "And here is the Red Saloon," she said, leading them into a room in the front of the house, "named not for its color but for none other than the celebrated Red Monk, whose nightly visitations in the summer of '62 rendered the room quite uninhabitable, and it should have remained so ever after but for the exertions of the lady of the house, in publicizing these events with spasms and vapors in every drawing room in the county. Her behavior occasioned such interest in the viewing of the place that her lord, struck with the happy notion of charging sixpence a head, so enlarged the family fortune as to enable them to take a house in Town, and lease the manor to a tenant entirely unalarmed by spectral visitors."

"Oh, miss, you mustn't!" uttered Tess, between gasps for breath. "I'll bust my laces!"

With a supercilious rise of her eyebrows, Lenora turned her back on the afflicted maid and made her stately way down the gallery, which was as barren as the entrance hall below. Suddenly, she stopped, dramatically indicating the blank wall midway down the gallery whose paper curled almost to the floor.

"Behold my Lord and Lady Helden, late of this Hall. These portraits are, as you no doubt have already perceived, by that master of masters, Sir Joshua Reynolds, and very like. Note the eyebrows," pointing to a diagonal crack on the plaster, "that swoop upward like those of the Devil himself—for I scruple not to own this indisputable similarity to his lordship's character—as well as," moving a step or two farther down the gallery to present another point on the peeling wall, "the dejection of his lady's countenance. You will agree it was masterfully done."

She turned with a politely superior air to her companions, and her gaze falling upon Mr. Ingles, she gave a studied start, narrowing her eyes and striding up to peer intently at his features, which were practically hidden under the growth of his hair.

"Sir!" she cried, after an intense scrutiny, "I declare myself betwattled! How it could have escaped me I know not, but you bear an uncanny resemblance to our distinguished hosts! Does he not, Tess?" turning to the maid, whose hands had flown to cover her mouth, and whose eyes twinkled with undisguised mirth. This Lenora chose to overlook as she continued, "Mark the eyebrows, Tess, and the look of gloom! Sir! I cannot mistake! You are the lost heir!"

As the two young ladies regarded him breathlessly—one from unabated giggles, the other in spurious interest—Mr. Ingles, who had watched her during these narrations with a not unappreciative gleam in his brown eyes, laughed again, a deep rumble that rolled up from his chest, rich and glad. Lenora stepped back in real surprise at how welcome the sound was to her heart. It was almost as if the house itself had rejoiced.

She exchanged a delighted smile with Tess, then hastened to school her countenance. "A thousand apologies, sir. I must, indeed, have been mistaken, for a laugh like that could never emanate from the descendant of the evil Lord Helden, and his desponding wife." She bowed her head courteously. "You are safe from the inheritance of so august a fortune."

His eyes crinkled in a grin, and Lenora caught a glimpse of excellent white teeth, before Tess flew to her side with the laughing entreaty that they move on.

"What shall we find next, I wonder," Lenora said as she walked arm-in-arm with her maid, following Mr. Ingles as he led them up a back stair. "A torture chamber, or an oubliette?"

"Oh, it's to be the King's apartments, which he visited one night when his carriage wheel shattered on the lane!" suggested Tess.

"Unworthy, Tess!" said her mistress deprecatingly. "Too mundane by half! It shall be the Madman's Chamber, where Lord Helden's insane brother, hidden from birth, lived out his days in tragic solitude!"

This elicited a burst of corroborative remarks from Tess, and the two young ladies, heads together, had settled all the details of the madman's existence by the time their footsteps carried them into the room at the top of the stairs. They stopped still, however, on the threshold, Tess emitting a tiny shriek.

They had come to the attics, and stacked against a garret just before them was a large painting of an eagle-eyed gentleman in a powdered wig, with a long, aristocratic nose and a receding chin.

"It's the Old Lord himself!" squeaked Tess, and she would have cowered behind Lenora had that young lady not taken her firmly by the arm and led her up to the painting.

"It is not himself, Tess, only his likeness," she said, "and so it cannot harm you. Do not tremble so, I beg of you."

They inspected the painting in silence, Tess dubiously and Lenora critically. "He does look formed for evil, I must say," was Lenora's verdict. "A brute and a coward. I wonder if all the Heldens were evil, like him, or if he was the first. I certainly trust he will have been the last."

She tipped the painting forward to look behind at the next, and gasped. "Here is one I have been longing to see," she said, pulling it to the side so that the others could view it.

It was of a pretty young woman with powdered locks drawn up behind her head, with several ringlets falling forward across a white shoulder. Her nose was straight and her mouth sensitive, and her eyes bore the most beseeching look Lenora had ever seen.

"This must be Lady Helden," she murmured, gazing in real sorrow at the sweet little face. "Perhaps taken upon her marriage. I fear, from her looks, she had an inkling of what awaited her here."

"I don't wonder she died, miss," added Tess in a low voice. "She looks fragile as a flower, and his lordship a hailstorm."

They looked on in mournful silence for a few minutes, until Lenora, having no desire to succumb to the blue-devils over a lady who was long beyond their help, thrust the painting behind its companion once more and straightened, looking about the room properly.

"Oh, Tess!" she sighed, grasping the maid's hand.

Chapter 10

THE ATTICS STRETCHED before them, a warren of cubbies and garrets covering the entire length of the house. Unlike the rest of the house, however, every corner of this floor held some other remnant of the past, either overlooked or deemed unsalable by Lord Helden in his haste to rid the manor of anything of value.

"Upon my honor, miss, it's a treasure trove!" cried Tess, her eyes starting.

As one, the young ladies looked a question at Mr. Ingles, who waved them forward with the declaration that no one else had any use for the stuff, then looked on in placid indulgence as they scurried in and out of corners, emitting cries of delight at their various discoveries.

"Tess, Tess!" cried Lenora, hastening to meet the maid with her hands outstretched. "It's the most delightful painted parasol you've ever seen—with the supports broken, but still—come see!"

"Oh, miss!" said Tess, in her turn, "A real malacca cane, broke in two—no doubt in one of his lordship's craggy moods—but I wonder if it couldn't be mended!"

"Tess, a chest full of old children's clothes!"

"Miss, the ugliest old urn you ever did see!"

Lenora, rushing from one discovery to another, was every moment more enamored with Helden Hall and its mysteries, and a glimpse at Mr. Ingles standing quietly near the door reminded her that she owed her present enjoyment entirely to him.

She went to him, her eyes shining. "I do not know what you must think of us, sir. I declare it's better than a bazaar, or a country fair!"

"Best not let it get out, or the heir will come hot-foot, demanding his property."

Lenora laughed, but said, "I fancy that would be a good thing, for the heir to come see what he is missing."

"Perhaps he knows too well what he is missing," he said, in a more serious tone.

She glanced down, a vision of the dark, brooding master she had imagined coming into her mind. "If that is so, then he must be made to see his mistake in neglecting his duty."

He regarded her quietly before remarking, "It is not such a simple matter, I think. The Old Lord's hold over this place would be untenable to the heir he never wished for."

"But it need not be so. Indeed, there is so little left of the Old Lord now that if the wallpaper were pulled down, and those horrid things in his bedchamber removed, any vestige of the former inhabitants would be gone. Then, whatever one did to this place would transform it completely, and I daresay the evil Old Lord's connection to it would be broken."

At that moment Tess called Lenora away to inspect a baby carriage without wheels, and Lenora was lost again in exploration. By the end of their adventure, the young ladies had unearthed a writing desk whose hinges had rusted shut, several tatty linens, a moth-eaten hoop skirt with ridiculously wide panneirs, two pair of boys' boots with the soles not quite worn through, three skittles, a cane chair without a seat, a torn kite, several woebegone children's toys, a piece of iron grillwork, and a pair of rusty garden shears.

The shoes Mr. Ingles graciously consigned to Tess, after her remark upon the shocking waste practiced by the gentry, when poor folk stood by without so much as a stitch on their feet all winter. Lenora was pressed to take the writing desk, which could easily be fitted with new hinges, and was quite a lovely thing besides.

"It is very heavy," said Lenora, hefting the desk. "I wonder if there is not something inside."

Mr. Ingles obligingly prised the desk open and they all were stricken speechless, gazing in wonder at a large, beautifully preserved family bible fitted tightly inside. Lenora itched to touch it but did not dare; this was no cast-off to be treated lightly. Mr. Ingles, however, felt no such compunction, taking the volume into his own hands and opening its heavy cover to reverently peruse the yellowed pages.

"What was it doing in that old writing desk?" asked Tess, looking over his shoulder at the inscribed family names.

"Depend upon it, the Old Lord knew it would be of great value to the heir, and being unable to sell it, he locked it away up here, in the hopes that the heir would never find it," offered Lenora. "At least we may be grateful that he was God-fearing enough not to attempt to destroy it."

Angling for a better look, Lenora cast her eye down the list of names, and started at one in particular. "Ingles—here is an Ingles!"

Mr. Ingles clapped the book shut, tucking it under his arm. "I'll take this for safe-keeping until the heir—"

"Mr. Ingles!" Lenora cried, stopping him. "There was an Ingles in that list. Are you—are you related to the Englehearts?"

His eyes shifted from the floor to hers and back again. "On the distaff side. Ingles is a maternal line—so I'm informed. It's how I got the position, after all. The circumstances—they wanted someone in the family, you see."

"Certainly," said Lenora, considering. "It is perfectly sensible in this case. And right that they should wish to assist a poor relation. How fortunate for you, sir. I am sure you are exceedingly grateful for the improvement in your situation."

He gazed back at her somewhat enigmatically, but did not answer.

She indicated the bible. "That is something the heir would wish to see. Perhaps when he is apprised of its existence, he will deem a visit worthy of his trouble."

"Why this great interest in the heir, Miss Breckinridge?" he asked, watching her through hooded eyes.

"It is nothing—that is, he must be brought to—" She stopped, aware of his close scrutiny. "I mean only that I cannot bear to see this noble house forsaken."

"You think the heir would change things, do you?"

"I am persuaded—he must want encouragement to overcome his reticence to do something."

A huff escaped him. "And you think to encourage him, Miss Breckinridge? When nothing and no one else has succeeded? Does that not strike you as a great piece of impertinence on your part?"

"It is no more impertinent than—" She stopped, having begun to feel distinctly uncomfortable under his examination. "Perhaps there is something in what you say, sir," she said at last, a little stiffly. "But you cannot wonder at my interest to try. It would be a great tragedy if the heir never took a proper interest in the Hall."

"Just what would you call a proper interest, ma'am?" he asked, placing the bible carefully on a window ledge and crossing his arms over his chest.

She lifted her chin. "A public claim of his property, sir! Until the heir has made Helden Hall his own, the Old Lord has won."

"You speak as if turning this place to account is a mere nothing," Mr. Ingles said stormily. "I will have you know, Miss Breckinridge, that you are wide of the mark. You have seen the state of this house, and you know the grounds are not much better; one would have supposed that might have opened your eyes, but you seem to live somewhere between the covers of a romance, and believe that all heirs are knights in shining armor, and that everything magically turns out for the best!"

Coloring, Lenora retorted, "I know that it is no easy thing to revive a neglected estate, sir! My brother has been doing it for years now, and I have watched him, and have learned a thing or two. It is hard work, and takes sacrifice and diligence, but it can be done!"

"And was his estate gutted and abused, and left derelict, as this one?"

"No, not quite—"

"Then you know nothing about it! Helden Hall is an albatross, and the heir's more likely to sell the estate and be done with it."

"Sell Helden Hall?" cried Lenora, horrified. "Never! He cannot sell it—Mr. Ingles, you do not know that he cares so little for his heritage. Surely he must wish to save it!"

"Must he?" he asked, his face red under the bushy beard. "And I suppose he must also be rich, and handsome into the bargain, eh, Miss Breckinridge?"

"That—that is neither here nor there, sir!" she stammered, feeling her cheeks grow warm.

"Oh, don't be shy, ma'am," he said in a coldly cajoling tone. "It's as plain as the nose on your face. You've set your heart on being mistress of this place, but not until your prince sweeps in and puts it back to rights, like in a faerie tale."

Lenora looked quickly away, huffing an unconvincing laugh. "What nonsense you speak, Mr. Ingles!"

"If it's nonsense I speak, then why do you take such an interest in what don't concern you?" he said angrily.

"Well, perhaps I have taken a fancy to this place," she said, boldly meeting his fiery gaze, "but it is high time someone did!"

His eyes narrowed and he shook his head. "It would take a madman to try to redeem this heap."

"It is not madness to retain and revere one's heritage, sir!"

He let out a short bark of a laugh, far from the chuckle he had favored her with yesterday. "I had no notion you held the family of Old Lord Helden in such esteem."

"You know I do not—that is, I have no opinion of the Old Lord, but his heir need not be so despicable—indeed, it is highly unlikely that he would be, for his own father was disinherited for being of a different mind than the Old Lord, which supposes that the present heir must have been raised up to be quite the reverse of his grandfather," she finished triumphantly.

"And what happens if he wasn't? What if he's as despicable as Old Lord Helden himself, and ugly, too?" he asked with grim sarcasm.

"I am only trying to be optimistic, sir," Lenora said, disturbed by both his unquenchable anger and his effortless exposure of the flaws in her fantasy. "If he is like the Old Lord, then he will not care a fig for the estate, but if he is merely misinformed or overwhelmed by the responsibility, then I wish him to know that I, for one, intend to stand a friend to him."

"Well, Miss Breckinridge," he said, towering over her like a thundercloud, "perhaps the heir don't wish for friends, and knows exactly what is what, because anyone in his senses can see that this wreck of a manor ain't worth looking at, much less throwing away good gold after."

And he stalked past her, disappearing down the stairs. Lenora stared after him for several astonished moments, until Tess crept to her side and asked in a shocked whisper if Miss supposed it would be proper for them still to take the boots and the writing desk away with them.

With a huff, Lenora abandoned the writing desk, saying tightly, "I shall not give Mr. Ingles the satisfaction of having me in his debt." At Tess's sigh, Lenora put out a hand to forestall her relinquishment of the boots. "You need not scruple to take those, Tess, no matter how wild a tragedy he decides to enact, for his argument is with me. Come along," she said, lifting her chin. "We are leaving."

Chapter 11

When the next day found Lenora sitting primly at home, and virtuously professing to be entirely at the disposal of her mother, Lady Stiles could not but be astonished. She had quite given up hope that her daughter would give over her infatuation with the Helden Hall caretaker, and had seriously considered removing to London at Christmas, counting on the distractions of town to sever the tie. However, when several days passed with Lenora remaining dutifully at home, very much on her dignity, and never once gazing out the window toward the Home Wood, Lady Stiles's hope began to revive, and she ventured to ask whether Lenora considered a house party to be preferable to celebrate the upcoming Christmas holiday, as opposed to a snug family party. When Lenora gave it as her opinion that a house party was exactly what was needed to liven up the dullness of her existence, and directly proposed that the families of two or three extremely eligible young men, including Mr. Dowbridge, should be invited, it was all that her mother could wish.

For the next fortnight, Lenora entered into all her mother's schemes for the entertainment of the party, and professed great delight at the list of young people invited to stay at Wrenthorpe Grange. Never once did she betray a hint of longing to visit the lodge of Helden Hall, satisfying Lady Stiles that whatever fascination Mr. Ingles had held for her was lost, and that the door was once more open to other, more suitable, admirers.

"I flatter myself that I have planned the perfect house party, Sanford," said Lady Stiles in great spirits one evening, as her loyal henchwoman assisted at her toilette. "I had forgotten how enjoyable it is to direct such an undertaking, and to have the staff to support one! What a time it shall be! I declare, I feel as giddy as a schoolgirl."

Sanford primly expressed the hope that Cook would be equal to the challenge, and ventured the suggestion that Branton, the butler, keep the sherry under his eye.

Lady Stiles gazed blandly at her maid's reflection in the mirror and answered, "As Blaine has been on her best behavior, I cannot but trust that all will be just as it should be." She stood, inspecting herself in the mirror. "I really do not know how you contrive to make me so elegant, Sanford! You are a wonder!"

In charity with all the world, Lady Stiles betook herself to the drawing room, where she was pleased to see that her husband, very handsome in dinner dress, was wearing the new embroidered waistcoat she had only just finished for him.

He took her extended hand and carried it to his lips, remarking, "My love, you've either caught another canary, or you've made a delicious discovery."

"My dear Joshua," retorted his wife, smiling, "if I am so easily read, I wonder that you still bother to try."

"Ah, but I do not know which of the two it is, and so must ask or wonder."

Receiving his kiss, she allowed herself to be settled onto the settee, and informed him that she was merely delighted with the successful preparations for the Christmas party.

He smiled thoughtfully, saying, "Much as it gratifies me to know you are happy, my dear, I had rather you had made a discovery—specifically, regarding Lenora. I cannot be quite comfortable about her. Her engagement in planning our Christmas party seems too earnest to be genuine, and it strikes me that she is striving to hide a disappointment."

"I am sure I do not know what you are talking about, my love," replied his wife, in some annoyance. "For you know as well as I that she has not singled out any young man as yet, excepting—but surely you could not mean him, for that was nothing."

Her percipient spouse glanced pensively at her. "If you refer to her interest in poor Ingles, my dear, you may recall that I was never convinced of its veracity. Indeed, I have for some time been persuaded that it was not to the Bluebeard that she has lost her heart, but to the romantic Helden Hall, of which he is caretaker, and to which, therefore, he is her passport."

"Good heaven, Joshua," cried his startled wife, blinking at him. "Do you really think so?"

He nodded gravely. "From her actions of the past month, I infer that she tried and failed in her purpose—the extent of which we can only conjecture—and has since thrown herself into your preparations as a distraction, a course which I'll not scruple to own causes me some misgiving."

"I see what you mean." Genevieve gazed into the fire, her brow contracted. "The strength of her energy is equal to the strength of her disappointment—which must, indeed, be very great."

"So I surmise. I fear that if she cannot reconcile herself soon, her present pace will be productive either of a nervous breakdown, or a rapid decline."

His lady cast him a satirical glance. "A decline would exactly suit her taste, and I am certain she should enjoy it far more than a breakdown. But I should not enjoy either, and would much rather find some way to arrest such an eventuality. I fear anything of the sort must wait until after the house party, however, for we may find out that the house party itself will do the thing."

"Indeed, I trust that it may be so, for, from what you tell me, there will be such a lively assortment of young people in the house that she will not find time to go into a decline."

"Exactly so, my love!" she replied. "But you have removed a great weight from my mind—you can have no notion! To be nearly certain that Lenora has no thought of Mr. Ingles gives me no end of joy."

Had she been privy to her daughter's thoughts at that moment, however, she may have suffered a shock, for they were full of Mr. Ingles. For many days following their confrontation in the attics of the Hall, Lenora had cherished nothing but righteous indignation toward Mr. Ingles for his ungentlemanlike behavior—though she told herself that she could not understand why she had expected such a coarse and uncouth man to behave like a gentleman in any case. Nevertheless, she had felt betrayed, for he had led her to believe that a truce had been called between them; indeed, she had come to the conviction that she had proven her goodwill to him, and he had reciprocated with his own, and their mutual agreement had, she had been persuaded, become something of a friendship.

Hence, she held that Mr. Ingles' sudden animosity toward her had been nothing short of treachery. His mocking accusations and harsh summation of her character she could view only as proof of his true and base nature, and the contempt she felt for his duplicity was evident in her inability for a sennight to call up anything even resembling a Christian thought regarding the odious caretaker of Helden Hall.

As time cooled her anger, however, a more subjective examination of their argument forced her to own that his accusations were, in actuality, true. She had fallen in love with Helden Hall, and by virtue of its potential, had imbued the heir with perfections which would enable him to fulfill the fantasies which she had created. And while this in itself was quite innocent, she had allowed herself to become so taken by these dreams that she had given no thought to the impropriety of expecting that they should come to pass, and had even been so smug as to disrespect Mr. Ingles' situation in life.

That part, at least, of their conversation she could not remember without a shudder; in pointing out the lowliness of his circumstances, and the gratitude he must feel to his superior relations, she had most cruelly mortified him. She was heartily ashamed of so thoughtlessly treating someone whom she had come to regard, even unconsciously, as a friend. How he felt toward her now she could not tell, but she imagined that he considered that, as she had so ill-used him, he was well within his rights to break off whatever agreement they had reached.

Lenora knew she must attempt to gain his pardon, but she was uncertain as to the propriety of even putting herself forward now that their tenuous relationship seemed at an end. She could not bring herself to ask for the advice of her family, for doing so would bring upon her both their censure and their disappointment, and she did not think she could bear it, in addition to her own. She would simply have to discover for herself some way that she could make amends.

The arrival of her brother Tom provided a welcome relief to the distress of Lenora's feelings. He came in his own curricle, with a groom seated beside him—a noticeable improvement to his previous mode of travel, which had been on horseback, and alone, having no groom to bear him company. Now, as he stepped down from the smart equipage, the groom having gone to the heads of the two magnificent bays, Lady Stiles beamed rapturously upon him and held out her hands to receive his exuberant greeting upon both her cheeks.

"Oh, Tom!" she cried, gripping his hands tightly and running her eyes down his fine figure. "How well you look! Lenora! See how handsome your brother looks in his new greatcoat."

"I expected you to say 'in his new curricle,' Mama," laughed Lenora, who had come out just behind her to meet her brother. "Or even 'his new rig,' or 'with these new horses!' Everything about you is new, Tom!"

The new man swept his sister up in a hug that carried her off her feet and around in a circle before she was released. "So I should hope, Nora, for I am reborn! Next month sees the last of our tenants, and I shall take up residence in Branwell Manor at last."

"Oh, Tom!" cried his mother again, as her eyes shone. "You have done it! But I always knew you should, and never doubted it."

"Well, Mama, your patience and frugality are as much to thank as my management," admitted her son, taking both her and Lenora by the arm and walking with them toward the house. "But I own I'm rather proud of what I've accomplished."

"You've every reason to be," came Sir Joshua's voice from the front door. He advanced toward them, his hand extended to Tom. "And I am certain we are all anxious to hear the details of your many successes."

They repaired to the library to exchange news from the last few months, for Tom was an indifferent correspondent, rather preferring to receive letters than to write them, and had much to tell on the subject of his improving fortunes.

"The farm is going on wonderfully," he apprised his audience grandly, accepting a glass of Madeira from his stepfather, and leaning against the mantle to warm himself. "The breeding was prodigiously successful—Mama, those three chestnut colts proved the most beautiful bits of blood and bone I've ever seen! I'd half a mind to keep them myself, but John Tansenby offered top price for all three, and intends to train them to drive unicorn! Daft idea, I think, but then my bays are prime goers, and I've nothing more to wish for."

"Very fine specimens, I must say," agreed Sir Joshua. "But I own I'm more curious about the farm. Have you extended into the west acreage yet? And how are your tenant farmers coming on with the barley?"

Their talk of farming carried on some minutes, until it wore out, and Tom suddenly turned to Lenora, saying, "What's all this I hear of your conquest in the neighborhood, Nora? I must say it don't surprise me at all, but what I want to know is if this local boy is worth a groat. When do I get to see 'im?"

"Tom, he's not one of your cattle!" cried his mother with a laugh. "You speak as if you think me incapable of distinguishing between proper and improper persons, and I can assure you I am not! Besides, I needn't remind you that Sir Joshua would have something to say if I was."

"I certainly would, you may depend upon it," corroborated her husband.

Tom hastened to reassure his parents that it was not their

judgment in question but that of his hen-witted sister, but when this sally failed to arouse a response in kind, three pairs of eyes turned to regard the intended victim, who sat staring off into the distance.

Tom shook Lenora's shoulder gently. "Nora! Where've you gone to?"

Lenora, who had taken the opportunity during the farming interchange to retreat into her tumbled thoughts, blinked at her brother for a moment, then straightened and begged pardon. "Woolgathering, I fear, Tom!" she said, smiling ruefully upon her onlookers. "That's what comes of boring on about farming at the height of the afternoon."

This successfully reanimated the conversation, and the family enjoyed much banter back and forth about Lenora's beau and his questionable merits, as well as his doubtful chances with her. But when they all retired to their employments before dinner, Tom followed his sister to her room and ensconced himself on the stool at her dressing table, threatening to stay there all the evening if she didn't open her budget to him.

"I don't know what you can mean, Tom," temporized Lenora, with as unconscious an air as she could muster. "I've told you all about my sole admirer, and that I have not the least tendre for him, and if you think I am so gooseish as not to know my own mind, I can tell you to your head, you are fair and far off."

"Coming it too strong, Nora," replied her brother promptly. "You've been up to something, beyond breaking this poor flat's heart. I know full well you don't care a button for him, which gives me a notion he's merely a screen for something much more interesting. Spill it, sis!"

"Perhaps I am simply bored of country life and have come up with a sort of game to liven up the scene."

Tom crossed his arms over his chest, challenging his sister with his gaze. "And perhaps I'm a great gudgeon who'll believe that his sister, who couldn't live a day without imagining herself and her bosom bow as the heroines of some novel, has suddenly given over all her dreams in favor of petty flirtation."

Lenora, who had been needlessly rearranging the contents of a shelf near her bed, paused at this. "As I no longer have a bosom bow about me, Tom, is it so wonderful that I have begun to cultivate other interests?" she asked coldly.

"I know you miss Elvira," said Tom in a gentler tone. "But I also know you must've found something to fill up the space she left behind, and your abstraction tells me it's gotten bigger than you can manage. Let me help you, Nora."

She fiddled a few more moments with the things on the shelf, torn between a desire to keep her stupidity hidden and another to throw part of her burden upon her brother's capable shoulders. All at once, she turned to regard him gravely. "You won't tell Mama? Or Sir Joshua?"

Tom declared himself ready to cut out his own tongue before divulging her secret to anyone, and she sighed, plumping herself down on the end of her bed. "Very well. I own I'd be glad of your advice, for I've made a mull of it, Tom."

The entire history of Helden Hall, before and after her coming into the neighborhood, then tumbled out, and if Tom was utterly bewildered at times, he nobly bore his confusion, upheld by the certain knowledge that his sister's methods of communication, while somewhat convoluted, should eventually put him in possession of all the facts in the case. He was not disappointed. After nearly half an hour's explanation, Tom wanted only a few moments of reflection to grasp the whole.

"You're in love with a caretaker?" he exclaimed.

"What?" Lenora gaped at him. "No! Tom, haven't you listened to a word I've been telling you?"

"If you can call it telling, Nora, for I'll not scruple to inform you that your notion of telling begs redefinition."

Lenora threw a pillow at him. "Tom, I clearly explained that Mr. Ingles has been very friendly and obliging, and that I've used him abominably ill! That is all!"

"Obliging, eh?" muttered Tom, throwing the pillow back to her. "Is that why he's on your mind so much, my girl, that you can't attend to even the simplest conversation without dreaming of him?"

His sister rolled her eyes. "You are the most bacon-brained young man I've ever had the misfortune to be related to. I do not dream of Mr. Ingles! My conscience is stricken, Tom—and if you ever troubled to listen to yours, you'd understand what that feels like! I have wronged a person, and I yearn to make it right, but have no notion how to go about it! That, and that only, is what is driving me distracted."

"Hmph." Tom considered her, his mouth working from side to side. "Well, I'll believe you this time," he finally said, "but you'd better take care not to let your conscience run away with you. Do you have any idea what a figure you'd make of yourself, falling in love with a common caretaker?"

With a groan, Lenora threw herself back on the bed, putting her hands over her eyes. "Leave off, will you, Tom? I—Am—Not—In—Love—With—Him!" She pushed herself back up, leaning on her elbows. "And I'm not going to fall in love with him! Do you understand? I care only for his feelings, as a fellow human being whom I have wronged, and if you want to help me, brother, you will tell me what a young lady can do for a young man to show him she is sorry."

"Well," said Tom, shrugging his shoulders, "there's not much you can do but tell him."

Lenora, in a few pithy words, gave him to understand that if that was the extent of his wisdom, he was welcome to leave, and to take it with him.

"No, I mean it, Nora," cried Tom, coming toward her with hands raised placatingly. "A man's honor is one of his tenderest spots, and if you've offended his, you ought to own your fault—though I don't yet know how you can do that, with propriety." He sat beside her on the bed and gazed ahead, deep in thought. Finally, he snapped his fingers, a smile lighting his face. "I have it. It's Christmas, isn't it? Everybody gives gifts at Christmas, and since he's a servant, and has no master, it would be highly proper in you to remember him with a gift. Something small, mind you!" he adjured her, with a finger pointed at her nose. "So the high sticklers will be satisfied."

"As I am not so totty-headed as to publish abroad that I mean to give Mr. Ingles anything, even at Christmastime, I can't see that it signifies," remarked Lenora acidly.

Tom turned to her with an injured expression. "I'm only doing my brotherly duty by you, sister, in ensuring the safety of your reputation. You may not publish abroad that you give a young man a gift, but he might, and then the tongues will wag, I can assure you!"

Lenora waved this consideration away. "If you knew the tenor of Mr. Ingles' relationship with the villagers, you wouldn't express such a dull-witted notion. What I should like to know, oh wise one, is what ought I to give him?"

"I don't think it much matters," said Tom, unhurt. "Something innocuous, like a handkerchief, or a fob—though, he don't wear a proper waistcoat, I'll wager."

"No, he doesn't wear a proper waistcoat," said the exasperated Lenora, but she did remember his lack of something normally kept in a waistcoat, and thought she knew what to do. Standing, she took her brother's hands in hers, pressing them with not quite spurious gratitude. "You have been a tremendous help, and I'm sure I have found just the thing. Thank you."

Though cherishing some doubts as to her sincerity, Tom accepted her thanks with proper condescension, and allowed her to pull him up and send him out of the room.

Just as the door was closing, however, he popped his head back in to say, "I'll go with you to present it to him, Nora, to keep all aboveboard, you know."

"That's very noble of you, Tom," replied his sister blandly, "but I don't fancy an elder brother hovering over my shoulder should make my confession more palatable to Mr. Ingles. It might, rather, put the very ideas into his head that we are so eager to keep from being spread abroad." Tom's eyes grew wide at this cogent notion, and he hastily attempted to revise his offer, but Lenora forestalled him, saying, "I believe I shall take Tess with me, my dear, so you need not tease yourself."

With this, he seemed to be satisfied—at least Lenora could have seen it had she troubled to regard his retreat before closing the door.

Chapter 12

THE NEXT DAY afforded Lenora the opportunity to make the purchase and, her mind relieved of the chief of its burden, she was able, without compunction or effort, to wholly give herself up to the enjoyable demands of a house party. The guests who arrived hard on Tom's heels found in her such a charming hostess that at least one male breast was filled unjustifiably with hope, and Tom found plenty of opportunity to quiz his sister for her hard-heartedness. Nevertheless, the house party was a resounding success, with the young people gaily occupied in every activity from charades and speculation and hide-and-seek on chilly days, to riding and archery contests on the mild ones. They even got up a scheme to climb Cooper's Hill, from the top of which could be seen the spires of Gloucester Cathedral, and Mr. Dowbridge boasted he could see even to Wales, so clear was the day.

On one of the last evenings of the party, a dance was contrived, though there were only eight couples, for Mr. Dowbridge's mother, Lady Mintlowe, played tolerably well, and declared it was her delight to make possible the enjoyment of so many by plying her fingers at the keys for hours together. As Mr. Dowbridge stayed at Miss Breckinridge's side with a coolly proprietary air, Lenora made it a point to dance with every young man in the room, including her brother, though she was so universally pleasing that Mr. Dowbridge, on whose arm she went in to dinner, spent the evening with the belief that he was forwarder in her affections than previously.

When he petitioned her for a second dance, Lenora thought it wise to plead fatigue, but was baffled in her attempt to fob him off by his accompanying her to the sofa where she sat to rest. Though not intending to be uncivil, she found her mind wandering from his polite conversation to a certain decrepit mansion, and the lodge that reposed in its shadow, and more than once he was forced to recall her to the present.

"Forgive me, Miss Breckinridge, if I bore you," he said at last, a trifle stiffly.

"Oh, no, Mr. Dowbridge, not in the least," she hastened to reassure him. "It is only that I am a little tired. Do go on about—the fifteenth century wing at Stinton Abbey was it?"

He smiled ruefully. "It is very stupid of me to go prosing on about my home during a ball. Tell me, Miss Breckinridge, what would you wish to speak about?"

Lenora, who had slipped again into her secret thoughts, started at that and said, "I do not know—that is, perhaps you will tell me if there are any secret passages at the Abbey."

He looked blankly at her. "Secret passages? If there were any, they are gone now. All such things were done away with during the renovations of the last century, I imagine."

"Surely your ancestors were not so barbarous as to remove all the secret passages?" insisted Lenora, deeply concerned at his offhand manner on the subject.

"It was for the best, you must agree, for who would wish for a guest or a servant to go missing because they were lost in a secret passage?" he said reasonably, his eyebrow raised.

Lenora regarded him with pitying exasperation, but agreed to it with a sigh.

Late in the evening, Lenora escaped the heat of the ballroom—and the blandness of her admirer—by slipping out onto the balcony at the back of the house. The cold night air made her breath into a cloud and, rubbing her arms, she walked to the balustrade and leaned against it, gazing out at the Home Wood. With the fixed resolution of making peace with Mr. Ingles, and the plan formed of how to do it, the prospect of the Home Wood filled her with tense excitement, and she longed to plunge into its groves at once. But of course, she could not. The muted music of the dance was carried to her through the walls of the house, and she knew that soon, her absence would be remarked, and her mother, if not her beau, would come looking for her.

With a last long look at the deepness of the wood, Lenora turned to re-enter the house, but a movement caught her eye, and she paused. There, at the edge of the leafless forest, outlined by the light of the moon, was a figure—a figure with bushy black hair, in a frieze coat. She took a sharp breath, staring hard at the figure to determine if it really was Mr. Ingles, but then he was gone, swallowed by the darkness as the moon was hidden for a moment by a cloud.

Lenora could think of very few causes that would bring him out on a cold winter night to gaze at Wrenthorpe Grange, other than that he was as anxious as herself to make peace—or that he wanted to see with his own eyes the frivolity and thoughtlessness of Miss Breckinridge's life as opposed to his own. Her chest restricted at that thought, but as her eyes strained after him, she made a decision, and slipped back into the house, through a side hallway, and up to her room long enough to pull a cloak over her dress, and to thrust a small package into her pocket. Hastening down the back stairs and through the servants' passage, she again exited the house and ran through the pleasure garden to the wood, taking care to stay in shadow.

At the edge of the garden, she turned into the trees, following the sodden path she had trod so many times this autumn toward Helden Hall, and rehearsing in her mind what she would say to Mr. Ingles. As it happened, she did not have far to go, for when she reached the Prince's clearing, there he stood in a pool of moonlight, head bent and shoulders sloping downward, the picture of dejection. Lenora burst into the clearing and he whirled about to face her, his bearded face impossible to read.

"Mr. Ingles," she began, but could go no further for a few moments as she recovered herself with great gulps of air. "Mr. Ingles, I have been wishing to speak with you."

His head nodded infinitesimally, but he made no other movement or sound, and Lenora stepped forward, all the eagerness she had been holding in for the last few weeks coming out in a rush. "Mr. Ingles, I must beg your pardon—I never meant to wound you with my thoughtlessness. It was silly—ridiculous—my imaginings about the Hall, and the heir. I let my fancy run away with me, and never considered your feelings, nor anyone else's. I ought not to have teased you about the house, nor should I have made you feel beholden to me in any way, no matter how I served you, for I would have helped you even without the hope of reward. And it was unconscionable in me to speak to you as I did, regarding your circumstances, especially when we had just become—that is, I had hoped we were something like friends."

This burst of candor hung in the still, cold air while Mr. Ingles stood watching her in silence, not a hair moving to give evidence of his feelings. Lenora shivered, her fingers wringing together under her cloak, and her heart beat heavily in her chest as she thought how undeserving she was of forgiveness, and how foolish she had been to believe he would wish to speak to her again.

"I am sorry to have bothered you, sir," she murmured, heat rising into her cheeks. She took a faltering step backward.

"No, I'm sorry," Mr. Ingles said abruptly, the words issuing from his mouth in a little cloud.

Lenora blinked hopefully at him.

He came toward her, his dark eyes fixed on her face. "Miss Breckinridge, I oughtn't to have spoken to you as I did. It doesn't matter what you think should happen at the Hall, nor what the heir is like, for you were right in that there's been shameful waste of good property, and there's no harm in wanting to help."

"You are too kind, sir, to treat my offenses so lightly," Lenora said quietly, "but I assure you, I will not forget your goodness, and shall do my utmost never to give in to thoughtless fantasy again."

A puff of steam emitted from his nostrils, indicating a huff. "It won't do to strain at impossibilities, ma'am."

Lenora opened her mouth to retort, but immediately closed it again, not to be undone by pride so soon as she had repented of selfishness.

"Besides," he continued, in a gentle, conversational tone, "the heir to Helden Hall must have so many troubles over his head as to be wanting a guardian angel like you, Miss Breckinridge."

She felt a blush infuse her cheeks. "It is ungentlemanly in you to rally me, Mr. Ingles." Then she recollected her spiteful thoughts on his not being a gentleman, and experienced a moment of confusion. But the relief of being back in charity with him had raised her spirits enough that she was presently able to add, with a smile, "Though I ought never to have aspired to such heights."

His eyes sparkled appreciatively. "It's a famous notion, I'd say, Miss Breckinridge. Poor man must be at his wit's end to decide what to do with this heap of rubble, and here you are just raring to take possession of the place and live off imagined elegance for the rest of your life."

"One has so much more hope for happiness," she returned, her chin raised, "when unfettered by worldly considerations."

"Oh, but I was forgetting the larder belowstairs," he went on ruthlessly. "That'll set you up for who knows how long. But you may wish to retrieve the honeypot from Tess first."

This elicited a gurgle of mirth from Lenora, which brought a gleam of grinning white teeth to Mr. Ingles' bearded face, and the two enjoyed a cozy chuckle in the middle of the clearing, puffs of steam wreathing about their heads.

When their laughter died down, Lenora sighed and said, "I must have been mad. I suppose the Hall makes people mad, for they say in the village that Lord Helden was quite out of his senses by the end of his life." Mr. Ingles raised an interested eyebrow and she elaborated, "Evidently, he was found more than once digging up the hedge maze in the middle of the night."

"I never heard that story."

She lifted her shoulders. "Looking for turnips. 'I'll get that turnip!' he'd say, but they carried him off to bed. Perhaps he mistook turnips for gold. I fancy you ought to beware, sir."

"I may already have overcome the effects of this madness, thanks to you, ma'am."

Her cheeks warmed and she shuffled a bit in the silence that followed, until at last she remembered her gift. She said, "I have something for you," but at that very moment he said, "I brought you something," and held out a boxy object wrapped in sacking.

After a momentary pause—wherein she considered whether it was proper to accept a gift from him, and instantly cast her scruples to the wind in favor of staying in his good graces—she accepted the package, and unwrapped the sacking.

"Oh!" was all she could say. It was the writing desk from the attics of the Hall.

"I replaced the hinges, just as you meant to have done," he told her, pointing to the lid.

She turned the desk to look with wonder at the new hinges, stricken dumb by the thoughtfulness of the gift.

He blew on his gloved fingers and said abruptly, "It's too cold to be standing so long. Dash it, you must be frozen!" He took the desk from her and set it beside him on the ground, taking one of her hands in his and chafing it.

She stared at his hands enveloping her own, thinking how lovely it felt to have one's hand held by such warm and gentle ones, until she suddenly remembered her own gift and said, "I have something for you as well."

He let go her hand as she reached into the cloak pocket and removed the small box, which he took almost reverently, turning it this way and that in the moonlight.

"I tried to think of something you would find useful," she explained as he opened the box to reveal a pocket watch. "Every gentleman should have a watch."

He gazed down at the watch, rubbing a forefinger along its smoothness. "It's grand," he said, in a somewhat muffled tone.

Replacing the lid on the box, he put it carefully into his coat pocket, and silence closed between them again, but it was peaceful and inviting. Lenora's teeth began to chatter, and she tugged her cloak tightly around herself.

"Come, I'll see you to the garden," he said, picking up the writing desk. She went willingly with him back through the wood, speaking very little but enjoying a sense of camaraderie as they moved together through the moonlight.

When they reached the pleasure garden, she said, "Thank you, sir. For the writing desk, which I shall treasure, but also for your forbearance toward me—in everything."

"You're welcome, Miss Breckinridge. Thank you for the watch. I'll cherish it."

She smiled a little nervously and held out a chilled hand. "Good night, sir."

Taking it in both his own, he bowed, and she turned away, but after she had gone only a few steps, he called out to her, "Miss Breckinridge, you may visit the Hall any time you like, and for any reason. No need to ask my permission."

"Thank you, Mr. Ingles!" she cried, smiling in delight even as she shivered in the moonlight. "Good night—and happy Christmas!"

Chapter 13

IMMEDIATELY UPON ENTERING the house, she was accosted by a junior maid, who informed her in carrying accents that the whole house was in an uproar for fear she was kidnapped and murdered, and then Blaine erupted from the kitchens just down the passage, to envelop her in a large, warm embrace, and to reproach her for scaring the wits out of everybody. She had only enough time to give the writing desk into the maid's hands with the instruction to have it taken up to her room, before she was dragged down the passage to the parlor, which was quite shimmering with the heat of a roaring fire, and pressed into a wing chair, her sodden shoes removed and her feet propped on a cushion, and a cup of steaming tea thrust at her.

Before Lenora could collect her wits, her mother had rushed into the room and fallen to her knees beside the chair. "Lenora! My love, we have been searching the whole house for you! Mr. Dowbridge and Sir Joshua—oh, and nearly all the gentlemen—had just resolved upon mounting a search party! How could you serve us such a trick? Oh, my dear, your slippers are ruined, and your hands are like ice!"

"Mama," Lenora said, "I only wanted some air—it was so stuffy in the ballroom, and the night was so lovely that I wandered a little too far."

"Wandered!" cried her ladyship, taking a blanket from the junior maid, who had just entered the room laden with quilts, and tucking it snugly around Lenora's slim person. "In the middle of the night, in ball dress, in December? What can you have been thinking, my love?"

Sir Joshua arrived on the scene at that moment and came to stand in front of Lenora's chair. "Are you alright, my dear? What happened to you?"

Sighing, Lenora set about calming her parents by telling them just enough of her adventure to seem plausible, but not enough to introduce new anxieties into their minds.

"Mr. Ingles brought you home?" remarked her mother, a crease appearing between her brows. "I wonder that he was in the wood, at this time of night. It is very singular. Do not you think so, Sir Joshua?"

Sir Joshua, regarding Lenora intently, merely said, "No, my dear, I do not, for he is caretaker of Helden Hall, which marches alongside the Grange, you recall. He has every right to prowl the Home Wood at any time he chooses." He took his wife's hand and raised her to her feet. "And he brought our Lenora home safe, which deserves our thanks."

Lady Stiles, silenced by the look in his eyes, had to be satisfied with adjuring the housemaid, who was still hovering about fringes of the room, to bring Tess to Miss Breckinridge at once, and to tell her that Miss was to be gotten to bed with a hot brick at her feet, and the fire built up.

"Now, finish your tea, Lenora," she called hastily, as her husband ushered her from the room, "and do not let Tess keep you up talking of your adventure!"

"But really, Joshua," said Lady Stiles an hour later, as she and her husband reposed quietly in her sitting room, after having reassured their guests and seen them off to bed, "you must own that there is something havey-cavey about Mr. Ingles just happening to be out and about, tonight of all nights, when Lenora takes it into her head to wander into the Home Wood and get lost."

"All I must own, my dear, is that I, for one, am exceedingly grateful that Mr. Ingles happened to be out and about, for Lenora is not generally so hen-witted as to submit herself to the elements in such an irresponsible way," replied her husband, in a tone of unconcern. "Which, I may remind you, could easily have been the death of her. But thanks to Mr. Ingles' intervention, the worst consequence Lenora will suffer from her indiscretion looks merely to be a trifling cold."

Pursing her lips, Lady Stiles was obliged to agree, but could not keep from muttering darkly about clandestine meetings and fortune hunters, and the inert attitudes of certain fathers.

Raising his head from the book that he had been calmly perusing, Sir Joshua regarded his spouse with an indulgent eye. "My darling Genevieve, I see that your prejudice against Mr. Ingles will not be repressed, and I should enter into all your feelings on that head, were it not that I am in possession of information that I now perceive I ought to have shared with you directly." He then proceeded to impart what Tom had divulged to him upon Lenora's disturbing disappearance, regarding Lenora's obligation to Mr. Ingles.

As Genevieve blinked at him, Sir Joshua lay his book upon a side table and rose, taking her hands and raising her to her feet, saying,

"It is Tom's opinion that she glimpsed Mr. Ingles in the wood tonight when she went out for air, and saw the opportunity to discharge her errand without bringing undue attention to herself—which, you need not tell me was an unfortunate miscalculation on her part—and far from taking unfair advantage of the situation, Mr. Ingles delivered our girl safely home, and in good time."

Genevieve, her brows lowered, looked down at his waistcoat, considering the delicate embroidery of her own making for some moments before remarking, "It is very disobliging of you to have all the answers, Joshua—but I must own you are right. I have allowed my prejudice to carry me away into fancying Mr. Ingles to be capable of all sorts of villainy, and blinding me to his very good qualities. For he may have behaved abominably at our first acquaintance, but he became almost conformable as we nursed him, which suggests he is not at all black at heart; and he may have been a drunkard but, by all accounts, he is no longer, and that is very much to his credit, for it shows a resiliency and a determination to do right."

"And it is very much to your credit, my dear, and to Lenora's, for nursing him so well," said her husband, bringing one of her hands to his lips and kissing it.

With a sigh, Genevieve stepped into his arms. "I never imagined I should be such a suspicious parent, Joshua, for all the time we were in London, I never felt the least concern over Lenora's admirers."

"In all fairness, my love, none of them were caretakers."

She raised her head and looked intently up at him. "And that, I think, is what I do not trust, Joshua. Lenora still does have romantical notions, however she tries to convince us otherwise, and I fear that in a flight of desperation to fulfill her dreams, she will force a relationship with someone entirely unacceptable."

Sir Joshua dropped a kiss onto her forehead. "We must hope that Lenora's experiences have taught her to be wiser than that, my love."

This reminder soothed his lady enough to allow the subject to be dropped and for other, more agreeable ones to be pursued.

―⁂―

To have her mistress confined to bed with an illness at last was the realization of a lifelong ambition for Tess. The tenderness of her watch care over the sickbed was second only to the morbidity of her prognostications regarding the dreadfulness of the illness with which she expected her mistress would be long afflicted. That her mistress should make a full recovery was never in doubt—merely Tess devoutly trusted that the process would involve many close encounters with Death, comprised of fevered nights and delirious days, wherein the faithful nurse's skill and devotion would figure most prominently, and to which care said recovery would be wholly ascribed.

Unfortunately for Tess, Lenora was possessed of as strong a constitution as her own, and was laid low for only five days, requiring very few hours of barley-water cloths bathing her forehead, and even fewer applications of mustard footbaths. The apothecary was not even sent for—a circumstance in which Tess secretly rejoiced, for though she held nothing personally against him or his profession, she was loathe to share any of the credit for Miss Breckinridge's recovery with someone who had, in her opinion, more than his fair share of victories at the sickbed.

When Lenora rose from her couch without even a lingering cough, her first determination was to make good Mr. Ingles' invitation to visit the Hall again, but in this she was frustrated by the first winter storm of the year, which deposited a surprisingly heavy blanket of snow onto the countryside. Not all her demonstrations of the healthfulness of fresh air and exercise to the recovery of invalids could work upon either of her parents' sensibilities to the degree that they would allow her out while the ground was thus encumbered; therefore, Lenora was obliged to turn her mind from the project for another sennight, whiling away her time as patiently as she could in games and other interactions with Tom and Tess.

At last, the snow melted away, and Lenora, well-bundled and admonished to minimal exertion, led Tom into the Home Wood and down the path to the Prince's clearing—which she nearly named to him, but stopped herself in time to escape his inevitable mockery. Tom was suitably impressed by the wood, and made several comments on the probability of good hunting there in the proper season, which Lenora accepted with equanimity, having been long resigned to the fact that he had no sensibility at all.

The sight of Helden Hall, in all its derelict glory, brought him to a standstill, and as he gaped in wonder, Lenora began to have hopes that she had misjudged him. But when his first comment, upon regaining his voice, was to marvel that the place hadn't been put to the hammer, she could only sigh and urge him on, around the house, to the lodge.

It was her daring intention to make Mr. Ingles known to Tom, to prove that he was, indeed, only a friend, and to further repair former inattention by this notice. But when her knock upon the door went unanswered, an inspection of the rooms through the dingy windows revealed them to be uninhabited, with the stripped bed and empty grate attesting to the likelihood of their having been so quite some time.

"I cannot understand it, Tom," said Lenora, as they turned away from the cottage and made their way back up the gravel drive. "Where could he have gone? From what I know of him, he has no family nearby, or he should have gone to them at Christmas, should not he?"

"No use worrying over it, Nora," replied Tom airily, pulling her arm through his own. "He's a grown man, and knows what he's about. No doubt he's gone for supplies, or touring the manor, or some such thing."

"But his bed has not been slept in, and the grate was swept out. Surely there would have been the coals of the morning's fire there, if he was to return soon." She mused in this way a few moments longer, but Tom did not attend, so she let it go, saying as they came up to the door of the Hall, "I only hope he left the door unlocked for us, for he did expressly invite me to come whenever I wished."

Her hope was not in vain. The knob turned at a touch, and the door creaked open upon the same eerily expectant emptiness she had found so enticing last November. With great nostalgia did Lenora lead Tom through the principal rooms of the house, indicating those areas that held superior interest for her, but to all these he gave only cursory notice. He wrinkled his nose at the kitchens, not even hazarding a guess for what the lone knife had last been used, nor did he favor her with any of his own surmises as to how the various empty rooms had once been decorated. He felt no shiver of ice creep up his back at the sight of the dead lord's rumpled bedclothes, and had enough improper feeling to suggest that Lord Helden's shoes could be put to some good use rather than rot in his wardrobe, untouched.

Overall, it was a depressing experience for Lenora. The house seemed lifeless without Tess and Mr. Ingles there with her. She had not even the heart to take Tom up into the attics, where he may have found something to pique his interest, and she led him back through the hall to the saloon, exiting the house through the back door to the veranda. As she turned to ensure the door closed properly, she was surprised to see a small note affixed to the door frame, with her name written in sprawling letters across it. Casting a quick glance at

Tom, who had noticed it at the same time, Lenora pulled the note free and, breaking the wafer, read the following:

> *Miss Breckinridge,*
> *I've been obliged to go down to London for a time—I know not how long, but rest assured that you are expected and welcome in the Hall, and if on further examination you still find it calls to your heart, you'll be pleased to know that I hope to bring you tidings of the heir before long. Content yourself that I'll leave you to reveal your plans for him and his house, if I should meet him.*
> *Your servant,*
> *James Ingles*

Color suffused Lenora's cheeks as she read this very impudent note, and she stuffed it into her muff before Tom could glimpse how familiar Mr. Ingles had been. Even so, he peered at her blushing countenance and asked her what was toward.

"Nothing—nothing, Tom," she replied with utmost unconcern. "Just a note from Mr. Ingles renewing his most obliging invitation to see the house, of which I have already availed myself, so we need not concern ourselves with it. Shall we go home?"

Chapter 14

If Tom found anything suspicious in this speech, the only sign he gave of it was a cocked eyebrow—which was entirely lost on his sister, as she had already set a brisk pace toward the overgrown lawn. He caught her up within two strides and said amiably, "I don't for my life see what has caught your fancy about that ramshackle building, Nora. It's shamefully run down, and would take a fortune to furbish up."

Lenora eyed him askance. "So I believe, and I could not expect you, of all people, to apprehend my feelings in the case."

"Oh, come down off your high ropes, Nora! I'm only speaking truth. Look at the place!" He pulled her elbow to make her turn to regard the great hulk, its boarded windows staring back like so many blank eyes. "How could anything so derelict be romantic?"

"That, my dear Tom, is exactly why you will never understand me. You've not the least notion what romance is."

She turned back and resumed her determined progress away from the Hall, and Tom, shaking his head as his gaze swept once more over the pitiful stone house, followed her. They made their way on the path to the Prince's clearing in silence, but Tom had been exercising his mind over the problem of his sister's fascination with the Hall, and astonished her by saying abruptly, "Perhaps it shan't take so much to put the place to rights."

Lenora favored him with a wry look, and he lifted his hands in self-exculpation. "I did not think, before, but the house itself is in good repair—only that one rotted place in the lower hall, and all those broken windows—but paint and wallpaper and draperies aren't too dear. The greatest expense would be the furnishings and the glazing—stap me if there aren't enough window frames to fill the treasury! But all the rooms need not be furbished up at the outset, only those that'll be most in use." Tipping his head to the side, he gazed into the distance and nodded in satisfaction. "Yes, I'm persuaded it wouldn't take too large a sum to see that place habitable, and then it would only take a few years of provident living, and putting the land to good use—bringing in tenants and hiring workers and such—to realize enough income to finish the job."

"I am persuaded you are right, Tom," said his sister, with a tart smile, "and so I shall tell the heir if ever I see him."

He laughed and tucked her arm in his, setting off toward home again. "I know, much use it does us to make any plans. Unless, of course, your fancy of marrying the heir comes to pass."

"Oh, that I had a pillow to throw at you!" she cried, pulling away from him and blushing furiously.

He cocked an eyebrow at her. "Well, it might not be a bad thing for you Lenora, nor for him, for now that Sir Joshua has settled thirty thousand pounds on you, it's bound to be enough to do the trick."

Lenora stopped still and stared at her brother in disbelief, the color draining from her cheeks as quickly as it had come. "Tom, is that true?"

It was Tom's turn to stare. "Never say they didn't tell you!"

Her look of shock was eloquent enough to confirm this, and he pulled his hat from his head to run agitated fingers through his hair. "What a cod's head I am! And all this time I thought you knew—joking about your suitor—" He broke off again as her eyes widened in mortification. He grasped her hand, pressing it. "Not that it makes a difference to him! I dare swear he don't know about it."

She snatched her hand away. "Do you suppose that Mr. Dowbridge is after my fortune? That I am incapable of attaching a young man on my own merits? Thank you very much, Tom!"

"No, no!" cried Tom, scrambling to retrieve the situation. "He seems quite taken with you—with you, yourself, and not any trumpery fortune you might have. You're quite a catch, Nora! Why, I've never seen you so taking as you were at the house party—a regular diamond, I'd say!"

Rolling her eyes at him, Lenora turned her back and marched pointedly away down the path.

Tom hastened to come up with her. "I wonder Mama didn't tell you. Or Sir Joshua. I suppose they have their reasons, but I think it's foolish not to at least warn you before you go off to London and make a figure of yourself."

"What do you mean by that, pray?" demanded his sister, stopping once more to confront him face to face.

"What I mean, Nora, is that countrified young men are one thing, but Town Beaux are a breed unto themselves." Her brows drew closer together, and she opened her mouth to argue, but he spoke over her. "Once you step foot in the capital, if they find out you're a wealthy woman, every dashed fortune hunter is going to try to cut a wheedle with you, and you'd likely never know it, what with that devilish romantic head you have! Sure as check, you'd attach yourself to some bottom dweller, thinking he's besotted with you, when it's your rolls of soft he loves."

"But if I should attach myself to Mr. Dowbridge I should be safe, is that it, Tom?"

He shrugged. "It's not for me to say, but if you attach yourself to Dowbridge, I wash my hands of you. Not that he's a fortune hunter—just an impudent dog if there ever was one."

"I shall take leave to inform you, Master Thomas," Lenora ground out between clenched teeth, "that contrary to your very flattering expectations, I have not become attached to any of the young men who have so obligingly dangled after me, countrified or no—or have you forgotten my adventures in London last spring? If you troubled your head to think, you would perceive that I have a brain, alongside my overactive imagination, and thus far it has not failed me completely, and so I will thank you to keep your cynical observations to yourself, and give me the credit that is my due!"

She whirled and continued down the path, leaving Tom blinking in the wood behind her.

After a period of stormy reflection, during which Lenora passed rapidly from anger to annoyance to grudging resignation, she was obliged to own that Tom's warning was, regrettably, appropriate. She was uncomfortably aware that before making her residence at Wrenthorpe as Sir Joshua's stepdaughter, she had never, in fact, been seriously pursued by any gentleman, and so she did not know if she could recognize true love in a suitor. Even Mr. Dowbridge's attentions were not much of a test, for she did not at all return his interest. Whether she would think to question the motives of a man to whom she were truly attracted, she did not know.

There was only one man she could think likely to be in this category, and that was Lord Helden. While he was at large, she could not imagine any other man capable of commanding her affections, for no matter how rational she thought herself, she suspected that as long as Helden Hall held sway in her heart she could give it to no other. The London season, which was fast approaching, would give her the perfect opportunity to test this notion, for if the heir had not settled at his estate, the next most likely place to find him would be in London.

Indeed, the possession of a fortune positioned her perfectly to act, as Mr. Ingles had so appropriately termed it, as guardian angel to the new Lord Helden, and she found it impossible not to become lost in a fantasy in which she saw herself, dressed in flowing white, coming upon his lordship, who had lost all hope and was wasting away in a pauper's den. After attending to his recovery, which should involve many applications of lavender water to his fevered brow—But here she was brought back to reason, as the feverish Lord Helden, suddenly and to her great disquiet, assumed the deep, brown eyes of the feverish Mr. Ingles, gripping her hand and uttering secrets through his hairy beard.

With some effort, she returned her thoughts to the responsibility she now carried under the weight of a fortune, resolving that if she were to find Lord Helden residing in London, as Mr. Ingles seemed to consider possible, she would not allow her heart to overpower her reason. He would be required, just as any of her suitors would be, to prove himself before she should consign her hand and fortune to him. He must also commit to restoring his estate, for she shared

Tom's opinion that it would not, after all, take much to make the Hall livable, and she would never consent to residing at any other house. When she again recollected herself in the midst of rapid calculations of how far thirty thousand pounds should go in furbishing up the Hall, however, she was forced to conclude that perhaps her mother and step-father had been right to keep the fact of her fortune from her.

The heavy snow had delayed the family's preparations to remove to London for the season, and now, midway through February, there was still a deal of packing and shopping to be done before the journey could be attempted. Once the ladies' numerous gowns had been delivered, and all the necessary accessories to their wardrobes procured, and the servants sent bustling about preparing the house for the family's protracted absence, Lady Stiles came into Lenora's room, ostensibly to assist her in packing, but her immediate dismissal of Tess from the room aroused Lenora's suspicions that this was to be no ordinary chat.

"My love," began her mother, taking the dress that Tess had been carefully folding on the bed and placing it in a trunk, "there is something of a delicate nature about which I wish to speak to you, before we are completely overcome by this whirlwind of preparations and find ourselves already in London."

Believing she knew what was toward, Lenora lowered her eyes and murmured, "Yes, Mama, what is it?"

Her mother arranged a few more articles of clothing in the trunk before continuing. "As this is to be your second season, my dear, I feel confident that you are much more up to snuff, as the saying goes. However, I cannot but feel that certain of your interests continue to be a strong influence upon you, and I must own to a slight anxiety over how you will choose to conduct yourself while we are in town."

"Mama," said Lenora reasonably, "I hope you do not suspect me of cherishing the same thoughtless fancies that brought calamity upon me last year—and not only me, but Elvira, as well. If you believe me to be so insensible as to have forgotten the consequences of my thinking the evil Duke to be romantic, I do not know how you could trust me to come within a hundred miles of London."

Lady Stiles smiled at this response. "No, my love, I could not think it of you. Indeed, that occurrence will not easily be forgotten by any of us, and I do not doubt your having learned a valuable lesson. I simply worry that—in light of recent events—" She hesitated, as if formulating her words carefully. "You are young and impetuous and romantic, which are attractions in and of themselves, and now you have—you have even more to offer a prospective husband—by way of maturity and experience, you understand—In short, you need not snap up the first offer that comes your way, my dear. You will certainly not be left on the shelf, so you need not fear to be discriminating in your companions."

Subsiding into uneasy silence, Lady Stiles regarded her daughter, who had listened quietly to what had been said. Indeed, Lenora, possessed as she was of Tom's intelligence, read much more into her mother's words than had been communicated, and thanks to her earlier reflections, was able to put the maternal mind at rest.

"You are right to speak to me on the subject, Mama," she said, "for I cannot pretend to be immune to flattery, and your warning, though mortifying, I will allow to be timely."

Her mother let out a sigh. "Oh, my dear," she said, enveloping Lenora in an embrace. "I wish only to see you happy—as happy as I am now—and not miserable, as I was in my first marriage."

This reminder of her mother's unbearably disappointing first marriage, which had begun with so much hope and had ended in disillusionment and despair, moved her to return the embrace warmly.

"Have no fear, Mama," she said with feeling. "I shall allow no evil Dukes nor stammering heroes to take my fancy this season. I promise, moreover, to conduct myself with the utmost propriety, and to bring to your attention any suitor for whom I feel the slightest tendre, well before my affections are fixed."

Her mother laughed at this, expressing her trust that Lenora would not behave so properly as to be insipid, to which Lenora concurred, and their discussion turned to the more light-hearted subject of what they were to do first upon arriving in the Metropolis.

The next day, the family set off to London, intending to take Branwell in the way, and to see first-hand the improvements that had been made by Tom's judicious handling. They were not disappointed, and as the movers had nearly completed the transition of Tom's things to the manor house—the tenants having vacated the week previous—the Breckinridges enjoyed a reminiscent afternoon going over the old house, and regaling Sir Joshua with the memories they had chosen to remember from among those they had rather forget.

Late the next morning, Tom took Lenora aside and placed two fifty pound notes in her palm, discarding her objections out of hand. "I had planned to give you your second season, Nora, but now that Sir Joshua has taken that responsibility, the least I can do is buy you some trumperies."

Then, adjuring her not to waste it all on diamond-studded slippers or some such sacrilege, he promised to visit at Easter and saw them off—Sally, the cook, having treated them to a fine breakfast, and pressed sandwiches and cakes and bottles of lemonade upon them for the journey to London, which would be accomplished in little over three hours, thanks to the four excellent coach horses that Sir Joshua had hired.

Chapter 15

SIR JOSHUA HAD taken a house in Curzon Street, facing the garden of Chesterfield House, the trees of which swayed alluringly above a high stone wall, while their own house boasted large apartments for entertaining, at the expense of a garden. Lady Stiles assured Lenora that this lack would be amply recompensed by the proximity of the house to the Green Park, to which she promised to walk with Lenora every day, if only to gaze upon the tree to whose infirmity they owed their present happiness.

"For if I had not been stranded in the tree by that broken branch, my love," observed her mother, "you should not have brought Sir Joshua to the spot, and he should not have discovered what a hoyden I was, and been straightway captivated."

"Perhaps not straightway, darling," interposed her husband, who had quite inopportunely entered the room just at that moment. As his wife glanced reproachfully at him, he smiled and continued,

"Some four-and-twenty hours had passed before it dawned upon me that I had been unable to banish that ridiculous and adorable picture of you, seated like a lost heron on the branch, from my mind." He dropped a kiss onto her nose. "Then, I was captivated."

While her parents argued their differing viewpoints on the precise definitions of "straightway" and "captivation," Lenora betook herself to her room, which overlooked the street and gave a tantalizing glimpse of the lovely gardens behind the wall of Lord Chesterfield's property. While Tess unpacked her trunks, Lenora gazed out across the garden to the rooftops beyond and wondered, if Lord Helden was in London, where he was to be found.

No matter his situation, his lordship could easily prove to be among the gentlemen of her acquaintance, for thanks to Sir Joshua's station, they moved in some of the best circles. Though she knew that her bosom friend, Elvira Ginsham, could not be in town this season, owing to her interesting condition and her husband's very laudable but vexing desire to keep his wife and unborn child wrapped in cotton wool, Lenora could look forward to meeting other friends in town. Mr. Dowbridge and his parents, Lord and Lady Mintlowe, had given many smiling assurances that they should follow hard on the Stiles's heels; and her friend Diana Marshall, who had enjoyed a light flirtation with Tom last season, was already in London. The notion that she might see Mr. Ingles in town occurred to her as well, and she was startled by the warmth with which it entered her mind, but she firmly banished it, for he could not meet with her when they moved in such disparate circles, unless by chance in the street.

But Lord Helden she could meet at almost any time, if only she knew what he looked like. As she gazed out at the lovely gardens behind Chesterfield house, trying to create an image of Lord Helden in her mind without it transforming into that of Mr. Ingles, she became aware that a gentleman had appeared under the trees, and was returning her regard with some interest. Startled and embarrassed, she raised a hand in an unconscious gesture of apology, then immediately dropped the hand as the gentleman, mistaking her gesture as one of greeting, tipped his hat very gallantly to her. Mortified, Lenora almost leapt away from the window, pressing hands to her burning cheeks, and fully convinced that the gentleman must think her abominably forward, to stare and then to wave at a complete stranger.

Tess, watching her precipitate retreat from the window, started forward. "Miss! Whatever's the matter? Are you unwell?" she cried, not without hope.

Lenora disclaimed any such thing, but when she dropped her hands to reveal red cheeks, Tess uttered a triumphant shriek. "Miss! Oh, you've taken the scarlet fever! No wonder you're overcome! I knew we should never drag you, just recovered from death's door, to this dirty, nasty, God-forsaken city! Here—"

Lenora batted away the outstretched hand of her would-be savior and said firmly, "I've no more contracted scarlet fever than you have, Tess! What a ridiculous creature you are! I merely—I saw something that took me aback, is all," she temporized, as the color ebbed out of her cheeks, leaving them pale but glowing with perfect health.

Disappointed in this proof of her mistress's regrettably strong constitution, Tess sniffed and returned to her unpacking, muttering darkly about London air and vermin carrying unthinkable disease, and young ladies given to dissipation and frivolity being struck down when they least expect it. These musings considerably lightened her mood, and she quite cheerfully set to arranging her mistress's dresses in the wardrobe while contemplating the gratifying probability of

Miss being too wasted to wear any of them, having been stricken by some nameless town disease, and relying wholly upon her faithful maid to nurse her back to health.

Lenora, meanwhile, dropped into a wing chair by the fire, where she mentally chastised herself for a ninnyhammer, for if she had not jumped away from the window, the gentleman, whoever he was, should not have had any reason to think ill of her. He had ever so calmly returned her salutation, and if she had merely faded out of his sight, walking casually away from the window, nothing could have been more natural than the exchange.

Groaning, she left the chair and returned to the window to peek carefully out at the garden across the street, but the stranger had been replaced by a sturdy young boy with a cricket bat. No doubt the gentleman was somewhere in the shrubbery, hunting for the ball. She wondered who he was, and realized he could be anybody—Lord Chesterfield, or heavens! He could be Lord Helden—for the Earl of Chesterfield knew all the world, she didn't doubt. No matter who he was, her situation was mortifying.

To think that she, who had so recently played a heroine's part—saving the life of a fellow creature not once but twice, and now looking to bring to pass the redemption of a noble house—could react so prudishly to so slight a misstep, bringing upon her the censure of a stranger, was almost unforgivable in her. Overcome by a mixture of helplessness and self-recrimination, she shuddered at the vision of herself being presented to Lord Helden at last, only to discover that he was this gentleman, and thought her a fast female whom he would scorn to know.

She shook herself, suddenly aware that she was once again staring, and stalked away from the window, informing Tess that she was going to see if her mama needed any assistance.

Lady Stiles, refreshed after supervising an army of servants in unpacking all the morning, responded to Lenora's inquiry with a proposal that they sally forth to that dazzling house of bargains, the Soho Bazaar. This expedition proved efficacious in relieving some of Lenora's emotion, as the two ladies spent what only last year would have seemed to them a shocking sum of money on such essentials as silk stockings at three shillings a pair, long gloves at two shillings a pair, and ostrich plumes at five for a guinea; and some non-essential bargains they simply could not ignore, including satin slippers for two guineas and a cashmere shawl for only five. They packed their purchases into the barouche and set off toward Curzon Street.

On the corner of Oxford Street and New Bond, as their coach was slowed at the turning by a surge of pedestrian traffic across the road. A group of ragged urchins, some in their gangly teens, descended as one onto the open stall of a bakery, plucking loaves of bread from baskets and rushing pell-mell in all directions away from the unfortunate proprietor. A very small boy, however, was not quick enough, and the baker, justifiably enraged, swooped down upon him, taking him by the scruff of the neck and shaking him until his eyes crossed and the dusty loaf fell from his hands.

"Stop!" cried Lenora to the coachman. "Oh, Jackson, stop at once!"

This order was quickly complied with, and Lenora, her heroine's ideals returning full-force, nearly tumbled from the coach to remonstrate with the fuming baker.

Recovering from her stupefaction at her daughter's astonishing behavior, Lady Stiles descended from the coach and stepped through the crowd that had gathered, to lend her assistance. Addressing the combatants in so diplomatic a way as to validate both party's concerns in the case, she had the satisfaction of observing the color slowly recede from the angry man's face, and he set the urchin on his feet, though he did not let him go.

"He oughta be whipped, ma'am," he ground out, yanking on the terrified boy's collar for good measure.

"But sir," cried Lenora, "he is starving! Just look at his poor body, so thin his clothes hang on him!"

"Half the world is starving, my dear," said Lady Stiles gently, turning then to the baker. "And we well know it is not this man's fault, nor the fault of any in his profession, that bread is so shockingly dear just now."

"Aye, and it'll be dear full long, ma'am, if those dashed MP's have aught to say for it!" thundered the man, shaking the poor boy in his anger. "I can't scarce feed me own family on what I take for this bread, and now this 'un's gone and thrown one in the dirt, and it must be me poor youngen's dinner!" So saying, he bent to retrieve the loaf, but Lenora was quicker.

Snatching the bread from the dust of the flagway, she held it to her chest and said, "We'll take this loaf, sir, and five more, if you please."

The baker blinked at her for several moments, then said, "As you please, ma'am, though I'd go bail you won't like that dirty one."

Lady Stiles stepped forward, reaching into her reticule to pull out a guinea. "Oh, you may depend upon it, we will not be bothered at all," she said, smiling and extending it to him.

"And we shall take the boy off your hands as well, sir," said Lenora, with a quick, pleading glance at her mother. "You may be certain he shall be dealt with."

The man's face stiffened, but after another few moments, he grunted and thrust the urchin toward her. "Makes no odds to me, ma'am."

Grasping the trembling boy's hand, Lenora coaxed him into the coach and climbed in behind him, followed directly by Lady Stiles with the other five loaves they had just purchased. Her ladyship gave the coachman the order to drive on and gazed with supreme unconcern on the street ahead, while wondering what on earth she was to do with a daughter who seemed suddenly bent on rescuing all the poor starving children in London, not to mention mollifying shopkeepers by purchasing half their wares.

Presently, Lady Stiles directed her coachman to turn onto a small side street and Lenora stiffened as her mother requested him to pull up next to a small chapel. The boy instantly set up a shrill resistance against their leaving him "on the Parish," saying he had a perfectly good house, and didn't need no churchman to lock him up. He quieted only after Lenora had assured him they would do no such thing if he did not wish it, watching warily as her ladyship instructed the coachman to take four of the loaves into the chapel and give them to the verger, to be distributed to the poor.

When the coachman had gone, she addressed herself in a kindly tone to the little boy at Lenora's side. "Well, young man, you have gotten yourself into a bit of trouble today, haven't you?"

He shrank back from her, his eyes unnaturally wide in his emaciated face. Lenora's heart was wrung, and she gently touched his cheek. "Don't be afraid! We shan't hurt you."

"No, my dear boy, we shan't hurt you," agreed her mother, picking up the dirty loaf Lenora had set on the seat and dusting it. "We shall take you to your home, and hope that if you can manage it, you will not steal your bread again."

His eyes rolled from one lady to the other. "Ain't no way to eat if I don't steal, mum!"

Lenora cast her mother a beseeching look, which Lady Stiles held for a long moment before asking the boy, "Have you no mother or father to feed you?"

He gave one emphatic shake of his head.

Her ladyship hesitated for a moment, then said coaxingly, "There must be something you should like to do to earn your bread."

The little boy shook his head again. "If I get a penny, the big boys take it. An' if they don't, Baxter will, sure as check."

The two women exchanged another pregnant look over his head, and Lenora bit her lip. Lady Stiles bent toward the lad and said gently, "Where do you live, young man?"

"In the coal bin at Baxter's, mum."

She said quickly, "Is Baxter your master?"

"Sort of. He didn't buy me, if that's what you mean."

Her ladyship, blinking rapidly as if something had got in her eye, nodded briskly and asked, "And where does Baxter live, my boy?"

"Up by the Tower Bridge, behind the slophouse."

"Oh, Mama!" uttered Lenora, her hand flying up to her mouth.

Lady Stiles looked out across the street, visibly swallowing against her horror, which was the more palpable for knowing that this small boy was but one of thousands living in unthinkable circumstances in the Metropolis. Lenora's soft heart and inexperience had put her in a quandary—they could not save them all. Sir Joshua was wealthy, but even his resources could not extend so far. But as she glanced back at the shivering child next to Lenora, she remembered the many times small kindnesses that had been shown to her own children after her first husband's death, and knew that she must do something for this one child, at least.

She blinked again several times, then set her jaw and looked once more at the boy. "What is your name, little man?"

"Ben."

"Do you like to live in the coal bin, Ben?"

He stared up at her as if she were mad, and shook his head slowly.

Smiling kindly, she said, "I thought not. But I suppose it is better than the Parish?"

His startled jerk and vociferous concurrence gave no doubt as to his opinion of the Parish. Lady Stiles cast a glance at her daughter, imagining the look on Sir Joshua's face when they returned home, then suggested thoughtfully, "Perhaps you should like to come home with us, at least until we can find you a better home."

Lenora gasped, then looked down at the urchin beside her, a smile trembling on her lips. "Oh, yes, Ben, should you like that?"

The little boy stared again at the strange lady across from him, then twisted to squint up at the younger one by his side, his forehead wrinkled. "But I cain't live with gentry morts!"

A surprised laugh escaped Lady Stiles, but Lenora simply patted the little boy's shoulder and said, "Certainly you could, Ben, as we happen to be the kind of gentry morts who wish to help little boys like you to be happy."

Lady Stiles smiled warmly at him. "Would it make you happy to eat a loaf of bread by yourself?"

"Would it ever," he piped, then clamped his mouth shut, a mistrustful look pinching his face.

Lady Stiles held out the last loaf she held. "There. That loaf is your very own."

He stared at it for a moment. "But it ain't the dirty one."

"No, it is not. I fancy that one will make a very nice meal for my housekeeper's son's pigs. But little boys need plenty of good, clean food to become strong men, so you shall not have any dirty loaves. Nor shall you have stolen ones."

"But—" he began.

But Lady Stiles interrupted him firmly, placing the loaf in his lap. "You will not have a need to steal any more bread, for we shall help you to find a new home where no one will steal your pennies."

The little boy, dubiously eying first one lady and then the other, as if convinced they meant at any moment to relapse from their generous mood and relieve him of his prize, tore a huge piece of bread off in his teeth, chewing it defiantly. As this merely earned him an encouraging smile from one and a satisfied nod from the other, his little body relaxed, and he gave himself wholly to the novel enjoyment of a rapidly filling stomach.

On the return of the coachman, Lady Stiles desired him to drive on to Curzon Street, and Lenora encouraged the urchin, between mouthfuls, to divulge sundry facts about his existence—namely that he'd been "love-begotten and left on the Parish," until Mr. Baxter had discovered him and invited him into his family. This horrid situation little Ben had been made unwilling to escape for fear of a worse fate in the workhouse, which evil place had been ably and colorfully described to him by said Baxter whenever the child had evinced a desire to better his situation. By the time they drew up in front of the house, Lenora was trembling with both rage and sorrow at the horrors endured so pragmatically by such a small child, while Lady Stiles prepared herself to relieve her daughter of the notion that she would be able to repeat today's performance.

Had Lenora been more in command of her emotions when she had flown to Ben's rescue, she may have been made aware of the crowd that had gathered, and spied a familiar face among them. Mr. Ingles, walking down Oxford Street, came upon the astonishing spectacle of two gentlewomen arguing hotly with a tradesman, apparently over the rights to ownership of a scrawny little boy. Interested, both in the cause of the argument and in the fate of the boy, Mr. Ingles found himself an excellent vantage point and prepared to be enlightened. No sooner had he settled himself, however, when the elder of the two ladies turned her face toward him, and with a start, he recognized Lady Stiles.

The realization that the other, young lady must be Miss Breckinridge hit him with surprising force, and he pulled himself back away from the crowd, to a discreet distance where he still had a fair view of the proceedings. As he watched, Miss Breckinridge turned to shepherd the boy into a waiting carriage, and Mr. Ingles caught sight of her face—a face that had haunted his dreams ever since he had left Gloucestershire—and he knew that he did not want her to see him—not yet. He was not ready to show himself to her, here in London, amidst so many fine people and places, for he feared she should despise him, and he could not bear the thought.

No, he needed more time—more time to maneuver himself into a position where he would be proud to introduce himself to her, and where she should have no qualm in owning him as an acquaintance. And so he kept himself hidden as the carriage rolled off down New Bond Street, though he watched it out of sight, and wished that he knew if she thought more of him than she did of this boy, or if he was just another object of her pity.

Chapter 16

BEN, AT FIRST restrained by uncertainty and suspicion as to his fate at the hands of these "gentry morts," quickly came to understand that, far from imagining that small boys existed merely to be used and abused, all that his benefactors seemed to expect from him was a modicum of respect and the performance of the simple tasks of a page boy. In exchange for this, he was given clean clothes and regular meals and a proper bed—not in a coal bin, but in a room at the top of the house with the other servants. These accepted his presence very well, for they were touched by the kindness of their mistress in taking him in. But Sanford was heard more than once to sniff when he was about and comment that the household was going to the dogs.

Still, Ben mistrusted his luck, and went silently about, apprehensively executing any errands they desired of him, but as it was borne in upon him that this was a very different establishment than that of Mr. Baxter, he began to laugh and to whistle and even to question out loud why he was wanted to fetch and carry while Branton, the butler, sat counting silverware.

"They's alus the same number," he confided to Simon, the footman, who had taken him under his wing. "Do he disremember?"

Chuckling, Simon said, "The thing is, he remembers too well, and must make sure no sneaking thief has taken something from under his nose. Someday, if you work very hard, you'll become footman, like me, and then butler in a fine house like this, and then you'll do the same, my boy."

But though Ben was excessively uninformed in the ways of the gentry, he showed admirable aptitude for learning, and Lenora looked with complaisance upon her protegee, involving herself in his household education, and revolving in her mind possible plans for his future. Her mother, on the other hand, was obliged to take a more practical view of the matter.

"It is not as if we can take in all the poor orphans in London," she had told her astonished spouse, when he had met Ben upon their return from the boy's rescue, and had instantly requested a private interview. "But once Lenora had taken his part, and he told us in what conditions he was forced to live, I ask you, what else was I to do?"

Sir Joshua fully comprehended her feelings, and said, "I fear that we have mistaken the direction of Lenora's romantical notions, for this paints her as less a lonely maiden and more a Joan of Arc. I need not tell you that we had better speak with her, and soon. Much as I would applaud our establishing a foundling hospital, I am persuaded that we would do better to support those with experience and resources already in place."

"Rest assured, my dear, that I am of the same mind. I intend to consult my dear friend Caroline Wraglain, who is well-versed in the charities available in London, and we shall come up with a plan for young Ben."

Approving this course of action, Sir Joshua pledged his support of Ben's continuing in the household as long as was necessary, and even went so far as to offer to take Lenora aside and discover how far her sudden philanthropic tendency was likely to take her. But when he had found occasion to do so, she seemed to him to have been quite humbled by the experience, as she assured him that "it is my furthest intention to begin introducing street urchins into the household, for though I wish I could, poor souls, I know that it would not answer."

Lady Stiles, observing with what alacrity Ben lent himself to his work, was greatly relieved in her mind as to the wisdom of welcoming him into her home, and she began to consider how best to provide for his future.

"To be sure, he is full young to be apprenticed," she confided to Lady Wraglain, after Ben had been with her nearly a sennight, "for I shan't consider abandoning him to any such trade as uses small children, for they all of them invariably do so barbarously, and I may as well consign myself to Perdition as hand him over to one of those masters."

"As it happens, I know of a situation that may do for young Ben," replied her friend, communicating to her the address of a Lady Hawkridge, whose son had established some three schools for orphans in healthy localities about the kingdom. "But I should warn you that the family is mad for philanthropy, and may very well drag you into their schemes, if you do not take care."

"My dear Caroline, need I remind you that I am now a woman of substance?" answered Genevieve with affected pride. "I can afford to support charity with more than just needlework, and am proud to do so."

"Yes, but does Sir Joshua desire you to run through his entire fortune, all for the likes of Ben?"

Genevieve chuckled. "For all he is so careful, he is the best of men, and would probably outrun even my interest in raising the prospects of the likes of Ben. But do not worry on that head, for although commanding the elegancies of life has gone a little to my head, I am very far from putting myself in the poorhouse, even so that others can be saved from it."

At that moment, Branton opened the door to announce not only Mrs. Marshall and Miss Diana Marshall, who were acquaintances made last season, but also the Right Honorable the Countess of Gidgeborough and her daughter, the Lady Athena Dibbington, utterly unknown to Genevieve.

Lady Gidgeborough was a small woman, whose features had never been more than pretty, and whose person, though clothed in the height of fashion, was nothing to merit the weight of her presence, which seemed to center her in the room. The Lady Athena, however, was a tall, elegant, and beautiful young woman who put Genevieve in mind of nothing so much as the fabled Ice Maiden, to whose untouchable grace Lenora had aspired for a short space during her last season. Lady Athena's well-formed person was enrobed in a white embroidered India muslin gown of exquisite make, beneath a high-necked Russian blue pelisse with ruffled trim, with a fringed Cashmere shawl that looked to be worth every penny of forty guineas draped negligently at her elbows.

Genevieve, thrown into a bit of a flutter at the arrival of such august personages, desired Branton to fetch Lenora directly, and upon her entrance, made the introductions. Gazing upon the alabaster brow crowned by smooth, dark locks, and the aristocratic nose set between large, imperturbable gray eyes, Lenora was quite as impressed as her mother had been, imagining that Lady Athena had sprung from the pages of a novel, and she was momentarily stricken with awe. But Miss Marshall slipped a hand into her ladyship's arm, giving her a roguish sidelong glance, and said in a low tone, "Come, Athena, I am determined you shall be friends, so none of your stuffy airs."

The stiffness relaxed on Lady Athena's face, and her mouth betrayed a twitch of humor. With a toss of her head, she allowed herself to be led to the sofa, and sat quite good-humoredly as Lenora and Diana renewed their acquaintance. Moments later, they were all startled by a bustling sound on the stairs, and Ben made his precipitous entrance into the room.

He ran directly to Lenora, crying, "Cook's a'going to boil my toad for supper!" and then burst into tears.

After some minutes of incoherency, Ben was able to make his trouble plain: he had found a toad in the garden and had brought it into the house, promptly losing it in the kitchens. He had been searching diligently for the creature when Cook had held it up by the leg, and announced that it would be frog legs for the master tonight. Horrified, Ben had come instantly to his preceptress, trusting that she would save his innocent friend.

With a vast deal of self-command, and despite the desperately muffled titters of certain of the ladies in the room, Lenora expressed her great disappointment in Cook's not recognizing the difference between frogs and toads, and after exacting from Ben a concurrence that amphibians had no business being indoors, and receiving the tearful promise that he would not bring more livestock into the house, lest Cook mistake them for delicacies—for though she was an Englishwoman and a Christian, she did still aspire to the heights of the gourmet, and if such things as snails and frogs were considered delicacies, one could not trust that other things would not be as well—Lenora assured Ben that Sir Joshua despised frog's legs, as Cook well knew, and Ben could depend upon it that Cook had not meant a word she had said, and had liberated the poor thing as soon as Ben had quitted the kitchens.

With this reassurance, Ben, bright-eyed above tear-stained cheeks, bounced out of the drawing room to make his amends with the cook, and the ladies were at liberty to give full reign to their mirth.

"What an enchanting little scamp, Genevieve!" cried Mrs. Marshall, when she could at last speak. "Wherever did he come from?"

Lady Stiles, having observed that her high-born guests had not joined in their delight, said with an expressive look to Mrs. Marshall, "Lady Gidgeborough and Lady Athena cannot be much interested in the antics of a little boy so entirely unknown to them."

Mrs. Marshall, recollecting her company, cast an apprehensive glance at her ladyship, with whom she had been fast friends for twenty years and more, and with whose vagaries—pride being the foremost among them—she was intimately acquainted.

Lady Gidgeborough, however, bestowing a languid smile upon Genevieve, said, "On the contrary, it is a pleasure, Lady Stiles, to witness firsthand the charm of your household. We all have our quirks, to be sure, and there is never anything so refreshing to a jaded palette as a child's liveliness. Is that not so, Athena?"

Her daughter replied blandly, "Undoubtedly, Mama. He is enchanting."

Lady Stiles said lightly, "Our Ben is new to the household, and already we know not what we should do without his cheerfulness to temper our humdrum existence. To be sure, he comes to us in a most unusual way, which you may appreciate."

Then, calculating on the likelihood of her ladyship's pride being built at least in part upon a sense of her own excellent charity, Genevieve launched into an eloquent recitation of Ben's story, and soon Lady Gidgeborough was in a fair way to condoning Ben's existence, at least in the Stiles household.

While the elder ladies' conversation wound into the sober realms of poor, lost orphans and wicked men with coal bins behind slophouses, Diana pronounced her delight at discovering that Lenora was back in town.

"That you should at all wish to leave such a romantic country as Gloucestershire is most astonishing, for London must be the drabbest place to you, of all people, Lenora! Though I am very glad you did come, for what should I do without you, even if dear Athena and Iris—Miss Slougham, you know—are in town this season. I must make you known to our friend Miss Slougham, dearest Lenora—if you should not dislike it!"

Lenora expressed her willingness for such a treat, and her friend, having never doubted it, went on to say, "For, you apprehend, our fathers went to school together, and could never be separated after, so Athena and Iris are like cousins to me! Even our names were meant to be a bond between us—all goddesses, for Iris is the handmaiden of Hera, you know—but it can be a sore trial! You would not believe the game that was made of us growing up!"

"I cannot tell what made that such a trial to you, Diana," interpolated Athena with a wry look. "To be called the Goddesses is nothing—at any rate, not for me, for it is all too true."

Diana let out a peal of laughter and bent conspiratorially toward Lenora. "You will get a very poor opinion of Athena if she continues in this odious way—but take my word, she has not the least harm in her." She cast a saucy glance at her friend and continued, "She is only thus when embarrassed, and anxious lest she should not show herself in the best light."

Athena did not look much pleased at this speech, and Lenora wondered at Diana's insensitivity, until Athena said, with exaggerated dignity, "You should stare, Miss Breckinridge, that I countenance such treatment, and from this Person, whose company I am obligated, through long acquaintance, to tolerate even in Polite Society."

Lenora, bewildered, knew not how to take this, but before she could feel too much discomfiture, she detected a twitch beside Athena's mouth, and perceived that Diana's eyes were crinkled with mirth.

"Oh, Lenora, pay us no heed!" begged Diana. "We were apart all last year, and have only just reunited, and I fear our spirits are far too high, for Athena, you know, was constrained by illness to miss last season—"

Athena abruptly blenched, and stiffened so visibly that Diana stopped instantly, looking conscience-stricken. "Oh, what have I done? Pray, pray forgive me, Athena! I never meant—"

"Do not distress yourself, Diana," said Athena in cutting accents, the personification of the Ice Maiden once more. "I should have known better than to repose confidence in your discretion."

"Oh, no, Athena! I should never betray you—" But sensible that she had done just that, Diana was overcome, and relapsed into remorseful silence.

Lenora, torn between burning curiosity as to why Athena should be so embarrassed at having it known that she was ill, and an earnest desire not to be caught up in a confrontation, said with an assumption of calm, "If your ladyship does not wish for your illness to be made known, there is nothing more to be said. I shall certainly not spread it about, and I am sure there are far more interesting topics we may discuss. You have not asked about my new home, Diana."

She then launched into a glib catalog of Wrenthorpe, its people, and environs, crowning it all with a highly colored description of Helden Hall. Diana was painfully attentive, but Lady Athena did not seem likely to unbend, and Lenora, straining to keep the conversation flowing, had the happy thought to mention that her brother had remained at Branwell.

The ploy succeeded; Diana reanimated, remarking blushfully that Mr. Tom Breckinridge must find it prodigiously dull by himself at the Manor, and wouldn't he enjoy a sojourn to town, for a change of scene? Lenora was only too glad to oblige her solicitude by recounting, with impressive detail, just how Tom had been spending his time, and rewarded her at last with the information that he could be expected in town at Easter.

By the end of this, Lady Athena had thawed sufficiently to express a hope that Diana would be a trifle less transparent in her sentiments, and Diana retorted that at least one had the heart to display sentiment, and Lenora, suspecting that she must be on her toes if she were to be part of their circle, breathed an inward sigh of relief that the crisis was over.

When Lady Gidgeborough rose to take leave, calling to Athena to accompany her, Mrs. Marshall signaled her intention to depart likewise, and Diana took Lenora's hand, pressing it with unspoken gratitude. Athena shook hands with Lenora also, saying almost with warmth, "It was a pleasure to make your acquaintance, Miss Breckinridge. I do hope you will favor us with your company at Mama's soiree Tuesday next."

Lenora, receiving a nod from Lady Stiles, assured Lady Athena that she would be honored, and their guests took their leave.

Chapter 17

THEIR FIRST SOCIAL airing of the season was to the Covent Garden Theater, whither Lenora went with Lady Stiles and her in-laws, Lord and Lady Cammerby, to see Miss O'Neill in a stirring performance that left every eye tearful if it had not succumbed to sleep. During the interval, while the elder ladies eagerly began a discussion of whether Miss O'Neill or Mrs. Siddons was the finer tragedienne, Lord Cammerby—roused from slumber by the chatter—sought refreshment in the tea room, and Lenora allowed her eye to wander over the myriad faces in the boxes opposite. Some of the occupants were known to her from her last season, and she received several civil bows, but many were strangers to her. She wondered if any one of these was Lord Helden, and if her deep connection to his house would help her to know him.

No such fateful connection occurred, but as she was about to withdraw her gaze, she recognized a gentleman in the forwardmost box, and started. It was the gentleman she had seen at Chesterfield House, his quizzing glass raised and directed at the crowd milling in the pit. Instantly, Lenora shrank back against her chair, but the notion that he could perhaps be the mysterious Lord Helden kept her eyes on his face, searching for some sort of sign to that effect. When none was evinced, she suddenly became conscious that she was yet again staring at him, and turned abruptly to her mother and Lady Cammerby, to join in their discussion. At that moment, however, the curtain at the back of their box parted, and Mr. Dowbridge and another gentlemen entered.

"How do you do, Lady Stiles, Miss Breckinridge," said Dowbridge, bowing over each of their hands. "I trust we don't intrude."

He was welcomed warmly, and Lady Stiles lost no time in making him known to Lady Cammerby, after which he indicated his companion, a tall, plain, but foppish young man with dark hair, saying, "May I introduce Lord Ratherton to your ladyship?"

His lordship bent gracefully over Lady Cammerby's hand, giving her a very good opinion of his manners, and was begged to be seated wherever he should be comfortable. As the only seats available in the box were next to Lenora, the gentlemen acceded to her request with visible satisfaction, and after paying civil heed to a rather convoluted anecdote from their kind hostess, turned all their attention upon her pretty young friend.

"You cannot imagine my satisfaction upon spying you here, Miss Breckinridge," said Dowbridge, removing his hat and placing it carefully upon his knee. "I've just arrived in town and had intended to call on you instantly."

"It's kind of you to say, Mr. Dowbridge, but I am persuaded you've such a large acquaintance here that you scarcely recollected such a poor friend as me," returned Lenora.

"Devil a bit," put in Lord Ratherton, looking askance at his friend. "I'd give good money on it he came to London only to see you."

Casting a repressive glance at his friend, Dowbridge said, "I'd be a poor friend, indeed, to leave any young lady I esteemed to make her way unprotected, for I have it on excellent authority that your brother does not come to town."

"My dear Mr. Dowbridge, your authority is only partly true," replied Lenora. "Tom follows us at Easter. And even so, I can assure you that I am far from unprotected."

"If all your friends admire you as much as Dowbridge, here, you'll not want for protection," offered the helpful Lord Ratherton.

"Indeed, Miss Breckinridge," said Mr. Dowbridge quickly, "I must count myself Tom's deputy, and as such, I am at your service."

Lenora, raising her brows a little at this sentiment, expressed her gratitude for his gallantry, but reminded him that Sir Joshua was very well able to provide her all the protection that was wanted.

Mr. Dowbridge, taken out of stride, nevertheless acknowledged that this was so, and after a brief, uncomfortable pause inquired, "Do you go to Lady Wishforth's ball, Miss Breckinridge?" At her assent, he asked punctiliously, "May I take the liberty of requesting your hand for the cotillion?"

Lenora consented and was immediately accosted by Lord Ratherton for the honor of her hand for the waltz. With a little laugh, she said, "I should be delighted, if my mama gives her approval, for I have only just met you, you know."

Mr. Dowbridge, who had looked thunderstruck at his friend's application, said quickly, "But do you intend to waltz, Miss Breckinridge? I should have thought it out of the question."

"Why should I not dance the waltz, Mr. Dowbridge? I am not a miss in her first season, after all. I was approved for the waltz last year at Almack's, and had Lady Mintlowe played one at our Christmas party, you should have seen me waltz without a care in the world."

Her admirer answered rather testily, "If I had known it, Miss Breckinridge, I should have asked my mother to play one!"

Not to be outmaneuvered, Lord Ratherton expressed a determination of applying to Lady Stiles for approbation of his prior claim, but Dowbridge countered with an expostulation on the impropriety of a couple so little acquainted performing such an intimate dance, and the discussion rapidly assumed the proportions of a quarrel.

Lenora, little knowing whether to be flattered or exasperated, said, "I fancy my mama ought to make that distinction, I thank you, sir," but as both her swains continued to argue, she was prompted to add, in a goaded tone, "Mr. Dowbridge, I begin to believe that you are jealous, which you have no right to be! Perhaps I shall decline to dance with you, too, to teach you a lesson."

"I am persuaded you could not use me so ill, Miss Breckinridge!" Mr. Dowbridge said firmly, and in a carrying tone that made the color come up into Lenora's cheeks.

Then Lord Ratherton whistled. "It's my belief the young lady is a minx, my boy!" he cried, and Lenora could not refrain from darting a glance out at the other boxes. Several eyes were upon them, but most horrifying was that of the mysterious Chesterfield House gentleman, considering her through his quizzing glass. The glass dropped immediately, and his gaze averted to the stage, but many members of the crowd in the pit had turned to look, and were murmuring to one another.

Lenora, rosy with mortification, shrank back, gasping, "How could you, Mr. Dowbridge? Lord Ratherton, pray mind yourself!"

The gentlemen made their disparate apologies, but Lenora could not hear them, being overcome by the desire for them to be gone and for herself to become invisible, and she rejoiced when Lady Stiles ushered the pair out of the box for the second act.

Her mother came to her side and took her trembling hand. "My dear, what can have overset you? I am persuaded that you are proof against the vulgar stares of a few Cits."

"Oh, Mama! It was more than a few Cits!" insisted Lenora, pulling out her fan and plying it with energy. "How could they expose me in such a way?"

"Pooh! It is already forgotten! Look," her mother said, directing her gaze at the pit, which was milling as its occupants searched for their places. "Their heads are once more full of opera dancers, and nothing else."

With a defiant swipe at a hot tear trickling from one eye, Lenora obeyed her mother, but her gaze lingered on the foremost box, where she had the comfort of observing that the gentleman's attention was firmly locked upon the parting curtains of the stage, as if nothing untoward had passed. She told herself that this was unsurprising, as the gentleman had little reason to be interested in a minor disturbance among persons with whom he was unacquainted, and had likely given it no more than a cursory thought. But as her indignation faded, it was replaced by her former fancy that he was Lord Helden, and though she tried valiantly to give the play her full attention, her eyes strayed toward the forward box more often than she would have liked.

The following Tuesday, Lenora and her parents set out to Lady Gidgeborough's soiree, which proved to be quite a dashing affair, with several officers in attendance, in addition to a group of more staid, mature individuals with whom Sir Joshua and Lady Stiles fell into conversation. Lenora stood uncertainly for some moments, until she was saved from looking no-how by Diana, who came delightedly to claim her, and to introduce her to a pale and slightly vacuous-looking young lady trailing in her wake.

"Dear, dear Lenora! What felicity that you are here, for here is Iris, and we may all be acquainted at last!" Tugging forward her companion, she said with light formality, "Miss Breckinridge, may I make you known to Miss Slougham?"

Miss Iris Slougham was fair, with auburn-tinged gold ringlets framing an oval face with pale blue eyes. The young ladies exchanged how-do-you-do's and curtseys, and then Miss Slougham, regarding Lenora intently, said, "You are not at all beautiful, and I am glad of it, for Athena's beauty is enough to be borne, do not you think?"

Lenora, taken aback, did not know how to look, and glancing to Diana for support, discovered her biting her lips against laughter.

Iris, looking from one to the other, sighed, "Oh my, I've muddled it again. I fear you will think me abominably rude."

"And we practiced so faithfully," said Diana, taking Iris by the arm in a comforting clasp, and leading them both to an alcove, away from the chattering groups. "Never mind. I am certain Miss Breckinridge thinks no such thing."

"On the contrary," Lenora hastened to reassure her, "I find, upon reflection, that I feel much as you do, only I had not considered it in precisely the same light."

"You see, Iris? Lenora sees things just as she ought," approved Diana.

"It is kind in you," said Miss Slougham, glancing behind at the group they had left. "I am always prodigiously stupid at parties, ever coming out with the wrong thing."

"Not so with the gentlemen," offered Diana.

"Certainly. With them I can say nothing at all."

Lenora, her compassion stirred, said, "But perhaps this is your first season? I am persuaded you simply lack experience."

Miss Slougham confirmed that it was her first season, her parents having at last put their foot down upon her insistence that she was too odd to enter society, and Lenora laughed. "Nonsense! You are only perfectly honest, and I find it charming!"

"Oh, I do like you, Miss Breckinridge," said Iris, smiling. "I daresay you are quite as good-hearted as Athena, who is not at all as high in her own opinion as she appears, I assure you."

"What Iris means to say, I am persuaded, is that we shall all be great friends," explained Diana laughingly.

"Yes," corroborated Iris. "I am glad Athena was so careless as to contract mumps last season, for I would a hundred million times more rather have my first season with you as a friend."

Diana, imperatively reminding Iris that she mustn't breathe a word about Athena's disposition to anybody else, towed her and Lenora toward a knot of people, chattering excitedly that there were a great many people to whom the latter must be introduced. There were, in fact, only two, and she was made known to Major Lord Prewhurst, a dark-haired Corinthian with striking blue eyes who seemed bent on monopolizing Lady Athena's attention. But when she turned to the last gentleman in the group, she found herself facing the stranger from Chesterfield House.

Her cheeks flushed and her throat constricted as the most recent scene at Covent Garden replayed itself in her mind, and she felt a trifle faint. Here was a man who had every reason to believe that she was ill-bred at best and fast at worst. If he was Lord Helden—it was not inconceivable, and her knees felt weak at the possibility.

Then Diana was speaking, and Lenora heard, above the pounding of her heart, "May I introduce Captain Mantell, who is at present residing with Lord Chesterfield."

Lenora was so ludicrously relieved that she was in danger of sinking to the floor, but Captain Mantell prevented this eventuality by taking her hand and favoring her with a gallant bow. "I believe we are neighbors," he said smoothly.

Lenora made a valiant effort to reply as smoothly but failed, for the looks of the others in the group belied that she had perfectly telegraphed the panic she had undergone. What they thought of her she dared not conjecture, but peeking up at Captain Mantell, whose unremarkable features were made handsome by the warmth and good humor of his expression, she thought that he, at least, wished her no ill-will.

Major Prewhurst, perhaps losing interest in the mini-drama that seemed to have come to an end, took up again the discussion of whether Kean could ever outshine Kemble on the stage, and as the others joined in, Captain Mantell bent his head toward Lenora, remarking in a confidential tone, "I fear you have been laboring under a misapprehension, and if I am right, I must admit it to have been a very understandable one, for who expects an earl to be twelve years old?"

A gentle laugh escaped Lenora, and she said, "You are too kind, sir, though I had not determined upon you being Lord Chesterfield, precisely."

"Then whatever has occasioned you such distress, I am sorry for it."

She shook her head. "It is only my own folly, sir, for you have been nothing but civil."

"I am glad to hear it," he said. "But I am also excessively curious."

She peeped up at him and he continued, "One tends to be after strange young women make a habit of staring at one."

Lenora's eyelids fluttered closed, but she found her voice. "Oh, sir! At the theater—you must forgive—but that day at my window—" Her hand came up to cover a flaming cheek. "What must you think of me?"

His chuckle made her look up again and he said, "My dear girl, you are far too serious! I think nothing more than that I surprised a thoughtful young lady at her window and had the effrontery to make my bow without an introduction."

"Y—yes!" she said, all amazement. "That is exactly how it was! You cannot think how I have been yearning to explain myself to you, since that first day, and yet how could I? And then Mr. Dowbridge and Lord Ratherton made me a such a figure—and I could only stare! I was certain you thought me a—a shameless flirt!"

Again, he chuckled, his eyes twinkling with merriment. "Unfair, Miss Breckinridge, to judge a perfect stranger so! Well, it has cost you dearly, for your one misapprehension has given birth to several more."

"Yes, it has," she admitted, so relieved by his easy attitude that her embarrassment began to melt away. "So, it is indeed the boy who is Lord Chesterfield? I declare I never should have thought it."

"It is very natural, and you may comfort yourself that you are not the first to have done so."

Lenora, grateful for his kindness, asked, "You are his lordship's relative, then?"

The captain shook his head. "I am a friend of the family. His cousin, Sir Edwyn Stanhope, is my good friend."

"How fortunate. Then it is only natural that you should stay with the Stanhopes when in town."

"I ensure an open invitation by agreeing to take his lordship to

Tattersall's and to Newmarket as often as he wishes. He is horse-mad, you see." Again, his engaging smile flashed. "You need not tell me it is abominably encroaching of me, for I know it very well."

"Oh, I would never say that, sir," retorted Lenora, having fully recovered her spirits. "Though some might think me ill-bred, I do sometimes comport myself with decorum."

"That was never in doubt, Miss Breckinridge," he said, with such sincerity that Lenora blushed, and wondered if her heart might be in any danger. But as they joined the others in conversation, his easy manners put her more in mind of Tom than of a romantic hero, and she knew that she was safe. He was not, after all, Lord Helden.

Chapter 18

A CHANCE SIGHTING OF a man possessed of a beard like Mr. Ingles—but who thankfully did not notice either Lenora's delight in perceiving him nor her disappointment in directly discovering he was not Mr. Ingles—recalled to Lenora that she had yet to receive word from him regarding Lord Helden. Had he not intimated that he would do so, and soon? A brief perusal of the note Mr. Ingles had left her at Helden Hall confirmed that he had been obliged to come to London, and had hoped to have tidings of the heir. That he had not yet sent her word was disappointing, but it did not take her long to recollect that communication between them would scarcely be possible in London, so carefully regulated as was society.

She conjectured that he had been called to London on business for the heir, for nothing else could have taken him from his home in the middle of January, and the notion that Lord Helden was to take his seat in the House of Lords suddenly occurred to her. If he had at last been prevailed on to claim the title, then perhaps he had summoned the caretaker to ascertain the practicality of reviving the ruin, in which case her services in convincing him would be imperative.

In light of this urgent possibility, Lenora resolved to cease waiting upon Mr. Ingles' leisure and to take matters into her own hands. If his lordship was to take his seat in the House of Lords, one of her noble acquaintance could easily confirm or refute it, and she would then be able to act accordingly, and not risk losing the critical moment.

Lord Ratherton was her most reasonable first choice, for though he had affronted her at Covent Garden, he had since shown such persistence in their acquaintance that she fancied he would like to be put to good use. This notion was not far off the mark, for Lord Ratherton had resolved that it would be to his best interest to make himself agreeable to Miss Breckinridge.

The Ratherton estate was sadly mortgaged, Lord Ratherton's esteemed father having had an unfortunate penchant for building and redecorating, without having the least head for it or for business—the combination of which should have ended in ruin, had he not very providentially fallen victim to an apoplectic stroke. The Sixth Baron, Lord Ratherton, had conscientiously tried to recruit his funds at hazard or horse racing, but these methods seemed never quite to succeed, determining him that marriage was his best bet for freedom from debt. He had soon been obliged to give up dangling after known heiresses, however, for they all seemed to possess rival suitors who were all too aware of the state of the Ratherton finances, and who felt no compunction in apprising their fair one of it as well.

Not one to be subject to dejection, Lord Ratherton had merely bided his time, and was rewarded when a rumor reached his ears at White's that a new catch was in town, a Miss Breckinridge, who was pretty, amiable, and rich, and a country-bred innocent besides. Looking into the matter, Ratherton discovered that, while nothing was generally known of Miss Breckinridge's fortune, some elder members of the club had it on good authority that her step-father, Sir Joshua Stiles, had come down handsomely by way of her dowry.

Having lost no time in being introduced to the paragon through his school chum, Frank Dowbridge, Lord Ratherton set down Miss Breckinridge's dislike of his raillery at the theater to mere crochets, and embarked on a courtship which consisted of his meeting her wherever possible, showering fatuous compliments upon her, and lacing all his conversation with gilded descriptions of his estate and holdings which, he flattered himself, would not fail to impress the country heiress.

About a week into this program, he went driving in the park, having obtained the intelligence that Miss Breckinridge meant to walk there with her maid during the fashionable hour of the promenade. He had completed the circuit only three times before he found that his information was good, and having caught the lady's eye, he pulled up to invite her to take a turn, revolving in his mind several blandishments to bestow upon her once they were moving.

But scarcely had he handed her up and settled himself beside her when she said, "You, my Lord Ratherton, are just the gentleman I had hoped to see."

Such an encomium came as no surprise to him, and he smiled rather smugly, ready to cast her into pretty confusion with one of his studied compliments, pausing only to exchange greetings with a dowager whose carriage was passing the opposite direction.

When he turned back to Miss Breckinridge, she remarked, "You, sir, seem to know everybody. Is it true?"

He looked at her in rather a startled way and said, "Should've thought that to be obvious!"

"I wonder, then, if you have heard of the Engleheart family," she inquired.

"Engleheart, you say?" he mused, gazing off between his horse's ears as he searched his memory. "Engleheart. Hmm."

"Of the Helden viscountcy in Gloucestershire, sir."

"Ah, yes, Helden," he said, unwilling to expose his ignorance. "Why didn't you say so before?"

Miss Breckinridge glanced swiftly at him. "Then you must know of the truant heir."

He opened his mouth, closed it again, and then said, "Oh, yes, the truant heir. He is…truant. Sad business."

"Sad indeed," concurred Miss Breckinridge, with feeling. "And so odiously mismanaged that it does not bear thinking of!"

"Undoubtedly," he readily agreed.

She smiled happily. "How fortunate that you should enter exactly into my feelings! For something must be done, and I am persuaded that you, my Lord Ratherton, are just the man to do it!"

Lord Ratherton hesitated, having on no account intended to include chivalrous performances in his courtship. "Not to be inquisitive, Miss Breckinridge, but may I know just what there is to be done?" he asked warily.

"Oh, nothing you would not like," said his companion. "I have a great desire to be made known to the heir. I wish only for you to discover if he intends to take his seat in the House of Lords, and if so, to make me an introduction."

He was astonished, and not a little dismayed. "But what can you have to do with this Lord Helden, pray?"

"He is Sir Joshua's neighbor, my lord, and has allowed his estate to slip into shocking disrepair," she responded quickly, as if she had anticipated such a query. "His negligence is a blight on the community, and he ought to be made to see his duty."

"Assure you, ma'am, not the least occasion for our interference in the matter," he said, relieved. "These things happen all the time. He surely intends to sell the estate and be done with it."

"Oh no, sir!" cried his companion. "That will never do! Helden Hall is such a—" She seemed to strive for words adequate to its description. "It is so noble a house, so rich in its history, that it must be retained by its rightful owner."

Lord Ratherton looked askance at her. "Splendid place, is it?"

"Oh, yes," sighed Miss Breckinridge, launching into a florid word-picture of the Palladian derelict, by the end of which Lord Ratherton sat staring at her in such undisguised disbelief that she was obliged to urge him to mind his horses.

"That is what you call splendid?" he asked incredulously, having narrowly avoided a dip in the lake.

She returned his look with one of surprise. "Certainly, sir. How can you question it?" He continued to look thunderstruck and she sighed, settling back against the squabs. "I should have known that you would not have read Mrs. Radcliffe. It is no wonder that you do not understand me."

Lord Ratherton, having only heard of Mrs. Radcliffe, did not understand her but, being possessed of a lively sense of self-preservation, was ready to overthrow all his own beliefs if it meant that the heiress should come to regard him with favor. Gathering his wits, he looked at the thing objectively and concluded that if he played his cards cleverly, this ridiculous fascination of hers was bound to put other men off, clearing the field nicely for his own machinations.

Pulling up the horses and turning toward her with a sympathetic expression, he said with great feeling, "Miss Breckinridge, my amazement comes only because the picture you've drawn is so romantic that it don't seem real." She looked at him askance, but not without interest, and he reached to take one of her hands, pressing it. "Say no more. I am at your service. Anything in my power."

Lenora, wreathed in smiles, returned the pressure of his fingers. "Lord Helden must be somewhere, for the viscountcy is not given up. Only find out if he is to take his place in the House of Lords. If so, then I may hope for an introduction."

"Certainly, Miss Breckinridge," he said promptly, though planning to do exactly the reverse. "The work of a moment."

Urging the horses to a trot, he resolved upon a stratagem that would speedily change this Lord Helden's place in her heart with himself, for he was not such a simpleton as to risk losing the heiress to a no-account lord, when it was plain as a pikestaff she was half in love with the very idea of him.

How ineffectual this course was, he could have no way of knowing, for he was too sure of himself to consider that the same rumor that had reached him would reach other ears. Miss Breckinridge had already begun to receive quite flattering attentions from several new acquaintances, a circumstance which gave Sir Joshua and Lady Stiles some anxiety.

"I own, my love, that I had not anticipated that a rumor of Lenora's fortune should surface so soon," said Sir Joshua after Lady Wraglain's rout party, where two gazetted fortune hunters had approached Lenora and vied for her attention.

Lady Stiles accepted a glass of claret from him, her brow furrowed in consternation. "It is excessively vexing, Joshua, to say the least. I had such high hopes of her having the satisfaction of attracting a husband who could have no other motivation than esteem for her, and now we will have the trouble of vetting all her suitors."

Sir Joshua poured himself a glass of Madeira from the decanter on the sideboard. "It may not be so troublesome, Genevieve. Lenora has shown herself proof against at least two gentlemen in recent months."

"Oh! Do not quiz me over Mr. Ingles, if you please!" replied his wife tartly, sitting in a wing chair near the fire. "I have long since recognized my mistake there, and acknowledged that I was a ninnyhammer to even think it. Such an uncouth man, and so hairy! But if the second gentleman you mean is Mr. Dowbridge, I cannot say I am sorry that she remains indifferent to him. He does not seem to me to be entirely fitted for our Lenora."

"I will own that you are right, my darling," said her spouse, "though at one time I took his part. He has so little imagination that I believe Lenora was bored of him within a month."

"But that is only to be expected," she said pensively, "while her new admirers may prove to have far too much imagination for my comfort."

Sir Joshua bent to kiss his lady's cheek. "Do not let it worry you, my love. I cannot believe that Lenora is likely to give her heart willynilly to the first, or even the second or third, gentleman who evinces some romantic qualities."

"Of course you are right, but Joshua, I cannot but be anxious for her," said Genevieve. "I fear she will be deceived, as I was, and make a choice that will break her heart."

Taking her agitated hand into his own, he said, "My love, do not forget that Lenora has two advantages that you did not. First, she has a step-father who is dedicated to her protection and happiness, and who will have something to say to any gentleman who aspires to her hand. Second, she has had the good fortune to have you as a mother. Your experience and example have been such an influence that I am persuaded we may have every confidence that she will carefully weigh her options in the end, and will not let her romantic fancies rule her final choice."

This seemed to pacify her, as he followed it by kissing her soundly, but after a moment she glanced anxiously at him. "You do not think it was a mistake to keep her fortune a secret from her, Joshua?"

"Not yet, my love," he replied. "Though it has come out, Lenora is still better off making her own way, unfettered by the vexations of wealth."

Chapter 19

MR. DOWBRIDGE PAID little heed to the majority of the gentlemen who had begun to dangle after Miss Breckinridge, for he knew that these frippery fellows could not hold a candle to his worth. He was not, however, so sanguine in regards to Lord Ratherton. Arriving at a card party with the sole object of monopolizing Miss Breckinridge's attention, he discovered her ensconced in a window seat, deep in discussion with that peer. Too well-bred to eavesdrop, he nonetheless found excuse to linger nearby, adjusting his cravat in a handy mirror, his ears catching the words "Helden" and "mansion" more than once from their general direction. When this scenario—varying only slightly in place and circumstance—played out again the following week, he began to suspect that he, having introduced Lord Ratherton to Miss Breckinridge, had nurtured a snake in his bosom. That his lordship, as foppish as he was pompous, could catch the lady's fancy had never entered his head, but the evidence of his own eyes could not be denied, and irritated him prodigiously.

When Miss Breckinridge had removed to London—where he knew himself to be the only gentleman from the neighborhood of the Grange—he had been all but certain of her heart; she herself had told him she had no beaux. He had not calculated on Lord Ratherton showing an interest, and the growing intimacy between his lordship and Miss Breckinridge now obliged Dowbridge to entertain doubts of his power over her. It seemed as though her fascination with Helden Hall had been more than a passing curiosity, but if that was Ratherton's hold upon her, Dowbridge fancied he knew how to act.

Inviting her for a drive out to Richmond, he broached the topic of Helden Hall with a comment upon its shameful use by old Lord Helden.

"Indeed, he was a fool to let it go as he did," he said, "and ruin both his name and his heir's chances at once."

"I am acquainted with your feelings on the subject, Mr. Dowbridge," replied Lenora, eying him askance, "and cannot feel that we have anything to say to it."

"It seems to be a subject upon which Lord Ratherton has much to say," he answered.

She raised an eyebrow. "Yes. He finds the Hall as romantic as I do myself, sir. I know you do not, therefore we need not discuss it."

He was silent for some minutes, as the fields and farms and walls of various estates sped by. At last he said, with barely controlled irritation, "I wish I knew why you are fascinated with that ruin."

"If you truly wish to know, sir, I find the house hauntingly beautiful, and think it tragic that the rightful heir has done nothing to redeem it."

To this, Dowbridge merely commented upon the likelihood of the Hall's falling down before the heir ever came to view it, and she responded that nothing so sordid could befall such a house. "It is quite a solid building, and shows not a single symptom of submitting to the elements. I am persuaded it will take much more than time to conquer Helden Hall."

"Then it may take its place with such monuments as Stonehenge and the Roman viaducts, for its time as a really useful dwelling has ended."

"But it has not," insisted Miss Breckinridge. "The house itself is perfectly sound, and needs only renovation to make it habitable. It would be a shame to leave it abandoned."

He huffed incredulously. "Only a madman would wish to inhabit such a house."

"Nonsense," said she, with supreme indifference. "Won't you let me take the ribbons?"

He was annoyed at her stubborn management of the conversation, and cast her an irritated glance. "Who is speaking nonsense now, Miss Breckinridge? I happen to have an eye to my own safety."

"Pray, how am I to improve my skill without experience?" she said coaxingly, her hand outstretched. "The road is clear, and I promise faithfully to pull up if another vehicle approaches."

"Whatever for? A lady need not learn to drive when she has a gentleman to drive her."

"But a gentleman cannot always be relied on," she answered in annoyance, tucking her hand back into her muff.

He glanced at her again. "I am persuaded that you cannot believe that to be universal, Miss Breckinridge. A gentleman with your interests at heart may always be relied upon."

"I suppose I shall have cause to rejoice when I find such a man, Mr. Dowbridge," was the clipped reply.

Dowbridge drove on in silence for some time, wondering if he had been misled. Her mother's spirits he had often deprecated, but he had never had cause to suspect that they had been passed on to the daughter, a circumstance by which he had set great store. The young lady who would become the future Lady Mintlowe must know her place, both in Society and at his side, and if he wished to be envied for his wife's vivacity in public, he did not at all aspire to continually be challenged by her in private.

Determined by this vein of thinking that it behooved him to assert himself, he said, "You would do better to forget about Helden Hall entirely. It's little more than a rubbish heap now, and should be knocked down if it won't fall down of its own accord."

"I'll thank you not to say such things to me," returned Miss Breckinridge, continuing obstinately to gaze out across the landscape. "The Hall has made a friend of me, and I'll not have it abused."

"A friend?" he repeated, not without a touch of mockery. "A very lucky thing to have you as a friend, Miss Breckinridge."

"Yes, it is, for I have determined to find the heir and make him take possession of it, and return it to its former glory."

"To what end, may I ask? How will the Hall—or the heir for that matter—thank you for undertaking such a task?"

She bestowed upon him a lofty glance. "You need not concern yourself with that."

An inkling of her meaning crept into his mind and, with it, a surge of jealousy. He insensibly urged the horses faster as he declared, "If you aim to be mistress of Helden Hall, I can tell you that you're fair and far off, Miss Breckinridge. Anyone with eyes to see can tell that heap isn't worth the trouble, and the present Lord Helden, wherever he may be, is a cod's head if he don't sell the land

and live off the profits."

He knew by the sparkle in Lenora's eyes that he had gone too far. Her hands clenched tightly in her lap, and she said with forced calm, "You know nothing of my aims, sir, and I say anyone is a cod's head who believes that the heir will turn his back on his rightful property. The manor has been in the Engleheart family for centuries, and he'll not give it up so easily, you will see!"

"And what makes you so certain, ma'am?"

"Merely my knowledge of the Englehearts. Any family possessed of such pride could not produce an heir who would tamely watch as his heritage is destroyed. The Hall knows it as well. It is awaiting its master," she said boldly, "as if it knows its time is coming."

His crack of derisive laughter brought her shocked gaze to his face, but he continued belligerently, "Its time is coming, depend upon it."

"I wish you will be quiet!" she returned, in high dudgeon. "Let us talk of something else, for I vow I shall have hysterics if I must hear one more horrid thing against Helden Hall!"

He clamped his mouth shut, and silence reigned for the remainder of the drive. At Richmond Park, they alighted, and Lenora, disdaining his arm, walked briskly beside him, speaking with stiff civility of the trees, the flowers, the air, the clouds—of everything and nothing—until Dowbridge fancied his hopes of her were winging away with the birds who took to the sky at their approach. As her manner remained formal, he was forced to reconsider his handling of her, and reluctantly determined that it would be more to his advantage to indulge her romantic imaginings a trifle—only long enough to fix her interest, at which point he could withdraw to a more dignified position, and she would naturally be obliged to follow suit.

When Lenora declared herself to be tired and turned resolutely back to the curricle, therefore, he gave no demur, but as he handed her in, he retained his clasp on her fingers. "If I have offended you, I am sorry, Miss Breckinridge," he said evenly. "I would not vex you for the world."

She took back her hand, regarding him dubiously for a moment, but then her demeanor softened, and she said, "Thank you, Mr. Dowbridge. If I have been uncivil, pray, forgive me."

He climbed into the curricle, nodding at the groom to let the horses go, and set them off down the road toward town, his mind revolving schemes to reclaim his place in her good graces. She did not attempt to interrupt his thoughts, and the silence lengthened, until he said at last, "One understands the fascination such a place as Helden Hall may excite."

"Does one?" she asked, arching an eyebrow at him.

He smiled ruefully at her. "Yes, Miss Breckinridge, if one tries, one can come to see it."

"I, for one, do not understand anyone who cannot. It is most romantic," she declared roundly.

"Most romantic," he agreed, staying on safe ground.

"Such a tragic past, and such a hopeful future," she continued purposefully.

He let this pass, inquiring instead if Lord Ratherton had perhaps agreed to help her find the heir. She responded that he had, which he took in good part, for this meant that Ratherton was not as dangerous as he had fancied, and his own suit was still favored. With this conviction firmly in his bosom, his spirits greatly improved, and it was without pretense that he spoke very cheerfully to her all the way back into town.

Dowbridge's continued aversion to Helden Hall was not unexpected to Lenora, but the discussion nevertheless discouraged her. His insistence that she had grossly misjudged the heir's desires gave her seriously to doubt the reliability of her plans for him and his house. Her strong attachment to the derelict, it seemed, had once again led her to fall victim to her own sensibility in transmuting the tragedy of Helden Hall into a romantic tale of her own concocting, and of which she was the heroine. Knowing too well how this sort of fantasy could go wrong, she wondered if she ought not to leave Lord Helden's redemption to Mr. Ingles, who now seemed of her mind, and could most probably be relied on to influence his master accordingly.

Lord Ratherton, too, had disappointed her. He had announced to her after only a week that no Writ of Summons had yet been delivered to any claimant to the title of Lord Helden, but when she had asked that he discover if the Committee on Privilege knew who the claimant was, he had failed time and again to satisfy her. His ardor for the project remained undimmed, but this only added to her growing suspicion that he was putting her off.

"For I do not mind telling you, Tess, that for a man of information, Lord Ratherton fails to impress," she said one evening as the maid readied her for a ball. "I should have thought that by now he could have answered me, but he has told me nothing to the point, notwithstanding we are so much in company. He will go on and on over the blackness of Lord Helden's character, and how ill he has used his nobility, until the time is gone, and we part."

"It's very bad, for it makes me to wonder, miss, if he might not like to help you," said Tess, considering the placement of a bunch of rosebuds.

Lenora sighed. "If I fear you are right, and I wish that he had refused my application outright. But it is all of a piece, I suppose. I knew him to be a thoughtless gentleman from the start, and it follows that he should also be a fickle one. Often I wish I were a man, Tess, and could act on my own behalf in such things."

"But if you were a man, miss, how could you be mistress of Helden Hall?" asked Tess, reasonably.

This question was unanswerable, and prompted Lenora to seek advice of the one gentleman she felt was entirely unprejudiced in the matter. Thus Captain Mantell, returning after a sojourn to Newmarket, was subjected to the thrilling tale of Old Lord Helden, and asked to give his opinion on what could be done.

"I believe I have heard something of the story, but I would have been on the Peninsula when he died," he said, as he walked with her in the Green Park. "As to what can be done, I expect the solicitors have done what they must, and more is not to be expected. We need not concern ourselves about the matter."

Lenora's protestations to the contrary were laughed away, and though she had half expected this would be the conclusion, she began to feel positively cross. "I had no notion you were so hard-hearted, sir."

"Hard-hearted?" he cried. "You mistake. Merely, I value my reputation." He cast her a remonstrative look. "It is you who are hard-hearted, Miss Breckinridge, to try to cozen me into such a ridiculous start. What a gudgeon I should look, prying into business that is none of my own!"

As this merely echoed her other friends' responses to the problem, she was obliged, though regretfully, to acknowledge its justice; nevertheless, she gave it as her opinion that those whose business it was were doing a pretty poor job of it.

This made him laugh again. "Yes, I suppose they are, having failed after two or three years to make the new Lord Helden assume the title and take his place in Society. But if they found it necessary to sail to India and back, and make inquiries there besides, one really must make allowance for such dilatoriness."

"You must be right," said Lenora, having never considered it in this light. "If he is still waiting to prove his claim, then there is still a hope of his taking an interest in his property afterward."

"Exactly, Miss Breckinridge. There is absolutely no reason on earth why we should interfere."

She accepted this meekly, her thoughts devolving upon Mr. Ingles, and his conjecture that the heir was likely overwhelmed with what needed to be done at the Hall, and his description of the estate as an albatross. All her former convictions of the heir being a victim of tragedy came back to her. "I cannot but feel compassion for the heir, sir," she said aloud. "He may be secretly yearning for someone, anyone, to reach out the hand of friendship, to lend a listening ear, to give wise counsel, and to judge impartially."

This merely served to convince Captain Mantell that Miss Breckinridge did not comprehend the meaning of impartiality—at least in this case—but the strength of her feelings worked upon him to such a degree that he drew her arm within his and said, "Any man would be lucky to have such a friend as you, Miss Breckinridge."

"Do you think so?" she said hopefully.

"I do. And I think it would be a shame to leave poor Lord Helden without one."

"Then you will help me?"

He smiled down at her. "I will try what Lord Ratherton has been unable to do. I've no doubt he has simply been remiss in communicating the urgency of his requests. But beyond that, my dear Miss Breckinridge, I can promise nothing, and I pray you will not pursue the matter farther."

With a sigh, Lenora agreed, but was grateful to him nonetheless, and they finished their walk in full charity with one another.

Chapter 20

As the season was now in full swing, Lenora was in constant demand, thanks both to her parents' social standing and to the rumors of her fortune. It seemed that everywhere she was the recipient of most distinguishing attentions, but she was not to be blinded. Many were pathetically transparent in their motives, but two at least were more flattering, though Major Prewhurst she knew to have been courting Lady Athena before her own arrival, and young Mr. Nicolas Tenby was as poor as he was attentive. Much as she would have liked to attribute their interest to her personal charms alone, she had not forgotten Tom's information, nor her mother's warnings, and so viewed each new gentleman acquaintance with a jaundiced eye.

Tom, arriving the week before Easter, was equally unimpressed with Lenora's court, being moved to expostulate. "Really, Nora, I had believed you to be more up to the knocker!" he said, cornering her in the corridor before dinner. "Didn't I warn you before ever you left Gloucestershire to beware such scaff and raff?"

"And who, Master Tom, are you calling scaff and raff?" demanded his sister.

"Nicholas Tenby, my girl, who hasn't sixpence to rub together," he responded without hesitation. "And my Lord Ratherton, who's nothing but a snirp, but he's not near so bad as that Prewhurst fellow," he screwed up his face as he said the name, "who's a sauce box if ever there was one! How can you be so buffleheaded as to encourage the advances of such a worthless set?"

Lenora was nettled. "And what do you know of the matter, Tom? If you had any sense, you would know that they are no threat as Sir Joshua is watching out for me. You would also see that they need no encouragement."

"That's just the trouble!" He eyed her shrewdly. "Have you let it slip about your fortune? It'd be just like you."

"It's just like you to suggest such a thing," sniffed Lenora. "I will have you know that I have scarcely given a thought to my fortune since you told me of it, much less breathed a word about it."

Tom huffed. "Well, I can't conceive of how you've managed to gather such a flock of ne'er-do-wells, my dear!"

"How complimentary you are, Tom," she replied tartly. "I cannot conceive what can have given you the notion that my suitors are ne'er-do-wells, for Mr. Tenby and Mr. Dowbridge are politeness itself, and Lord Ratherton—well, he is perhaps less than unexceptionable. But as for the others—there is no harm in being admired, if I do not return it. They cannot get my heart if I do not give it them."

He eyed her calculatingly. "As I've a notion you've set your cap at the master of Helden Hall, I'll have to agree, my goose, but I'll be bound if he doesn't turn out to be just such a one as all these others! But if he proves to be younger than fifty and no wider than he is tall, you'll let him wheedle into your good graces nonetheless, all thanks to that deuced romantic imagination of yours! Gothic ruin indeed! You're a zany if you don't cut the lot of them!"

"Then I would be in the suds!" she retorted, irritated by this sweeping indictment of both her intelligence and Lord Helden's character. "I am not some great lady, able to pick and choose my companions with no care for the consequences! If I were to go about giving the cold shoulder to every man I suspected of being a fortune hunter, it would put an end to all my chances quicker than you could stare."

She pushed past him, but he caught her at the landing, saying in a coaxing tone, "Here, Nora, don't take a pet. I know it ain't your fault those ramshackle fellows are after you, but it wouldn't harm you to give some of them the go by. You're worth more than they deserve, you know."

She sighed. "Tom, I appreciate that you are trying to help me, and that you desire only my happiness, but I wish you will give me credit for having more sense than to fall in love with the first gentleman who pays me flattering attentions."

Tom, eying his sister with some misgiving, gave it as his opinion that chits in their second season were no more worldly-wise than kittens, and he'd be dashed if he left her to the wolves.

This very characteristic brotherly solicitude caused her to unbend somewhat, and with a wry smile, she drew his arm within her own, compelling him to continue with her down the stairs. "You need not be so anxious, Tom. Recollect, there are no longer wolves in England. My suitors really are quite like lapdogs and I am more likely to pat them on the head than to fall under their spell."

While Tom still had his doubts, these gradually faded as he watched his sister comport herself in society, and could discover not one lover-like symptom about her. Indeed, he was forced to admit that Lenora was almost businesslike with her beaux, treating them with a friendly tolerance that would—he admitted to one of his cronies over a half of daffy—have driven him to despair. That none of them did was a source of uneasiness to him, until he was privileged at Whites to hear the same rumor that Ratherton had, and if he hadn't been so busy pursuing his own quarry, he might have spent the whole of his time in town in trying to scotch it.

Miss Diana Marshall, being a party to nearly all of Tom's thoughts on the subject, began to have a great curiosity to know what Lenora was about, what with her indifference to her many suitors, and this unknown Lord Helden and his derelict Hall. She recalled Lenora having mentioned a haunted house in her neighborhood, but was nearly affronted that she had not divulged the existence of its mysterious master, or more to the purpose, the hopes she had in him, and was determined to find them out directly.

She had not long to wait, for they were often in company, and one day soon after Tom's arrival she found herself with the other Goddesses and Lenora, walking in the Green Park, when Iris observed that she had never witnessed such cavalier treatment go unpunished as Lenora pleased to pay her admirers. Before Diana could voice her own views, Lenora found an unexpected ally in Lady Athena.

"Don't be hen-witted, my dear Iris," her ladyship said, gazing blandly down her nose at her friend. "Lenora merely is not such a simpleton as most young females."

"But what will be the end of it, Athena?" asked Iris, more curious than adamant. "Lenora will likely drive away all her prospects, and will live out her days an old maid, like me."

Lady Athena favored her with one of her satirical looks. "Such is always a possibility, my dear, however, it need not be the case in either instance. Our dear Lenora is merely taking advantage of an opportunity, and making as much use of several very worthless young gentlemen as they will allow her to do. It need not follow that they will be her only suitors. Indeed, it is very unkind in you to suggest such an eventuality."

Iris protested that Lady Athena was putting words into her mouth, and that not everyone was as mercenary as she, but Diana, intending to answer both Iris's concerns and Athena's insinuations said, "Indeed, she is not the least mercenary, for I am persuaded her aim is to find true love!"

This brought all three pairs of eyes to Diana's face, including Lenora's, which made her blink, and protest, "I do not know if I am right, precisely. Only Tom assured me there is an extenuating circumstance in the case."

Lenora, unprepared to corroborate any such thing, hastily disclosed her very disinterested resolve to unite Helden Hall and its rightful master.

"And perhaps," added Diana, with a sparkle of delight in her eye, "to add a third to the union."

Lenora colored, and could only incoherently disclaim.

"Perhaps is not the best of assurances, however," opined Athena in a deprecating tone. "Perhaps Lord Helden will prove to be a red-faced wastrel, and seventy."

"And perhaps he will be gallant and young," returned Lenora, her reserve forgotten in defense of her hero. "If he is the lost grandchild of old Lord Engleheart, he is certainly not yet thirty."

"Perhaps," allowed Athena, "but whether he be gallant or young or charming or even alluring, he will still be ruined, and no good match for any young woman of sense—even if she have a fortune."

This last was delivered with a sly look, but Diana cried, "Nonsense!" quickly enough to banish the question that had hung momentarily in the air. "Only think how romantic for a young lady to sacrifice all to an alliance with a worthy young man in poverty! I can think of nothing more heroic!"

"Oh, yes," Iris murmured. "To starve with the man you love is better than to prosper with a man you cannot esteem."

"All the benevolence in the world does no good if it brings ruin upon the bearer." Athena sniffed. "I still say it would be a waste of perfectly good prospects, to throw them away on some faceless nobody."

Bridling, Lenora retorted, "But he is not nobody, Athena! He is a nobleman, and his estate, though laid to waste now, is not irredeemable in the least. With good management, Lord Helden could regain his fortune in a handful of years, and all with only a modest outlay."

Lady Athena eyed her with open incredulity. "You have certainly put much thought into the matter, my dear. I wonder if Lord Helden will approve of your taking such an interest in his personal affairs."

Diana—inured to Athena's snubs, but recognizing that Lenora was not—abruptly turned the conversation back again by musing, "I wonder, will he be tall and fair, or stocky and dark?"

"Why not tall and dark, like in the novels?" put in Iris. "Tall, dark, and handsome is what the hero always is. Though, I prefer fair men."

"I wonder that you claim to prefer men at all, the way you shrink from the very sight of them," snapped Athena, irritated.

"Hush, Athena," said Diana, soothingly. "Not everyone was born to be comfortable in company with the male sex. To the general run of women, they can be quite intimidating, and bewildering."

"And so demanding of one's attention," agreed Iris, unruffled. "One is ever expected to hang upon their words and say pretty things and laugh when it is proper and—and never say what comes naturally to mind. I declare, it is enough to send one distracted."

"Well, if one is not to be overcome in the company of gentlemen, one must make a push to try, and one will discover soon enough that one has nothing to fear," said Athena, in a slightly softened tone.

"That is why I feel no compunction in treating my admirers as I do, my dear Iris," said Lenora, glad to have the subject changed, "for I have come to see that they have only the power over me which I allow them, and unless I become a shameless flirt, my holding them at arms' length will do them no harm, and may even do them some good."

⁂

It was not to be supposed that Tom should not take notice of the small urchin who had taken up residence with his family, nor was it possible that Ben should long be unimpressed by Tom's superiority. Within days of his arrival, Tom had secured to himself Ben's everlasting loyalty by defending him to Branton, after a plate of strawberry scones and Devon cream laid out for the Mistress had been violated. That Tom had committed this depredation himself was never thought of—by the staff, at least—and the friendship being therefore cemented, the pair bade fair to become inseparable.

Ben became indispensable to Tom, delivering notes to his cronies in town, fetching forgotten articles from various parts of the house, or wheedling fresh-baked buns from Blaine. Tom never failed to reward the boy upon the completion of each task, and Ben amassed an impressive collection of buttons, rocks, dice, string, and other sundry small articles that somehow had found their way into Tom's pockets, for the sole purpose of being passed along into Ben's hands. However, when Ben's hero-worship led him to scale the pantry shelves in search of treacle—for Tom had inquired in an off-hand way if there were some to be had—he only narrowly escaped a dangerous fall, and broke a china bowl, which enterprise earned not him but Tom a stern warning from Lady Stiles, who was not blind to her son's rather thoughtless influence over the boy.

After this, Tom charged Ben most straightly to refrain from doing him any more favors, and to confine his usefulness to direct orders, which assumed a more purposeful mien, such as delivering posies to Miss Marshall as she walked in the park with Lenora. Daily forays into the kitchen continued, however, for the cook turned an indulgent eye on Tom's and Ben's tricks, saying with a chuckle, "Boys will be boys, and they are my boys." This view would have been extraordinary—Tom having never resided in her house, and Ben being merely a visitor—but that Cook had lost a son in the Peninsula, just Tom's age, and that Sanford had taken a dislike to Ben.

Contrary to her prognostications, there had been no incidents to prejudice the lady's maid against Ben, but she could not forgive the theft of the scones, which she herself had tenderly placed on the tray to be served to her ladyship. The outcome of this misunderstanding was that a furious Sanford had penetrated to the kitchens to vent her mortification on Blaine, to whose indulgence she laid every mischance that had occurred since that vile imp had beguiled her mistress into keeping him in the house. The resulting altercation, beginning in icily civil tones and escalating to shrieks which echoed throughout the house, convinced Lady Stiles that she was about to be deprived of two excellent servants, and all through her folly, for it was at last borne in upon her that her clear responsibility had been to nip the rivalry in the bud at its earliest stage, no matter the risk to their sensibilities.

Her ladyship was not destined to lose either servant, however, through the pride of both, for neither would leave while the other might stay to be victorious. Thus, Lady Stiles entered into quite the most horrid week of her life, navigating a household where her maid and cook refused to acknowledge each other's presence, and where every moment seemed to be taken up in trying to smooth the ruffled feathers of one or the other.

One benefit that arose from this outburst was that Ben, recognizing in his childlike way that he was somehow the cause of this calamity, redoubled his efforts in carrying out his responsibilities with a precision and determination that engendered in Lady Stiles the desire to keep him on in the household, if only to prove his worth. This development pleased Tom no end for, having received news that necessitated his early return to Branwell Manor, he had the happy thought to charge Ben with the care of Lenora, whom he had no scruple in stigmatizing to his small henchman as a hen-witted peagoose, who couldn't tell the difference between a gentleman and a gaby.

Chapter 21

LENORA, TO WHOM every passing day was one less that she knew the mind of the master of Helden Hall, eagerly awaited Captain Mantell's information. Knowing that the captain had planned to take young Lord Chesterfield to the races at Galleywood Common for a few days, she was obliged to exercise great self-control to keep from accosting him before he would go, and in this sacrifice she was rewarded. The day before his projected journey, he paid a call in Curzon Street to confirm that the Committee on Privilege knew that the heir was one Phillip Engleheart, and were waiting only on the last few pieces of corroborating evidence in his favor.

As may have been expected, this news sent Lenora into a flutter of apprehension. Unlike the moment when she faced the stranger whom she had fancied could be Lord Helden, but who proved to be the captain, she had more than a breath to prepare herself, and to think through all the mortifying facets of her situation. The distraction of her mind was so great that she could hardly thank Captain Mantell as she ought, and feared that she said many unintelligible things. As soon as she was at liberty, she rushed away to her room, where she paced the floor, deliberating over her sensations.

Until this moment, she had told herself that her motives regarding Helden Hall were of the purest; she wished only to save the manor from ruin and to see it properly beloved by the heir. But the agitation which assailed her was accompanied by the many visions of Lord Helden that she had entertained in the preceding months, of his feverish brow, and his warm, dark eyes, and his impassioned avowals of undying devotion. She had been unable to entirely put aside these dreams—which had nothing to do with altruism, and everything to do with the secret wish of her heart to become mistress of Helden Hall—and now she worried that her desires were as transparent as they were improper.

Ever since Mr. Ingles's reproof in the attics of the Hall had humbled her, she had held herself aloof from the idea of becoming mistress of the ruin, but had continued to be beset by dreams of Lord Helden, of coming to his rescue, and of capturing his heart in the true romantic style. She had indulged these fancies because they were not real, and she knew they were not reasonable; and yet, they had influenced her thoughts and words to the extent that Tom and the Goddesses, at least, had divined the truth.

Now, as she considered that Lord Helden not only existed but was any moment to make his appearance in the ton, she was once more awakened to the impertinence of her fancies. She knew nothing about this Phillip Engleheart. Tom's and Athena's cautions to her now lost their irritation and became alarmingly real. He could be old, or grossly vulgar, or married, or vilely greedy like his predecessor for all she knew. The enormity of her folly threatened to overset her, and she could only trust that his lordship would never come to know how material a role he had played in her fantasies.

As yet, Mr. Ingles was the only being who could positively betray her, for he both knew her inclinations and knew his lordship. However, Mr. Ingles had promised that he would not divulge her secret, and she knew him to be honorable, which knowledge held such comfort that she was presently able to sit at her dressing table and consider the matter more dispassionately.

Lord Helden did not know—and need never know—of her audacious ambitions in regard to his property. She had been unguarded, perhaps, with her brother and her friends, but they would not betray her, and she would take better care in future. Thus, she need not draw back from a meeting with him, for though the very thought of what she had undertaken to achieve at his expense now made her physically ill, that could all be forgotten, in time.

Upon reflection, Lenora determined against revealing her information to Tess, for this, she was persuaded, should precipitate one of Tess's rapturous moods, which in turn would bring on a renewal of all Lenora's horror and self-loathing—a circumstance which she felt she would rather avoid. Tess would discover the existence of Lord Helden soon enough, and until that eventuality, Lenora would do all in her power to prepare for it.

In this state of expectation did she approach every social event, wondering if this would be the one at which she would at last meet Lord Helden, but a sennight passed without seeing or even hearing of him. By the night of Lady Wishforth's ball, she had resolved to forget all about him, for she was persuaded she would crack under the strain of the expectation that he would appear.

She was assisted in this resolve by the alacrity in which her suitors greeted her upon her arrival in the ballroom, and the speed with which her dances were nearly all claimed. After satisfying the demands of the first gentleman, moreover, she was accosted by Iris, paler even than usual and visibly distraught, who hastened toward her from an alcove and clasped her hands in her own, saying under her breath, "I am so glad you are come, for I would not be here for the world!"

"Good gracious, Iris, what do you mean?" returned Lenora, stupefied.

"I mean that I am in the deepest despair!"

Though still new to friendship with Iris, Lenora nevertheless knew enough of her quirks not to be made uneasy by this claim. Pulling her friend back into the safety of the alcove, she calmly desired to be told what she could do.

Iris whispered urgently, "My mother has threatened to marry me off to Sir Isaac Hornaby if I do not make myself agreeable to at least three eligible gentlemen present tonight, and so I must jump in the river!"

"Do not say so, dear! I am persuaded there will be no need for that," Lenora said firmly. "Who is Sir Isaac Hornaby?"

"He is a friend of Papa's, and looks like a toad," answered her friend, adding in desperation, "He licks his lips, as if I were a tasty morsel and he'd like to gobble me up!"

Lenora stifled the urge to laugh, and merely pressed her friend's hands reassuringly. "Then you must never be made to marry him, dearest, and I trust that your mother is not serious in carrying out her threat."

"But you do not know my mother!"

Following the direction of Iris's darting glance, Lenora turned to see the turbaned woman holding court with several exceedingly haughty-looking matrons near the refreshment table, an immovably stern set to her countenance. A little shaken, she turned back to Iris. "It does look dire for you, my dear. Do not you think, under the circumstances, that you could make a push to at least speak to some gentlemen?"

"It does no good, you must believe me," said her friend. "I cannot think of anything but outrageous things to say, then my tongue seals to the roof of my mouth, and I can't—" As if on cue, her speech became sticky and suspended altogether, and her eyes became glassy.

"Pardon me, Miss Breckinridge," said a low voice behind Lenora, who turned to find Mr. Nicolas Tenby smiling behind her. "I believe I have the honor of the next dance."

"Oh, you must excuse me, sir," said Lenora, placing herself firmly between Mr. Tenby and Iris, who stood as if one who was stuffed. "My friend is overcome by the heat and I must not leave her."

He glanced past Lenora's shoulder at Iris. "Surely, her chaperon ought to be apprised of her condition. Allow me to go—"

"No!" cried Lenora, grasping his arm. Then she said with a pacific smile, "It is only a passing faintness. She will be better directly, I thank you."

After extracting from her a promise to stand up with him for the boulanger, Mr. Tenby went away, and Lenora set about comforting her friend, persuading her to sip a little champagne, and attempting to persuade her that the prospect of a gentleman's coming to speak to her was not terrifying in the least. This gambit failed signally, driving the color from Iris's already pale face, and Lenora, in desperation, embarked upon a discussion of matron's headgear, which was calculated to divert even the most tenacious mind. By dwelling long and gravely upon the merits of four-foot ostrich plumes to short and plump figures—during which Iris finished the champagne and took up another glass—Lenora was at last successful in softening Iris's reserve to the point that her color returned, and after only a few more very silly observations, she smiled and even laughed. A gentleman or two took notice of them, and Mr. Tenby, returning to claim Lenora for the boulanger, commented with genuine pleasure on the recuperation of her friend.

Iris—not unaffected by the champagne—thanked him with a gentle smile, and caught the eye of Mrs. Slougham who, ever watchful from her knot of cronies, bestowed upon her child an approving nod. Iris swayed a little, blinking at this encomium, then her countenance brightened, and she allowed Lenora to proceed into the dance, giving herself over to the care of Lady Stiles.

Lenora, congratulating herself on a job well-done, enjoyed the boulanger immensely, but an even greater victory awaited her. Their dancing done, Mr. Tenby returned Lenora to her party, but instead of pursuing some other young lady, turned to her pale and wide-eyed friend and requested the honor of a dance. Lenora instantly put out a hand to support Iris, lest she balk, but needn't have been anxious—Mrs. Slougham chanced to look over at just that moment, and the effects of the champagne still lingered. After only a long moment's hesitation, wherein she seemed to be somewhat muzzily weighing her options, Iris gave her hand to Mr. Tenby, and allowed him to lead her onto the floor.

Lenora, entering the same set, watched her friend in no little trepidation, sensible of several horrible eventualities should Iris experience a relapse, but as it transpired, she managed a very creditable performance in the country dance, in part because it was too energetic to require much speech from either partner. At the end of their two dances, Mr. Tenby delivered her back to her friend, and Iris was somewhat stunned, though as much from exhilaration as from incredulity at her success.

"Oh, Lenora," said she, "I hope I have not made a fool of myself. I declare, I could not string two words together while we danced!"

"But perhaps that is a good thing, my dear!"

Iris flashed her a recriminating look and Lenora tutted. "I only meant that one ought not to place speaking above dancing at a ball. What is more to the purpose, your mama observed the whole, and looked very pleased. I trust Sir Isaac Hornaby is soon to be forgotten."

Iris's eyes flew up to Lenora's. "Oh, my! Sir Isaac had quite gone out of my head. Oh dear," she murmured with a hunted look.

"You must not retreat into yourself again, Iris," chided Lenora gently. "You must make your mother forget her promise by proving to her that this is not a singular occurrence."

Iris's color fluctuated, and she swallowed, but Lady Stiles, who had overheard the whole, instantly engaged to take Iris under her wing, and led her to a group of military men with whom her husband was chatting, giving her every appearance of being a part of the conversation. Iris, compelled as much by Lady Stiles's gentle encouragement as by her mother's eagle-eyed looks, managed to smile quite naturally throughout the discussion, though she never unclosed her lips.

Lord Ratherton, whom Lenora had not met with for several days, came to claim the next dance, having been denied by Lady Stiles the waltz.

"Good gracious! It seems an age since last we met, my lord," said Lenora, as they took up their positions. "I wonder how you can have used your time."

"Well you know, Miss Breckinridge," he said, all smiles. "I have been untiring in my promised pursuit of the mysterious Lord Helden!"

He then launched into his usual rhapsody over the decrepitude of Helden Hall and the lassitude of its master, but Lenora had heard enough of what he believed Lord Helden's shortcomings to be, and cut him short.

"Perhaps it would interest you to know, my lord, that while you have been pursuing mysteries, Captain Mantell has discovered the answer to my question."

Looking much like a hare in the face of a hound, Lord Ratherton swallowed and said, "How resourceful of him, I declare! And what did he discover?"

She told him. With a smile frozen on his face, he performed his steps in silence for some little while before answering.

"Yes, well, that is a new development. Assure you! Nothing of that kind to be heard of until—when'd he tell you? Yes, just recently. Excellent news. I congratulate Captain Mantell. And you, to be sure."

Looking blandly up at him, Lenora said, "And so you need no longer trouble yourself over Lord Helden. I thank you for your efforts, and regret only that they should have cost you so much time. Time, too that was wasted. Such a pity."

"Nothing wasted, my dear ma'am," he insisted. "Go to the ends of the earth for you—that is, a pleasure and an honor to be of service."

"I fear it must have been a great bore to you, sir. Dear me, if we meet in future, what will we find to talk about, I wonder?"

"What do you mean, Miss Breckinridge?" he said, staring at her. "We've a great many things in common—a love of—that is, I find your delight in—we both enjoy—" He stopped, flicking his gaze desperately about the room in search of inspiration. "We both love to dance."

Her acknowledgment of this spurred him on. "And good society and conversation." Again, she agreed, and he continued, "And a dedication to noble causes."

Here, she raised an eyebrow, but before he could panic again, she relented, saying, "True enough, my lord. Where there is fellow feeling, there is always friendship."

His relief was patent, and he led her back to her mother with a spring in his step, which was only arrested upon the sight of Captain Mantell making his way purposefully toward Miss Breckinridge. Thinking quickly, he tried to shield her from his view, suggesting that she should like some refreshment, or a breath of fresh air, or—But she had caught sight of the captain and excused herself with a cheerful "good-bye" that sounded to his ears like a death knell.

"Ah, Miss Breckinridge!" said Captain Mantell, taking her outstretched hand. "I am in luck tonight. It is good that this is not Almack's, for Willis would have locked me out, it being past eleven o'clock, and I came on purpose to see you."

"How delightful! But it is not yet midnight, and so you are only fashionably late. Are you just returned from the races? How did Lord Chesterfield like it?"

He confirmed that they had returned that morning, and had had a splendid time, saying, "I have had quite a full day, and should not have come at all, but that I met someone—that is, I have information that I know will interest you excessively, and I could not wait."

His words acted strangely upon her, for they struck her with both excitement and dread, and the color fled from her cheeks. Exclaiming at this, he led her quickly to a chair and took up her fan, plying it vigorously until she was able to tell him, with near-perfect truth, that she was better.

205

"Forgive me, Captain," she said with an assumption of calm she did not feel. "The heat—I was overcome. But pray, what could be so pressing that you would go to the trouble of putting on ball dress and coming to find me?"

He smiled, returning her fan. "It may be a trifle, but I do believe it is better that you hear it now from me, rather than in the gossip columns tomorrow."

He paused, as if to allow her to prepare herself, and she bent all her energies to dispelling the notion that he had guessed her fascination with Lord Helden to be more than altruistic, and had come to disabuse her mind as to his youth, his beauty, or his availability. This was rather a more energetic exercise than she was at present capable of performing, however, and she soon gave it up, desiring him to tell her what he had come to say, despite the disquiet of her mind and the pounding of her heart.

"Merely that I have met Lord Helden," he said. "He is here, in London, and his Writ has been delivered. He will take his seat in the House of Lords at the end of the month." He hesitated, looking at her once more as if to gauge her fortitude thus far.

Though this was not much more than she had been expecting for the past several days, she feared she would succumb to palpitations if he did not simply tell her the rest. She was saved this mortification, as he instantly continued, "And if it is not too much to ask, he has expressed a desire to meet you."

Chapter 22

Lenora had just enough command of herself to declare she was agreeable to meeting his lordship, when the captain said, looking around, "Ah, here he is now. It looks as though he has already made the acquaintance of Sir Joshua."

Lenora was afterward grateful that her heart did not stop altogether, though it seemed to cease beating for an interminable time as her mind froze and the dancers whirled in slow-motion before her. Before she knew what was happening, Sir Joshua came smilingly forward, saying, "Lenora, here is a gentleman who is eager to make the acquaintance of his neighbors, and whom I am certain you would like to know." Then he stepped aside to reveal a tall, young, dark-haired man with brown eyes, who tugged at the cuffs of his impeccably tailored blue velvet coat as his gaze dwelt on Lenora's face.

The introductions were made while Lenora, fanning herself with alacrity, could hardly put two thoughts together. Here was Lord

Helden—what was she to do? He was bowing over her hand, he was young and well-looking, and had wanted to meet her! Then he was smiling cordially and saying something—she did not catch it. She should respond—but how? She should smile—would he know it if her smile was forced? He was speaking to Captain Mantell—their voices were a buzz in her ears—then Lord Helden had turned to her and was asking her something. The color fled from her cheeks as he held his hand out to her—had he asked her to dance with him? Everything in the room faded to a blur.

"By all means, Lenora, dance with his lordship," said her step-father, giving her a little push.

The room burst into life again around her, and Lenora mechanically extended her hand, letting her fan drop to dangle from her wrist by its cord. Lord Helden took her hand, leading her out onto the floor, and clasped her waist as the orchestra struck up a waltz. A waltz—as her first dance with the heir to Helden Hall! The color blazed into Lenora's cheeks again, and she kept her eyes trained on Lord Helden's white and gold waistcoat, unable to command her feelings. What would he think of her? Would she betray herself? She was sensible of the necessity to make a good impression, but her tongue felt fat, and her mind could think of nothing but that the intricate embroidery of his waistcoat looked almost foreign.

They moved in the steps of the waltz for some time, and Lenora—she knew not how—did not falter, though she felt his eyes upon her face and never ceased to wonder what he could be thinking of. At last, he said, "I believe it is customary for persons who dance together to make some attempt, at least, at conversation." Her eyes flew to his face, and she saw his brown eyes laughing down at her. "Or do I frighten you, Miss Breckinridge?"

"Certainly not!" responded Lenora, so quickly that she was forced to add "my lord" as an afterthought, which refreshed the heated color in her cheeks. Her eyes returned to his waistcoat.

"I did not think so," said his lordship, in a reflective tone. "You do not strike me as a hen-hearted kind of girl."

She murmured something about his being so kind, and he continued, in the same thoughtful tone, "But perhaps you are not frightened by such mundane things as lords. Perhaps there are other things that would frighten you—ghosts, for example."

Again, her eyes flew to his, and her mouth formed a shocked O. Had Mr. Ingles told the heir of her visit to Helden Hall? A blush of mortification kept her cheeks aflame, and she began to repent her agreement to be introduced to the heir. How could Mr. Ingles have used her so? She would have something to say when next she saw him.

She became aware that he was looking expectantly at her, and she said with tolerable dignity, "It would be a strange thing if one were not afraid of ghosts, for they would be terrifically horrid if they were real, but that is neither here nor there, for ghosts are not real, and only appear in novels."

Her eyes dropped once more to his waistcoat, and another silence ensued as they moved through the dance, broken at last by his remarking, "It was embroidered by my mother." He was rewarded with another view of her face, and he added encouragingly, "She loved fanciful designs."

"But your mother could not have—she is—she is not—" Again, Lenora dropped her eyes, but this time to her feet. "Forgive me, my lord. I do not know where my wits have gone."

"She embroidered a kurta for me as a child," he said gently. "It is a kind of long shirt, and I only recently had it made up into a waistcoat."

She glanced up, and his smile and earnest gaze emboldened her enough to say, "It is lovely work, and your repurpose of it a fine tribute to her memory."

His smile deepened, and she was struck by the warmth of his eyes. She was drawn into them—they were exactly as she had envisioned them all these weeks, for Mr. Ingles had warm, brown eyes. Perhaps this was an inheritance from the Ingles side of the family. Her eyes roved over his face, which was slightly tanned, and handsome, but not in the ordinary style. His jaw was square and he had a dimple in his left cheek when he smiled, and his hair waved naturally over a short forehead, tumbling down on one side to touch a rather bushy eyebrow.

The eyebrow quirked up, and he said playfully, "Do you find my face as lovely as my waistcoat, Miss Breckinridge?"

She felt the heat creep into her cheeks again, but replied, "On the contrary, I do not, though the work was at least half done by the same master. I should not try to have it remade, however. It is well enough."

"You are too kind," he said, his smile widening into a grin, and showing good, white teeth.

A crease appeared between her brows as she considered what was so alluring about good, white teeth, and remained as they twirled about the room.

"I fear I perplex you, Miss Breckinridge."

She blinked, waking from her reverie, and denied being perplexed, or that anything at all was the matter. "Merely woolgathering, my lord."

His brows rose. "Is my conversation so boring? I would not have it so for the world. Of what do you wish to speak? I am at your service."

"I beg you to speak of what you like," she said quickly. "Perhaps you might tell me how you—how you like Helden Hall."

He looked out over the dancers. "It is a discouraging sight, to say the least. Enough to give one the blue devils," he said, with a rueful half-smile.

"But it is nonetheless a noble place, and deserves that its master should care for it," replied Lenora, more boldly than she had expected.

It seemed that it was his turn to have trouble meeting her eyes. "I do not disagree with you, but one's wishes may not always be feasible."

"Surely you mean to make a push to redeem your estate, my lord," she said quickly.

He brought his gaze to rest on her countenance—a look that spoke of hope and despair and longing all at once—and Lenora's heart skipped a beat. This was the moment she had envisioned many a time—Lord Helden, desperate, and she his only hope—and yet, she could not bring herself to speak. Her mouth suddenly felt dry, and the thought of his being a fortune hunter like so many of her suitors chased itself about in her brain. She knew nothing of him but stories and rumors, and though they at one time had inspired her ambition, she now knew they were nothing upon which to base a future.

She swallowed with difficulty. "It must be daunting for you, my lord, but you will find a way in the end, I am persuaded."

He agreed quietly with her, and she changed the subject, chattering on about the delights of town life until the waltz ended and he led her back to her mama, leaving her to her churning thoughts. If he was a fortune hunter, he had good reason—but did not every fortune hunter believe his reasons good? How great a difference was there between a man who must marry money, and a man who sought to do so?

Lenora pressed a trembling hand to her heated cheek. If only Mr. Ingles were here—she could consult him on his master's motives. He could advise her, and perhaps they could join forces to discover if Lord Helden's character was good, and if he did, indeed, wish to redeem his estate.

But Mr. Ingles was not here, and the very idea that he could ever be was ridiculous. How out of place he would be, here among such finely dressed people, with their impeccable manners and graceful limbs, and his rough speech and hairy face—though he did have fine white teeth to rival Lord Helden's.

She sighed, and a voice from beside her interrupted her thoughts.

"That sigh does not bode well for my dance, Miss Breckinridge."

She turned to see Mr. Dowbridge looking at her with something like concern, and she forced herself to smile, shaking off her deflated spirits. "Nonsense, sir. I am good for hours yet, and never go back on my promises."

He expressed his relief, leading her out into the set. They took their places at one corner of the square for the cotillion, and as they awaited their turn, Lenora glanced about to see if Lord Helden was anywhere near, having a great desire to know with whom else he should dance or converse. Her partner, having tried unsuccessfully to engage her in conversation, soon requested her to tell him what was wrong.

"Oh, nothing, sir. Forgive me," she answered quickly. "It is only that I have made a new acquaintance whom I am trying to puzzle out. Strange how a person can be so like what one expects, and yet so unlike."

"The man you were dancing with just now? I do not know him."

She turned startled eyes to him. "But his name you know as well as your own, sir. The probabilities of his character have been canvassed throughout your neighborhood for the past several years. He is Lord Helden."

Mr. Dowbridge regarded her somberly. "I begin to understand your distraction of mind. You have met your hero at last."

Lenora disclaimed that he was any such thing, but Mr. Dowbridge remarked that he hoped his lordship proved to possess more depth of character than his predecessor.

"Surely, it is not a question, sir," said Lenora, but was kept from saying more by the movement of the dance.

After they had completed the figure, Lenora took up the defense of Lord Helden's character once more, but Dowbridge stopped her, saying, "You know nothing of him, Miss Breckinridge, and I trust that you have better judgment than to leap to conclusions."

Silenced, Lenora looked about again, as if the sight of Lord Helden could vindicate her assessment of his character.

"I believe he has gone into the card room, Miss Breckinridge," said her partner coolly.

Lenora cast him a sideways glance. It was not surprising that he should be out of humor, as he had no opinion of the Englehearts or of Helden Hall, but she thought it hard that he should be the one to be her companion after her first meeting with a man whom she had longed to know, leaving her no recourse but to stifle her curiosity and suppositions. They finished the dance in silence, and Lenora wondered if their friendship, which had only just survived the idea of Lord Helden, would survive his reality.

For two days, her thoughts jumbled in her head, and it was only in the expectation of a visit from Lord Helden that Lenora was prevented from going entirely distracted. But he did not come. Though she waited at home, pleading fatigue so that she should not miss his call, he did not come—a circumstance which boded ill for his character, to her mind. If Lord Helden was a proper gentleman, he should call on her just as any other gentleman would after having made her acquaintance.

Her other admirers, however, did call, among them Lord Ratherton, with flowers and a box of Lenora's favorite sweets. His visit was a trifle over the correct fifteen minutes, so ardently did he pursue the commonplaces he had prepared, and Lenora did her utmost to pay him proper attention, but she was too full of wondering why it was that Lord Helden did not come.

As the days passed, she was watchful at every rout and picnic, card party and theater, hoping to catch sight of Lord Helden's face, but without success; yet not a single day went by without some whisper of his being seen by someone at some place. Lenora was justifiably annoyed by this circumstance, for she could not but feel slighted by this sign of his neglect.

She was not destined to find much sympathy with her friends. As she sat in company with Diana and Iris at the Countess of Dewsbury's rout, while Lady Athena circulated with her mother amongst the more notable ladies present, they clearly overheard one of the young ladies in a group nearby say, "I declare, Lord Helden is the most handsome gentleman! I saw him riding in the park yesterday, and he has the most excellent seat!"

Dimples peeping, Diana murmured to Lenora, "Your Lord Helden sounds a fine figure of a man, my dear."

"He is not my Lord Helden," replied Lenora, a blush suffusing her cheeks.

"But he will be, soon enough, I'd wager," said Iris, contemplating the fringed tablecloth. "No man could withstand the attentions of a young lady who has set her cap at him."

The color fled from Lenora's cheeks as both she and Diana turned shocked gazes to Iris. "I have not set my cap at him, Iris," Lenora declared stiffly.

"Pray, forgive me, I misspoke," Iris stammered in confusion. "You merely will raise no objection, if he will have you."

It was perhaps fortunate that Lady Athena chose this moment to return to her friends, and to change the direction of the conversation, though not the subject. "It seems Lord Helden is not seventy, after all, Lenora," she said. "I felicitate you."

Annoyed, Lenora answered, "You need not rally me, Athena. Lord Helden may be young and available, but he has hardly fallen at my feet."

"Which is why I felicitate you, my dear," said her ladyship blandly. "For otherwise, I should feel obliged to caution you."

"Your solicitude is moving, but there is no need, I assure you. I have cautioned myself amply."

Lady Athena raised an elegant eyebrow. "I should say no more on this head, but as matters stand, I feel an overwhelming responsibility to disabuse your mind. No, hear me out, Lenora, for once, I beg. Lord Helden is of noble blood, but there are distasteful rumors surrounding his maternal parentage, which mar his eligibility for any young lady of quality. Even disregarding this, the destruction effected by his grandfather is enough to put off the discerning, for any taint of scandal could ruin his chances of finding a foothold in Society. If you wish to make an eligible match, I would caution you to think twice before looking Lord Helden's way. There are many other gentlemen with less beleaguered estates who would welcome your charms, if you would but throw yourself in their way, rather than his."

"I have no intention of throwing myself in the way of any man, much less one with a beleaguered estate," snapped Lenora, who abruptly excused herself to go stand by a window to cool her heated countenance, all the more consternated for knowing that until the past sennight, her intention had been to do exactly that.

Lady Athena's intelligence of the rumors dismayed her, but she did not give much credence to it. As time went on with no visit from Lord Helden, however, Lenora found herself dwelling more and more on the ominous unknown. What if he was ostracized by the ton and was forced to leave London? What if he proved to be a wastrel, or a gamester, or worse, had inherited his grandfather's despicable pride? What if his one dance with her had somehow left him with a disgust of her?

Chapter 23

Iris, who observed the next day that she had always wished to visit someone in Bedlam, but did not believe Athena would countenance Lenora's residence there, attempted to ease the perturbation of Lenora's spirits by inviting her on a drive through Hyde Park. Iris was a fine whip, being quite at ease with animals who had nothing to say and cared not what she said to them. They had chosen to drive out early, before the regular traffic converged on the park, and Ben, fancying himself a tiger, perched up behind, taking his role as Lenora's protector so seriously that any stranger caught ogling her or her friend met with a stare so ferocious as to make him think twice before being so foolhardy as to approach.

There were few riders in the park, and even fewer vehicles, and Iris set the pert gray mare at a smart pace down the carriageway. They had been discussing Iris's success at the ball, that maiden insisting, "I hardly know what happened. I do not know what Mr. Tenby thought of me."

"He must have told you something of what he thought, for I distinctly saw you smile at what he said," Lenora said.

"He very kindly complimented me on my steps," admitted Iris, shrugging. "I am persuaded he meant only to put me at my ease, for I had just trod on his foot. But he is very gentlemanly."

Lenora laughed. "Whatever his meaning, I believe you have made a conquest."

"Oh, no!" cried Iris, horrified. "Do not say so, for I shall never be able to speak to him again!"

"My dear Iris, then I shall not say so," soothed Lenora. "I shall only say that you have accomplished a great thing. At one time, dancing with Mr. Tenby should have been quite impossible, but now you can never again question whether you will die if a man asks you to stand up with him, for you know you will not!"

Iris considered this, a smile tugging at her lips. "No, quite the reverse. I felt more alive than I have in a twelvemonth after dancing with Mr. Tenby."

"And I suspect that he—"

But Iris was not to know what Lenora suspected Mr. Tenby of feeling or doing, for at that moment, a scrubby youth leapt out from the brush at the side of the lane, darting in front of the mare and causing her to rear up and sidle, tossing her head. The reins were torn from Iris's hands, and the urchin, adding insult to injury, shouted and jeered at them, encouraging the already panicked horse to bolt. The young ladies were thrown back against the squabs, and Ben nearly lost his seat, shaking his fist at the boy and shouting curses which were blessedly incoherent beneath the trampling of the horse's hooves.

Before the ladies had time to be more than terrified, however, another set of hooves came pounding up beside the gig, and a rider on a glowing chestnut mare came up beside the horse, reaching a hand down for the harness and pulling back, effectively halting their headlong flight. As the mare came snorting to a stop, Lenora and Iris clutched at the sides of the seat, gasping for breath until they were able to collect themselves enough to thank their rescuer.

He had slid off his horse to gather up the loose reins, and when he turned to bring them back, Lenora cried out in utmost astonishment, "Lord Ratherton!"

A smile that could only be described as exultant turned up his mouth, and he presented the reins to her with a bow. "I believe these are yours, Miss Breckinridge! Lucky that I was riding so closely behind you. Little did I know the felicity that was shortly to be mine in coming to the rescue of two such lovely maidens."

Lenora took the reins doubtfully, passing them to Iris. She had never seen him exert himself so much in all their acquaintance, and she was not unaccountably surprised.

Gathering her wits, she said, "It was very lucky, to be sure, my lord. We are indeed grateful for your presence of mind! You certainly have saved us."

"I'd've got the horse to stop, miss!" cried Ben behind her, and Lenora turned to say that he may well have, but he may just as well have fallen and gotten trampled beneath its feet, adding soothingly that it would have broken her heart, and that it was much more desirable that Lord Ratherton put himself in harm's way than her dear, sweet Ben.

His lordship gave an overly hearty chuckle. "Yes, I'm simply another gentleman to be used as Miss Breckinridge chooses. Listen well, young man, and learn what hard-hearted creatures females are, before it is too late!"

Ben scowled, but Lenora replied lightly, "His lordship is funning, Ben. He knows I meant that a grown man would be in less danger of injury, and he would never be so ungallant as to suggest otherwise."

This sent Ratherton into a morass of explanation and exculpation, which ended only when Lenora at last was able to make him understand that she bore him no ill-will, and he smiled very brightly, taking leave far more formally than was necessary. His erstwhile beneficiaries gazed after him in bewilderment as he trotted down the lane.

Turning to Iris, Lenora burst into giggles at sight of her face. "Exactly my thought, Iris! What an odd rescue that was!"

Iris took up the reins again, saying, "One can only reason that if one is to be thrown into danger, one would rather be rescued than not, and if it is by a coxcomb, so be it."

"But that will never do!" cried Lenora. "None of our favorite heroines would stand for it, but would send him away into the wings, and await the knight errant! Now, where can he be, I wonder?"

Iris smiled in return, and the pair continued their drive without further mishap. When Lenora had got home, however, and sat before her dressing table while Tess helped her dress for dinner, she could not but feel decidedly unsettled at the encounter.

"I do not know whether it is my nerves still on end, or Lord Ratherton's unaccountable behavior," Lenora mused. "It was so odd, as if he were playing a part."

"Ooh, but miss, it's straight from a novel—mercy! He saved you from wild horses—leastwise, one horse! But he did you a signal service, like one of King Arthur's knights!" cried Tess, clasping the hairbrush to her bosom.

Lenora's brow creased. "Yes, I suppose he did, though it did not seem in the least romantic. Rather, it was shocking, and frightening."

She ruminated over this notion while Tess continued to brush and pin up her hair, but was unable to come to a satisfactory conclusion. "I do not know the meaning of it. Am I fated to feel that every romantic situation into which I am thrust is a counterfeit? My abduction last season ought to have been romantic; however, it was nothing of the sort. And now this."

"Perhaps it is a warning, miss," Tess offered in a dreadful whisper.

"Yes, but of what?" replied her mistress, in no expectation of an answer, but rising and making her way ruminatively down to the drawing room.

Five days after the Wishforth's ball, Mr. Dowbridge called, and his entrance into the drawing room was peremptory. By the grave set of his countenance, Lenora could perceive that he was in a black mood, and prepared herself for more aspersions on Lord Helden's character.

"I fear you are not of a mind to hear me, Miss Breckinridge, but I must speak. Something of import has come to my knowledge regarding Lord Helden, and I feel it incumbent upon me to inform you of it. What you do with the information is your concern."

With utmost civility, Lenora thanked him for his consideration, but begged to be told what could possibly be of such moment.

He turned away, pacing to the door and back, his face grim. "This will not be easy for you to hear, Miss Breckinridge, and I beg you to believe that it gives me no enjoyment to say it: Lord Helden is a sham."

Lenora stared narrowly at him, in utter disbelief at this claim.

"It is true," he said, in a low, fierce tone. "He is no more a nobleman than that urchin your mother is housing."

"That is a ridiculous charge, sir," said Lenora, indignant. "He could not have received a Writ of Summons without sure proof of his identity."

"I do not know how he has done it, but that proof must be forged! I happened to see him in company with some officers, and they all called him Ingles! You stare! He is none other than that drunkard of a caretaker, who has had the audacity to impersonate a nobleman, thinking we none of us would be the wiser!"

Lenora's cheeks had gone white. Mr. Ingles' face resolved itself in her mind, the day he had taken her through the first floor of the Hall, and had laughed at her comparison of old Lord Helden's features to his own, his eyes crinkling at the corners and his white teeth gleaming from beneath the mass of beard. Her breath caught at the likeness—could it truly be that he was Lord Helden?

Dowbridge ranted on. "I see that this news has affected you as it has affected me. The effrontery of the man! To place himself at our level—to steal what is not his!"

She had been affected, but not as he had supposed. Her mind was racing to discover if Mr. Ingles had, in fact, used her so deceitfully. Had she not given him ample opportunity during their visits together to reveal himself as the heir? But her justice reminded her that her motives at the time had been unclear, as much to him as to herself, and so she could not expect that he would trust her with his identity before he was ready to reveal it to the world.

Moved at last to speak, she said, "I implore you to be more careful of your words, sir. What you claim is extremely serious, and must be considered rationally. Though he is Mr. Ingles, he could still be what he claims."

Dowbridge's gaze snapped to her face. "Are you so lost to all reason as to be taken in by a charlatan? How comes it that you wish to defend him?"

Lenora leapt up. "Your anger does you a disservice. When you are calmer, you will see that it is no easy thing to pull the wool over the eyes of the Committee on Privilege. Think, Dowbridge! To what lengths must Mr. Ingles needs have gone in order to fabricate his authenticity? It is impossible."

He was silent some minutes, his jaw working as she paced in front of him. "You say it is impossible, yet you cannot believe he is Lord Helden," he said at last. "I can see by your agitation that you cannot credit it. Your reason tells you that stranger things have happened than that an upstart, whose indolence has given his mind too much reign, and whose cleverness is hidden behind a drunken exterior, has plotted to overthrow the very laws that keep our kingdom orderly and great, and has done well enough almost to succeed!"

"Perhaps," said Lenora, still pacing, "but Mr. Ingles is not such a person. He is no criminal."

"How do you know?" Dowbridge demanded.

"I simply know!" cried Lenora, facing him. "I tended him for many days, and saw how much goodness he had hidden in his heart."

Dowbridge turned away, disgusted. "I cannot listen to this—"

"You must! You must not breathe out such slander against a man you know nothing about." She reached a hand to touch his shoulder. "This unreasonable anger is beneath you, Mr. Dowbridge."

Her visitor returned her intent gaze, his anger slowly draining from his body. At last, he said stiffly, "Forgive me. You are, of course, right."

He turned the hat in his hands, his head bowed as if preparing himself to say something difficult. Then he raised his head to say gravely, "I allowed my emotions to govern me, but only because I should not for the world see you injured."

Lenora's breath caught at the look that he gave her then, so full of intensity that she felt as if it would push her over. Before she could think of anything to say, however, he took her hand and brought it quickly and briefly to his lips, then quitted the room, leaving Lenora to cope with her many and varied emotions.

She flung herself down on the sofa, only to jump up again and pace about the room for several minutes. Mr. Dowbridge must be in love with her. Certainly, she had known of his preference for many months, but that look! It had left nothing to doubt. It had likewise given her nothing to rejoice over, for there had been no tenderness or passion in it, only possessiveness, and it had almost frightened her. She did not think that her idea of love was the same as his.

But Mr. Dowbridge's sentiments must move aside, for if he had so easily discovered Lord Helden's true identity, it would take no time at all for the fact to spread through London, and then Mr. Ingles must bear the consequences. It was only left to consider what those consequences might be. Would he have done something so rash and dangerous as attempt to impersonate a nobleman? She could imagine that the situation was indeed a tempting one, and the family bible might have given him all that was necessary to prove his claim. It may have contained histories, besides the names, with birthdates and places that would come in useful.

But she could not credit it. Mr. Ingles was not that kind of man— she knew that without a doubt. And the Lord Helden she had danced with was a perfect gentleman. How could a rough, coarse, uncouth man suddenly become well-versed in etiquette and possessed of refinement, unless he had been raised and educated so? His years in the army could very well have driven him to hide his finer virtues, and had he not—though briefly and under the influence of spirits— claimed himself a gentleman, at their first meeting?

That Dowbridge had so quickly believed the worst was worrisome, however, and the more she reflected, the more anxious she became. How many others would do as he had done, and would their suspicion be without foundation? Was it possible that Mr. Ingles was a consummate criminal, so conniving that he could touch her heart, even as he played the drunken fool?

Distressed, she took refuge in her room, sinking down into the chair by her fire and gazing unseeing into the flames, her hands wringing in her lap. She was discovered in this attitude some time later by Tess, who instantly perceived that she was in the grip of some sudden and ghastly malady. Rushing to her mistress's side, she shrieked, "Don't leave us, my dear miss! I'll save you!"

Lenora, starting violently, cried, "Good heavens, Tess! What are you going on about?"

"Oh, miss! Oh—you're back from the dead! Thank the Lord!"

Batting away Tess's hands, which were outstretched to clasp her to her faithful bosom, Lenora snapped, "What nonsense! I do not understand you!"

"You must stay quiet," uttered Tess, watching Lenora in fascination, "or you may be taken again. But never fear—I am here to save you!"

With most ungrateful asperity, Lenora adjured her maid not to be a zany and, pushing to her feet, stated that if Tess truly had her welfare in mind, she would leave her in peace. To this, Tess responded that she should never quit her mistress's side at such a dangerous time, and Lenora was forced to take her by the shoulders and shake her.

"Tess! I was merely thinking, for I have a thorny problem, and I am at my wits' end to know what to do about it. Mr. Ingles is in London professing to be Lord Helden, and I do not know if it is true, or if he will be taken up by the magistrate and transported."

"Good Lord, miss, I never!" responded Tess, correctly interpreting this cryptic utterance. "To think that such a hairy man could be Lord Helden!"

Lenora shook her head. "And yet he is Lord Helden. At least, I must believe so, for though he has been so rough and rude, and was a drunkard, and a common soldier, and—and so very hairy—I do not believe that he would do so dangerous a thing as to impersonate a nobleman! It defies reason."

"That it do, miss, and I wonder that he'd have the pluck to try it! He'd have to be bold as brass! But if he fancies himself a gentleman, there'll be no stopping him, for he'll be living too high to wish to leave off."

"You are right, Tess! He will soon be ruined!" responded Lenora, startled. "Who knows how he came by the money to rig himself out in fine clothes and set himself up as a gentleman in town, for even if he is Lord Helden, it cannot last for long, and when he comes to the end of it, he may be driven to desperation to keep up his appearance! He may turn to gaming, or to thievery—or worse!"

As neither young lady liked to think what could be worse than thievery, they did not attempt to envision such vice, but bent their minds to discover a way to save the unfortunate gentleman. At the end of a half hour, however, they had come up with only one solution: Lenora must seek Mr. Ingles out and confront him.

How to do this was another problem, but was solved rather speedily by Lenora, who proposed to write to him, requesting an interview. Tess, with much respect at her daring, declared her full support of this impropriety, as it was for the sake of saving a man's soul, and offered her services as messenger. These were declined, however, for Lenora did not repose much trust in Tess's ability to remain incognito, instead suggesting that Ben, who was already an adept messenger boy, should perform the task.

This satisfactory conclusion having been reached, Lenora set the plan in motion, finding no resistance from Ben, who wasted no time in discovering his lordship's whereabouts by the simple expedient of asking all the pageboys at the principal hotels if they had seen a new swell about by the name of Lord Helden. He returned triumphant to Lenora, who had labored long to compose her letter, which was comprised of two lines:

> *Mr. Ingles,*
> *I must see you. Have the goodness to meet me tomorrow morning at 9 o'clock in the Green Park, near the lodge.*
> *Lenora Breckinridge*

She read over this short missive, and then, feeling anxious at the license she had taken, added a postscript:

> *I will bring my maid.*

This assertion of her respectability eased her mind, and she sealed the letter, remembering to address it not to Mr. Ingles, but to Lord Helden, Limmer's Hotel, and gave it into Ben's hands.

Chapter 24

THE NEXT MORNING, Lenora was up betimes, and with the able assistance of Tess was successful in ensuring that her exit from the house went unremarked. With the maid in tow, she closed the distance between Curzon Street and the Green Park in excellent time, all but ignoring the maid's protests at her unnecessary speed, and arrived at the bench by the lodge with a quarter of an hour to spare. Gazing about in bemusement, and realizing that she was quite winded, she proposed to sit, and had scarcely done so when Lord Helden came striding around a bend in the path ahead and stopped, a look of surprise on his face.

"Mr. Ingles!" cried Lenora, for now she could easily trace the features of the caretaker in the gentleman's face and figure.

He tipped his hat and came toward her. "I wondered when you would know me, Miss Breckinridge. I am pleased to find that you were as eager as I for this interview."

She blushed, and hesitated a moment, discomposed by his easy assurance. "I feel strongly that I must speak to you. I must know if you are truly who you claim to be! Forgive me," she said, averting her eyes, "I fear I am impertinent, but I must know, for if you are not, I doubt not but that you have undertaken this enterprise without comprehending fully the repercussions which will certainly overtake you, and I beg you to reconsider, before it is too late."

He nodded, a rueful smile playing about his lips. "I see. Perhaps an introduction is in order. Phillip Jaymit Engleheart, Lord Helden, at your service," he said, executing a bow.

"But you are James Ingles, a caretaker," said Lenora, in urgent accents. "How do you come suddenly to be an Engleheart?"

"I am, truthfully, Miss Breckinridge, both," he replied simply. "I was raised to believe my name was Jaymit Ingles, which we changed to James when I went to school, and have gone by that name all my life. My father apparently threw off the Engleheart after my birth, when his father would not recognize his marriage, and so I did not know anything about them. Even after I discovered I was Lord Helden, it seemed natural to carry on under the name with which I was most comfortable, for I could not be much of a nobleman with hardly more than a name."

The simple sense of this explanation soothed her. It certainly was more reasonable than what she had often read in her Gothic romances, where young men had not seemed troubled at assuming a strange new identity, when they had been one thing all their lives, and were suddenly expected to be another. They were always assisted in the transition by grand estates to match their grand titles, whereas the present Lord Helden had not been.

"Then you truly are Old Lord Helden's grandson," she said.

"I am."

"And you never knew it."

"Until last year, no."

His answers were so straightforward that her disbelief was quite vanquished, but she could not help observing, "Something in your circumstances must have changed, for you certainly look the nobleman now, my lord."

He glanced down at his splendid dress and raised his arms, turning and posturing. "This? Yes, in London it seems clothes make the man. Of course, a title helps as well."

"And how does a mere Mr. Ingles, with nothing to his name, become the possessor of such a fine coat by Weston, and boots by Hoby, and a fashionable beaver?" she pressed, gesturing to these articles.

"Do not forget the haircut!" he put in, removing his hat. "I paid a great deal for it—but I believe it to have been a bargain, for it was such a haircut!"

She smiled, despite herself. "I declare, I never imagined such gentility could be hidden under that beard. If it had not been for the lack of hair and refinement of accent, I should have known you immediately, depend upon it."

He chuckled. "I knew it would be so. I scarcely knew myself! But we are ahead of ourselves; I came this morning fully intent on making a clean breast of it—indeed, I have been most eager to tell you how I came into funds. But shall we walk? I am much better at forming my thoughts when I am in motion. I believe it is something I learned in the army."

She professed herself willing, and took his arm, walking with him in the direction of the reservoir.

"The money was a legacy from my grandfather," he said, and smiled at her look of incredulity. "Truly, he left it to me. In the hedge maze."

"Now you are quizzing me."

"On the contrary! You told me at our meeting during Christmas of the rumor that he had gone mad and was digging in the hedge maze, and it struck me as singular. The next day, I received word that my solicitor had gotten the proofs back from India that he needed to proceed with my application to the Committee on Privilege, and he requested my presence in London without delay. I never needed money more, so I went to the maze and began to dig about, on the off-chance that luck would favor me at last."

She had stopped walking and stood gazing at him in amazement. "And you found treasure?"

"For a long while I found nothing and was ready to give up the idea. But the watch you gave me fell from my pocket at some point, and when I retrieved it, I perceived that the spot where it had fallen seemed as if it had lately been disturbed. So I dug there."

Lenora gazed at him in disbelief. "Your grandfather had buried something there? He was not digging for turnips, but was burying gold?"

"Yes, guineas. A box of golden guineas. I fancy that he had not been able to spend it, and so he buried it to keep it from my father—the turnip he was speaking of, no doubt. But it came to me, in the end."

"I cannot believe it! Thwarted by his own selfishness!" Lenora huffed a laugh. "What a fitting end! And so you came to town. This legacy must have been a grand one."

"I wish it had been, but it was not. It was enough for me to live comfortably here for a few months, as befits a nobleman, but more importantly, to transact certain estate business that has needed attention these several years."

She murmured her understanding of this, but a crease formed between her brows. "You left Gloucestershire in January. Why did you not come sooner into Society?"

"It was quite an undertaking to make the transformation from Mr. Ingles the caretaker to Phillip Engleheart, Lord Helden. I have spent the better part of four years striving to forget I was a gentleman, for without means to live as such, it was nonsensical to retain the airs of a gentleman. You well know there were several habits I had picked up that would not do in Polite Circles. "

She accepted this and walked on in silence, a question fretting her until she could no longer disregard it. "What will you do when your grandfather's legacy is spent?"

"I do not know," he said, with a troubled look. "That will depend on circumstances."

His distress, and the look on his face, so moved her that she knew an impulse to take him in her arms and soothe away his worries and fears, and to promise him all her worldly goods, if only she could share his life and Helden Hall with him forever. The strength of the impulse shocked her, and she stared as if seeing him for the first time. However, he had not evinced the same feeling, and the sensation passed within moments, so she tore her gaze away, giving not the slightest hint of how she had been affected, though the experience left her a trifle breathless.

Having reached the reservoir, they turned onto the meadow, where they ambled along in a comfortable way. She asked him questions about his childhood in India, and he surprised her with the intelligence that much of his childhood had been spent here in London, for though his father had wished to cut all ties to England, he had become convinced that his Anglo-Indian son would be better off there.

"Mixed race persons are treated very differently in India than they are here," he explained. "The East India Company has its fingers in so many political pies that its governors feel it necessary to protect the British sovereignty by depressing all ties to Indians. It makes being Anglo-Indian very uncertain in India. But the stigma has not yet become so strong here."

Lenora put her other hand on his arm in a comforting gesture. "How lonely for a little boy to grow up outside his culture, and even more so without his mother."

"There was quite a bit of English culture in our home as well, but I did miss India very much at first. I missed my mother the most, but there was nothing to be done about that, as she had died by the time I went to school. But Mrs. Swaythe, the excellent woman with whom I boarded, was as much like a mother as I could wish. I thrived in her care, for I enjoyed learning—I attended Merchant Taylor's School—and it was during my last year there that I learned of my father's death. It was so sudden that I can only suppose he had been unable to arrange matters satisfactorily, for I was left with very little money, and at the age of seventeen was forced to look to my own support."

"Did not Mrs. Swaythe offer you a home?"

"I wanted to be up and doing, acting on my own behalf—a desire I suppose I inherited from my father. I did not want to be beholden to anyone, and I was very restless with uncertainty. My father had a cousin—the only English relative I knew—who was in the army, and he agreed to sponsor my enlistment in his regiment. So I went to Spain."

"You must have witnessed true heroism—indeed, any soldier who fought in the Peninsula is a hero, sir!" she said with feeling. "Were you at Waterloo?"

"I was at Waterloo, ma'am," he said. "And though my regiment was responsible for keeping a platoon of French cuirassiers from escaping, I regret very much, but I cannot claim to have been a hero at any time during the war. I was more often the beneficiary of heroism."

His solemn tone alerted her that this was a hallowed subject, and she kept a respectful silence. After some minutes, he said quietly, "My father's cousin, Lieutenant Woodley, died protecting me and others, at Orthez."

She remembered her compassion for him, when she had first met him in the autumn in the Home Wood, which was kindled by his having been through so much as a soldier. This memory made her even more sorry for her subsequent insistence that he repay her very trifling service to him, and she blushed for herself.

Perhaps sensing her subdued mood, he said, glancing sideways at her, "The sacrifice of one's life is not the only way to save another, Miss Breckinridge. Sometimes small acts of kindness can be just as heroic."

Her blush of mortification changed to one of gratitude, and after some moments, she said self-deprecatingly, "I could never claim heroism in present company, sir."

"Nor could I," he said, adding ruminatively, "though I did sustain a wound in battle."

She eyed him askance, saying, "A gentleman never boasts, sir."

"It was a very trifling wound," he returned, in the humblest of accents.

Unable to resist a smile, Lenora thought it prudent to return to Lord Helden's story. "Pray, how did you discover you were Lord Helden of Helden Hall?"

"My cousin told me my grandfather was some sort of lord, but that it was best I not think of it, for my father had been cast off. So I did not think of it. After my discharge, I had nowhere to go but back to London, where I was little better off than before the army. I eventually was forced to sell everything I had of value, including the watch my father had given me for my sixteenth birthday. I was lucky enough to find work at the docks, and last summer I saw an advertisement announcing my regiment's being awarded the Waterloo Medal. When I went to claim the award, the Engleheart solicitor was waiting, with the news that he had spent the last two years tracking me down, as I was Lord Helden of Helden Hall, Gloucestershire. I was persuaded it was too good to be true, and when he told me what state the property was in, I knew it was so."

Lenora quietly digested this before saying, "I own I am glad that you came to the Hall nevertheless, and that you did not lose hope."

"That I did not lose hope was entirely your doing, Miss Breckinridge. I had, in fact, lost all hope, and was prey to the most miserable, self-pitying thoughts you can imagine. They led me far too often into drink—but you know about that. Your coming, and being such a bother—No, do not blush! You see, that is how I perceived you at first. You made me reconsider the Hall's potential and I greatly resented you for it. But even such a hardened one as I could not resist your great kindness to me, during my illness. Your enthusiasm became infectious, even though I tried to deny it, and I began again to hope."

Lenora could not but be pleased at this, but was too conscious to be able to form a reply. They had arrived back at the lodge, and Tess, who had been following at a discreet distance all the while, stood expectantly by the bench, and Lenora was awakened to a sense of the time. Regretfully, she acknowledged to herself that prolonging her absence would cause comment at home, something which she wished to avoid, at least until she had sorted out her feelings. Therefore, though longing to continue their dialog, she turned resolutely to her companion and thanked him for their meeting, explaining that she must be off home.

Lord Helden took her proffered hand. "May I call on you, Miss Breckinridge?"

"Certainly, though I had not supposed that you wished to do so, sir, as you did not call after Lady Wishforth's ball."

He looked down at her hand, that lay so neatly within his own. "It was craven of me, I know. But I could not bring myself to face you again, after your coldness to me."

"Coldness?" cried Lenora, unconsciously pressing his hand. "I was suffering agonies of mortification, with the shock of finally meeting Lord Helden—that is, you—and the weight of my impertinence so heavy on my mind. I was persuaded every moment that you would guess that I—" She stopped, the color rushing to her face with the recollection that Mr. Ingles knew full well what she had striven to hide from Lord Helden.

He clasped her hand, which she was trying to withdraw, and said with a gleaming eye, "What was it you thought I would guess, Miss Breckinridge?"

She gasped, covering her face with her free hand. "I do not know—it is of no consequence."

But he would not allow this, his smile growing to a grin as he pressed her to tell him, and she blushed hotter. "For shame, sir! Oh, you are odious and—and impossible! Release me at once! I will go!"

She turned her back adamantly to him, and when Tess advanced to lend what aid she could to her mistress, he tugged her toward him, bending to her ear and saying gently, "Lord Helden is not in the least offended by your having fallen in love—with his house."

Then he released her hand and, touching his hat, bid her and Tess good day.

Chapter 25

LADY STILES RECEIVED quite a shock the next day, when Lord Helden arrived in her drawing room and declared that he was none other than Mr. Ingles. Her disquiet was great, for the prejudice she had cherished against the caretaker these many months would not go tamely before the noble appearance and bearing of the gentleman before her. He outstayed his half hour in telling the whole of his story, which went some way in reconciling her to his nobility, but the fact remained that he was as penniless as he had been before, which did not bode well for Lenora's good sense holding out against her romantic proclivities.

She could only hope that he and Lenora would not be much thrown together, but she was soon to discover that this was a forlorn hope. His lordship, having made his debut, was just the sort of well-bred and handsome young man that any hostess would wish to grace her saloons, and possessed the added distinction of mystery. Everyone was soon talking of him, and he was soon to be seen everywhere.

Walking in the park a few days after their private meeting, with Tess and Ben trailing along behind, Lenora came upon his lordship mounted on a handsome grey, and riding in very good style toward her.

He reined in instantly upon coming abreast of her. "Good morning, Miss Breckinridge! I see you have your entourage with you, as is right and proper."

"To be sure, sir!" replied Lenora in a dignified manner. "I hope I will never be accused of being fast by wandering about unattended."

"If my memory does not deceive me, I recall your having a different attitude in the Home Wood."

Lenora sniffed. "Surely you do not expect that I should behave in town as I am wont to do in the country."

"Certainly not! I only wonder," said he, dismounting to walk with her, "if Tess and Ben ever become tired of wandering about with you."

Ben piped up that he never, but Tess shushed him, saying in an under voice that his lordship wasn't speaking to them, only about them, and was only quizzing, besides, which brought on further questions as to the unaccountable things the Quality were permitted to do.

Over this discussion, Lenora said to Lord Helden, "As I am often accompanied by a gentleman, Tess is not obliged to tramp after me too often, and Ben comes along whenever it suits him."

"Oho!" cried Lord Helden. "I see I am to be humbled, and it would be vain to offer myself as a desirable companion amid so many."

Looking archly, Lenora replied, "Oh, indeed, you may save yourself the trouble, for I have experience with your companionship on wandering walks, at least through woods, and unless my memory misleads me, it was more work than I presently engage for, I assure you."

His answering chuckle reminded her of the warmth of his eyes, and the beauty of his teeth, and she was forced to avert her eyes.

"Do you ride, Miss Breckinridge?" his lordship inquired next. "I have never seen you on horseback."

She answered, "Indeed, I do, and have my mare at my disposal."

"You must allow me to accompany you sometime, if it is not asking too much."

She raised an eyebrow. "Perhaps I am not convinced that you would be a better riding companion than walking."

"How better to prove my merits than to test them?"

She laughed at this, but instead of answering his inquiry, she asked if he had bought his horse or if he borrowed it.

"You think to catch me out, Miss Breckinridge," he replied sagely, "but you will not do it. No, I did not spend an enormous sum only to purchase and house and feed this animal. He is a friend's hack, and I am doing a great favor by exercising him regularly. So you may not accuse me of frittering away money on an extravagance that I could be putting toward my future."

Coloring a little, she said, "You do not truly believe me capable of such a trick, sir. I had no doubt it was something of the sort. But what friend of yours can have lent you such a fine animal?"

"Captain Mantell," he answered, letting this reference to his poverty of acquaintance pass. "He was a friend to my cousin Woodley, and showed me great kindness when I had just come into the army. He was a passing acquaintance, really, but when we met in town, he was good enough to take notice of me, and has made a friend of me."

"Certainly! I know the captain well," said Lenora.

"Indeed, he seemed to know much of my story, Miss Breckinridge."

She lifted her chin. "It was no secret, and he seemed to feel just as he ought about it."

"Then perhaps he may tell you if I am a proper person with whom to go riding," he said, touching his hat. Then he remounted and bid them a good day.

Lenora, watching him trot away, could not help but admire his seat, and think that perhaps she had been unwise to tease him, rather than accept his offer outright. But she suffered no ill-will from him, for in the following days, wherever they met, whether at a ball or a card party or the opera or the theater, as soon as their eyes met, she was conscious of an almost tangible understanding that he would seek her out and they would spend however much time was correct to the situation conversing or dancing or generally enjoying one another's society. Lenora had never felt more comfortable in a gentleman's company, nor so content.

Thus, when Mr. Dowbridge accosted her at an al fresco picnic given by Mrs. Marshall, and demanded to know what she was about giving her attentions to that impostor Ingles, Lenora was in no mind to indulge his jealous crochets, and told him so in no uncertain terms. His response was as vitriolic as it was absurd in a man bent on securing her affections, but in addition to making her very angry with him and ensuring that she had no wish to see him for several days at least, he did plant the insidious thought in her head that Mr. Ingles had something to hide. The rise of rumors to the same tune over the ensuing days encouraged this thought, and as she considered what ought to be done, Lord Helden's recommendation that she apply to Captain Mantell for answers seemed to her exceedingly propitious.

Having engaged to accompany the captain to a balloon ascension in Hyde Park, she waited only until they had entered the park and backed the vehicle into a spot with an excellent view of the proceedings, before she unburdened herself to him.

"You must have some notion of my consternation regarding these rumors, sir," she said, "for I know Lord Helden—that is, I know Mr. Ingles, and have come to count him as a friend."

"It is most distressing, Miss Breckinridge," agreed Captain Mantell. "He is fortunate indeed to have a friend in you."

"But I have only very lately come to know him," she continued, "and though I believe him to be an excellent man, there are many who do not, and I do not know that I am equal to withstanding their arguments."

Her companion rested a thoughtful gaze on her. "Then I hope you will be guided by me. I think it is a great piece of impertinence for anyone to assert that a man who has successfully laid claim to his inheritance, through a solicitor who is trained in the law and would detect an impostor thirty miles off, besides receiving his Writ from the Committee on Privilege, who know exactly what questions to ask and what proofs to require, should not be what he claims to be."

"Certainly," replied Lenora. " It is easy to not give any heed to the whispers that he is illegitimate. It could not be possible that his father and mother were not married before his birth, or he would not have been proven the rightful heir to the Engleheart estate, or to the title, and to claim otherwise is ridiculous. But Captain, could it be possible that he has taken another man's place? That he is truly merely James Ingles, a distant relation who has successfully placed himself in Phillip Engleheart's shoes?"

Captain Mantell's brow furrowed, but he answered readily, "If he has, it has been very long in the making, for his cousin told me four years ago, in a camp near Orthez, that Ingles's father was the heir to a viscountcy, but that he had been cast off, and the estate wasted almost as soon as James was born. If that is not a faithful description of the Helden estate, I know not what it could be."

"Oh, Captain!" cried Lenora, eyes shining. "You have relieved my mind! That is as good as proof positive, to my mind, and is all that was required. To have another witness to his testimony—I feel ashamed that it was necessary to my trust, but how could I know otherwise?"

He comforted her on that point, and in the silence that followed, they turned their attention to awaiting the great moment of the balloon launch.

It seemed to be still many minutes distant, and the captain turned to Lenora, saying, "I feel certain I am right in assuming that you take as great an interest in Lord Helden's affairs as when you first asked me about him."

A trifle conscious, she answered, "I have always felt a—a connection to Helden Hall that will not be denied. Now that Lord Helden has revealed himself to Society, I feel a great curiosity to know how he will approach the problem of his estate, and a desire to encourage him in whatever way possible."

"Hmm," replied her companion, and she was anxious lest he question her motives. But when he continued, it was in an entirely different vein. "There is much in what you say about connections. I do not believe in fate, but I have felt a connection like what you describe, and which has persisted through all my attempts to suppress it. I begin to feel that this connection is one I must endure, for I fear it will never be requited."

Lenora, intrigued by this strange utterance, was made to wait for further elucidation, for they were interrupted by a distant relation of the captain, a spinster with a fiddlestick for a tongue and an eye to scandal, who stopped to exclaim upon his delightful companion, and to point out to Lenora her great good luck in having snared such a catch.

As the lady strode away, Lenora, covered in mortification, knew not where to look, and if she had not glanced up to find Captain Mantell equally shocked, she should have crawled under the curricle on the spot. But the horror in his eyes so exactly mirrored her own that she found courage to say, "Captain, pray do not think—I have never—there has not been the slightest hope—Oh, dear!" Gathering her wits, she rushed on, "I lay no claim to your affections, nor should I ever wish to!"

Here she could not meet his eye, but Captain Mantell let out an explosive sigh and said, "Oh, Miss Breckinridge, you relieve my mind excessively! For one terrible moment, I thought that I had given you reason to expect—I should never wish you to believe my intentions to have been—in short, I have never cherished romantic feelings toward you!"

Lenora's relief expressed itself in a strong desire to laugh, and laugh she did, with the captain wholeheartedly joining her, until their eyes flowed with tears and their neighbors looked askance at them. At last, pressing a hand to her side, Lenora declared that there was nothing so good as a laugh to ease one's worries, and they were able to bring themselves into tolerable order.

After a companionable silence, Lenora asked, "What was the connection you were speaking of, before we were interrupted, Captain? Or shall I not ask you? You need not share if you would rather not. I will not press you, but I own I am curious."

"If I had no wish to share it with you, I should not have mentioned it. That would be badly done, don't you think?" His smile faded a little as he gazed unseeing toward where the balloon stood ready to launch at any moment. "Her name is Emily. We were childhood friends, but were separated when I went to school, and I did not see her again until I returned home from the Peninsula."

"But you thought of her."

"Indeed, I did, every day. But thinking was not enough. She is lost to me, and I do not know that it is not my fault. I never told her of my feelings."

Lenora gazed at him in dismay. "She is married?"

He looked down, fiddling with his gloves.

"How sorry I am, sir, truly," said Lenora gently. "I like to believe that a connection based on love is fastened at both ends. If you cannot forget her, it should follow that she, likewise, cannot forget you." Her eyes flicked up to his. "But I suppose that notion would not comfort you."

He smiled wryly. "Not under normal circumstances, Miss Breckinridge, but at this moment I will take comfort in the kindness of your intent."

The signal was then given for the balloon to launch, and their attention was claimed by the amazing spectacle of a contraption of silk and reeds being lifted into the air by heat, and taking two brave—or foolhardy, as the varying opinions ran—persons up into the atmosphere to tempt death and fate for an hour or two. Lenora was struck by the parallel of the event to both her situation and that of Captain Mantell, and was very thoughtful on the drive home.

As he handed her down from the vehicle, Captain Mantell pressed her hand. "Do not despair for me, Miss Breckinridge. I am in earnest when I say that I take comfort in your kindness. I am newly disappointed, but am young, and time will heal my wound, you will see."

Smiling encouragingly, she bid her attendant good bye and went up the steps of her home to pour the details of the ascension into her mother's ears, dwelling long on Captain Mantell's many excellent qualities.

"I had almost convinced myself that the captain could be the one, Joshua," Lady Stiles said to her husband later that evening. "But she is no more in love with him than she is with Mr. Dowbridge, and it is very disheartening."

"How so, my dear?" inquired her spouse, as he adjusted his neckcloth in the mirror. "I find it refreshing to have a man of sense so often in company with our daughter."

"I very much fear she will end by marrying Mr. Ingles—that is, Lord Helden—just so she may waste her fortune on that barrack of a ruin."

"Lord Helden is a fine young man, my love, and as good a catch for our Lenora as any—indeed, better than most of her suitors, for I am much mistaken if they are not all, to a man, in the basket."

"Except, perhaps Dowbridge," she said, "who is only palatable in small doses. I should go distracted if she were to marry him, Joshua."

"Do not fret," Sir Joshua told her, kissing her forehead. "We will await events, and perhaps be better pleased with the result than we at present have cause to hope."

Chapter 26

On the strength of Captain Mantell's testimony, Lenora not only put aside her own doubts, but strove to blight all others' suspicions by being seen in Lord Helden's company as often as was seemly. She accepted his invitations to ride in the park, and took care to encourage this exercise during the fashionable hour. On one of these excursions, he asked if she never drove, like other young ladies who tooled their phaetons on the drive and, laughing, she told him that she was very indifferent at the ribbons, much worse than she was in the saddle.

"I was accounted quite a whip in the army," he remarked casually. "It was often my lot to drive supply wagons through the most execrable conditions, and our horses were generally recalcitrant creatures. I may not drive to an inch, but I can handle a pair over any road you wish. Perhaps I can teach you."

She considered. "You will not be the first to make the attempt, my lord, but perhaps, with those very odd credentials, you may possess some mysterious skill to make you the last."

It would also be an opportunity to widen the reach of her campaign to show that Lord Helden was all the crack, and they were soon often seen driving together. This stratagem was effective, but not in the way she had supposed, for those who took notice were chiefly her admirers, who were less apt to take a new rival to their bosom than to curse his name.

Lord Ratherton was one of these, who, having given much thought to Miss Breckinridge's dismissal of him at the Wishforth's ball, recognized that his suit was in peril. Though activity of any sort was abhorrent to him, he had determined that the time had come for chivalrous performances. Miss Breckinridge's persistent fascination with the newly arrived Lord Helden, without engendering in him the violent jealously that frequently overcame her other suitors—notably Mr. Dowbridge—had taught him that romance was the way to her heart, and after consulting various volumes by Mrs. Radcliffe, he had set forth on a course of action which, he had flattered himself, would impress Miss Breckinridge with the conviction that Lord Helden was not worth her while, when a truly romantic hero stood ready for the taking.

After orchestrating the rescue in Hyde Park, his next endeavor was to invite her with Diana and Iris—Lady Athena being above his touch—and some of his own cronies to an evening at Vauxhall Gardens, where they partook of shaved ham and chicken in a supper box, and danced to the orchestra beneath the stars in the Grove. Lenora, not overly moved by these delights, nevertheless enjoyed rediscovering the gardens, and could not help but wonder what it would be like to lose oneself in the dark walks with someone she truly loved.

Before she had gone farther in her imaginings than to envisage Lord Helden, however, she found herself alone on one of these paths with Lord Ratherton, the other gentlemen having whisked her companions away elsewhere. Turning to remonstrate with his lordship on leading her into such an improper situation, she was forestalled by the appearance of a masked ruffian, who leapt from the shadows, waving a pistol and demanding their purses. Lenora stood blinking at the wiry little man, thinking he must know very little of pistols to handle one in so irresponsible a fashion, but Lord Ratherton, unimpressed by the danger, lost no time in placing himself between her and the man, and declared that the thief had better stand down or he should be made to be sorry.

Disregarding this warning, the masked man lunged at his lordship, using his pistol rather like a sword, but Lord Ratherton brought his arm down hard across his opponent's weapon hand, knocking the pistol from his grip and sending it skittering off the path. The ruffian shouted in anger and leapt at Lord Ratherton, his hands outstretched as if to choke him, but his lordship coolly sidestepped his attacker, bringing his fist up at the last moment and neatly felling him with a blow to the face.

Lenora gazed down at the man—who looked very small and oddly familiar—lying senseless in the grass at the side of the path, and felt a twinge of pity for him. But Lord Ratherton, dusting his hands, came to her side to inquire as to her well-being, and desiring her to allow him to lead her back to the main walk directly, with apologies for his inability to allow her time to recover herself, as the villain might awaken at any moment and renew his demands. She accepted this solicitude with absolute calm, having never been tempted to swoon or go into hysterics during the whole of the encounter, and was not surprised in the least to find their party awaiting them near a cluster of lights on the Long Walk.

In contemplating these stirring events, Lenora could not but be sorry that Lord Ratherton was the hero of them, for it seemed owing entirely to this fact that she was gripped by none of the sensations she would have expected. Perhaps if he were darker, and a bit more broad, with fine white teeth and warm brown eyes, she could have felt something like romance, but as this was impossible, such thoughts merited little of her time. It was far more enjoyable—that is, it was far more important to pursue her virtuous goal of clearing Lord Helden's name, and so Lord Ratherton was forgotten for the time being.

It was readily apparent to Lenora that her plan thus far did not seem to be as efficacious as she would like in repressing the gossip about Lord Helden. As the problem exercised her mind of how better to achieve success, she at last hit upon the notion that if he could but put Helden Hall in order, his retractors would be silenced, for who but the true heir would care to take on such a daunting project? She broached the idea while he tutored her driving on the way to Richmond—a feat which was accomplished in Sir Joshua's gig, with Ben perched up behind, and on little-used side roads to avoid possible collisions due to her ineptitude.

"If you could but find a genteel occupation, my lord, it would be very good for you," she declared, causing the horses to veer only slightly as she glanced to see how he took it. He seemed nonplussed, and she explained quickly, "So that you could redeem your estate! Is not that what you desire to do, above all else?"

He tipped his head. "Perhaps not above all else, ma'am, but it is a high priority. I own I had not considered taking up work to do it, however, which I see now was short-sighted of me. It could be the simplest thing in the world, to go into trade, or to join the navy."

"Not the navy, sir," said Lenora quickly. "That would not do, for you should be gone for months or years at a time, and could never see to the job properly. No, you must not think of the navy. But a trade—did you learn anything useful while in the army?"

"I learned many useful things in the army," he said, with a half smile. "But I do not think that any of them could translate into gainful occupation."

"You could become a secretary to a great man, I am sure," offered Lenora, but again she was declined, being reminded that he had not gone to university, and so had not the credentials to prefer him to any great man. She would not, however, be deterred. "A clerk, then. Surely you learned enough at school to write up tables and calculate sums."

He squinted, considering. "I believe I know enough of sums to be certain that a clerk's wages would scarcely refurbish the gatekeeper's lodge, much less the Hall."

This was daunting, and Lenora was hard-pressed for some minutes to think of another avenue to explore. "I don't suppose you should like to take orders," she said at last, and his sidelong look was enough answer for her. "No, I did not think you would. I cannot think what is to be done."

"I have thought of a very simple solution," he said. "I should marry an heiress."

Lenora looked quickly at him, indignation flaring in her bosom, but he was all innocence, with a maddening twinkle in his eye, and her color rose. "Certainly, sir, it would be simplest, and if that is all you care for, you must do as you wish. However, one must be prepared to sacrifice something or other in the case of heiresses, for all too often they are insipid, or simpering, or worse, expensive. What a trial, to go to the trouble of marrying money, only to lose it all on gowns and horses and carriages and houses in every principal resort! But you must be the judge. Have you one in your eye?"

He protested that he had not, but opined that as he had been so recently introduced into Society, she would be in a better way of pointing one or two out to him. This she declined to do, declaring that she knew too little of his tastes to trust herself in a recommendation.

"That is easily mended, Miss Breckinridge. I'll tell you my requirements." And he counted off on his fingers. "She must be pretty, she must be genteel, she must ride and have an excellent seat—though as to driving, I am indifferent—she must have spirit, and she must be to me something of a guardian angel."

She blushed rosily and loosened the reins, urging the horses faster. "I have never heard of such a woman, upon my honor, sir. I had not thought that one in your situation could have such nice notions. Really, there is nothing for it but to dig up the entire garden at the Hall, to see if your grandfather left you any more legacies."

Before he could favor her with his opinion on this solution, however, they came within sight of an imposing and dreary mansion so like those in Lenora's favorite novels that she involuntarily drew up, gazing at the structure with undisguised admiration.

"Have you ever seen anything so horrid?" she cried in delight, her consternation with him forgotten. "Such lichen and ivy, and dim, brooding windows! It has given me gooseflesh, I declare, and the thought of entering fills me with delicious foreboding!"

"Indeed, I would not venture," agreed her companion.

She looked quickly at him, "But you are not afraid! You have entered Helden Hall many a time without a particle of fear. Ghosts and shadows are as nothing to you."

"In front of a lady, I was obliged to act with more courage than I felt, Miss Breckinridge, but you said yourself that I hid much behind my beard," he said gravely. "Depend upon it that whenever we entered the Hall, I was all of a tremble for fear of Mrs. Matlock's ghost."

"Mrs. Who?" she asked sharply.

"My grandfather's housekeeper." He shivered. "I've learned she was reckoned a most redoubtable lady, and would brook no nonsense from anybody. One speck of dirt on her floors—"

"It is ungentlemanly to quiz one when one shares one's innermost feelings," said Lenora with a toss of her head, and preparing to proceed down the road.

"Why do not we walk up to the place, and go around it?" suggested her companion abruptly. "Perhaps you might point out the desirable features that should be kept or added at Helden Hall." She merely looked askance and he added, "I should not like to be remiss in any detail, once the renovations are begun."

"That is a subject for your heiress, my lord," she answered loftily.

"No, no. I am persuaded she will not know the half of what you do of Gothic ruins."

"But Helden Hall is quite different, sir. Surely you see that," she said, exasperated. "It is a ruin that is to be reclaimed, not a hulk that has always been horrid. Its beauty lies in its present hopeless state, which must not for the world be allowed to remain, or—or—" The idea was so unthinkable that she struggled to find words. "It must not be."

After a pause, he said, "But I was made to believe that you admired a house like this," gesturing to the imposing mansion, "and abominated neat and ordinary dwellings."

"Yes, but one does not wish to live in such a place as this," she said reasonably. "That would be beyond endurance. Imagine, day in and day out to be faced with specters and skeletons and evil retainers at every turn? Ugh!" She brushed all these unpalatable visions away. "Every house must have its mysteries, to be sure, but they must not exceed what is acceptable. If I am to live at Helden Hall, it cannot be—"

She stopped short, flushing to the roots of her hair and unable to even peek at her companion's face. Not a sound came from him, and after a few moments she jerked into motion, saying, "But you may depend upon it that I have long recognized the impertinence of that notion, sir, and have quite given it up, never fear. My, how the time has flown. We must be getting back," and loosed the reins.

But in her haste to turn the horses around, she ran the gig up onto the berm, and would have upset them, had not Lord Helden, with great presence of mind, thrown his weight to the side, righting the vehicle just in time, and upon his polite request, seconded by Ben, Lenora willingly acceded possession of the reins to him for the homeward journey.

This experience having taught her that she must be more on her guard, Lenora resolved to spread her attentions more generously, and accepted a rather urgent invitation from Lord Ratherton some days later to drive out to Windsor.

Their object was ostensibly to view the castle, and he sweetened the prospect by engaging to allow her to try her skill at the ribbons along the way. Very much like Lord Helden, Lord Ratherton seemed only too willing to offer his tutelage, and to be at pains to show himself both an apt and a patient teacher. She suspected their journey to the castle took rather longer than he had engaged for, however, for he hurried her along the North Terrace to an inn, where he fidgeted as she partook of refreshment, and seemed relieved to hand her into the curricle at last for the drive back to London. This odd behavior, much like one with a great secret, gave Lenora to expect that something interesting was in store, and she tried to imagine what it could be.

Her previous two outings with him had proven to be terribly exciting, and after the second, she had felt a general curiosity to see if this dramatic trend would continue, but her exertions on behalf of Lord Helden had cast all such secondary considerations into the shade. Now, however, she was at leisure to think what he could be about, and came to the conclusion that if his motives were what she guessed, there was no harm in throwing herself heart and soul into the farce.

So it was with more delight than amazement that Lenora perceived, on the lonely stretch of Hounslow Heath, three riders wrapped in greatcoats galloping toward them, with pistols upraised and shouting such homely and exciting words as, "Stand and deliver!" and "Mind yer barkers, coves!" That these words were delivered in accents not wholly free from those of a gentleman, Lenora allowed to pass, so thrilled was she to be a participant in a scene any number of young ladies had relished on the page. Intent upon shaming even Mrs. Siddons in the role of damsel in distress, she shrieked and gripped Lord Ratherton's caped greatcoat, begging him to save her from the marauders, and artfully affected a swoon onto his shoulder.

This seemed to cast him into disorder, for the curricle came instantly to a stop despite the thunder of hooves that converged directly upon them, and Lenora valiantly held her insensible attitude as the hoof beats ceased and the horses snorted and pawed, and a general unease filled the air. His lordship uttered, "Blast!" several times, adjusting his position as if unable to decide where to turn, until his fair burden would have fallen across his lap, had he not caught her rather awkwardly in his arms.

Then a vociferous conference ensued between all four men, regarding the ill luck that had made her faint away just when things were getting interesting, and whether it would be more propitious to wait until the lady awoke, and to resume the charade, or to call it off and make a story of it later. Two of the highwaymen, thinking of their dinners, were in favor of the latter, but were shouted down by the third—seconded by Lord Ratherton—who made the point that to give up now would be a shame, after all their preparation, not to mention a waste of good blunt gone on the costumes. This recalled the others to their former enthusiasm, and with exclamations of brotherly loyalty, they staunchly agreed to see the thing through, passing the time until her recovery in adjusting their costumes to each others' satisfaction, and placing themselves in an appropriately frightening posture for when their victim awoke.

Lenora, judging by their eventual silence that it was time to reward their perseverance, stirred, and felt herself propped instantly back against Lord Ratherton's shoulder. Her eyes opened upon a scene calculated to make any gently-bred maiden's blood run cold, with three hulking ruffians on horseback advancing upon her, their hoods drawn down to obscure all but their scowling mouths in unshaven jaws, their frieze coats and trousers travel-stained and worn, and their pistols—surprisingly similar to gentlemen's dueling pistols—trained upon her. Suitably impressed, Lenora gave a dramatic start and a squeak, and regained her clutch on Lord Ratherton's coat.

"Oho!" her stalwart companion cried in manly accents. "Oho, ye villains, think you to get the better of me? I think not! Never fear, Miss Breckinridge, these ruffians shall not harm you!" With that, he pulled a pistol from his coat pocket, adjuring his groom—who had remained inexplicably silent through the proceedings—to follow his example, and without further ado, fired over the highwaymen's heads.

The first shot made Lenora jump, but she was better prepared for the second, and apart from covering her ears and hunching against the coming explosion, showed admirable fortitude in the face of such a shock, especially in one who had fainted dead away only minutes earlier. She watched in appreciation as the highwaymen scattered, their capes flying in the wind and their horses rearing and plunging, and as they disappeared into the horizon she so far forgot herself as to clap her hands, turning to Lord Ratherton with a rapt expression.

"Bravo! Bravo, sir," she cried, taking his hand and shaking it firmly. "An excellent performance. I declare I was never so delighted in my life!"

"Yes, well, I always thought such men were cowards," said his lordship, puffing up his chest and replacing the pistol in his pocket. "Never could see what there was to frighten people so about highwaymen."

"No, no," agreed Lenora, schooling her expression to one of grave consideration. "And now you have given them something to ponder, as they reflect upon their lives, and perhaps they will be moved to better themselves."

This drew a sideways look from her companion, but he answered her affirmatively, saying that naturally they should have much to think on after such a fright as he had given them, and wouldn't all the world be grateful that he had made the Heath a safer place, finally giving it as his opinion that they should be getting back to town. Lenora readily assented and settled into her seat, prodigiously satisfied with the day, and wiled away the hour in contemplating what had transpired, and in interspersing Lord Ratherton's monologue with reflections on what the highwaymen could have done had they wished to be truly odious—for she was no novice to the formulation of romantic scenes—to the vast entertainment of the wooden-faced groom perched up behind.

Chapter 27

Tess was in raptures over her mistress's adventure, which Lenora wasted no time in telling her that evening. "Ooh, miss! It's just like a novel! I'm all a tremble that they actually pointed their guns at you! But I suppose you wasn't in any real danger, so I needn't feel so—only what will his lordship think of next?"

"I do not know," mused Lenora, idly tying up her nightdress. "He will meet with some difficulty in improving upon the highwaymen, to be sure, though that scenario was not even as perfect as it could have been. He ought to have had one of them take me onto his horse and ride away, so that he must have given chase to rescue me, but I fear he has already overtaxed his imagination, Tess. It is perhaps well, however, for I mustn't encourage him. Though I am certain he is a horrid fortune-hunter, and certainly deserves a set-down, it would be improper in me to trifle with him."

This dispassionate view of the matter would have vastly

discomposed her swain, could he have had an inkling of it, for he viewed the continuance of her society as encouragement, and congratulated himself that he had made very good progress toward the enslavement of her heart. Lady Stiles, however, was less pleased with the use Lenora had made of her time, and was sometimes of a mind to make her daughter give up the acquaintance with Lord Ratherton entirely.

"For he is nothing but an opportunist, Joshua," she complained to her husband the next afternoon. "It is plain as can be that he has heard of her fortune, and cares only for that!"

"Yes, my dear," replied her husband, "though his methods are excessively original. In light of the fact that he seems to be quite overpowering her with romance, I should think you would be grateful that she is not taken in."

Genevieve looked dourly at him. "If I could but be certain of it, I would say it is the greatest joke, but I am persuaded that she has enjoyed herself hugely. However, I fancy she is safe enough from any attachment there, now that she has met Lord Helden."

Sir Joshua drew her into his arms and said, "Perhaps, but we may take tolerable comfort that Lenora will not easily be taken in by any fortune-hunter, even Lord Helden, should he prove to be one as well. I own that our Lenora has surprised even me, my dear, in her perspicacity this season, and that is saying something."

Mr. Dowbridge was not as sanguine as Miss Breckinridge's parents concerning the matter. He had reason to believe his chances superior to those of Lord Ratherton, but Lord Helden he knew to be a formidable opponent, for Miss Breckinridge had shown herself too naive and romantic to recognize a wolf in sheep's clothing. It was becoming tiresome, to be sure, to be yet again obliged to to remove the scales from her eyes, but he flattered himself that his patience and devotion could not but be rewarded.

Having successfully prevailed upon her to go driving with him in Hyde Park, Mr. Dowbridge's patience and devotion was instantly tested by young Ben, who erupted from the house just as Lenora was being handed into the smart curricle, and cried, "May I go as tiger, miss? Please, miss?"

Lenora's indulgent smile was lost on Mr. Dowbridge, who had turned to the eager little boy in astonishment. "What the devil? Does he think you've gone soft in the head?"

His fair one stiffened. "Not a bit, sir. He often accompanies me on drives."

"You are not serious!" exclaimed Dowbridge, eyebrows leaping.

"I know he is full young to be a tiger," replied Lenora defensively, "but he has never been in danger of falling off, and is very good with the horses."

"How can you stomach such an ill-favored creature?" demanded Dowbridge, eying Ben with distaste.

"I'm right here, govnor," piped Ben from the steps.

Bridling, Dowbridge muttered, "I'm well aware of that!"

"Well, I hears you!" pursued Ben, crossing his arms over his small chest. "And I don't like what you's a-saying."

"Certainly you do not, Ben," Lenora said, frowning at Mr. Dowbridge's back. "You must excuse Mr. Dowbridge. He is not often in company with children, and does not know how to act."

Her swain's gaze shifted to her, incredulous. "Miss Breckinridge, I know very well how to treat children, and this one is impertinent. How dare he suggest that we should carry him about with us, in the full view of Polite Society?" Her cast of countenance made

263

him pause, and he said, with a little huff of laughter, "We could never live it down."

"Perhaps you could not, Mr. Dowbridge," returned Lenora in a tone very close to icy. "I, however, should not regard it—as if such a thing could weigh with me! How can you be so stupid?"

Dowbridge gaped at her, as the realization dawned that Miss Breckinridge was perfectly serious, and was very close to thinking him an ass. Recognizing the prudence of regaining mastery of the situation, he shut his mouth abruptly and strove for a cajoling tone. "My dear Miss Breckinridge, forgive my surprise. I merely was not prepared to have the company of a child on our outing. Surely you cannot feel it necessary to bring him along to play propriety?"

"Indeed, I do not, sir," was the reply. "I only wonder at your incivility. The child is harmless, and my particular friend. You must beg his pardon."

Their gazes locked for a pregnant moment before Dowbridge turned stiffly, his jaw clenched. He bowed his head, touched his heart, and said crisply, "I beg your pardon, Master Ben."

Ben huffed. "Tain't nothing to me, guvnor. But you'll excuse me a-saying as I 'spected different out of a gentry cove with so bang up a team as you got there!"

"Ben!" cried Lenora, halfway between laughter and censure. "Do not injure your position, my young man. When one is in the right, one never holds oneself above another."

"You don't say," the boy replied, scrunching his mouth to one side as he considered. "Then I won't go with you, govnor, just to show you as I'm right." And with a decisive nod of his tousled head, he turned and stomped into the house.

Dowbridge stood for some moments staring after the young boy, unable immediately to resolve his feelings on somehow being bested by a street urchin, and it was with a tight smile that he at last turned to Miss Breckinridge and suggested they get on with the drive.

By the time they reached the park, Lenora was able to excuse Mr. Dowbridge's lapse in good breeding, setting it down to lack of experience and surprise, for she knew well that not everyone liked children—especially those plucked from the gutter, for while Ben's manners had improved a great deal during his stay, he still was fairly uncouth, and much as she disregarded it, he also was not what one would call taking. This had never bothered her, for she had felt an interest in Ben from the moment she and her mother had rescued him, but she did not imagine that everyone could do so, at least not without coming to know him. But this she would leave for another day, being sensible enough to recognize that Mr. Dowbridge would not suffer much more aggravation today.

After such a beginning, their conversation went on a little stiffly at first, but after they had been accosted by several of Lenora's male acquaintances walking or riding in the park, Dowbridge said somberly, "You seem to have gathered quite a following, Miss Breckinridge. I count myself fortunate that you would condescend to drive with me today."

"Phoo! What a thing to say to a good friend, Mr. Dowbridge," replied Lenora, taking care to emphasize the amiable nature of their relationship. "I should always have time for you, and count myself the fortunate one."

Considerably emboldened by this statement, Dowbridge said, "Do you grow tired of the attentions of all these Town Beaux, then?"

"Not in the least," was the glib reply. "It can be very amusing to be courted and cosseted, I declare, even if it is by fortune-hunters. They are often very useful."

"You find them amusing and useful? Is that all you care for them?" His hands had tightened on the reins, causing the team to slow.

"Certainly. As I have no plans to marry at present, I see no reason to single any one out."

She turned to see that, contrary to her expectation, he wore an expression of triumph, and he made as if to speak, but shut his mouth again, glancing quickly between her and the road ahead as a satisfied smile widened on his face. At last he said, "I thought it my business to warn you against them, but I see I have been far afield. It is they who ought to be warned against you!"

Relieved that his euphoria was not for a different, unfounded cause, she said, "Exactly, sir! It is lucky that you need not be warned against me!"

"Indeed!" he said, with considerable feeling, and pulled the team to a stop. Turning bodily, he snatched her hands into his own and said, "Miss Breckinridge, what you have been saying fills me with joy, for I had begun to question your preference for me, and now know I need not have feared. I shall not betray such weakness again, and will ensure it by declaring my deep admiration for you!"

Lenora, astonished at his sudden ardor, and her own mistake, tried to regain her hands, but he held them the more tightly, threatening even to take her into his arms until she cried, "Mr. Dowbridge, this is most improper! Pray, release me at once. We must not be seen in a public place in such an attitude!"

"It is entirely appropriate, now that I have declared myself," was his assured answer.

"I have not accepted you, sir!" she said firmly. "And I never shall!"

"But you have encouraged my suit—"

"I have done no such thing!" she said, valiantly attempting to command her heightening emotions. "I expressed most clearly just now that I have no intention to marry anyone at present."

"But you meant none of those wastrels—"

"I meant none of my suitors, sir, including you!" she returned, tugging at her hands and glancing about to see if anyone had noticed their impropriety.

"You cannot mean that," he said, holding her hands more tightly. "You do not know what you are saying, Miss Breckinridge."

"I wish you will cease to insist that you know me better than I know myself, and take me at my word!" she cried, abandoning all pretense at calm. "I do not love you, and cannot marry you, so you must let me go!"

He let go her hands abruptly, his earnestness changing rapidly into irritation. "You shrink from being seen clasping hands with me, but would not regard the consequences of being seen with that ill-favored urchin your mother has adopted? I see."

"Ben is not ill-favored!"

"He is as ill-favored as he is ill-mannered!" he retorted, letting the horses go.

The curricle bowled forward, throwing Lenora back against the seat. She clapped a hand to her bonnet, which threatened to be whisked from her head, and cast a glowering look at her companion. "There is no occasion for such spite, sir. Ben is not to be blamed for your folly in thrusting me into a situation I find most discomposing. I do not know how you can have mistaken my affections!"

Mr. Dowbridge's mortification burned in his face. He set his jaw and would not look at Lenora, focusing his attention on the path ahead, and Lenora followed suit, gazing impassively out at the scenery, brightening falsely only when called upon to greet acquaintances in passing. As they completed the full circuit of the park, however, her ire began to soften, for she had had time to think, and to apprehend how one of his temperament could have been misled by her buoyant spirits.

Hazarding a glance at her companion, she perceived that his countenance had settled into a glum and disappointed look, which touched her heart. "Mr. Dowbridge, pray, forgive me. I spoke hastily, and have pained you greatly, I fear." He shot her a sideways glance, but no more. She persevered. "We are good friends, are we not? May we not continue so?"

"How can I trust that you will not use me as you have your other beaux?"

"Because you are not like my other beaux, sir," she replied.

"And yet you will not hear my suit."

Patiently, Lenora answered, "I will not hear your suit because I cannot love you, sir—not in the way you seem to wish. For that I am deeply sorry. You must believe me."

His jaw worked. "I believe you, for I have not far to go to find the reason for your refusal. Lord Helden." The name ground out from between his teeth. "But I will tell you that you have clung to that fantasy far too long, Miss Breckinridge. I should have imagined an intelligent young lady such as yourself would give up such a useless dream, in the face of the stark realities—and I flattered myself that I could play some part in dispelling your ridiculous notions of becoming Lady Helden and redeeming that wreck of a house before it was too late. But you are blind, Miss Breckinridge."

Lenora protested that she had long abandoned that impertinent notion, but it was to no avail, for he plowed ruthlessly on, only casting angry glances at her as he drove his team at a smart pace up the track. "You are obstinately blind to the opportunities that await you—nay, the opportunities that even now lay strewn at your feet—in favor of some romantic fancy that will shatter at any moment, leaving you bereft and disappointed."

This was too much for Lenora, who had shown what she felt was ample sympathy in light of his mortification in being refused. She had known that he was not romantic, and she had long been aware that he did not view Lord Helden—or his home—in a favorable light, but that he would throw all this in her teeth, calling into question her reason and intelligence, was provocation she could not bear.

"How right you are to show me my faults, Mr. Dowbridge," she said with barely suppressed anger, "for that is, after all, what friends do, no matter that it is not their right to interfere. How glad I am that you would not allow any scruple to stand in the way of your duty."

Drawing his brows together, he said, "You may believe that I took no pleasure in it, Miss Breckinridge, except in the expectation of improving your future happiness."

"Which you have no say in, sir!" she cried, incensed. "How dare you accuse me of blindness, when you cannot see what is in front of you? When will you perceive that treating me like a child has not made me love you?"

He blinked at her in astonishment, but did not answer, as he had just then to turn the curricle out through the Stanhope gate and down the street. By the time this was accomplished, his companion was a smoldering statue beside him, and he preserved a thoughtful silence until he drew up outside the house in Curzon Street. When she stood to climb down from the vehicle without assistance, he grasped her wrist, saying, "Stay, Miss Breckinridge. You must hear me, for only a moment. We have both given way to anger, and are in no temper to be reasonable now, but please believe that your words have not been unheeded." He sighed. "I know I must apologize, but do not know how to do it. I have much to consider, and hope to present myself next to you with a clearer understanding. If you will forgive me, may I have the honor of a dance with you at the Tenby's ball?"

Slightly mollified, Lenora nodded her acquiescence and allowed him to hand her out of the curricle, but was still too angry to do more than bid him good day at foot of the steps. She was some time in ridding herself of her irritation, but as she had agreed to dance with him, she made an effort to move toward indifference, which she hoped to achieve by the day of the ball, but it was difficult going. Their encounters so often ended in a quarrel of some kind that she could not for her life understand why he could imagine himself in love with her—and if that was his idea of love, then she was doubly repelled by the thought of matrimony with him.

But he was her near neighbor, and a friend of sufficiently long standing to merit her forbearance, and she resolved to continue his friend, but resolved equally that it would not be her doing if after this day he felt that he was more to her than that.

Chapter 28

Tom returned to town the following day, hard upon the heels of a rumor that his sister was encouraging the advances of not one, but two gazetted fortune hunters.

"I thought you were more up to the knocker, Nora!" he said, following her into her room after tea. "To be chasing after Lord Ratherton, who's got more mortgages than I can count, and is a worthless fribble besides!"

Lenora stared at him. "I do not chase him, Tom, and whatever horrid crony it is of yours who told you I did, he is the worthless fribble."

"Do not try to deny it, my girl! Mama confirmed that you're forever in his company, three times in the last fortnight!"

She pressed a hand to her bosom in mock dismay. "Three times in two weeks! Heavens, then I must practically be betrothed to Lord Helden, for he has been in my company twice as often."

Tom rounded on her. "He's another one that I take exception to, Nora! Just because he's the owner of that drafty old pile you've fallen in love with, don't mean he's a proper person to be with. There're all kinds of rumors about him, which will stick to you, and that I won't stand!"

"How can you think me such a goosecap, Tom, when you are a gudgeon?" she said. "Lord Helden's claims have been substantiated by the Committee on Privilege, which is more than enough for me, sir, to discount any of the hateful rumors that have sprung up about him. He is merely new to Society, and the quizzes will have it that his past is a scandal, but it is not so."

"And how are you an authority, young lady?" asked Tom, crossing his arms over his chest.

Lenora raised her brows. "I happen to know his lordship better than almost anyone in this town, Tom, and have gotten the assurance of the one person who knows him better—Captain Mantell, who knew him in the army—that he is as good a man as could be wished."

Tom humphed, but said, "I suppose I'd better present myself to this Lord Helden and find out for myself."

"Or perhaps you should ask Mama to present you, Tom, for she—and Sir Joshua—have met him, and have yet to warn me away from him." She turned to ring the bell for Tess. "A pity that you made the trip to town for nothing, my dear. Or did you not know that Diana Marshall has gone to Brighton?"

"Oh, her papa developed a nasty cough, so they've quitted Brighton early," was the careless reply, and he left the room before she could ask how he could be privy to such information.

She entered the drawing room on the night of the Tenby's ball to find Tom alone, reading a newspaper. Looking up, he whistled and said, "You're looking as fine as fivepence, Nora!"

Pleased by this praise, and feeling that it was not altogether undeserved, she swept herself gracefully into a chair beside him and replied, "You look well yourself, my dear. It seems we have both outdone ourselves."

His eyebrows went up a fraction. "And how many of your suitors shall I have the pleasure of setting down tonight, eh?"

"None, sir, I thank you," she said, smoothing the embroidered gauze overskirt of her pale yellow silk gown.

He folded the paper carefully, saying, "Is that because none will be attending the Tenby's ball, or because none will be coxcomb enough to press his suit upon you, knowing your inimitable brother to be present?"

"It is because Lord Helden has been called out of town, and I am well able to handle Lord Ratherton, I thank you, dear," she said.

"You'll pardon that I'm not such a knock-in-the-cradle as to believe you," said Tom, returning to his newspaper.

This she did not dignify with a reply, but went through dinner in a ruminative mood, setting off in subdued spirits to the ball. The rumors surrounding Lord Helden had continued, and she feared he had left town because of oppressed spirits. Having only experienced two seasons in London Society, Lenora did not know for certain how long such rumors could go on without corroboration, but she wished that she could do more for his lordship than be seen in his company, and refute the rumors, for not many respected the authority or sense of a chit of a girl.

Lord Ratherton, too, had weighed upon her mind, as his attentions had become rather too pointed to ignore. Twice since their adventure on Hounslow Heath he had sent her flowers, and though she had sent the first back, with a carefully worded note that she had hoped would set him right without wounding him, the second offering had arrived a few days later with no note and no card, but Ben's secret smile when she questioned him as to the sender told her that her note had not been taken to heart.

Thus ran Lenora's thoughts as they drove to the Tenby's mansion in Grosvenor Square, where Tom abandoned her upon arrival to advance his own pursuits, namely, to seek out and monopolize Miss Diana Marshall. Lenora was immediately claimed by Mr. Dowbridge for the cotillion that was forming, and her mood aided her in making good her resolve to treat him with nothing but friendship, though she was left fagged, and he a little grim about the mouth when they parted.

Her next partner was Lord Ratherton, whose solicitous inquiry as to her impaired spirits so revived her charity with him that she agreed to the subsequent suggestion that they stroll about in the garden for the next half-hour, in order to refresh herself in the cool of the evening. He ushered her outside onto the veranda and into the gardens, which had been lit by several lanterns hung about on shepherd's hooks. He found a stone bench hidden by an arching shrubbery, which was a trifle more secluded than she would have liked, had she not been too caught up in wondering what it was about her that had captivated Mr. Dowbridge.

Lord Ratherton took her hand and gazed adoringly at her. "Allow me to tell you that your eyes are like stars, Miss Breckinridge."

Startled out of her abstraction, Lenora did not allow it, withdrawing her hand to emphasize this.

"But you must, my dear Miss Breckinridge, allow me to speak," he said quickly, shifting so that she could not easily escape the bench. "You can't have misunderstood my attentions to you of late."

Disheartened that she had so greatly miscalculated her charms, Lenora replied, "Pray, my lord, say no more. I fear it is you who have misunderstood me—and I am very sorry for it. My note to you only this week stated clearly—Please believe that I have never meant anything but friendship by you."

"You don't mean it—can't mean it!" he cried, leaning toward her as much in earnestness as in desperation. "Told me at our last outing you'd never enjoyed yourself more!"

"And I did!" said Lenora, inching away from him on the bench. "But enjoyment of one's company is not love. There is so much more to that emotion which, I am persuaded, our relationship lacks."

"What fustian!" insisted his lordship, moving close to her once more. "I've shown you true romance! No lengths to which I'll not go!"

"But that was all a sham, sir! You cannot deny it!"

Only momentarily deterred, he possessed himself of her hands and, bending close to her face, said huskily, "You must understand, no one'll cherish you as I do already."

Lenora, appalled, leapt to her feet, wrenching away her hands. "Pray, sir, believe me when I say that I do not return your affections, and can never do. It pains me to be so plain, but there it is."

His lordship, scarcely attending, jumped up and said in a rush, "Only say you will you marry me, Miss Breckinridge, and I'll make you love me!"

She inhaled sharply, and he rushed on, as if hoping to forestall her next reasonable argument. "And I'll fulfill your dreams, of course—all of 'em! Already laid plans to make over one of the cottages on my estate in the Gothic style, so you may wander over it any time you like—no doubt any number of ghosts will collect there, if you wish it."

"You mistake my dreams, sir, if you believe that will fulfill them."

He snatched her hands again, kneeling before her. "Prepared to believe anything you wish, if only you'll consent to be mine!"

"My lord, I will do no such thing!" she huffed, tugging at her hands in an effort to disengage him. "Get up, I beg you, before someone sees you in that ridiculous posture."

He stood quickly, but took her swiftly into his arms. "Anything you desire, my dear, my delight—"

"Unhand me, sir!" she hissed. "If you knew me at all, you would know that this is no way to win my heart!"

Ignoring her protestations, he attempted to kiss her, but all at once, Dowbridge leapt from the shadows, and Lord Ratherton was felled by what Tom would surely have described as a wisty castor. Lenora, eying her inert suitor with dismay, was startled when Iris swept past Dowbridge and took her by the arms.

"Lenora, the nerve!" said Iris, her glare at Lord Ratherton clarifying her meaning. "You should have hit him yourself!"

"Would that I had," said Lenora, squinting in the darkness at Dowbridge, to whom now she must feel herself obligated.

Turning his back upon his handiwork, Dowbridge bowed to Lenora and said, "Forgive me, Miss Breckinridge, for subjecting you to such a barbarous scene, but I believe it to have been necessary."

"I suppose there was nothing for it," Lenora said, thinking rather gloomily that she had no opinion of romantic scenes where the hero was all wrong.

A moan and a thrashing from the ground behind Mr. Dowbridge warned them that Lord Ratherton had regained his senses, and he leapt to his feet, growling, "How dare you hit me? D'you think to rise in her estimation by doing such a cawkish thing?"

"I could not have sunk myself lower than you have, my lord!" spat

Dowbridge. "How dared you touch her?"

Lenora stepped quickly forward. "Gentlemen, you must not fight! It is unnecessary!"

"It's no concern of yours!" ground out his lordship, and Lenora bridled, until she saw that he was glaring not at her, but at his opponent.

"Where a lady is in distress is any gentleman's concern, my lord, or did you not perceive her discomfort?" returned Dowbridge in equally menacing tones.

"A mistaken notion she'd taken into her head—"

"One under which I must be laboring as well, as I found you ensconced so privately and in such an attitude—"

"I meant no harm to Miss Breckinridge, and take exception to your tone, sir! You're not, after all, her protector!"

"Perhaps not, sir," replied Dowbridge, pushing nose to nose with his lordship, "but I have even greater claims upon her!"

Lenora, who had drawn to the side with Iris, stiffened at this, but the gentlemen took no notice, and carried on as if they were alone in the world.

"I suppose you mean to claim her fortune!" spat Ratherton, leveraging his superior height to loom over his opponent. "But you never will, for you wouldn't know how to woo a dairy maid, much less an heiress!"

"My lord!" cried Lenora, her face going white.

Again, she was ignored as Dowbridge exclaimed with icy hauteur, "I have no need to employ such arts with Miss Breckinridge. Our relationship is of long standing, and is based upon friendship and trust!"

"You have no need to employ arts, sir," interpolated Lenora angrily, "because they will do you no good, as I have told you!"

"How dare you speak of trust?" sputtered Ratherton, oblivious to her.

Dowbridge also continued his tirade. "I imagined you to be unfamiliar with the word!"

"You question my honor, sir?"

"I believe some few of us here do, my lord."

"Perhaps you will allow me to speak for myself!" cried Lenora.

Lord Ratherton did not even glance at her as he clenched his fists, his face purpling. "Then name your friends!"

Iris exclaimed, tightening her hold upon Lenora, who was fairly bristling with outrage. "Stop!" Lenora commanded, glaring at the rivals. "Stop, I say! For shame!"

The gentlemen paid her no heed, and Lenora, trembling with indignation, put Iris's arm under hers and swept away down the path, leaving the men to finish their quarrel how they would. At the entrance to the ball room, they were met by Mr. Tenby, who promptly reminded Lenora that she was promised to him for the quadrille.

Lenora, feeling rather that she would like to die than to spend one more minute with a member of the male sex, smiled dazzlingly upon him. "Forgive me, Mr. Tenby, but I cannot dance at present. A—a bunion, I fear." Her eyes glittered dangerously, and she scrupled not to enlarge this perfidy. "Iris desires nothing more than to dance the quadrille, however—do not you, my dear? How fortunate that you are, as yet, unpartnered."

So saying, she thrust Iris forward, and Mr. Tenby, covering his confusion with gentlemanly grace, proclaimed himself honored to stand up with Miss Slougham, and Iris, to her own astonishment, accepted, too shocked by recent events to be frightened by a mere dance. She was led into the set just as Tom, who had been given the intelligence that his sister had disappeared with Lord Ratherton several minutes previous, marched up to Lenora.

One look at Lenora's icy countenance told him all he wished to know, and he said curtly, "Where's the scoundrel?"

"You are too late, Tom," managed Lenora, her nostrils flaring in an effort to steady her breathing. "It seems I have no end of protectors this evening. Dowbridge has him in hand."

"Indeed?" he said through clenched teeth.

Lenora held up a staying hand. "I forbid you to interfere, Tom. Things are just as they ought to be. They have challenged each other to a duel, and if all goes well, they will relieve us both by killing each other."

Tom blinked at this, then huffed. "Nothing less likely. Dowbridge won't risk the law by doing more than graze his lordship, and if Ratherton can hit the broad side of a barn at twenty paces, I'm much mistaken. But you're not pleased? Ain't a duel romantic, or some such nonsense?"

Lenora deigned not to answer this, instead stalking off to the refreshment table, where she took up a glass of lemonade in a slightly shaking hand. After a few restorative sips, she began to regain color, and she turned to her brother, saying, "It is a great deal of nonsense, Tom, as you say. To hear them squabbling over me like two grubby schoolboys over a toy—for I assure you, I can be no more than that to either of them! Oh!" She tossed off the rest of the lemonade, her eyes sparking. "I could have wrung their necks myself!"

Remarking the paleness of her cheeks, Tom tucked her hand firmly in his arm and patted it. "That's good. You see now. There are more fish in the sea, depend upon it. But I hope you perceive by this that you're not quite up to snuff yet, my dear."

Annoyed that he may be right, Lenora was relieved to find Captain Mantell coming to claim her for the country dance. He, at least, could be trusted not to treat her as a mongrel dog does a bone, and she said as much to Tom when he looked as if he would refuse his approbation. The captain, sensing her need to be distracted, threw himself into the lively dance, encouraging her to match his activity, and by the end of the half-hour she had recovered herself tolerably enough to meet Mr. Tenby for the cotillion without disgust.

Chapter 29

LORD HELDEN, RETURNING to town the day after the ball, quickly learned that the gossips had not been favorably inclined toward his abrupt removal. Not only was he an illegitimate pretender, but his craven escape had proved it. That he had returned betimes was nothing—once a criminal, always a criminal, and nothing but a new scandal would drive that conviction from their heads. But he had grown up in London among the children of Society who mimicked their elders in everything, and so this attitude did not surprise him any more than it discouraged him. He had other, more pressing worries upon which his energy must be bent.

His sojourn to Portsmouth had yielded less than he had hoped. The information that had arrived with the last of the proofs from India had taught him to hope that good news was forthcoming—Sir Thomas Raffles had promised a messenger to arrive in England within the month, with intelligence regarding his father's property.

That messenger had been purported to have taken the ship that had docked three days earlier in Portsmouth, but when James had arrived, he had received only a note to the effect that the messenger had been obliged by illness to remain some weeks in Lisbon, and would send word as soon as he was well enough to sail.

That the man intended to take passage directly to London held some comfort, for then James would not be obliged to travel far perhaps for nothing, but it was nonetheless disheartening that he had still to wait weeks, perhaps months longer to know if he had any hope of an inheritance from his father. Such a boon would greatly diminish the brooding cloud that hung over him in London, and which threatened to overshadow everything he had worked toward with Miss Breckinridge.

There, he had high hopes. There were rumors she had a fortune, and with men of Lord Ratherton's ilk flocking to her like flies to honey, he had begun to wonder if it were true. An inheritance from his father would set him apart from such men, give him more of a chance to win her affections, and to bring his plans to fruition. He must make her trust him—that was his entire focus. It would all come to naught if she did not trust him.

Tom, finding London intolerably flat after Mr. Marshall had rallied and carried his daughter back to Brighton, discovered pressing business on his estate, and again committed Lenora to Ben's care, adjuring her not to be hen-witted while he was gone, though he had to own that Lord Helden, whom he had had occasion to meet, did seem to be a right one. Lenora took this placidly enough, but could not repress a tiny quiver of triumph at his commendation.

That evening, Tess remarked, "He is handsome, miss," as she pulled Lenora's hair into a complicated twist on the top of her head.

Lenora started, having been lost in a reverie wherein Lord Helden's brown eyes played a large part. "Who is, Tess?"

"Lord Helden, to be sure, miss—or Mr. Ingles as was," Tess replied, around a mouthful of pins. She placed them carefully and then continued, "I declare I can't take my eyes off him when he comes around, for wonder at the change. So horrid and hairy as he was, and now so gentlemanly and fine. My, but he do look like a lord!"

"That is because he is a lord, Tess," said Lenora. "We must forget that he was once in such a bad way, for it is all different now."

"But half the town is talking about it, miss," said Tess, in a matter-of-fact tone, "and it is true."

Exquisitely sensible of this, and of the necessity of quashing such rumors, she answered firmly, "Only parts of it, Tess! He was acting as caretaker to his own estate, but only out of exigency—it was not what he was born to. He was born the heir to the Engleheart estate, and it was all the work of his despicable grandfather that he found himself in such straights as required him to live in so humble a way."

This was enough to quiet Tess, who still cherished the hope of having her mistress raised to be a Lady, but the Society gossips were another matter. It seemed that everywhere she went, Lenora was to hear whispers of Lord Helden's questionable heritage, or his incredible poverty, or his unsavory character, and though she was persistent in treating all these rumors as ridiculous, she was shocked at how they had grown.

"It is as if someone is deliberately trying to blacken his character, sir," she said to Captain Mantell, as they walked in the park one day. "The rumors ought to have died down by now, oughtn't they? But something seems to be stirring them up."

Her companion grimly agreed to this, shaking his head. "That is the way with Society, however, ma'am. It is most unfortunate that no other scandals have arisen to overshadow The Usurper Lord. But one will, depend upon it. At the very least, the rumor cannot outlast the end of the season."

"I hope that is true," sighed Lenora. "For if nothing changes, I greatly fear Lord Helden's reputation will be irreparably damaged." Then, feeling she had been too transparent, she said quickly, "No one deserves to be treated thus unfairly, to be sure."

After a pause, Captain Mantell said with a mildly conscious air, "Lord Helden is a good man, Miss Breckinridge. I am glad you wish to see him right in the eyes of the world, for he certainly needs such friends as you."

Coloring, Lenora averted her face, but willingly acknowledged that Lord Helden was her friend, and proclaimed that he would have her untiring support. She was glad when he turned the subject, though it was to take leave of her.

"I must return home, and do not believe I will be coming back," he said, with a solemn set to his jaw. "I have had news—news that directly impacts my friend, Emily—that is, Mrs. Crowther."

Lenora glanced up at him in concern. "I hope it is not bad news, sir." His look convinced her it was otherwise, and she said after a pause, "If it is, then your bringing it to her must give her comfort."

"Yes, that is my sincere hope," he said with a tight smile.

She was silent, wishing she could tell him that all would be well, but his situation was too complex for her to assert such a thing. At last, she said, "Then I wish you godspeed, sir. And my best wishes for your happiness, and Emily's well-being."

The reminder of his tragic circumstances distracted her from her own concerns for an afternoon, but all too soon she was to recollect them, for she was subjected to a repetition of the rumors about Lord Helden that very night at Lady Malvern's ball. It came first from the lips of a brainless rattle with whom she had agreed to dance the cotillion, and instantly declaring such a claim to be false, it was all she could do to complete the set in tolerable charity with the gentleman, whom she had no difficulty in believing had been imposed on. But she returned to her party only to be pained by it again, this time by Lady Athena.

"I am glad that Lord Helden has not come tonight," said she, "for his appearance would set fire to all these rumors, and I am sick to death of them."

"Thank you, Athena!" cried Lenora with sincere relief. "I had not dared to hope that you would think as I do on the matter."

Her ladyship turned bland eyes to her. "You mistake me, my dear. I merely find the matter tiresome in the extreme. But I can see by your looks that you are put out by your favorite's fall from grace. I did warn you, did not I, that there was something off about him? Perhaps you could have been spared some part of this mortification had you attended to me then."

"Your solicitude is unnecessary, my lady," replied Lenora tersely. "There has been no mortification felt, for there is no truth to these rumors. I have never been so vexed in my life! That so many people of information should allow themselves to be duped by idle chatter!"

"You are not the first person in the world to have been wrong in your estimation of character, my dear," replied Lady Athena. "It is no shame to own fault in this case, for no doubt you were blinded by both naivete and partiality—the last of which I could never understand."

"No, and none could expect you to, Athena," returned Lenora, fanning herself vigorously. "The day that your affections are engaged will be one to go down in the history books. But that is neither here nor there, for it is not partiality that has brought on my indignation, but a natural sense of the injustice of such rumors being spread, and so carelessly. It could do material harm to his lordship, and he does not deserve it."

Lady Athena's reply was lost in the bustle of Iris coming to join them, and she squeezed herself between them, the better to speak with Lenora. "They have gotten to you, Lenora? I can see they have. What nasty rumors, and they trip off everyone's tongues! I do not for a moment believe them, and told Tenby so, when he was so obliging as to dance with me." She took Lenora's hands in her own. "I will do everything I can to scotch them, though I may offend everyone I speak to, for I cannot stand to have such a taint attached to your beloved Helden Hall!"

She was up and away before Lenora could retort that it was not her beloved Helden Hall, it was Lord Helden's, and she was left to bear Lady Athena's knowing looks and laughing disdain until the happy thought of escaping to the refreshment table got her out of the room. As she sipped lemonade, she was met by Mr. Dowbridge, whose civil apology for his ridiculous conduct the week previous, with the assurance that the duel had never taken place, was so much more welcome than were the caustic rumors of Lord Helden that she accepted his suggestion that he escort her out into the garden, to escape the insufferable heat of the house.

They went out across the veranda and to a bench where Lenora sat to give monosyllabic responses to his attempts at conversation. He was not a man to be easily daunted, but her manner was so terse that he soon gave up, turning to pluck the leaves and petals off a nearby flower bush.

"I suppose I can guess what has you blue-deviled," he said at last, in a tightly controlled tone. "Lord Helden has set the ton by the ears, has not he?"

"What do you mean?" demanded his companion, at last directing her gaze at him.

"His appearance in Society, so sudden and unaccountable, has set tongues flying."

"You blame him for these rumors? It is ridiculous. I cannot imagine why you continue to believe him an impostor!"

"Oh, I have given that notion up, never fear. I merely think that, had he set about it differently, there would have been no cause for suspicion," he said calmly. "But what more can one expect from a man raised in so strange a way? He has no notion of how to go on."

"No notion—" repeated Lenora, flaring up. "He is every bit the gentleman that you are—if not more, for he does not go about casting aspersions with no proof excepting baseless rumors and wild prejudice!"

His fingers crushed the bloom they were holding and he turned to her. "Do you have an interest in that man's affairs?"

"You know that I do!"

He shook his head. "I do not mean mere curiosity, Miss Breckinridge. What I mean to know is, have you come to an understanding with him?"

She blinked, and colored as his meaning became clear. "No! There has been nothing of that kind. My interest is merely in upholding the reputation of a blameless gentleman—something that I should have imagined to be the duty of us all."

He regarded her steadily for a long moment, then said, "You mistake me, Miss Breckinridge—I meant no disrespect to Lord

Helden. I meant merely that he is unaccustomed to our ways, and too innocent of the pitfalls in Polite Society, to have an easy time of it. That is all."

Pacified, she took a moment to calm herself, then said, "Forgive me, sir. I see that I have wronged you, and you do not know how glad I am to find it out. It is too true, what you say. Society is an odious monster, with no compassion and too little self-control. I am heartily sick of it."

"It is fortunate, then, that the season draws to a close," he said, shrugging and looking away. "Do you intend to spend the summer at Wrenthorpe? Or do you follow the Regent to Brighton?"

"I do not intend to follow the Regent in anything, I will have you know, sir. I believe my mother and Sir Joshua intend to return to Wrenthorpe, and I gladly go with them."

He then petitioned her for the next two dances, and Lenora accepted, reentering the ballroom with a defiant air that became even more pronounced upon her perceiving Lord Helden amongst the company. He came to her after Dowbridge had returned her to her party, and she gladly engaged to dance with him, gliding smilingly into the next set. All eyes seemed to be upon them, and Lenora stared them all down while Lord Helden's eyes remained fixed on her face.

After some time he observed, "You almost rival Lady Athena with your Great Lady airs. Am I to know what—or who—has vexed you?"

"Nothing but the stupidity of the ton, my lord," she said, her eyes bright and hard. "Had you a pleasant evening? I do not think you were here earlier."

"Dear me!" he said. "Is it as bad as that? I thought the rumors had not gained so much credence as to give anyone connected with me anxiety, but I see I am much mistaken."

Lenora was shocked at his complacence. "My lord, are you not concerned by what is being said? I cannot imagine you to be insensible of the injury that such rumors may do—nay, already have done. Everything must be done to dispel the danger before it is too late."

He smiled down at her. "With what other motive could I come here tonight? I must be seen mingling, dancing, laughing—in a word, unconcerned by gossip."

"That is exactly what you have done, time after time, and yet it does nothing!" She could not keep the note of desperation from her voice. "What if they ruin you?"

"They do not have the power to do so, Miss Breckinridge," he said, his eyes bright and warm. "I am who I claim to be, so soften your smile, talk pleasantly to me, and dance without a care in the world. A few more weeks, and my name will cease to be interesting. You will see."

She still marveled at his serenity, but his great good sense was the balm she had needed, and she took pains to comply with his directions. He continued to regard her with almost tenderness in his lovely brown eyes, and she felt her worries become lost in their depths. Their two dances were the most delightful she had ever known, and Lenora fell asleep that night on the conviction that Lord Helden was not only the bravest and wisest man on earth, but also the handsomest.

Chapter 30

In the morning, Lenora received both flowers and a note from Lord Ratherton, which she summarily threw into the fire, and a visit from Lord Helden. For him, she put on her brightest smiles, talking away the half hour very agreeably, and as he rose to leave, without ever having alluded to the rumors which had so agitated her last night, she was comfortable in the persuasion that they would both weather this very well, and bid him farewell with a light heart.

Dowbridge appeared just after Lord Helden had gone, and surprised her by inquiring after his lordship's spirits, in light of his disagreeable circumstances. With renewed charity for him, Lenora told him Lord Helden was very well, and inclined to shrug off the rumors, which he viewed as inconsequential, and she accepted with alacrity Dowbridge's invitation to drive out. Hastening to her room to change her dress, she met him in the hall, and was not unaccountably shocked to find him hobnobbing with Ben.

"This young man has agreed to come along as chaperon," was Dowbridge's response to her inquiring gaze, and Lenora, blinking away her surprise, expressed her complete approval of the scheme, leading the way down the steps to Dowbridge's well-appointed curricle.

The drive was uneventful, but much more enjoyable than Lenora had anticipated, owing both to her uplifted spirits and to Dowbridge's lightened manner, which extended itself so far as to include a reference to the desirability of Ben's accompanying them more regularly, and Lenora, with mingled amazement and approbation, agreed. She left him at the end of the drive to trip up her steps in the conviction that his was a character that she had taken much for granted, and she repented of it.

Over the next week, Lenora saw much of both Dowbridge and Lord Helden, and experienced a degree of satisfaction with each that, though wholly owing to disparate feelings, secured them in her good opinion. Dowbridge acted the perfect gentleman, never crossing the line nor referring to her rejection of his proposal, thus encouraging Lenora to believe that he had given up his suit, and increasing her comfort in his company. Furthermore, he proved himself an unwavering friend through the steady support of Lord Helden's morals and merits wherever the disagreeable rumors were met with, while Lord Helden's graceful disregard of what was being said against him so strengthened his cause that Lenora fancied she could perceive fewer disapproving looks cast his way when she was in his company. The day of his taking his seat in the House of Lords came and went, with nothing to mar its legitimacy, a circumstance which gave her such sensations of satisfaction that she could not but share them with Dowbridge when next he called to drive out with her.

"You must allow me to commend you, sir, for your very kind part in this success," she said to him with a glowing countenance. "For without your efforts, I am persuaded Lord Helden would not have met with so much forbearance. Your good offices have approved him in the eyes of many."

He nodded, taking a corner at a decent clip, which earned him a shout from Ben as to the advisability of his watching himself. Laughing, Dowbridge said, "If you are to become a tiger someday, young man, then you must learn to hang on tight, and not give opinions that may injure you in the eyes of your master."

Nevertheless, he slowed his horses, for they had entered into a part of town that was very busy, obliging him to slow even further at every crossing. It was at one of these that Ben suddenly uttered a strangled cry, and to Lenora's horror, she turned to see him carried off in the arms of a burly individual in a black coat whose collar had been turned up to obscure his face, and whose hat was pulled so low over his head as to preclude all possibility of recognition.

"Mr. Dowbridge! Stop! Oh, pray, turn back at once!" was her anguished cry. "Ben! We must go after him—he is being kidnapped!"

Dowbridge, with a smothered oath, turned the vehicle as quickly as he was able, which was not very, as the traffic just at that spot was considerable, and there seemed to be a never ending stream of pedestrians who felt inclined to take advantage of his stopping to crowd into the roadway. At last, however, he succeeded in turning the curricle, and they dashed off in the direction the burly man had taken, but their pursuit was in vain—Ben was nowhere to be seen. Up and down the surrounding streets they drove, Lenora calling after Ben, heedless of the looks cast her way, and craning her neck to see as far as possible down the side streets and alleyways.

"He cannot be gone, Mr. Dowbridge," she insisted, after what seemed like hours of searching. "I will not believe that he is gone forever!" And she gave way to tears.

Dowbridge instantly pulled up the team in a quiet side street, and put his arm around Lenora, allowing her to turn toward him and cry into the lapels of his coat. "Do not give up hope, Miss Breckinridge. I will take you home now, but will return immediately to this spot, and will search until I can search no longer."

Wholly overpowered by her emotions, Lenora conceded to this plan, accepting his handkerchief and drying her eyes only to wet them anew. By the time Curzon Street was reached, both his handkerchief and her own were so sodden that he bid her keep them both, adjuring her again not to despair. With broken thanks and a sorrowful heart, Lenora clasped his hand tightly, giving him a speaking look before treading up the steps to break the news to her mother.

Lady Stiles was at her dressing table preparing for dinner when Lenora came into the room, her aspect one of stunned desperation. Her ladyship jumped up, nearly upsetting her powder box, and greatly annoying Sanford, who had been arranging her hair and who now stood glaring at the intruder with hairpins protruding from between her lips.

"Oh, my dear, what is the matter?" cried Lady Stiles, leading Lenora to a chair and hanging solicitously over her. "You look as though you had seen a ghost! Are you ill? Tell me what has happened!"

"Mama," murmured Lenora, nearly exhausted by her emotions, "Ben has been kidnapped. He was taken just now from the back of Mr. Dowbridge's curricle."

Lady Stiles sank to her knees beside Lenora, her stunned gaze riveted on her daughter's face. Lenora continued in a subdued tone,

"We made chase but could not follow them. Oh, Mama, I am sure it was his old master, that horrid, odious Baxter, and he will be made to sleep in the coal bin, and we shall never see him again!"

She subsided into weeping and her mother, rising unsteadily to her feet, turned her sightless gaze toward Sanford, and shocked them all by fainting dead away.

The uproar that ensued was indicative of the extreme abnormality of Lady Stiles exhibiting this sort of weakness, she having never done so in all of Lenora's memory, nor her maid's. Sanford flitted about the room, searching for the vinaigrette, and Lenora rallied herself to call a maid to bring burnt feathers, and to send instantly for a physician and Sir Joshua, who was at his club.

Despite this upheaval, the news of Ben's disappearance spread like wildfire through the house, for Sanford's movements to relieve her mistress were accompanied by dark mutterings on the event, which she held to be solely responsible for her ladyship's present state of insensibility, and nearly every servant was thrown into disorder either by this news or by Lady Stiles' incapacity. It was nearly three quarters of an hour before relative peace was restored—Lady Stiles had been revived and was shut up in her bedroom with Sir Joshua and the physician; Lenora had been taken to bed attended by a watchful Tess; and Blaine, who had stood stunned for a full five minutes upon hearing that little Ben was gone, had rather violently gone back to work over the stove, merely sniffing a great deal amidst the crash of pots and pans, and muttering her grief over her sainted lamb lost in this heathen town, and at the mercy of cutthroats and villains.

Sanford, descending to the kitchens to prepare a tisane for her mistress, had witnessed Cook's initial response, which made her look even more disdainful than usual, and she carried out her errand without a word to the distraught woman, but as she ascended the stairs to Lady Stiles' bedchamber, she was heard to utter that if the villain who had made this mischief knew what was good for him, he would give up the boy, and quick-like, for no family deserved to be broken up and set at sixes and sevens, and she wouldn't stand for it, no matter that the boy was a great bother and nuisance.

The evening passed as if in anticipation of a funeral, for if anyone had the heart to speak, it was only in whispers, and her ladyship and Miss had both cried themselves to sleep. The morning brought Tom, whom they had sent for by express, and whose wild appearance attested to his state of mind. He set about being very much in the way in his anxiety to be of use, and when Dowbridge arrived late in the morning, to say he had found nothing, the entire household rejoiced at Tom's engaging to join him in the search.

"You must not despair, I entreat you," said Dowbridge, bowing over Lenora's hand. "I have alerted certain acquaintances of mine, who know others with a knack of discovering secrets, and who might succeed in putting us on the trail of our quarry ere long. We will apprise you instantly of any news."

So saying, he and Tom quitted the house. The day passed in a languor that made time seem to stand still, while there was much sniffling and subdued remembrances of Ben's cheerful eagerness, requiring the maids to be continually at work to provide a supply of fresh handkerchiefs to all the principal ladies in the house, for even Sanford had occasion to wipe away a tear, though why she should mourn Ben's absence was a mystery to all.

That evening, however, was to bring the first sign of hope, for Tom arrived with news—but his mien suggested that his intelligence was of a disturbing nature. Lenora, who was first to welcome him, felt a a sudden foreboding at sight of his face, and was obliged to sit quickly down beside her mother, who had at last been suffered to leave her bed and sit in the saloon, propped up by pillows and with Sir Joshua ready at hand.

"Dowbridge has discovered Ben's whereabouts," Tom said, with a gravity so out of keeping with his character that his listeners were instantly at attention. "He is being held in a house near the dockyards, where Dowbridge is at this moment keeping watch."

He hesitated, and Lady Stiles inquired urgently, "Have you seen him? Is he well? Tom, is he unharmed?"

"I haven't seen him. I went with Dowbridge to the house, and watched for some time—" Here he stopped again, glancing with a concerned eye toward Lenora, who blanched at the look, and steeled herself for what her heart warned was to be a blow. Tom looked down and continued, "We saw only two people enter the house together: a burly man who, I am told, answered the description of Ben's abductor, and the other was—Lord Helden."

Chapter 31

LADY STILES CRIED out, and Lenora, whose chest felt as though it had suddenly gone hollow, could not find breath enough to make a response. She swayed in her chair, a hand going out to grip the armrest until her knuckles went white, as the import of his words penetrated to her brain. Lord Helden was at the place where Ben was being held prisoner. Lord Helden apparently knew Ben's captor—possibly from his former life as James Ingles.

But it did not make sense. She heard herself say, "It could not be Lord Helden. He was called from town two days ago."

Tom turned to her with a deeply disturbed expression. "It was he. As sure as I'm standing here."

"Oh dear," murmured Lady Stiles, and she glanced at Lenora, who sat staring sightless before her.

Countless possibilities clamored in Lenora's imagination. Lord Helden could easily have returned to town—or he could never have left it. And he had told her himself that he had worked at the docks, before he had learned of his inheritance. Still, it was entirely possible that he could know Ben's captor, yet not know of Ben's captivity. He had not been apprised of the circumstance, for he had been gone. But it was also entirely possible that Lord Helden not only knew of Ben's captivity, but had orchestrated the whole using his absence as a pretense, and meant to use the boy as leverage—for what, she could not say.

Tom went on. "Dowbridge hopes to discover a way to free the boy without recourse to the law, for that, as you may surmise, could involve us all in the discomfort of public scrutiny, which would be distasteful at best. He assures me that his associates, who informed him of the boy's whereabouts, may be useful also in that direction."

Benumbed, Lenora nevertheless joined with her mother in charging Tom to carry their thanks to Mr. Dowbridge, expressing their willingness to be summoned at any time to do anything that was thought necessary for the safe return of their young charge. As soon as Tom had gone out, she escaped to her room to consider what could possess Lord Helden to do such an odious thing as to abduct a small, helpless—but by no means friendless—boy. Ben was no one to anybody, except to the Stiles household, and the only use for his ransom was to influence them in some way. But Lord Helden already held great influence there, at least over Lenora. Why he should feel it necessary to obtain such a security, she could not conceive, unless he had no notion of the strength of her feelings for him, which she found difficult to believe.

A more troubling idea occurred to her then, which turned her blood cold. Perhaps the rumors of his unworthiness were true, in a way. Perhaps, even if he were of noble blood, and the true heir to the

Engleheart estate, he had been ruined by his misfortunes—or, worse, had been tainted by the blood of his despicable grandfather—and was indeed no better than the loathsome drunkard she had once thought him to be. He may easily have discovered the existence of her fortune, as had Lord Ratherton, and his conscience, if her fears were true, would offer no scruple against his hedging his bets, as it were, and providing himself security against the possibility of her discovering his true character and refusing to bestow upon him her hand and her fortune.

The more she considered this possibility, the more conflicted she became. On the one hand, she had only to conjure up the image of Lord Helden, smiling down at her with those warm brown eyes, to instantly reject the awful notion as utterly false. On the other hand, the recent resurgence of rumors, and her own admission of concern over them, would have alerted an unscrupulous man to danger, and moved him to take this shameful step in the hopes of forestalling the inevitable revulsion of her esteem when his true character would have become known. That he should not consider that an attempt at forcing her acceptance, despite the knowledge of a tainted character, would rather make her more disgusted by him and in no way likely to accede to his demands with any tenderness of feeling, caused her again to doubt, but her agitation of spirits would not allow her to entirely dismiss the idea.

The rest of the day passed as some sort of a nightmare, and Sir Joshua stayed with them, to uplift the ladies' sagging spirits with his own quiet optimism and to make himself useful. When Lenora suggested that he might go with Tom and Dowbridge to rescue Ben, he maintained that his attendance upon those gentlemen would be both unnecessary and undesirable, as too many in the party would undoubtedly alert Ben's abductors to their having been discovered. Lenora was brought to see the good sense in this, and Sir Joshua, therefore, spent his time in supporting his wife and daughter, and in listening with unfeigned kindness to the cook's lamentations over the godlessness of a city that could harbor the likes of such villains as would carry off innocent boys and leave their homes desolate.

That afternoon, as Lenora sat in anxious rumination over her needlework, a note was brought her by the footman, who informed her that a small urchin had brought it "for the young lady what lives here." Knitting her brows, she opened it and read:

> *My dear Miss Breckinridge,*
>
> *I hope this missive finds you tolerably well, though I am certain my news will make you feel much better. I have discovered the whereabouts of your young friend, Ben, and will only too willingly disclose them to you, if you will but meet me, alone, at ten in the evening, at the church by the dockyards, and engage to satisfy one stipulation, which I will reveal at our meeting. I know I may rely upon your secrecy, for you know what is at stake.*
>
> *Yours, etc.,*
>
> *Lord Helden*

The shock of receiving such a letter held her spellbound for many minutes, for not only was she amazed at the contents—at once conciliatory and threatening, and in all ways impertinent—but she was struck by the style and look of the letter, which impressed her with such a dreadful conviction that she could not move. At last, however, she forced her limbs into motion, and went upstairs in a state of bemusement, going immediately to her writing desk and removing a letter contained therein. Again, she sat staring, first at one letter, and then at the other, for several minutes, her head revolving what she had not wished ever to have confirmed, but which could not be denied, lying in neat print before her very eyes.

Suddenly, her mind found some sort of equilibrium, and she put the letters away, drawing out a clean sheet of hot-pressed paper and pulling her pen from the standish. Writing quickly, she dashed off a short missive to Tom, apprising him of the astonishing letter and desiring him to come home instantly. Rising, she went out of the room, nearly colliding with the footman, who brought the tidings that Sir Joshua had requested that she wait on her mother in the drawing room.

Lenora's almost fierce answer startled the boy. "That is excellent, Simon. I will go to her directly, but do you deliver this letter, and we will see if we cannot get the best of the traitor after all."

So saying, she hurried down the stairs, leaving the footman to wonder who the traitor was, and why Miss must speak in riddles when things were already so terribly mysterious.

The dockyard church was a dismal building, tucked between two tall, dingy warehouses, and surrounded by a forbidding iron fence. Had she been in another mind, Lenora should have thrilled at the sight of it, and fancied all sorts of Gothic horrors awaited her inside its solemn walls, but her imagination being wholly caught up in the meeting to come, it could not be spared to the church.

"I never thought I'd be meeting a murderer, miss," breathed Tess, who sat across from her in Sir Joshua's carriage, peeking through the blind at the deserted pavement. "What my mother would say—oh! My heart is like to burst!"

"He is not a murderer, Tess," replied Lenora, with a calm she did not feel. "He is only an abductor, and soon will not even be that."

"But he always will, miss! He took poor Ben, and if he gives him up, he still took him in the first place."

Lenora allowed this to be true, but held to the conviction that a gentleman who was so misguided as to resort to abduction, and failed at it, was more likely to vanish into the undistinguished shadows of obscurity than to embark on a career in villainy. This particular gentleman, she maintained, whose reputation was at stake, should invariably retreat from his course once they had done with him.

"I still get the shivers," replied Tess, unwilling to relinquish the terror of the moment. "There's no knowing what else he may have done, before this, for we don't rightly know what he could have been doing before you made his acquaintance, miss."

Lenora, perhaps fatigued by her maid's raptures, merely hummed a reply, and kept watch out her side of the blind. The pavement, however, was still empty, disappearing into the deep shadows on either side of the church door, and when she consulted her watch, she saw that he was late. She did not know how much longer she could stay patiently. Her body quivered with want of activity, but knowing that her part tonight was as a bystander, she forced herself to remain quiet, tapping her feet on the floor of the coach to relieve some of her pent up energy.

At last, Tess cried out that someone was coming, and Lenora peeked out to see a figure striding along the pavement toward them, a link boy in his wake. It took all her will not to throw open the door and confront Lord Helden herself, and she clenched her hands in her lap, keeping her eye trained on his approaching figure outside.

Before his lordship came abreast with the coach, however, another figure detached itself from the shadows and intercepted him, stopping him with a hand held up. Lord Helden, by his expression, took exception to what was said next, and retorted angrily, but his words, and the words of his accuser, did not penetrate the glass of the window.

Yearning to have some part in this confrontation, yet knowing it to be imperative that she did not, Lenora pressed her ear to the glass, but could not discern more than a few words. She heard "snake" and "eyes have been opened" from one, and what sounded like hot denials from the other. At last, Lord Helden turned on his heel and stalked away, and Lenora quickly let down the glass at the approach of the other figure.

"I have called his bluff, Miss Breckinridge," said Mr. Dowbridge in a low, decisive tone. "He knows we are onto him, and is no doubt headed to remove Ben to a new location. But he will not succeed. I am off to follow him, and depend upon it, I shall deliver Ben, safe and sound, to you tomorrow morning."

Her eyes glittering, Lenora had time only to look her thanks before he was off into the shadows that had swallowed his quarry. Turning to Tess, she smiled triumphantly. "Now, we will see if all can be done as we have planned. I wish I were a man, but perhaps it is best I am not, for if I were to follow after them, I should not be responsible for my actions once Ben is taken into the open, and I am certain of his guilt. Oh!" she cried, lifting clenched hands into the air, "The perfidy and the maliciousness, and the inconstancy of man! It is said that women are more susceptible to weakness of that kind, but I tell you, this proves that misbegotten notion wrong."

Whether Tess followed any or all of this speech Lenora did not wait to determine, tapping the roof of the coach in a signal to the coachman to return to Curzon Street, and the two young ladies settled to their own meditations as the coach was given to the swirling shadows of the passing night.

Chapter 32

THE FOLLOWING MORNING, after having slept uncomfortably, Lord Helden at once made up his mind to approach Miss Breckinridge and confess all. There were many things he had not told her, wishing to save her from disappointment—or from disillusionment—but he saw now that he had been mistaken to have kept the whole truth from her. It did not signify what mortifications he may have to endure, for he flattered himself that, once all had been revealed, her natural compassion and generosity would overcome any disgust she may be inclined to feel, and then he could work to make her love him.

That she was already kindly disposed toward him, he had begun to believe, despite Dowbridge's increased attentions of late, but that gentleman's words to him last night had left him in doubt. She had been terribly upset by the rumors that had been flying about him, but these had quietened of late, and he had anticipated little more trouble from that quarter. So Dowbridge's claims that Miss Breckinridge had discovered his lies—and was disgusted enough never to wish to see him again—he would not credit. It was true that she had, in maidenly modesty, disclaimed any desire to become Lady Helden, but she had also encouraged James's attentions of late, which indicated with near certainty that Dowbridge had been grossly misled by jealousy. And though James's circumstances were not nearly as felicitous as those of Mr. Dowbridge, he would not give up the hope that, if all else failed, Miss Breckinridge's love of Helden Hall would make her his at last.

In this optimistic frame of mind, he made his way on foot to Curzon Street, coming within sight of the house just as a smart curricle drove up beside him. He turned his head to see Dowbridge smirking down at him with a mocking gleam in his eye.

"Will you never give up?" he inquired, holding his dancing pair with an effort. "One cannot imagine what you hope to accomplish by forcing your irksome presence upon our fair acquaintance, after what I have told you."

"You cannot stop me, sir," James replied irritably.

Dowbridge laughed. "Perhaps not, but I can detain you. It happens that I have an appointment with Miss Breckinridge, which I flatter myself shall render your visit moot. You may choose to follow me if you wish, but I fear such an action will merely precipitate an unpleasant scene, which we should all desire to avoid. You'd do better to try your luck back where you came from, where, no doubt, there is a lady who, unlike the lady in question, will not take exception to your antecedents!"

On this valediction, he gave his pair the office, and off they went down the short remainder of the street, to pull up in front of Miss Breckinridge's residence. As James watched, Dowbridge hopped down from the curricle, leaning back in to lift out a smaller figure in his arms. He turned toward the house just as the front door opened and Miss Breckinridge herself flew down the steps, almost throwing herself at Dowbridge in her apparent ecstasy.

James stood, staring speechless at this wonderful reunion, until Miss Breckinridge at last stepped away from Dowbridge, who set down the smaller figure and followed her into the house. As the door closed behind the happy trio, Helden's heart thudded from somewhere in the vicinity of his boots, his mind refusing to believe that all Dowbridge had claimed last night was true, though his eyes had witnessed the proof of it. Miss Breckinridge had chosen Dowbridge over himself, and there was nothing he could do about it but give her up forever. In absolute despondency, he turned back the way he had come, retracing his steps while giving way to ruminations which would have alarmed anyone who could read his mind, had there been anyone who cared enough for him to try.

※

Lenora, having kept watch at the window, was the first to receive intelligence of Mr. Dowbridge's arrival, and hastened to the door, throwing it open and flying down the steps, to catch Ben to her in a fierce embrace. As Ben was in the arms of Mr. Dowbridge, this was both awkward and improper—though she was in no mind to care for that—but Mr. Dowbridge's suggestion that the happy reunion could, with advantage, be accomplished within doors, seconded by Ben's vociferous complaints that she was squashing him to jelly, quelled Lenora's ecstasy enough to release her hold on her young charge, and all three mounted the steps on their own power.

Having reluctantly given Ben over to the care of a maid—who was almost instantly relieved of him by Blaine, who came bustling up the stairs at the sound of his piping voice in the hall, and who snatched him to her bosom with a great many blessings upon his and all the heads who could be responsible for his return—Lenora led Mr. Dowbridge into the drawing room, where there were assembled Sir Joshua, Lady Stiles, and Tom. Mr. Dowbridge bowed grandly and pressed Lady Stiles' hand with a self-assured smile.

"This has all come to a most surprising end, sir," said she, gazing enigmatically up at him from the sofa.

"It is most gratifying to have been in any way a part of restoring your family's happiness," returned Mr. Dowbridge. "In serving to both enlighten and relieve you, I have received the greatest honor, I assure you."

"Relieved we are, most certainly," said Sir Joshua gravely. "The return of our young Ben, whole and hardy as he is, has answered our highest hopes, but it is hard to ascertain whether this, or the enlightenment which has come to us through these events, will be the longer-lasting blessing."

"Ah! Yes," said Dowbridge, seating himself upon a chair and regarding his hosts with a somber countenance. "The discovery of such duplicity among your friends I am sure has been a sore trial, and it was with the utmost reluctance that I should have been the instrument of revelation to you, had not circumstances placed me as the only means by which you could be both righted and undeceived. I saw it as my duty, however, and may only be pleased by the happy result."

"As are we," agreed Sir Joshua, crossing his arms across his chest. "But as all is well that ends well, I will not beat about the bush. You cannot be insensible of our great curiosity, Mr. Dowbridge, to know if you bribed the individual who abducted Ben, or if he was one of your—er—less exalted acquaintance?"

Dowbridge gave a visible start. "Pardon?"

"And how did you entice Lord Helden to enter a certain house near the dockyards with that man? Was he actually the same man, or another person entirely—an acquaintance of his lordship who conveniently fit the description of your friend?"

Their visitor had gone quite white. "I do not have the pleasure of understanding you, sir," he said, his voice trembling ever so slightly.

Sir Joshua shook his head. "You must forgive my disbelief in such a weakness prevailing in the brain that was able to refine so plausible a scheme."

"You are under a grave misapprehension, sir," said Dowbridge, jerking to his feet. "Lord Helden is the one to whom you must direct these questions—he is indisputably—"

"Do you take us for fools?" cried Tom, stepping angrily forward. "How much more drivel do you intend to spout, to no purpose? We know the whole, and there is nothing you may say to bamboozle us."

The blood rushed back into Mr. Dowbridge's face, and his nervous gaze flicked from one face to another, finally resting once more on Tom's. "What are you saying? You saw Lord Helden enter the house where Ben was imprisoned—you saw his captor—"

"I saw Lord Helden enter a house, and with a burly individual whom you claimed was Ben's captor, but it was not his lordship who led me back there last night—"

"For I followed Lord Helden directly back to his lodging," interpolated Sir Joshua calmly.

"And it was not Lord Helden who removed Ben from the house and transported him to your lodging," finished Tom.

"It means nothing! Lord Helden sent a note—to Miss Breckinridge!"

Dowbridge appealed to Lenora. "You wrote to Tom of it, Miss Breckinridge! It proves his complicity!"

"Do you refer to this note?" inquired Lenora coolly, pulling the paper from her reticule. "It would have indicated his complicity, had it been written by him. But it was not."

"How can you know this? Did he deny it? You cannot trust him—he is a—"

"I know it was not written by him," cut in Lenora, her voice unsteady with emotion, "because it is not in his hand. This is Lord Helden's hand, sir, and it is not at all alike." She produced another note for Dowbridge's inspection, and his eyes flew from one to the other in disbelief. "I fancy," she added, "if you were to write something just now, we should find a similarity, however."

Flushing, he cried, "If he did not do this thing, he should have done another! He is an impostor, and is not worthy to be among us—is not worthy to aspire to the hand of such a one as you!"

"One such as I? Do you mean an heiress?" returned Lenora in indignation. " Lord Helden is more honorable than you ever will be, for he at least never pretended to love me! I shudder to recall that I once called you friend—you, who are false to the bottom of your heart!"

Mr. Dowbridge stared at her in disbelief, then at each of her companions in turn. Then his countenance underwent an ugly change. "I never should have pursued you, no matter the size of your fortune!" he retorted, abandoning all pretense. "You are nothing but a Jade! Carrying on a clandestine correspondence, with a man of James Ingles' stamp—"

But he was not destined to finish this declaration, for Tom hit him hard enough that he nearly lost his footing, and when he flung himself back at his attacker, Tom floored him with a hard right. He stood over him, his look venomous, as Dowbridge writhed on the carpet, his eye blackening and blood oozing from a cut on his lip.

After a long minute, Tom looked up, blinking. "I beg your pardon, Mama, Nora. I suppose I ought not to have subjected you to such an exhibition."

"I'd lay odds they enjoyed it," said Sir Joshua, smiling wryly.

"Indeed, I did," said Lady Stiles decisively, then held a hand out to her husband, indicating that she was ready to remove to her sitting room.

"Many thanks for doing the job so neatly, Tom," added Sir Joshua. "You'd better see to it he is removed from the premises. If his father weren't such an old friend, I'd have him consigned to the magistrate, but I doubt the neighborhood could bear such a scandal. It is to be hoped that he has learned his lesson." And he led his lady from the room.

Dowbridge groaned while Tom got him to his feet, but he offered no resistance as he was escorted out.

Chapter 33

BEN ENJOYED SEVERAL days of coddling by everyone in the house, excepting Sanford, who merely sniffed when she passed by him, though once a maid swore she saw Sanford pat his head, but could never be certain. Blaine kept him by her side all the day long, pressing sweets and buns upon him, and listening with glowing eyes to his recital of all his adventure in the Bad Man's house, and nodding sagely when he declared that he had always known that Dowbridge to be a wrong'un.

Within two days of the affair, Lord and Lady Mintlowe and Dowbridge, with all their entourage, were heard to have removed from town, and a day following that, Iris arrived to take leave of her friend, charging her most straightly to keep her apprised of any changes at Helden Hall, or with its master. To this, Lenora colored delicately and promised to do her poor best.

Lady Stiles, in the relief of having Ben restored to her, resigned herself to Lenora's tendre for Mr. Ingles—or rather, Lord Helden—and joined her husband in the sanguine hope that he should prove to be as adept as Tom in turning a neglected estate to account. Their complacency, however, was short-lived, for Lord Helden did not appear at the house, and Lenora's confidence dwindled into pensive anxiety. She expected to see Lord Helden—she anticipated his coming every day—but the days passed, and he did not come. Her taste for society all but vanished, and the few delights offered by the waning season held little fascination for her, especially after it was borne in upon her that the master of Helden Hall had unaccountably withdrawn, not only from her, but from Society.

At last Lenora prevailed upon Tom to write to him, but when his letter was returned unopened, and his sister seemed truly inclined to investigate matters herself, Tom offered to pay his lordship a call, and went off with Ben to his address. Within the hour, they returned with the intelligence that his room at the hotel had been let to another gentleman, and that Lord Helden was gone.

Bewilderment was the only word to describe Lenora's sensations on hearing this news. Why he should have occasion to leave London before the end of the season, and when his attentions to her had become so marked, she could not fathom. He had known of Lady Stiles's intention to remain fixed in Curzon Street at least a few more weeks, and Lenora could not but feel ill-used at his quitting town without so much as a take leave.

As she considered the singularity of his sudden departure, she recalled the night at the dockyard church, when Dowbridge had confronted him, and wondered again what had been said. She imagined Dowbridge must have flung some baseless accusations at his lordship, but could not conceive of why that would drive him from town when the horrid rumors had not done so.

She was at last forced to admit the idea that perhaps she had chased him away with her wide-eyed, romantic, silly notions. He had never, after all, given definite indications of an attachment to her. He had flirted and hinted and made her feel very comfortable in his company, but so too had Captain Mantell, whom she knew never to have cherished romantic sentiments toward her. Her fascination with Helden Hall may well have led her to believe Lord Helden's intentions were more than what they were, and perhaps he had known it, and this was why he had removed early from town.

The contemplation of these ideas was so mortifying that Lenora succumbed to a decline which, contrary to her mother's expectations, was not the least enjoyable to her, but dreary in the extreme. She wished to be done with everything, to run away to nowhere. She longed for a change, but dreaded it at the same time. Nothing and nobody held any interest for her, and food was a burden.

Tess, at first delighted by her mistress's malady, lavished every care upon her that a girl of her resource could muster. Hot baths, smelling salts, hartshorn and water, tisanes, and basins of gruel each made their appearance in Lenora's darkened bed chamber, and as quickly were discarded. Not one to be easily deterred, Tess rubbed Lenora's feet and wrapped her in blankets that had been warmed by the fire, and brushed her hair for half an hour together, and read to her from her favorite Gothic novels.

But Lenora could not appreciate these as she had done in the past, for her loss of James Ingles had at last taught her what true romance was. She found that she cared very little for the romance depicted in books, of daring deeds and high-flown vows—like those of Lord Ratherton, that had entertained but not fulfilled her—and her opinion of the happiness promised by the acquisition of wealth was nonexistent. But now that it seemed lost to her forever, she did care very much for the comfort and security assured by love, for the oneness of purpose and mutual respect engendered by a deep and lasting attachment, which she had believed had subsisted between herself and Lord Helden. But it seemed that she had been mistaken, and she was certain that, in the absence of this kind of attachment—this kind of romance—even the deep connection she had felt for Helden Hall—the connection she had been persuaded was her destiny—was hollow and meaningless.

It was at this point that Tess began to feel real anxiety for her mistress, and redoubled her efforts to reclaim her from the depths to which she had withdrawn. She approached Tom about the possibility of his discovering whether Lord Helden had loved Lenora or no, and very nearly rang a peal over him when he told her he wasn't such a gudgeon as to make a fool of himself, even for his only sister. She turned instead to Ben, asking him how likely it was that he could find a stray puppy or a kitten that wasn't too mangy, and hadn't any fleas, that they could wash up and present to their mistress.

"For she's as lovelorn as any young lady could be, Ben," wiping a tear from her eye with a corner of her apron, "and I'm that close to despairing over her ever coming back to us, unless that Lord Helden can be made to come up to scratch!"

"I don't know as how he could be," remarked Ben, squinting up at her. "Since that wrong 'un, Dowbridge, told him she don't wish to see him no more."

Tess, stunned at this revelation, required him to explain instantly where he had come upon this information, and was outraged to find that he had overheard it over a week ago, when dozing in Dowbridge's curricle upon his return home. With a cry, she swooped upon the startled little boy, grabbing his shoulders and looking him fiercely in the eye. "Do you tell me you knew all this time that that—that villain made Lord Helden believe Miss didn't like him?"

Ben managed a nod, and Tess put him from her in disgust, promising to deal with him in unspecified terms and at a later date before flying up the stairs to Lenora's bed chamber and throwing open the door, flinging wide the drapes and drawing a moan of protest from her mistress.

"Miss!" she cried, unheeding of Lenora's distress. "Your Tess will cure you at last, for I've just found out that Lord Helden didn't leave on account of anything you done, but what that horrid, odious—oh! I could wring his neck! That Dowbridge drove him off, with lies about you not liking him, and Lord Helden is likely wandering the ruined manor, bewailing his lost love and wishing he were dead!"

Lenora blinked at her, two spots of color coming into her wan cheeks. "What are you saying, Tess? Who told you this?"

"That scamp Ben heard it when he was supposed to be asleep in the curricle, when that—that man brought him home, and he stopped and talked to Lord Helden, who was on the street, and told him you was wishful of never seeing his face again! Why Ben didn't see fit to part with that information until now, I'll never know, nor will I forgive him!"

"You will forgive him, Tess, because he is my hero!" cried Lenora, jumping up from her bed, and swaying a little as her unaccustomed legs wobbled beneath her.

Tess, indignant at this gross misapplication of recognition, stared at her mistress for a full minute before declaring, "If he is, I don't know why, miss, for it's not him who's been fetching and carrying, and bathing you and reading to you, and brushing your hair til his arm's like to fall off! If he's to get credit for curing you, all for saying a word he'd ought to have said days ago, then I'll take myself off back to my mother, and see if she can make use of me!"

"No! Tess, my dear, dear Tess!" responded Lenora, leaning on the bedpost. "Ben's heroism pales next to your own! It needn't even be said! You, my dear Tess, have shown more patience than a Pamela, and more kindness than a Camilla! You know I could never do without you, and I beg you will not forsake me, just when I will need a faithful companion to support me in reuniting with my one true love!"

This speech mollified Tess enough that she sniffed, and said that she hoped she wasn't so ungrateful as to know what her duty was.

"Excellent," said Lenora, as she groped toward the dressing table. "I must dress! Oh, dear, my head—fetch me some food, Tess. I am getting up!"

When Lady Stiles received the intelligence that her daughter had not only risen from her bed, but was at that moment consuming a hearty repast, she repaired instantly to the invalid's bedchamber to behold the event with her own disbelieving eyes. Lenora greeted her mother with the desire to know when they should return to Wrenthorpe Grange, to which her ladyship responded that they had formed the immediate intention of a removal.

"Thank you, Mama! May we go tomorrow? Tom may take me in his curricle, and I shall not mind the distance at all. Tess is even now packing a portmanteau. Oh, please, may I go instantly?"

"Certainly, my dear! Though we cannot possibly be ready tomorrow. But if Tom is agreeable, you both may go as soon as you are ready. But my love," said Lady Stiles, with some hesitation, "I trust you recollect that the Mintlowes have already left town, and may be at Stinton Abbey."

"It doesn't signify, Mama," replied Lenora. "I am not so unreasonable as to expect that Lord and Lady Mintlowe should remove from their home simply to save me embarrassment."

"It is something I could hope they would do, however, to save themselves embarrassment, for it was their son who perpetrated a very great evil against us, and not the other way around."

Lenora acknowledged this was so, and asserted that she cared not what the Mintlowes did, for she had washed her hands of Dowbridge and that was that.

"Well, my dear, if you are certain, for I cannot deny that I also wish to go home, for something has happened, beyond this very regrettable affair, that has given me a very determined dislike for London." Lenora looked an inquiry, and her mother, looking once again as though she had swallowed a canary, continued, "Sir Joshua has discovered that he is to be a new father, and he is very anxious that the mother of his child should be safe at home before any other danger may befall the family. Under any other circumstances, I should have argued against him, for I hate nothing more than to be taken from pleasure to be wrapped in cotton wool, but after the events of the last few weeks, I own I shall be glad to be coddled and cared for and generally spoilt for a time."

Stunned, Lenora stared at her mother for several moments before exclaiming, "Mama! Is that what made you swoon? Good heaven, I don't know whether I am on my head or my heels! And that is why Sanford was so emotional. I shall have a little brother—or sister—it does not signify which! It could be both! I shall love them and care for them—you will see what a good nurse I shall be!"

"Dear me!" cried her mother, laughing. "Pray do not wish twins upon me! For a woman in my time of life to be breeding is accounted very precarious, and I will thank you not to increase my danger by doubling my burden! If Sir Joshua heard you, he should lock me in my room and never allow me out of bed, for which I would never forgive you!"

"Oh, Mama, pardon me," said Lenora with a delighted smile. "You know I would never wish you harm. But I do intend to be of the greatest use to you, even after—"

"After?" asked her mother, with a lift to her eyebrows.

"I will only promise that, whatever occurs, I will always be of as much use to you as I can," answered Lenora lightly, returning her attention to the plate on the tray before her.

Chapter 34

AS IT TRANSPIRED, it was some few days before Lenora ventured forth through the Home Wood toward Helden Hall, for no sooner had she gained the conviction that James Ingles loved her, than she began to doubt. If he loved her, why had he not come to the point in London? He had not lacked opportunity, and unless she was mistaken, she had given him ample encouragement. But perhaps he had taken her protestations that she had given up the notion of being mistress of Helden Hall too much to heart, in which case Dowbridge's intelligence, though wrong, could have decided him against her, and even a knowledge of his rival's perfidy might not be enough to reignite his interest.

She went round and round with this kind of thinking until, driven nearly distracted, she felt she could not stand four walls crowding her any longer, and resolved to end her uncertainty once for all, and discover James's feelings. Her feet fairly flew down the path she had taken so many times last autumn, and after very few minutes, she found herself once again at the edge of the riotous lawn leading down to Helden Hall. The once-beloved sight had little power over her as she plunged through high summer grasses, caring not that her skirts were all over drenched in dew and patterned with clinging enchanter's nightshade and petals of red helleborine.

She came around the front of the house, scarcely noticing the dismally staring windows and lichen-crusted lintels in favor of craning to see if smoke came up from the chimney of the lodge. There was none, but she went on, even as the uncertainty of her reception sent her heart drumming. If he did not wish to see her, she did not know how she would bear it, but not knowing would be worse, she was persuaded. Recollecting his smiles and quizzing humor, and the way he looked at her as they danced, she reasoned that he was, at the very least, a friend to her, and could not refuse to see her, if he was there. So she went to the door and knocked.

There was no answer. Her heart thudding in her chest, she peered into the dingy windows, and saw the bed neatly made, brogues tucked beside it, and a bowl sitting on the hob, over coals that glowed on the hearth. He was here—it must be he! She knocked again, and again, then stopped herself—she was acting the fool. He was not in the cottage, and she need not beat down the door merely out of impatience! She would simply have to come back another time.

Turning, she wended her way back up the rutted drive until she found herself in front of the Big House again. She looked up at its beloved facade, counting the broken windows and tracing the vines of ivy that hung green and glorious across the frames. Would he ever redeem this beautiful place? Was that why he had returned, to do what little he could, and bide his time? If only he could know just how much she longed to help him, to support him—to love and be loved by him.

The door creaked, and her eye fell to regard it—had it creaked open? Stepping closer, she saw that it was slightly ajar, and her pulse pattered in her throat. He must be inside—did she dare follow him? Of course she did. He had given her carte blanche months ago, and nothing had occurred to nullify that, even if he did not love her. Besides, if she did not speak to him today, she would die of uncertainty. Steeling her courage, she pushed open the door and went into the gloom.

Once more in the lofty entry hall, Lenora gazed about, searching for clues as to where he had gone. Surely, not upstairs. Only empty rooms were upstairs. And downstairs held only the dismal kitchens. But everywhere was empty and dismal. She shuddered. The Hall was as pathetic and forlorn to her now as it appeared to other people, and she longed for it to be restored, so that light and laughter and noise and bustle could once more exist in its rooms, and all the despair and loneliness and shame it had known would be buried forever beneath a new and virtuous life.

She walked through the hall to the corridor and, peering through an archway into the saloon, perceived a figure sitting in the middle of the floor. Her breath caught, and a fearful excitement thrilled through her body, down to her fingertips, so that she was obliged to take a deep, steadying breath before striding into the room. Her footfalls were deadened by the dust that billowed about in the light breezes from the broken windows, but his head turned almost as soon as she started toward him. His eyes widened, and he leapt to his feet, brushing the dust from his breeches and staring at her as if she were a ghost.

"Well, Mr. Ingles—my Lord Helden." She gave a nervous laugh. "I fear I shall never know what to call you now. Here is where I came to know you as Mr. Ingles. But without the beard, and with proper clothes," she indicated the buff breeches and dark blue coat and elegant cravat he wore, "you are much more Lord Helden to me."

"Helden will do, if you please," he said, with a catch to his voice. He cleared his throat. "I had not heard you were at Wrenthorpe, Miss Breckinridge. Do you come with—erm—with your family? Or with—"

"I come with my family, of course, sir. With whom else should I come?"

He scratched the back of his neck. "I imagined you might come with Dowbridge, to his family, as a matter of course."

"As is the case with so many London rumors, that is one which was exaggerated," she said. "May I sit down?"

"It's all over dust, Miss Breckinridge. Your gown—"

"Is already all over dirt and flora, so a little dust ought not to make a difference." She sat on the floor, arranging her skirts neatly over her ankles as he took a place beside her. "How suddenly you quitted town! We were all astonished, but then, we had a bit of an adventure to take up all our attention, and may have missed your take leave. But perhaps you did not know—Ben was kidnapped."

He started. "Kidnapped? Young Ben? But why? And who—"

"He was snatched from the back of the carriage by some brute with a turned up collar," she continued in a conversational tone. "We could not follow him, and despaired of ever finding him again. It was all very distressing, and not at all what they say it will be like in novels. But so it is always, it seems. We were thrown completely into an uproar, and then there was so much waiting and wondering, while Tom and Dowbridge searched for him, that we quite fell into the dismals. It was all I could do to keep my imagination from running wild. That is, until I received a note that shed a clear light upon everything."

"A note? From whom?"

She smiled sweetly. "From you."

"I?" he repeated, puzzled. "But I never wrote to you. Not in town."

She agreed with him. "And that is how I knew the note in question was not, in fact, from you, but from someone else trying to blacken your character with me, and I very quickly apprehended that it must be Dowbridge."

"Dowbridge," he repeated, with an edge to his voice. "I received a note as well, saying that someone I had been looking for wished to meet me at the dockyard church, but when I got there, it was Dowbridge who met me, and he told me—never mind. It does not signify."

"But it does, for if he told you that I wished to cut your acquaintance, it was untrue. You must see that now."

He looked fixedly at her. "He did tell me that. He claimed that you believed the rumors about me, that you had discovered that I had been lying to you, and that you had washed your hands of me."

"You must pardon my very great disappointment in you for believing him," said Lenora deprecatingly, "when I had only ever shown you my constant support."

"I believed him because—" He sighed. "Because I had been—not lying precisely—but keeping the full truth from you. I hadn't told you everything of what I was doing in London, and what I hoped to accomplish, so that I could be worthy to aspire to—" He stopped, looking down. "I went to see if I might not claim some property my father owned in India. The money I found here in the hedge maze was just enough to cover reasonable expenses in London, and to

327

make inquiries and pay the lawyer's fees. It seems to have come to naught, however, for I have just recently been informed by a friend in India—he knew my father, and he pledged to act for me if he could—that my father's property was seized in a riot after he died. It was this friend's messenger whom Dowbridge claimed wished to meet me at the dockyard church. Sir Thomas—that is his name—had previously sent me news through this messenger, who met me in a house near there. "

"A burly individual?" inquired Lenora.

"Ye-es," he replied, looking askance at her.

"Then unless you are certain the messenger was indeed from Sir Thomas, I advise you to question his veracity."

He stared hard at her. "Dowbridge?"

She shrugged. "Very possibly. I do not know for certain. I only know that Dowbridge was on hand, with Tom, to witness your meeting with this messenger, and claimed that the man was Ben's abductor, and that the house into which you went was where Ben was being held captive—which you must know made things look very black for you."

He smothered an oath. "I only hope Dowbridge does not come within a hundred yards of me, for I cannot be responsible for—" He muttered something and turned away. "It does not signify, for it changes nothing."

"I beg your pardon?"

"Dowbridge told me I was not worthy of you. And I am not." He threw out his arms. "I am as you see me. Despite all my machinations and plans and dreams, this is all I can boast of princely raiment, and this ruin is my only castle. If I were to offer you all my worldly possessions, even along with my heart, I could not offer you a greater insult."

Lenora regarded him, her eyes bright. "That is the most nonsensical speech I have heard in my life." She stood, and brushed off her skirts. "Insult indeed. Do you love me?" He scrambled up beside her, blinking in his astonishment. She put hands on her waist and enunciated, "Do you love me or do you not?"

"I—I love you more than life itself! But it makes no odds! There is nothing I can do."

"You are either the most poor-spirited gentleman I have ever met, or you are a cod's head," she said, primming up her lips.

"Lenora—Miss Breckinridge, you must see that as romantic as such circumstances should appear in a faerie tale, it will not do in real life. I can offer you nothing!"

"You must have a very odd idea of insults, for you can think very little of me if you believe I should count your heart as nothing."

"A heart cannot shelter you, and feed you," he retorted.

"And this house, nay, the whole of the estate—do you count it as nothing?"

"As long as there is no money, it is only a liability and an expense," he said gruffly.

"Then your arguments are at an end, for if you have no money, I have enough and to spare for the both of us."

He looked as though this was no surprise, but lowered his brows and gazed sternly at her, taking a quick breath to remonstrate.

"Give me no protestations that my fortune is not to be touched," she said, forestalling him, "for that is quite the most ridiculous notion of all. What else, pray, shall I do with thirty thousand pounds? For that is what Sir Joshua has settled upon me, and I am persuaded it is more than enough for two people to live on. And if we practice some economy, and live in a small home like the lodge, I daresay there shall be plenty left over to bring this place about."

"Live in the lodge?" he ground out. "Who is the cod's head now? What kind of gentleman would take his bride to live in the lodge?"

"I have plenty of experience with living on little means, for we did so for years at Branwell Cottage, and I assure you I will do very well. Indeed, I should find it excessively romantic! And Tom shall advise us, for he knows just what to do to make an estate profitable, so you must not fret on that head."

"Oh, and I suppose Tom will live in the lodge as well!" he said, his voice rising. "You must be mad, to think I should give in to such foolish notions!"

But she punched a finger at his chest. "You grossly misjudge my determination, sir, if you believe I will not do anything in my power to be mistress of Helden Hall! I have been in love with this house since my first sight of it last autumn, and dashed if I won't haunt the place as much as any ghost if you mean to deny my wish!"

They stood, defiant blue eyes boring into smoldering brown ones, until he jerked her into his arms and kissed her, hard and long, while she threw her arms about his neck and kissed him equally as fiercely. After some time, their embrace became more tender, and it was many minutes before they drew apart, to gaze upon one another in wondering delight.

"We must decide where to put the oubliette," he said at last, with a half smile.

Lenora tilted her head. "I have already determined that it shall go where I put my foot through the floor. But we must look about for a skeleton to put in it, for I refuse to have actual prisoners languishing in my own home, with their cries forever keeping me awake at night, and frightening away the servants."

"When did you become so practical, my love?" asked his lordship, all admiration.

She put up a hand to adjust his rumpled cravat. "When I discovered that no Gothic romance could compare to my love for you, James Ingles."

His look softened. "Would you truly live in the lodge with me, for the sake of Helden Hall?" he asked, brushing a stray lock of hair from her cheek.

"Yes," she answered, "but not for the sake of the Hall. I would live in a barracks with you, or in a hut, or in a jungle under the stars—or on the moon, if it came to that."

He drew her to him again, saying, "I trust it will come to that, and often," and proceeded to make her very much inclined to agree.

If you enjoyed this book, I hope you will share it with others! Please consider leaving a review on Amazon, Goodreads, Bookbub, or any other review site you like. Reviews are the best way to help people find their next favorite book, and are incredibly appreciated. Thank you!

Author's Note

My purpose in writing Regency fiction is not to become an apologist for the time, nor to impose a modern perspective on history, but to represent the period as accurately as possible. Sometimes this exposes the less than elegant or agreeable realities of the time, but I find that representing these points in true color, rather than trying to make them better than they were or show why they were so bad and wrong, can actually facilitate our finding solutions and overcoming effects with greater success. Most of my research, however, is just plain interesting.

The opening scene of this story takes place in the Bricklayer's Arms, a true-to-life posting inn on the corner of the Kent Road and Bermondsey New Road in London. This inn is no longer extant, having been replaced by houses, but it holds a special place in my heart: my ancestor was employed there as a potman—which is a serving man—in 1811. When I discovered this, I turned to my copy of *The*

Epicure's Almanack, which is a listing of all the eating establishments of any note in all of London, published in 1815. There I found that the Bricklayer's Arms was a major coach stop, and offered "a most comfortable repast either in the style of a hasty dinner or a flying lunch." It was such a thrill finding this connection that I just had to use it in my book.

The seven year-long struggle to free Europe of Napoleon's rule had been so overwhelming that his final defeat at Waterloo marked one of the greatest victories of all time. The Prince Regent, seeing the victory as England's, decreed that all those who had fought at Waterloo and the surrounding battles were to receive a reward in the form of a medal (boasting the Prince Regent's profile) and a monetary prize equal to 2 years' military pay according to rank. The only problem with this recognition was that it effectively dismissed the contributions of all those who had fought in the six years leading up to Waterloo, but who had retired or were not called upon to fight after the Peninsular War. This neglect by the Prince Regent added to the already difficult circumstances prevailing in England because of the high costs—emotional and financial—of the war.

The Peninsular War was paid for primarily by raised taxes and tariffs on various imports. After the war, Parliament imposed the Corn Laws, which prohibited the import of foreign grains until the price of British grain rose sufficiently to bolster a struggling economy. While this strategy helped the wealthy landowners, who realized the profits from the sale of their grain, it only further depressed the economy by raising the cost of food for the working classes, who then stopped buying manufactured goods so they could afford to feed themselves. Riots and general unrest ensued, but since the voting members of Parliament were mostly landowners, legislation to revise or repeal the Corn Laws continually failed to pass. The Reform Act of 1832 extended voting rights to the merchant class, who had a vested interest in increasing trade, and the Corn Laws were finally repealed in 1846.

The title of this book is a play on the 1791 Gothic romance by Ann Radcliffe, *Romance of the Forest*. A romance in the time of the Regency was a fantastic tale, usually set in the past, where the action was not possible in real life (similar to a fairy tale). They were typically filled with fainting damsels in distress, dastardly villains bent on abduction (but oddly preferring marriage to rape), and downtrodden heroes who ended up the long-lost heir of some rich lord. Gothic romances added paranormal elements, horror, and suspense to the mix. Romances such as those penned by Mrs. Radcliffe were responsible for the decades-long craze for sensibility—a deep response to emotion, whether in oneself or in one's environment. Sensibility bore a strong resemblance to what we now term drama—or the tendency to overreact to or overdramatize anything and everything. Hence Marianne Dashwood's extreme reaction to Willoughby's abandonment, and Lenora Breckinridge's fascination with Gothic fantasy tinged with danger.

Many Regency stories rely on the trope of an entail to complicate matters of heredity and fortune, and my story is no exception. But while most people know what an entail is, it seems that there is a lot of confusion over how to break one. It turns out that breaking an entail was not doing away with it, but recreating it. An entail was formed for three generations: the present owner, to his heir, to his heir; then it would legally end. If either of the first two generations wished to change things, they would have to agree to collude in a farcical legal battle, called a "common recovery," with an imaginary opponent—often played by a clerk or paid actor—who supposedly had laid a claim to the estate. With an outside claimant, the entail would no longer be legal, and thus it would be broken until the claim could be decided. But the imaginary claimant would not appear for testimony, and being found in contempt of court, would lose his claim to the estate. Then the current owner and his heir would recreate the entail, making adjustments such as selling off land in order to free up money, and the new entail would then carry to the heir's second generation. In *Pride and Prejudice*, Mr. Collins, unlike a son of the Bennets, could not be expected to collude in breaking an entail as it would likely reduce his inheritance. In my story, James Ingles' father refused to collude with the Old Lord, so the entail carried to James, where it naturally ended. Entails were outlawed in 1833.

When we think of British relations with India, most of us instantly envision colonial officers and their memsahibs lording it over the natives. But this supremacist attitude was a long time in the making, and did not develop in England until well after the Regency era, which ended in 1820. In India in the 1700's, officers of the East India Company (the ruling body of the British in India) were encouraged to intermarry with Indians, and the children of these unions were generally treated as full British citizens and given posts of importance within the EIC. But as political tensions in India fluctuated near the turn of the century, the EIC tried various approaches to depress rebellion and widen the divide between the rulers and the ruled, including restricting benefits for Anglo-Indian children. This led to mistrust and prejudice from both Indians and the British toward children of mixed race, and by the time of the Regency, it was very hard to be Anglo-Indian *in India*. In *England*, however, due to difficult travel and communication, these political tensions were not yet felt, and mixed-race children of gentry or nobility were not regarded as inferior. Therefore, during the Regency, Anglo-Indian children were often sent to England to live because they were more likely to be accepted and thus be successful. This tolerant period, unfortunately, was fairly short-lived, as the advent of steamships and the telegraph increased interchanges between the two countries, and by the 1830's, strong prejudices against Indians and Anglo-Indians began to develop in England, culminating in the typical colonialist attitudes of the Victorian era.

If you want to go more in-depth with me on these and other Regency history topics, visit my blog at judithhaleeverett.com.

Sources:

"Military Info," *Napoleon Series*, https://www.napoleon-series.org/

"Waterloo Medal," *Wikipedia*, https://en.wikipedia.org/wiki/Waterloo_Medal

"UK, Military Campaign Medal and Award Rolls, 1793-1949," *Ancestry.com*, https://www.ancestry.com/search/collections/1686/

"Corn Laws 1815," *Cove Collective*, https://editions.covecollective.org/chronologies/corn-laws-1815

"Corn Laws," *Britain Express*, https://www.britainexpress.com/History/victorian/corn-laws.htm

"Common Recovery," *University of Nottingham*, https://www.nottingham.ac.uk/manuscriptsandspecialcollections/researchguidance/deedsindepth/freehold/commonrecovery.aspx

William Dalrymple, *White Mughals*, Penguin Books, 2002.

Michael Herbert Fisher, *Counter flows to Colonialism: Indian Travellers and Settlers in Britain, 1600-1857*, Permanent Black, 2006.

C. J. Hawed, *Poor Relations*, Curzon Press, 1996.

Acknowledgements

THANK YOU TO my readers, returning and new, for coming with me on this journey. I hope that this book lived up to at least some of your expectations, and left you excited for more.

I had so much fun writing this book, but I would be a liar if I claimed it was easy. There were many weeks of grueling hard work, late nights, frustration, discouragement, and tears, and if it weren't for my excellent support people, I would definitely have decided that my calling in life was actually to be a gardener.

To my writing group, Nichole Van Valkenburgh, Amy Beatty, and Julie Frederick, for all your patience and feedback and encouragement and kind words when I needed them most—thank you!

To the PR Queen, Laurel Hale, for sharing your vast knowledge of the marketing monster, and talking me down from ledges and away from minefields, and always making me feel like I am doing you the favor—you are a treasure!

To my walking buddies, Cynthia Hart and Marianne Hales Harding, you don't know each other but you both have helped me no end by listening and validating and letting me share my ups and downs in a safe environment—bless you both!

To my beta readers, Signe Gillum, Emily Menendez, Elizabeth Prettyman, Cynthia Hart, and Diane Paredes, you are amazing! Thank you for taking the time out of your busy schedules to show me how I could polish up my story.

To the brilliantly talented Rachel Allen Everett, who designs the covers for my books—you nailed it again, and I am so grateful you take the time in your busy life for my commissions.

And last but definitely not least, to my family. To my kids, who speak with confidence of my books "taking off" and only sometimes complain when it's leftovers again (they almost never complain if it's pizza, though). And to Joe, with whom I would live in a barracks, or in a hut in the jungle, and very often do live with on the moon. I love you!

Sneak Preview of
Forlorn Hope
Book 3 of the Branwell Chronicles

It was clearly his sister's fault that Geoffrey had lost his boot in the woods, since it was she who had suggested they wade through the stream separating their property from that of the Chandry estate, and if he had not removed his boots to do it, it was because Clara had not given him time to consider. On the path home, his wet shoes had chaffed his ankles, so of course he had removed them and carried them by the strings. But one of the boots had fallen, and Geoffrey had not noticed at all, and at Miss Gillies' stern look when they returned to the schoolroom, he knew he must search through the wood until it was found.

As Clara had caught a chill from her wet feet, she could not even accompany him the next morning, but Geoffrey was made of sterner stuff, and he set off to find his boot. His search took him nearly to the stream again, and knowing that he had lost his boot after crossing the stream, he was turning back to overlook his path again, when the sound of singing stopped him. He stood still to listen carefully, and determined it was coming from the Chandry side of the water, and it sounded so sad, so faerielike, that he was intrigued.

He crossed the stream, this time removing his shoes—old shoes that pinched anyway and were a relief to leave on the bank—and wound through the trees following the sound of the music, trying to keep silent on his bare feet. He finally came upon a very small clearing almost like a bower, with drooping tree branches forming a low roof and bushes grown up around to form walls like a hedge. The song seemed to be emanating from within the clearing, and peeking through the foliage, Geoffrey saw a girl, thin and pale, with large mournful eyes and lank brown hair tied back inexpertly behind her ears with a ribbon. She sang to herself, a haunting melody, as she worked with twigs and leaves and grasses to form an intricately detailed faerie village in the dirt.

Fascinated, Geoffrey crouched down and watched her movements far longer than he realized until, all at once, his muscles seized with cramp and he lost balance, falling with a crash into the brush wall. When he had scrambled up and peered back into the clearing, the girl was gone. He smothered an oath and stretched to see over and around the bower, but could find no sign of the mysterious girl. Muttering to himself, Geoffrey climbed into the clearing and leaned down, his ear almost in the dirt, to see into each cunningly wrought little house in the girl's make-believe village. They were works of art, so cleverly designed, but something was missing.

"This village needs some life in it," he declared to the surrounding trees, and he set to work.

It was not until two days after that, as he sat silently watching the clearing, that his efforts were rewarded. The girl came to the bower, silent and cautious as a deer, and froze when she saw the telltale signs that someone had disturbed her property. But she quickly appreciated that the disturbance was in good faith, for she knelt down to closely inspect a tiny twig horse placed beside one of her houses before picking it up, taking in all its details with her large eyes. She replaced the horse, scanning the surrounding bushes as if for another sign of the trespasser, and Geoffrey pulled his head back from his peep-hole, holding his breath as her glance swept past. When he dared to peek again, he saw the girl crafting a miniature figure with long hair and a leaf dress. A distant gong sounded several minutes later, and only then did she put down her handiwork with a regretful sigh, turning with a wistful glance at the shrubbery to make her way toward Chandry Manor.

Geoffrey needed no more encouragement. He slipped silently into the clearing and gathered twigs and grass to create a tiny boy with bark trousers. He set the boy next to the little girl and gazed thoughtfully at them, then wove a little basket and put it between them. Slipping back through the bushes, he ran to the stream bank and searched until he found a lovely white pebble shot through with milky swirls, and took it back to the clearing. Placing it in the basket, he considered a moment more, then scratched a message in the dirt by the feet of the boy and girl—"Friends?" Grinning at his handiwork, he finally heeded the rumblings of his stomach and ran off toward home.

He arrived several minutes late to dinner in the schoolroom, sliding into his seat and almost simultaneously spreading his napkin on his lap and spearing several slabs of ham onto his plate. Miss Gillies glanced at him but continued to observe her own plate.

"Welcome, Master Geoffrey. Did you enjoy your outing?"

He swallowed a mouthful. "Yes, Miss Gillies, very much." He reached for the lemonade and only then noticed Clara glowering at him from across the table. He paused uncertainly, then his hand dropped and he slumped back in his chair, remembering. "Oh, Clara, our battledore and shuttlecock game! I forgot! I'll play with you tomorrow."

She colored, then looked down at her plate and pushed her food about with her fork. "That will do nicely, thank you, Geoffrey."

The tone of her voice gave Geoffrey pause. "What else have I done?"

Miss Gillies glanced from one to the other, but held her peace as Clara dropped her fork onto her plate with a clatter. "If you don't wish to spend your precious time with me, you should simply say so, and not run away."

Geoffrey was aghast. "Why would I run away from you? I forgot, Clara, that's the long and short of it."

She looked up at him, tears running down her heated cheeks. "But you just went and sat in the woods, Geoff! I saw you!"

"You followed me?" Geoffrey demanded, slapping his napkin on the table.

Miss Gillies put a hand out to each of the children, quelling them with a look. Clara gulped and stared down at her fingers clenching in her lap while the governess gazed steadfastly at Geoffrey. "Clara went to find you when you missed your appointment. When she did find you, your manner was curious enough to make her watch you."

Geoffrey ground his teeth in frustration, but he closed his eyes and mastered himself with a deep breath. He had to think quickly; he could not have his nosy little sister ruining his new friendship. Suddenly inspired, he opened his eyes and looked with what he hoped was frankness at his sister. "I was watching a fawn."

Clara's face instantly cleared. "Oh, Geoff! May I come see it, too?"

Consternated, Geoffrey compounded his mendacity. "The mother will have moved it by now, depend upon it."

"Perhaps not!" His sister bounced in her seat. "May we go and see? I promise I'll be silent as a mouse!" Her blue eyes pleaded with him, and when Miss Gillies looked at him as well, urging him with a raised brow to his duty, he knew he must see it through.

"Very well," he said. Clara's joy was unbounded, drawing from him a tiny smile. "Tomorrow."

Clara's eagerness for their adventure was evinced in her appearance directly after breakfast with a hamper, which she had cajoled the cook into packing with sandwiches and lemonade, to which she had thoughtfully added some tulip bulbs dug from beneath the hedge. Her excitement caused Geoffrey a pang but, fortified by the chivalrous thought that his deception would somehow protect the mysterious girl, he manfully led Clara in circles until she was quite lost, then set her to watching for the fictitious fawn in an entirely different clearing until the sandwiches had been eaten and the lemonade drunk and Clara's remarkable patience finally wasted. As she tramped gloomily ahead of him on the path toward home, he comforted his conscience with the sure knowledge that Clara would doubtless forget her disappointment in a day or so.

But Geoffrey, sneaking out the side door that very afternoon while his sister was in her music lesson, returned to the original clearing and was made to wait only a quarter of an hour before the girl came, kneeling in front of his message, and delightedly reaching to take up his doll boy, turning it in her hands. She replaced him and picked up the basket, fingering the pebble and holding it up to the filtered sunlight. At last, looking shyly around the edge of the clearing, she called quietly, "Are you there?"

Geoffrey's face flushed. He had anticipated this moment, but had not thought it would come so quickly. Taking a deep breath, he steeled himself against her being frightened away again, and crept through the brush into the clearing.

The girl faced him with both her hands up in a warding gesture, and her eyes wide with uncertainty. He stopped abruptly, sitting down cross-legged at the edge of the clearing and smiling as kindly as he could. "My name is Geoffrey. Our property abuts yours. That way," he said, pointing back toward the stream.

He was glad to see the girl's breathing slow a bit, and then she smiled faintly, lowering her hands. "I am Emily," in a gentle voice hardly above a whisper.

Geoffrey thought she looked as fragile as one of Clara's porcelain dolls. Cautiously, he pointed to the pebble she still worried in her hand. "Do you like it? I found it in the stream."

She nodded, coloring faintly. "It's lovely." She placed it back into the little basket as he inched forward.

"Your village is so cleverly done. You inspired me," he said, gesturing to his horse and boy. "I thought it needed some life."

She gazed thoughtfully at the small creatures and said, "Yes, now it has purpose, my village."

Her shyness seemed then to be dispelled, and the two became fast friends, with the tiny village as the hub of their united imaginations. Geoffrey soon perceived Emily to be the more creative, but she was also the more skittish, almost to the point of paranoia. She grew to trust him implicitly, but sudden sounds in the wood or movements in the brush startled her so unnaturally that her new friend began to wonder if she wasn't touched in the upper works, as his elder brother Francis would say. Indeed, one time she would have fled from the clearing, uttering breathless half-sentences about "them" and "find me," but for Geoffrey's quickness in catching her hands and holding them firmly in his, while speaking soothingly until her trembling subsided.

"Forgive me," she had said, looking up at him with clear, gray eyes that had nothing of the lunatic about them, but only gentle fragility.

Geoffrey had smiled at her, but she had withdrawn her hands and looked away. "My father says I inherited a nervous condition from my mother."

Geoffrey never made mention of the incident, to her or to anyone, but over the several weeks of that summer, he came to recognize that Emily was one who would be misunderstood by the majority of society, and he secretly was glad to be the only person in the neighborhood who seemed to know of her existence.

But this consolation was rudely torn from him one day in the village, when two of his fellows began talking of the Waif of Chandry Park.

"I've heard its moaning myself, late at night," said Shelby Frean, the Squire's son, relishing the rapt attention of the other boys.

"Well, I've seen it!" put in Billy Thornton, puffing out his chest. "Pale and skinny thing with huge eyes like a frog's."

Shelby waved him away. "No, that's just the daughter."

"Sir Anthony don't have a daughter, clodpole!"

"Of course he does," said Shelby in an authoritative tone. "She's the reason Lady Chandry's dead, and that's why the old gager keeps her locked up, because he can't stand the sight of her, you gudgeon!"

"Well, if she's locked up, then why'd I see her with my own eyes, eh, cawker?"

"Because she's made a pact with the Devil, and can move through walls, but only when the moon is at the full, you—"

But the others never heard what name Shelby had concocted for Billy for, in a trice, Geoffrey was on him, pummelling him with his fists and shouting, "Take it back, you snake!" The other boys were no more surprised than Shelby, who only had sense enough to curl up and yell, "Gerroff!" while the others stared slack-jawed. Were it not for Colonel Mantell's groom, who came striding across the street at that moment to grab up Geoffrey by his coat collar, there may have been very little of the Squire's son left unbruised by the encounter.

Unceremoniously dumped into the chaise next to his rigidly disapproving mother and morbidly delighted sister, and forced to endure Clara's sniggering all the way home, Geoffrey thought to beat a hasty retreat to his room upon reaching the Hall.

But in this he was forestalled by his mother, who halted him with the words: "No, no, Geoffrey! You shall not get off that easy. Your father will wish to see you, instantly! What can have possessed you to behave in such an oafish way? I declare, I was stared out of all countenance! All the village high street gaping at us, no doubt wondering what back slum you were brought up in! Oh, I shall never live it down!"

The boy had little choice but to go directly to his father's domain, a study on the first floor whose walls were adorned with various hunting trophies and a life-sized painting of a more youthful Colonel Mantell in full military regalia, medals glittering upon his manly chest. A single bookshelf was full of manuals on hunting, boxing, riding, and all other forms of outdoor sport, and a fine oak case held an assortment of guns, some antique, others glaringly new.

Geoffrey stood in embarrassed silence, eyes flicking about this shrine to masculinity, until Colonel Mantell raised his eyes from the letter in his hand only long enough to ascertain the identity of his guest. Lowering them again, he said, "Well?"

The boy cleared his throat. "I was in a fight today, sir."

The Colonel immediately put down his letter, an eyebrow raised at his son. "A fight you say? What sort of fight?"

Geoffrey swallowed and looked at the floor. "An affair of honor, sir. With Shelby Frean."

"The Squire's son?" His father stared at him for several interminable seconds, then suddenly threw back his handsome head and laughed out loud. "I knew you had it in you, boy!" he crowed, wagging a finger in his son's direction as he stood and strode around the desk to stand in front of the utterly surprised boy. "Who was in the right, son?"

Geoffrey gulped. "I believe I was, sir. He—Shelby—said something—I mean, insulted a lady, sir."

The Colonel's eyebrows shot up and he whistled low. "Ah, that's the landscape is it? I should think at twelve years of age you're a little young to notice the females."

His son flushed scarlet. "She's not a female! I mean—we're just friends, sir!"

The Colonel chuckled knowingly. "Well, well, my boy, and who is this lady?"

Geoffrey glared at his toes. "Emily Chandry, sir," he mumbled.

"What was that? Speak up, boy!"

He threw back his shoulders and looked defiantly into his father's eyes. "Emily Chandry, sir!"

A slightly pained look crossed his father's features but was quickly replaced by an indulgent smile. "No matter, son, it's a good start! Defending a lady is a high and mighty purpose, and I'm proud of you, boy!" He took his son's hand and pumped it in both of his, then ruffled the boy's hair and, with a final chuckle, went back to his letter. Thus dismissed, Geoffrey fled to the refuge of his room to contemplate the perversity of parental priorities.

Subjected thereafter to many winks and knowing looks, and the occasional clap on the shoulder in passing, Geoffrey tried in vain to reconcile his father's spirited support of his exploit with the conviction in his heart that his defense of Emily had been honorable. But to his mind, his father's approval served only to reduce the nobility of the deed to mere posturing, thus tarnishing any satisfaction he could have gained from it, and rendering the thought of repeating the action untenable.

But these struggles besieged him only in his real life, for merely entering the clearing in the woods lifted every care from his shoulders, and pulled him into a delightful world of fancy that insensibly sustained him. Emily knew nothing of the affair in the village, and her continued trust in him, despite her nervous condition, allowed his chivalrous feeling to blossom despite his disillusionment, and he came to view his time with her as a noble act in itself, though he could not bring himself to tell anyone about her.

At the end of this enchanted summer, Geoffrey was summoned to his father's study and, aware that his parent had grown less and less pleased with him over the last few months, and having overheard him discussing heatedly with his lady something that had to do with the insipidity of Nature as opposed to masculine pursuits, he presented himself with some trepidation.

Colonel Mantell glanced up from the newspaper he was reading, adjuring Geoffrey to sit down, then shuffled the pages a bit and muttered over their contents before at last folding the paper and gazing thoughtfully at his son.

"Well, my boy, you're nearly thirteen."

"Yes, sir."

"Your mother and I are agreed that it is high time we sent you off to school."

Geoffrey gasped. "But Mama said last year I am to have a tutor, sir!"

His father harrumphed in disgust. "School was good enough for Francis, and it'll be good enough for you! You're no more sickly than he was, whatever your mother says—I'll not have a weakling homebody for a son." He pushed himself to his feet as he spoke and began pacing behind his desk. "I thought you were finally showing some spirit when you flattened young Frean last May, but since then I've not seen a single likely spark in you. All you do is wander about in the woods, staring at wildlife or some such nonsense, not even taking a gun or a slingshot!"

"What would I take a gun for, sir?"

Colonel Mantell turned a severe eye upon him. "That is precisely the kind of claptrap I mean to cure you of, son, and no nincompoop tutor will do it for me. You will go to school, and learn what it means to be a man!"

Geoffrey, surrounded by the fruits of what it meant to be a man, and facing his principal example of what manhood had to offer, believed he could do very well without it, but there really was nothing he could do. Within two weeks, during which time he was given no leave to wander in the woods, he had been fitted out with new clothes and books, and prepared as much as was possible by his governess for what challenges awaited him. On the fateful morning, the Colonel bid him goodbye with a buffet on the shoulder, while his mother adjured him not to act in any way unbefitting his station, and with a mournful wave to Clara and Miss Gillies, he mounted into the chaise and set off toward Shrewsbury School in Shropshire.

Judith Hale Everett is one of seven sisters, and grew up surrounded by romance novels. Georgette Heyer and Jane Austen were staples, and formed the groundwork for her lifelong love affair with the Regency. Add to that her obsession with the English language and you've got one hopelessly literate romantic.

You can find JudithHaleEverett on Facebook, Twitter, and Instagram, or at judithhaleeverett.com.